NAMASTE and CODE All Day

ALLY WILLIAMS

Proofreading by Chelsea Adams.

CONTENT WARNING

This story contains explicit sexual content, foul language, mentions of emotional abuse, addiction, and a description of sexual assault (please skip chapter three if you would rather not read SA content).

Playlist

P!nk - Walk Me Home
The Band CAMINO - I Think I Like You
Jesse McCartney - Blow Your Mind
Mimi Webb - Little Bit Louder
The Head and the Heart - See You Through My Eyes
A Great Big World - I Really Want It
Calum Scott - Heaven
Rosa Linn - SNAP
New Rules - Happy Ever After You
Spencer Sutherland & Meghan Trainor - Chicken Little
P!nk - TRUSTFALL
Fitz and The Tantrums - Feeling Good
Betty Who - I Love You Always Forever

For the girls who know.

OCTOBER

1

GABI

His hand grasps my arm as a car whizzes by, horn blaring.

The metal misses me by inches and I stumble backward, thrown off balance. He pulls me into his chest, holding me as the car speeds off into the distance. They slam on the brakes as an afterthought when they come to the stop sign at the end of the street and then whip through the turn, disappearing quickly around the corner.

"Jesus, Gabi, are you alright?" He turns me around, looking me up and down, and for a shocked moment I'm surprised that there's nothing sexual behind his gaze. And then I realize he's looking for injuries.

"Yeah, I'm fine." I look at my hands, my arms. *I'm totally fine.*

My heart thumps at a wild pace, a sheen of sweat now coating my body when only a minute ago I was complaining about the chill in the air.

"Are you sure?" His brow is furrowed, his eyes dancing across my face.

I nod, pushing my hair back over my shoulder. I realize

as I do that my hand is shaking, and his eyes follow the movement; he sees it too.

I clear my throat and smooth down my dress. Across the street, a couple holding hands walks a small fluffy dog. They watch us, murmuring to each other, and then the woman shouts to us, "Are you alright?"

I nod, waving to her. "Yeah, I'm fine, thank you!" They nod and continue on their nighttime walk. I turn back to Zeke. "I can't believe they're driving that way through a residential neighborhood," I scoff, turning back toward the street with my head on a swivel, searching for other speeders. "They're going to kill somebody."

He follows my lead, his piercing blue eyes searching the road as I lead us across. He stuffs his hands in his pockets, his enormous frame looming in my periphery, and the look of concern plastered on his face slowly melts into his usual scowl as he falls into step beside me.

"So what was it you were saying about not needing me to walk you home?"

I cross my arms and throw him a glare, his smirk annoyingly charming. "If anything, you held me up twenty minutes, putting me perilously close to danger. If I had walked home by myself, I would have been nowhere near that car."

"*I* held *you* up twenty minutes? You were talking to your sister for an hour before you were finally ready to go. I got through an entire drink waiting for you to finish chit-chatting."

He's not wrong. Stephanie talks like Newton's first law of motion—at a constant velocity until acted upon by an external force.

I hold my chin up. "I never asked you to walk me home."

"No, you didn't." He knocks my elbow, a smile falling across his face. "But I don't mind."

I can't help but grin back at him. He looks intimidating, all tall and broad with a shock of dark hair and full of sharp angles—a pointed nose, high cheekbones, thin lips. Yet his smile brings a softness to his face that's as welcoming as his scowl is intimidating.

My apartment complex looms in front of us, a mass of glass and concrete in the form of stacked, cube-like apartments that look out over a central courtyard. The building takes up the entire block by itself.

"Why do you do it, though?" I ask, crossing my arms as the chill sets in again.

"Why?" he repeats, his eyebrows furrowed.

"Yeah, why do you always walk me home?" From every game night our girl gang crashes. From every night out with our little group of friends. From every event that puts the two of us in the same place at the same time. "Not that I don't appreciate it. But I live here, you know? Where else can you walk alone if not your home?"

He rolls his eyes. "Gabi, we're in the middle of the city. It's one thing to walk around after dark. It's another to be walking home in—*that*—close to midnight." He glances down at my dress, and I cross my arms tighter over my chest.

"I walk home after dark all the time. From yoga. From happy hour if we get drinks after work. It's nice of you—don't get me wrong. It just feels unnecessary if every other night I'm out here all alone, anyway."

He shrugs. "Well, when it's within my control, you get home safe," he starts. "That, and Charlie bothers me if I don't send a confirmation, so I can only imagine how that conversation would go if I told him, 'eh, didn't feel like taking her home tonight.'"

I roll my eyes. "Of course it's because of Charlie."

Charlie and I work together, but over the years our relationship has grown from casual acquaintances to best friends. And after one asshole boyfriend and one jerk of a client, Charlie's taken it upon himself to Make Sure Gabi is Okay. Constantly.

And apparently it's rubbing off on Zeke.

"He's just looking out for you."

"I don't need to be looked out for." It comes out a little sharper than I intended.

"Of course you don't," he snaps back and then smiles sweetly at me when I whip around to give him a piece of my mind.

"I carry pepper spray."

He nods. "And I could probably throw you over my shoulder and jog home with you if I really wanted to, so excuse me if I don't think pepper spray is enough protection."

We reach the gate to the courtyard, and he leans casually up against the wall, waiting for me to punch in the code. A gust of wind rips by us and he tries to condense his body inward. He's wearing only a dark T-shirt against the crisp October air.

I bite back my smile, watching him. So intent on making sure I get home okay when he didn't even have the foresight to wear a jacket.

I fix him with a look. "So because I'm blonde and wearing a dress, I'm not qualified to walk myself home past a certain time of night?"

He rolls his eyes at me. "Put in the code, Gabi."

I smile, leaning up against the gate, mirroring his stance. He raises his eyebrows at me. "No, I want to hear your answer. I walk home every night by myself. I want to know why I suddenly become a burden when *you're* around."

He sighs. "What time do you get home from yoga? Eight? There are still people around at that time. This is different— you're wearing *that*, you've had a couple drinks tonight, you obviously can't cross a road by yourself, and you're on my way home anyway."

I stick my chin in the air. "I get home at nine from yoga and sometimes I'm wearing less than I am now, especially if it was hot yoga."

His eyes drift down, taking in my bare legs and pausing at my chest. I'm much more used to the look he's giving me now than the one of concern he gave me only a few minutes ago when I nearly got hit by a car.

Although... not from him, I realize.

He doesn't look at me like that.

At least, he hasn't before today.

Then again, I essentially asked him to.

I suddenly feel on display and pull the ends of my skirt down. His eyes jump back up to mine, the hint of a smile on his face.

"Sounds like I'm neglecting my duty, then."

"What I'm trying to say is that you don't *have* a duty."

He nods as another gust of wind rushes by and we both shiver. "Gabi, can you please punch in the code so I can go home?"

I do as he asks, pushing the gate open with my hip.

"Good night, Gabs," he says, leaning in and giving me a quick one-armed hug, his scent getting lodged in my nose. Fresh laundry and something musky that makes me want to hold on just a second longer.

He waves over his shoulder as he walks away, stuffing his hands in his pockets, and I do my best to shake off the thought of him. It's been too long since I've been with anyone—he's hugged me plenty of times before and I didn't feel the need to cling to his skin, breathe him in.

I close the gate behind me, hip-checking it into place because it gets stuck easily, and continue along the pathway to my apartment, my heels clacking as I walk. The courtyard is deserted at this time of night, but the lights from the apartments surrounding it are bright, fuzzy silhouettes of the residents visible behind the glass as they move about their apartments.

I push through the stairwell door and head up the stairs to my apartment, my footsteps echoing off the concrete walls.

I dig my keys out of my purse as I reach my door, but just as I've isolated the right one in my fingers, I hear a cough from behind me.

My hair stands on end as I turn around.

"Hey, Gabi."

My breath catches in my throat. "Dustin."

My hand rests on my purse, very aware of the can of pepper spray inside it. There's no wind in here, but I can't help wondering if the spray will hit me too. I remember reading on the package that it can stay in the air for a few minutes after being used.

I should have done more research. I should have practiced.

He's in front of my neighbor's door, wearing an old sweatshirt and jeans, and his dark eyes find mine, a hint of longing in them. He's thinner than the last time I saw him, his short brown hair mussed and unkempt. His thin lips stretch into a smile as he moves a step closer to me.

As my heart rate slows, I realize I'm being ridiculous. Dustin isn't a threat—an asshole, yes; a manipulator, yes.

But he's never gotten physical with me. I don't want him here, but I also don't think he'd intentionally physically hurt me.

When we were dating, he stole money from my purse and gaslit me well enough that sometimes I *still* wonder if I made it all up, but my habits haven't changed that significantly over the past year, and after him, I magically had a lot more money left over each month. I cling to the memory of finding a stolen prescription pad in his backpack—that, if nothing else, proved there was something going on that was far beyond my control.

I'm embarrassed to admit that even knowing he was writing himself prescriptions, I forgave him for it. He wasn't doing anything *to me*—at least, nothing he couldn't explain away.

It was the guilt he laid on me for hanging out with my sister and Charlie too often that finally made me snap. I felt the wedge he was trying to stick between me and the people I cared about the most, and I realized I couldn't do it anymore. I needed their support *because* of him, and he was doing his best to rob me of that, too.

Probably because he knew that *they* knew that he wasn't good news.

But I don't think they ever knew just how bad he truly was.

In a way, I'm thankful that he wasn't just stealing from me. I would never have had the guts to confront him about that because I just wasn't sure. I would think I had a twenty in my purse, but when I mentioned it in surprise he'd remind me of the last place I went where I used cash. That twenty was probably what I used.

He always had an explanation.

But we broke up before I could confirm it. Before I could catch him in the act or work up the nerve to confront him.

In hindsight, it all feels so obvious.

"I was on my way home and ended up passing by," he says, taking another tentative step toward me. "I wanted to see you."

"You should have called."

"I was worried you wouldn't want to see me."

I cock my head to the side. "So it's better to show up uninvited and take the choice away from me?"

He takes a step forward, and I take a matching one back.

"Gabi, come on. Don't twist my words like that. I just wanted to tell you that I miss you."

I don't know what part of this to tackle. I don't want to get him angry by being combative, but it feels like my only option here is to insist I'm *not* twisting his words, or tell him that I don't miss him at all. Neither one seems like it'll make him leave.

He may not have been physical with me in the past, but I also haven't seen him in almost six months. Who's to say he won't be now? I don't feel comfortable fumbling with my door in front of him; he could be next to me in a second, pushing his way in behind me, and I definitely can't use my pepper spray from *that* distance.

"Dustin, I have a really early morning tomorrow. If you want to talk, why don't we meet somewhere tomorrow for lunch?"

"Gabi, I'm here now. Come on, don't you miss me too?" He takes another step toward me, but it's one step too close. His eyes follow my hand as I reach into my bag and whip out the pepper spray, holding it at arm's length in front of me and aiming for his eyes. I don't pull the trigger yet, but I will if he gets any closer.

"Gabi, what the fuck?" He backs up to the end of the hallway, and I take the opportunity to unlock my door, the pepper spray held protectively in front of me.

"I don't miss you. Don't come back here. Don't call. Okay?"

"Gabi," he whines, taking another step closer. I close the door behind me, locking the dead bolt and pulling the chain over. My heart thumping wildly in my chest, I grab onto the edges of my kitchen table and push it up against the door, just in case.

I still hear his footsteps outside the door. "Gabi, let me in. Come on, you don't need to be embarrassed or anything. That was cute, with the pepper spray. I'm not mad. I get it, you've been without someone protecting you for so long that you feel like you have to protect yourself. That's great, honey. Honestly. I'm proud of you."

His words send a shiver down my spine. Not because of *what* he's saying, but because of the girl I used to be who might have fallen for them.

I know better now.

I know what his game is. That he'll stand outside my door all night telling me some version of what he thinks I want to hear. *Of course I'm not angry with you for threatening me with pepper spray. I'm sorry I freaked out a little—I was just surprised. You've come such a long way, Gabi. I'm so proud of you for protecting yourself like that. But honey, I'm not the one you need protection from. I'll do that for you. Let me in. Let's talk for a bit. Keep your pepper spray out if that makes you feel better.*

And it will go on, and on, and on, until I finally open the door. We broke up so many times before it finally stuck, for exactly that reason.

I hate the version of myself that listened to him.

I block out the sound of his voice and dial Charlie. I

vaguely consider weighing down the kitchen table, just in case he does try to get in, but he's not the type to use force. At least, not in my experience with him. In his head, he's the good guy, and—at least in the past—good guys don't use force.

Just their words.

"Hey Gabs, you get home okay?"

"Yeah. Listen, can you stay on the phone with me for a couple of minutes?"

A door closes in the background. "What's wrong?"

"Dustin is here."

"At your apartment?"

Dustin shouts again, and I slip into my bedroom, locking the door behind me. I can't imagine what my neighbors must be thinking; I'm going to have to apologize to them tomorrow. I'm sure that's occurred to him too, that at some point I'll be so concerned about keeping the peace in my building that I'll let him in just to shut him up.

It wouldn't be the first time.

"Yeah, I mean, he's outside my apartment. I don't know why. I left him out there and I'm just going to ignore him. The doors are locked and I have my pepper spray, so I'm fine. I just don't want to have to listen to him alone."

"Gabi, I'm coming over."

"NO!" I shout. I slip into my closet and close the door behind me. The sudden silence deep within the padding of my clothes is a relief. "Charlie, please just stay on the phone with me for a few minutes. He can't stay out there all night."

"He can't?"

"Charlie. I'm telling you I'm okay. I need your words right now, not your actions."

He's silent for a minute. "This is making me really uncomfortable."

"I'm sorry. Is my distress bothering you?"

He sighs. "I'm sorry, Gabi. Yes, of course I'll stay on the phone with you."

I hear noise in the background—Annabel, the girl who managed to wrap playboy Charlie around her finger. Her words are muffled and unclear, but her voice is unmistakable. The line goes silent for a moment, and I realize he's muted himself. He's probably telling her what's going on.

I suddenly regret making the call, especially since I can't hear anything—in my apartment or over the phone—at the moment.

"Alright, Zeke is on his way back. He'll be there in two minutes."

"Charlie!" I lean into my clothes and slowly sink down to the ground, wrapping my arms around my legs and resting my head on my knees.

"Annabel heard me say I was coming over and called Zeke before I could say anything! But honestly, I'm glad she did. And technically, I didn't go against your wishes. Annabel did."

I hear her say something in the background and roll my eyes.

"Charlie, you're making this into a thing that it doesn't need to be. I just needed a little bit of comfort, not a brigade."

"Sorry, Gabi. Hey, can we give him the code to your courtyard? He says he's a block away, Annabel's on the phone with him."

I sigh, pushing an old dress out of my face. "Yeah."

"Is Dustin still shouting at you?"

"Um, hold on, let me get out of the closet."

I hear directions being given in the background and slowly drag myself out on my hands and knees to listen.

"You're in the closet? What were you going to do, sleep in there?"

"Yeah, if I had to."

"Gabi," he scolds, and there's a hint of pity in his voice that I *hate*. "Zeke's outside your door. He says he doesn't see anyone."

"Okay." And now I feel even stupider. I caused an emergency phone train and the emergency isn't even here anymore.

I unlock my bedroom door, putting Charlie on speakerphone as I climb up on my kitchen table to get a look out of the peephole.

And there he is. Dark hair, tall frame, his eyes roving across the hallway, his head on a swivel, and his phone pressed to his ear—Annabel, if I had to guess. He leans against the doorframe, his chest rising and falling rapidly. He must have run here.

"Zeke's here," I say. "Bye, Char."

"Text me when he leaves, okay?"

"Yeah, okay. Bye."

I slide off the kitchen table and push it back out into the middle of the kitchen—it's lopsided, but I can fix that later. I undo the chain, unlock the dead bolt, and open the door.

"Hey," he says, and his eyes run up and down my body the same way they did when the car flew by me. "You're okay." An appraisal rather than a question.

"Yeah, I'm sorry. I freaked out and thought calling Charlie was a good idea."

"Why didn't you call me? I was two blocks away?"

I shake my head. "I don't know, I didn't think about it. I just wanted a voice to distract me, you know? I didn't need you to come running. He's not, like, violent or anything. Just an asshole."

Zeke cocks his head at me. "Somebody showing up at your apartment who you don't want there is enough to come running. Especially with all this," he says, motioning to the stairwell and the courtyard beyond. "I guess I thought the courtyard was a safe space, but I take it he knows the code?"

I nod. "We were together for almost two years. He knows the code."

"You should talk to management. Have them change it."

"I doubt they'll do that. There are fifty apartments off this courtyard. People will revolt if they change the gate code."

His eyes narrow. "If I lived here, I would rather not have an unwelcome guest in my courtyard, regardless of the reason. It kind of puts all the residents at risk, you know, not just you."

I shrug. "Maybe I'll email them."

"Please do."

I nod. "Okay."

He's quiet for a moment. "So are you okay?"

I let out a long breath. "Yeah, I'm okay."

"Do you want me to stay?"

I shake my head. "No, I'll be fine. I really didn't need anybody to come for me. I just wanted a voice, you know?"

"You know you don't need to feel bad about people caring that you're alright."

I give him one short nod. "I know, Zeke, and if I was actually in danger, I would have called you."

He cocks his head to the side. "Would you have, though? Because if you're scared enough to hide in the closet, you're probably in danger enough to have called me."

He has a point there.

"I promise that instead of hiding in my closet next time, I'll call you."

"Thank you." He glances around the hallway as if he's searching the shadows for someone hiding within them and turns back to me. "You're sure you're alright?"

I give him a look.

"Okay, okay. You're alright," he says, holding up his hands. He takes a step back, away from the door. "I'll be on my way."

He turns to the stairs and starts heading down.

"Thank you," I call after him, and he pauses, smiling at me through the iron of the railing.

"Anytime, Gabs."

2

ZEKE

By the time I get back to my apartment, I'm no longer tired. Leaving Charlie's, I was worried I'd fall asleep on the trolley home, but after my sprint back to Gabi's, I'm wide awake. Calls like that prey on everything I fear most, especially when I'm not hearing it from the source.

I walk instead. I need the movement to quell the jittery feeling running through my veins. If I had already been on the trolley by the time Annabel called, I might not have made it in time. There's no saying whether my presence helped—I didn't see anyone lurking—but that doesn't mean *they* didn't see *me*.

I don't exactly look nice.

And I use that to my advantage as I shove my hands in my pockets, the wind whipping my skin as I walk home. It's not a nice area that separates Gabi's neighborhood from mine, so I stay along the main road with its streetlights and bright storefronts.

Hopefully tonight was just a misjudgment on her ex's part and she won't hear from him again. Maybe he was a little drunk and thought he could shoot his shot. I don't know much about him, but the next time I see Charlie, I'll ask. There was a lot of reassurance going on tonight, that Gabi is just fine and Dustin's not a concern.

But you don't hide in your closet from someone who's not problematic.

Something more is going on there that she hasn't told me.

Then again, people don't usually freely share the most intimate details of their past. Gabi and I are friends, but not close enough to suddenly start asking about her past relationships.

Maybe we should be closer.

I do know Charlie well, though, and he's protective of her in a way that I haven't really seen before. At least not before Annabel.

That must mean something.

I round the corner to my building, goose bumps prickling over my skin as another gust of wind hits my neck. It's that weird time of year when the sun is hot midafternoon, but the nights are brisk. If I knew game night was going to last this long, I would have dressed a little warmer.

I push into my apartment and throw my keys on the counter, flipping on the kitchen light. I pour a glass of water and lean over the granite countertop for a moment, unlocking my phone and shooting off a quick text to Gabi.

ZEKE

Still okay?

GABI

Still okay. Thanks Zeke.

I nod, even though no one can see me, and do a quick

scan through my texts to make sure no one else in my life needs saving before heading into the living room and sinking into my leather armchair.

I lean my head back and close my eyes.

And then I hear a noise.

I straighten, my ears tuned to a swishing noise that *must* be coming from somewhere inside my apartment.

I get up quietly, keeping my glass in my hand in case I have to smash someone over the head with it.

Is the noise coming from my bedroom?

I walk down the short hallway off the living room, and as I pass my office, I realize the noise is coming from the other side of the door. I pause, listening.

One hand clenching the glass of water and the other hand on the door knob, I push it open.

She screams.

I scream.

"Jesus Christ, Kelly!"

"God, Sneak, can't you knock?"

My sister holds her hand over her heart, long red hair trailing over one shoulder and a mess of makeup smudged across her face, blurring her little freckles. She's wearing one of my old T-shirts, which she must have rooted around for quite a bit because I haven't worn it in years.

I let the door swing open, the room coming into view.

The futon that lines one wall is pulled out, a pile of blankets haphazardly thrown on top of it. A glass of water sits on the floor precariously close to my sister's foot, and next to it, a sleeve of crackers is ripped open, crumbs spilling out onto the carpet.

At least it's not on my desk. After one too many spills, Kelly's been banned from eating or drinking around my tech setup. I'd rather run the vacuum every time she stays than have to buy new equipment.

"You have to tell me if you're staying over! How did you even get here?" My racing heart slows.

She shakes her head, still coming down from the scare. "I took an Uber."

I hate when she does that. And tonight, I was one neighborhood away from her. I could have easily walked an extra couple of blocks to Uber with her.

When I moved to the city, I chose a location where I could get a nicely sized apartment and still have access to nightlife. I didn't consider the possibility of Kelly one day crashing here.

I'll be fine walking around North Philadelphia by myself, but Kelly isn't even old enough to drink yet and thinks that with a smile and her high school track records, she can run away from any problem that might arise.

I need to move somewhere safer if she's going to keep popping up like this.

Of course, I might be a little too primed for this after what happened at Gabi's.

I let out a long breath. "Why didn't you call me?"

She shrugs. "You told me you had game night tonight. I didn't want to interrupt, but Carly has people over and they're being so *loud*. I didn't need a ride, just somewhere to crash for a night."

Kelly huffs as she sits on the edge of the futon, reaching for another cracker.

Judging by her smeared makeup and the fact that she's wearing my clothes, I can only imagine there was a heated conversation that drove her here. She and her roommate have been butting heads since moving in together, mostly because of Carly's party priorities and Kelly's sleep-deprived crabbiness.

"Text me next time, okay?"

She nods and then fixes me with a look. "Knock next time, okay?"

"I'll knock if you text."

She narrows her eyes. "Deal."

"Good night, Kell," I say, pulling the door closed between us.

"Good night, Sneak."

GABI FLASHES into my mind as soon as my eyes pop open.

I wake with a mild hangover that I'll blame on her and Charlie—Gabi, for chatting with her sister for so long, and Charlie, for taking that opportunity to pour me another whiskey and shove it into my hand.

I grab my phone off my nightstand and text her.

ZEKE

Still good?

I don't expect a text back right away. It's early.

I take a sip of water from the glass on the nightstand, tepid from sitting overnight. Light leaks in around the edges of my curtains, and I try to determine the likelihood of actually falling back asleep. Despite all of my attempts to prolong my nights—dark furniture, blackout curtains, white noise—I always wake up just a little too early.

Which would be fine—I'm used to it by now—except Kelly's here, and she's holding my laptop hostage in my office while she sleeps.

I'm currently trying to plug through the rest of a troublesome website for my favorite deli, owned by a sweet senior couple who's lived and worked here since before the questionable north end of Northern Liberties was cool. If Kelly weren't here, I'd be hammering away at it in my office, and there's a chance I could finish by this afternoon.

But since she is, I pull on a pair of sweatpants, grab my water, and tiptoe downstairs. The light is brighter down here, the big windows spilling streams of sunlight out over the dark leather and the thick Oriental rug underneath the coffee table.

I start a pot of coffee, using the trendy crème brûlée-flavored grounds Kelly bought me when she tasted my preferred "ass water" coffee. I cringe at the sound of the water gushing into the pot and hold my breath for a moment as I wait to hear if I woke her up.

When it's done, I pour myself a cup and fall into the couch, mindlessly scrolling and waiting, waiting, waiting. For Gabi to text me back. For Kelly to wake up.

I let out a long breath and sink further into the leather. I'm not good at sitting still. At focusing on nothing.

But I will take this sort of waiting over the endless waiting of an office job, any day.

After college, I worked for my then-girlfriend's family's accounting firm. And at the time, every moment was an exercise in patience. Waiting on clients. Waiting for tax season. Waiting for copies to be made or forms to be filed or payments to clear.

To think I almost chose a girl over my passion.

If that's the price of love, I don't want it.

I'm happy where I am.

Freelance web design isn't the sexiest of jobs. It's stressful, and there's no one to fall back on but myself.

But at least it's not accounting.

I top off my coffee and sneak back into my bedroom to throw a T-shirt on. I usually love mornings where I can get up and knock out a good chunk of work before most people are out of bed.

But Kelly has my damn laptop.

And I could have sworn Gabi was an early riser. She should have gotten back to me by now.

Some memory snags in my mind, her blond hair thrown across dark sheets, a sleepy smile in the early morning sun.

I pause, my coffee mug halfway to my lips. *That's not a memory. That's an intrusive thought. An intrusive daydream?*

The image passes through my head again. Gabi turning toward me, wrapped in a T-shirt that's far too big for her, long bare legs twisted in my—

"Nope," I say aloud. I shake the thought from my head.

And then I hear movement. I must have spoken louder than I intended.

I go to my office door and knock gently. "Kell?"

"Yeah?"

I push open the door. She's lying in a tangle of blankets, her phone inches from her face as she scrolls.

"I just need my laptop," I say, skirting the futon and pulling it from the charger.

"Mom and Dad want to know if you want breakfast."

"Right now?" I pause at the door.

She nods, her eyes still on her phone. "They're on their way into the city."

"Here?"

She looks at me. "Well, yeah. We're both here."

I guess I won't be getting any work done this morning after all. "Sure."

Kelly gets down most of a cup of coffee while I run through a double-time version of my morning routine.

When they text us they're here, Kelly flies through the door to greet them, and I check my phone again, hoping Gabi's name will appear, before shutting the door and locking it behind us.

My mom's red hair is braided over her shoulder as she steps out of the car, an older and more refined version of my sister. She wraps Kelly in a big hug, and then turns to me to do the same. I feel the imprint of her lipstick on my cheek and do my best to surreptitiously wipe it off when she turns away.

My dad walks around the car, clapping me on the back in greeting. He takes off his driving glasses and hands them to my mom to keep in her purse, and gives Kelly a quick hug and a kiss on the head.

As we walk down the street toward the diner and I check my phone yet again, a sense of unease settles on me.

I remind myself that Gabi is *probably* fine. But I struggle to follow the conversation happening between my parents and Kelly, my mind constantly drawn back to my phone.

It would have been so much easier if I had brought her home with me and tucked her between my sheets so I knew she was okay.

I shake off the thought as we reach the diner, Kelly leading the way and holding open the door for the rest of us.

We sit down at a booth next to an oversized display of pies, and a portly older woman comes by to take our drink orders. I wonder for a second if Kelly is going to try to sneak a Bloody Mary as her gaze slides across the drink menu.

And then my phone buzzes in my pocket. I whip it out, far more anxious for an answer than I should be, and a wave of relief washes over me.

GABI

Still good Zeke, you can stop worrying now.
:)

I can hear the sarcasm in her voice, even over text.

"And for you, hun?" the waitress asks, turning to me.

Relief pumps through my veins as I say the first thing that comes to my mind. "I'll have a Bloody Mary."

Kelly shoots me a look that tells me I'll be drinking very little of it.

3

GABI

The yoga studio is on the second floor of a converted townhouse. The stairway is long and steep and opens to a dimly lit room outfitted in warm oranges and reds, sheer curtains blocking out the last few tendrils of light as the sun sets.

It's quiet, aside from the breathing of ten ladies lined up in two rows through the room.

We move back into downward dog and slowly, as a group, sink into child's pose.

These classes are one of the few things that relax me. Something about the focus it requires calms me, almost like someone telling me to focus only on the stretch of my limbs magically melts the stress away.

I never meant to become a *yoga girl*.

During college and in the years after, I was a gym girl. I lifted weights and took spin classes like they were magic beans. Something about the physicality of pushing myself quieted the noise in my mind, and once I combined that with the mental focus of yoga, there was no going back.

When I was still reeling from my breakup with Dustin, I

came to the studio every night for whatever class was available—vinyasa, power, hot, yin. Knowing that I needed an outlet and a safe space, I bought myself a monthly pass and decided anytime I was upset, I would go do yoga. Any yoga.

It was only supposed to be for a few months. A little indulgence to carry me through a rough time. But then a few months ago, Frankie Carver happened, and the monthly pass was here to stay.

Just the thought of him sends a shiver down my spine.

He was an ideal hookup—a jawline that could cut glass, deep brown eyes that weren't afraid meet my gaze, and thick, mouthwatering muscles lining every inch of his body. It was only months after Dustin and I had broken up, and he seemed like the perfect rebound.

And if we ended up really connecting, that would be okay too.

Charlie and I sell advertising to people who have too much money and can't find anything good to do with it. Charlie's the main salesperson on our team—he's good at schmoozing—but I'm the one who does the research on who we're selling to. So while he gets to show up for a fancy dinner on the corporate card, I'm the one who knows the client he's meeting with has been sued five times in the past ten years for discrimination. Or uses his wife as a punching bag when things don't go his way.

And before we met up with Frankie for dinner, I joked to Charlie that Frankie Carver was one of the few clients I'd be willing to sell without him.

At the time I wasn't kidding, but I shudder to think what might have happened had Charlie not been there.

After a dinner of surreptitious flirting and footsie under the table, I headed to the bathroom. I had to find a way to send Charlie home without making it obvious what my plan was. And sure, screwing a client isn't the *greatest* plan in the world, but I certainly wouldn't be the first person at that table to do so.

Frankie slipped in when I was stepping out of the stall, and I paused, startled to see him in the women's bathroom.

Something happened in that moment, a great reconciliation of what I was planning versus what I had gotten myself into.

I smiled and laughed as I washed my hands, drying them with one of those fancy, thick paper towels. As I threw it in the trash, he wrapped one arm around my waist, bending down and kissing me so lightly that for a moment I forgot we were in the women's bathroom. That only a few seconds ago, it had struck me as inappropriate that he was here at all.

And then he spun me around, pressing me up against the counter, his leg pushing forcefully between mine.

A noise of surprise jumped from my throat that he smiled at.

"Frankie, not here," I whispered, smiling at him, laughing it off.

"Come on, Gabi, you know you want to."

His hand weaved into my hair, resting on my neck and pulling me to him.

"Not here," I repeated, turning my head from him. I gave him a playful, scolding look.

"Gabi," he whined, pulling my hair so he could kiss me again. He pressed harder into me, and my heart thumped in my chest. His hands moved down my hips, one reaching behind me and fiddling with the zipper of my skirt.

My hand followed his, interfering with his movements.

"Frankie. Not here," I said, finally. Forcefully.

He grinned at me—a grin that only a minute or so ago, was charming. Boyish, even.

It only took a second for that charm to completely evaporate.

"Don't worry, babe. I pulled one of the mop carts up outside the door. Everybody will think it's being serviced," he said and then paused, chuckling into my neck. "So I can service you."

I swallowed to avoid dry heaving.

"Stop," I said, pushing on his chest, but he didn't budge.

It was then that I realized how lucky I had been with Dustin.

Dustin, who despite being an emotionally manipulative asshole, had never cornered me in a bathroom and forced himself on me.

Frankie leaned in again, forcing his mouth on me as he pulled on my skirt, but he couldn't get it to budge. He started grabbing at my shirt instead, untucking it, and I seized the opportunity while there were a few inches of space between us, to slam my knee into his crotch.

He howled. I ran.

It was only when I got back to the table and Charlie's bewildered gaze swept me that I realized he had ripped my shirt. And a minute later, when Frankie returned to the table, it dawned on me that what transpired in that bathroom wasn't something we could ignore.

Frankie was *pissed*.

And the normally cool and collected Charlie became a ball of rage.

Around the time his fist connected with Frankie's face, I started crying.

Charlie stayed with me afterward. He talked to the police with me. He took me home and made me a cup of tea.

He offered to stay the night on my couch too, but I needed to be by myself at that point.

I needed to retreat into my apartment and not come out for a few days.

And when I finally did, I went to yoga.

Corinne turns the lights brighter, ending the class with a gentle "Namaste."

I sit up on my heels, taking a few deep breaths and savoring in the last few moments of class before everyone makes a mad dash to the cubbies that line the wall for their bags and shoes.

Gemma is on my right side, Natalie on my other. They live in the neighborhood and also have monthly passes, and after seeing each other in so many classes, we've become our own little group. We all have our own lives to focus on outside class, but every once in a while we make a trip to a bar down the street for a drink. Once in a blue moon, Corinne joins us too.

"God, I needed that," Gemma sighs as she stands up from her mat. She takes a sip of water, rolling her neck. "Taylor has been screaming bloody murder all week and god, it was so nice to just not *hear* anything for a while."

Gemma is a stay-at-home mom of a two-year-old girl named Taylor. If her husband gets home early enough to take over parenting duties, yoga is her first stop. She has big, curly brown hair that she wrangles into a braid for class. She plays with the ends of it while toeing the edge of her mat, folding it over.

"Me too." The memory of Frankie Carver threatens to make a comeback in my mind. I push the thought away.

Chatter in the room grows as Corinne strikes up a conversation with a few younger girls who are on their way out the door. Temple students, if I had to guess.

"Do we have an unhealthy addiction?" Natalie asks, reaching up and adjusting the high puff atop her head. She sits cross-legged on her mat, staring at the burning candle Corinne left on a stool at the front of the room.

"Yes." Gemma and I speak at the same time.

Natalie laughs, slowly coming to her feet.

We roll up our mats and make our way to the edge of the room where our things are scattered. I do the velcro on Gemma's mat straps and she does mine. Natalie, the chaotic one, simply shoves her mat haphazardly into her oversized tote and calls it a day. We pull on our sweaters and our shoes, and adjust the post-yoga hair that's always a little unpredictable.

"Hold up a minute before you leave, ladies!" Corinne says, eyeing us as she blows out the candle.

She rushes over in a wave of spandex, her sheer shawl billowing out around her as she pads almost silently toward us. She's a little older than us, her black hair tied into a loose braid over her shoulder, her skin a deep tan color. One arm bears an intricate tattoo filled with cherry blossoms and Japanese lettering.

She takes a deep breath when she reaches us, meeting each of our gazes before speaking. I haven't ever seen her so serious, and it spurs an unpleasant feeling in my gut that she's about to tell me something I don't want to hear.

"So I wanted to talk to you ladies."

Natalie's brown eyes are narrowed, fixed on Corinne's face.

Corinne sighs. "I don't even know how to say this."

Gemma glances at me, her face pinched.

Corinne shakes her head, her braid falling behind her shoulders. "I guess I just have to say it." She puts her hands on her hips and bites her lip. "The studio will be closing in six weeks."

My heart stops. A lump builds in my throat. "What? Why?"

She smiles sadly and shakes her head. "For a long time now, I've been thirsting for something more. I love this studio, but I need to follow my passion and continue growing in my career. So, for the next few months, I'll be teaching future yoga teachers at a studio in Center City. If all goes well, I might reopen—maybe a school just for that. But for now, I'll be closing. Your month ends on the thirty-first but you girls feel free to keep coming until we close."

"You can't close," Gemma sputters.

Corinne's eyes dip. "I'm sorry."

"We need you."

"I know, Gemma. But I have to step into the next stage of my life. It's time." Corinne reaches forward and squeezes her shoulder. "You girls should consider doing the teacher training. All three of you would be great at it."

Gemma's eyebrows pinch together. She doesn't have time to do teacher training with all of the responsibilities of motherhood.

"And hey, someone else might come along and open this right back up. You might never know the difference!"

"It's not the yoga. It's you," Gemma says, and I'm not sure that she means it as nicely as it comes out. She's pouting, her face pink, as Corinne pulls her in for a hug.

"I'm sorry, Gem."

"Well I'm sad you won't be here anymore but I'm happy for you," Natalie says.

I nod, realizing I'd been stunned to silence with the news. "Yeah, good for you, Corinne." Gemma's eyes flit between us, as if searching for a way to be happy for Corinne despite the devastating news.

"Thank you, ladies. Keep in touch, okay? And keep up your practice."

She squeezes Gemma's hand again before turning back to the front of the room, her focus shifting to her post-class cleanup.

Gemma's eyes are wide as Natalie and I direct her to the door.

"I can't believe this," Gemma says. Natalie heads down the stairs first, then Gemma, then me.

"I know, it sucks," Natalie says, reaching behind her to grab Gemma's hand.

"No, this place was *my* place."

We push through the door at the bottom of the stairs and enter the small walkway that snakes along the side of the building, the door slamming shut behind us.

"We'll find somewhere to go," I say, giving her a quick hug.

She turns to me, her eyes wide. "Promise me."

"I promise," I say, taken aback by the forcefulness of her request. I guess I wasn't the only one who found solace here. Maybe in the same way this studio quiets my brain, it grants Gemma a small relief from the pressures of her own life.

She sighs, shaking her head. "Okay."

We continue single file down the walkway to the street.

"I'm mad," she says.

"Me too."

"How dare Corinne follow her dreams."

Natalie and I laugh.

"I hope I didn't come off as unsupportive," she says, pausing as we get to the gate.

"You didn't," Natalie says, catching my eye.

Gemma grimaces, noticing our look. "Okay, I have to go back in and apologize." She lets out a grunt of frustration as she turns on her heel and heads back up the stairs.

"Poor girl," Natalie comments, unlatching the gate and pushing through.

"She'll be okay. We'll find another place," I repeat.

Natalie smiles and throws her arm around my shoulder for a quick hug. "We will. Text me, okay?"

I nod. It's not lost on me that it's the first time she's told me to keep in touch. We're all attached to this studio in our own weird ways.

But it's nice to think that even though the end is coming for this place, it's not coming for us.

I smile as Natalie waves a chaotic goodbye and heads in the opposite direction, toward her apartment. She hikes her bag up on her shoulder, her mat nearly spilling out, and stuffs her hands into the pockets of her sweatshirt.

I zip my jacket closed, turning into the October wind.

And it takes me a second to realize Zeke is standing right in front of me.

"Hey," he says, stepping out of the shadows. He had been leaning up against the facade of the building, scrolling through his phone. He locks it and slips it into his back pocket. He's dressed warmer today than he was the other night—a dark, thick sweater with dark jeans.

It dawns on me again how intimidating he looks at first glance—a tall, broad shadow with eyes that could bore holes right through you.

But then he smiles, and his whole menacing demeanor turns soft.

"What are you doing here?"

I realize I've stopped walking in the middle of the sidewalk, and take a few steps toward him to allow a couple to pass us.

He shrugs. "I was in the neighborhood. You mentioned you walk home from yoga by yourself, and I just thought you might like some company."

I nod, not totally believing this story. "Really?"

"Really."

I debate telling him I don't need company. It really isn't a dangerous walk *at all*. This feels different from him walking me home from Charlie's or whatever bar our group ends up at on the weekend.

It seems more intimate, somehow.

"Okay."

We fall into step beside each other.

"So how was yoga?"

I sigh, giving him an overdramatic frown. "The studio is closing."

His eyebrows rise. "Why?"

"The owner––who is also the teacher––has decided that she wants to do teacher training instead."

Zeke's eyebrows knit together.

"Like, she wants to teach yoga teachers, not us yoga peasants."

"Ah." He nods.

"Which really sucks because her studio was the best around. I don't know what I'm going to do with myself." I look both ways before we cross the street, the memory of last time's near-fatal collision burned into my memory. "She said we should join her class. Do teacher training with her."

Zeke cocks his head at me. "You should."

"It takes up so much time."

I've looked into it before. Some programs last months, some weeks, but the requirements are all the same to get a basic certification—two hundred hours, no more and no less. It's a big-time commitment.

"Yeah, but it's something you love, isn't it?"

That's a loaded question. "It brings me peace."

He nods. "So it's more than something you just *enjoy*."

I shrug noncommittally. "I mean, I enjoy it. I enjoy the *crap* out of it. But the past few months have been really hard, and it's become something more to me. Like if I stop going, I might actually lose my shit. That's why all this"—I motion behind me to the studio—"is a little overwhelming."

"Maybe that's a reason you *should* go."

"To teacher training?"

His eyes dart back and forth as we cross another intersection. "You know, take control of your own destiny," he says, somewhat mockingly.

"What if it doesn't bring me peace anymore?"

"What if you can make your own peace?"

I narrow my eyes. "You make an interesting argument."

He flashes me a quick grin. "I was in your shoes once."

"I didn't know you were such a yoga fiend."

He snorts. "When I first started freelancing, I had the same thought. Will doing it for a living ruin it for me?" He shrugs. "I mean, there was a lot more to it than that. I kind of exploded my whole life when I decided to start freelancing, but I wouldn't take it back for a second. Sometimes I think back on how close I was to just staying the course in my boring accounting job, and I get that feeling in my chest like I narrowly missed death." He glances at me. "Or something."

I nod, thrown by his candor. He turns his face to the sky, one side lit by the streetlights above, the other shrouded in darkness. "I guess all I'm trying to say is that I know how it feels. That hesitancy to step beyond just enjoying something for what it is."

We're silent for a beat.

"And you never regret it?"

I watch him carefully as he speaks. "There are times I've wondered if I couldn't have gotten used to what my life was before. But no, I never regret it."

The only sound is that of our shoes against the pavement.

I feel like I'm in *The Matrix*, faced with a red pill or a blue pill. Zeke's already taken the red pill. *Will I join him or continue as I am?*

"Can you do one-off classes with your teacher and a couple other girls or something? Like an under-the-table sort of setup?"

His question catches me off guard. "Uh. I don't know, I'd have to ask. I never really thought about it."

"She might just be bummed out about the administrative stuff, you know. It might not be the 'teaching peasants' thing," he says with air quotes. He gives me another grin that I can't help but mirror back to him.

I shrug. "Maybe. That'd be nice."

"That's part of what bums me out—invoices and scheduling and formalities. But I have some really cool clients— that's what really keeps me going. She might just need a break from all the mindless tasks. You should ask her about it."

I shrug. "Okay. I'll ask."

"Speaking of asking," he starts as my building looms ahead of us, "did you talk to management about getting the gate code changed?"

I grimace. "No."

"Do it, Gabi."

"I will."

"There's no reason to be nervous going into your own home."

I sigh, stepping up to the gate. "I know. It's just embarrassing."

He cocks his head to the side, his eyes watching mine. "Why?"

I shake my head, punching in the same code I've always punched in, and pushing through. "I guess because I made a bad decision in ever letting Dustin in, in the first place. And my bad choice is the reason why someone will inevitably get locked out. Someone is going to be bad-mouthing the young blonde who doesn't know any better. Someone is going to whisper, 'I think that's her, she's the reason Cindy or Becca or George got locked out for two hours and missed baby Zelda's christening.'"

He blinks at me, and I realize that I probably let out a little too much of the crazy. My breath catches in my throat as he nods.

"Have you ever thought that perhaps in that situation, it's not your fault for getting a new code—which probably should happen at a regular cadence *anyway*—but their fault for failing to write down or remember four measly little digits?"

I sigh. "Zeke, I know I'm nuts. I know I need to ask. What's one more day, you know?"

"One less day you have to worry about a psycho ex showing up."

"He's not psycho." Even as I say the words, I know how they must sound to him. Dustin isn't a threat. He just gets in places he shouldn't be sometimes. Apparently.

Zeke rolls his eyes. "Gabi."

"I know."

We reach the stairwell to my apartment and my heart hitches up a beat. The past few days—since Dustin—I've been carrying my pepper spray in one hand, my keys in the other.

Not that he's a threat. Just *in case.*

But I don't want Zeke to see that. I don't *need* to do that if he's here, right?

We head up the stairs, our footsteps echoing around us. I surreptitiously look up, searching for signs of anyone else in here with us. I glance at Zeke and see he's doing the same, his hands in his pockets so casually, like he's trying to give off an air of calmness just like I am.

"Thank you," I say as we step onto the second floor.

He smiles. "You're welcome." He throws a glance behind us.

"Get that code changed, okay?"

I slide my key in the door and unlock it, pushing it open. "I will."

He smiles as he winds his arms around my shoulders, pulling me in for a quick hug. It's a friendly hug—nothing suggestive about it—but I can't help leaning into him for a moment, the scent of soap and something deeper and muskier drawing me into him. My heartbeat slows as I take a breath into his shoulder.

"Good night, Gabrielle."

I pause as he steps away from me. "Gabriell*a.*"

His eyebrows shoot up, his eyes wide.

"Oh my god. I'm so sorry." He weaves a hand through his hair, taking another step back. "I've only ever heard anyone call you Gabi, and I didn't think to check if that was an *ah* at the end."

"It's okay, it happens a lot. Most clients call me Gabrielle anyway. I don't usually correct people at this point."

"Gabriel*la*."

"You got it."

He shakes his head. "I'm going to have to repent for that in some way."

I raise my eyebrows. "It's not that serious."

He rests his hands on my shoulders. "Gabi, just like you need to insist on the gate code getting changed, you should insist that people call you by your name."

I roll my eyes, but at the same time, my focus swarms around the heat of his hands on my shoulders.

"Well, I corrected *you*, didn't I?"

"Correct your clients too. That's not cool."

"Well, it's that or a paycheck."

He narrows his eyes at me. "No, it's not. Any good person wouldn't want to call you the wrong thing."

I resist the urge to tell him that most of my clients are not really *good* people. I wouldn't go so far as calling them all *bad*, but I also wouldn't lump most of them in the *good* category, either. The majority are entitled men with bank accounts thickened at the expense of others.

"Point taken," I say.

His hands leave my shoulders, and he takes a step toward the stairs. "Well, good night, Gabriel*la*."

"Good night, Zeke."

He takes a few steps down and disappears into the first floor. I head into my apartment and flip the dead bolt behind me as the door at the bottom of the stairs clangs shut.

As I turn toward my apartment, the only thing I can focus on is the warmth of my shoulders where his hands just were.

NOVEMBER

4

ZEKE

I've been walking Gabi home from yoga every chance that I get.

Over the past week or so, she's been stuck in my head like a song on repeat. Her teacher training. Her hesitancy to get her gate code changed. The way she doesn't correct people when they get her name wrong.

But there's also something incredibly charming about her. Something that has me yearning for what comes after game night. For that moment when we hear the distant ding of an elevator beyond the apartment door, the girls' murmurs growing louder as they approach.

Until then, I double-check that Kelly will not be needing a ride tonight—her roommate is going out rather than hosting—and pour myself another whiskey. Next to the bottle, Henry leans across the counter, his nose to his phone and his glass hovering just beneath his lips. He owns a T-shirt shop out in the suburbs, and one of his employees has been texting him nonstop tonight about making an update to their website that would allow for a one-page checkout flow. Henry already floated the idea to me–in about two seconds–and it's something I can take care of pretty quickly. But in the meantime, he has to calm down the overexcited employee who came up with the idea and reassure them that the change *will* happen. Just not right this second.

I take my fresh drink over to the large windows on the far side of the apartment where, beneath us, the lights of the city twinkle. Charlie stands only a few feet away, his eyes drawn to the lit up streets below us.

I can't help but wonder if he's imagining where Annabel is right now. I thought the nagging feeling in my stomach would go away with Kelly's confirmation that she won't be needing me.

But now my brain is stuck on Gabi, like I've folded her into my small collection of people I worry about, and I can't fully relax until I know she's good too.

"Where do you think the girls are?" I ask Charlie.

He shrugs, taking a step toward me.

"Last I talked to Annabel, they were heading to Concourse." He points out the window, angling so I can see where he's aiming. "And if I'm remembering correctly— where it is in relation to the Comcast Tower—it should be right at that traffic light."

I crinkle my eyebrows. "They're going dancing?"

Charlie shrugs. "I guess." He's quiet for a moment before he speaks again. "Gabi said you've been walking her home after yoga."

My face goes hot. On any normal day, it just feels like a part of my schedule. I've started to look forward to our walks like a nightcap after a long day.

But something about hearing it from Charlie's mouth makes it sound like something more than a friendship.

"Yeah, she's right near Kelly so it works out."

Charlie nods. "That's nice of you. She doesn't like leaning on people."

"I can tell." I take a sip of my drink. "Should I be worried about that guy?"

"Who, Dustin?"

I nod.

Charlie shrugs. "I don't know. He was nice until he wasn't. Or maybe I just didn't pick up on it. She became this shell of a person when she dated him, and it probably took me longer than it should have to realize what was happening. We talked about it eventually, and it seemed like she *knew* on some level that he wasn't a good guy. Maybe she just didn't want to admit it." He shakes his head. "She still dated him for months afterward, but one day she hit her breaking point and flat-out cut him off."

"Good for her."

Charlie nods. "She's got willpower, that's for sure. When she makes up her mind, she goes all in."

I take a sip of my whiskey. "Remind me to never get on her bad side."

"If I haven't gotten on her bad side yet, I think you'll be fine."

"Alright guys, we're ready!" Kick shouts from behind us.

We turn to see him arranging game pieces on the table, Oliver with a scowl on his face on the couch next to him.

Oliver is the artist of the group and takes it upon himself to draw our game boards. He works a stuffy corporate job through the week where he busts his ass for one promotion after another, and on the weekends, the easygoing, fun-loving guy we knew in college comes out to play. I've caught him on work calls before and it's such a stark difference from his usual goofy self that sometimes I wonder how he keeps up the appearance.

He smooths out the hand-drawn game board, making a point to fix the bent corners while Kick sorts, shaking his head. As the writer of the group, he butts heads with Ollie often, mostly because Ollie crafts a storyline to fit into his elaborate game boards, whereas Kick wants a story with immediacy, conflict, and clear direction––regardless of the bounds of the game board.

Oliver tugs on the game board, lining it up with the edge of the table, and the game pieces Kick sorted get jumbled up in the process. His jaw ticks as he side-eyes Ollie, but he doesn't say anything––he just picks right back up where he left off.

I sigh, taking another sip of my whiskey.

Something tells me this is going to be a long night.

5

GABI

Tonight is a girls' dinner, and Steph has steered us toward a new Thai BYOB she's been wanting to try. Afterward, we'll head back to Annabel's and see how game night is going.

At least, that's the inkling of a plan that I've been trying to set into motion all night.

Until our server stops by to apologize for the swamped kitchen and lets us know he'll be giving us a discount on the meal so we should feel free to pop over to the liquor store across the street for more wine while we wait.

"I'll get it!" Steph is moving before he finishes his sentence.

His eyes follow her movements as she dives into her bag for her wallet and stands, winding between close-set tables until she disappears through the front door. Her hair is a wavy blaze of yellow-blonde billowing behind her as the heels of her boots clip-clop across the wood floor.

Steph is good at that—grabbing attention and holding it effortlessly. I always do things "right." I get my hair light-ened, wear the appropriate clothes for the occasion, come prepared to any and all meetings or outings, keep my nails clean and usually manicured.

Yet Steph blazes in with last night's makeup on her face, her hair a wild mess that she leans into rather than fixing, and throws on whatever's first in her closet without bothering to check if it matches her shoes.

And she always looks perfect. My little sister, the free-flowing, free-loving version of me who sees my anxious mess and makes a total mockery of it.

When she returns from the liquor store, she takes to refilling our glasses. Our dinners show up a few minutes later, our server delivering them with a flourish and asking if we need anything else. If I'm not mistaken, I see his eyes linger on Steph again. We thank him, and he moves on to his next table.

"You know what we should do?" she asks once he's gone.

I don't mean to catch Annabel's eye, but I do.

"We should go dancing!" she says, taking another sip of her wine. "Wouldn't that be fun?"

"Oh, we should!" Mari says. She's Annabel's best friend, another victim of The Great Elevator Breakdown in which Annabel also met Charlie. Talk about trauma bonding.

Mari is a little pixie with sharp, delicate features. She's like Annabel's shadow, that same dainty body type, but with shiny dark hair she's been growing out over the past few months and now cascades down her back in waves. She and Steph are like two peas in a pod, always ready for the next adventure, while Annabel and I want to go home and start our skincare routines.

And then there's Carrie, who plays the role of Switzerland like it's her job. She has that big, curly blonde hair that she just can't tame, and equally big blue eyes that can pin you from across the room. She's a chronic observer, content to listen and smile and enjoy.

"We're not near any good dancing places," Annabel says through a bite of her food. The polka dot bow in her hair falls over her shoulder as she eats and she quickly jerks her head back to stop it from slipping into her food.

"We're near tons of good dancing places!" Mari says. "I'm definitely partial to the Gayborhood, but I will accept neon lights and ball pits and straight men if that means you guys will go."

I know the bar she's talking about. Every time we go there, we get ogled like zoo animals. But it's right around the corner from Charlie's.

Charlie, who's hosting game night right now. With Zeke.

The thought of him walking me home later sends a little shiver of warmth down my spine.

It's not that I necessarily *expect* Zeke to walk me home, but it's almost like *he* does. Whenever we all end up at Charlie's, I can sense his eyes on me, like he's reached that point in the night when he's ready to go and he's just waiting for me to get there too. Like it doesn't even cross his mind to leave without me.

If it was anyone else, I would assume he expects something from me. But he never makes a move.

He's been walking me home from yoga almost every night, emerging from the shadow of the building with a smile on his face and falling into step beside me. He asks me about my class and I ask him about Kelly, and we walk in companionable conversation until we reach my door, where he gives me the sort of hug I've found myself craving more of in the moments after, when I shut my door to his footsteps echoing down the stairs.

"Come on, just for an hour!" Steph says, her big eyes finding mine.

She knows if she can break me, the rest of the group will go.

Annabel's looking at me too, her eyebrows raised.

"Fine, just for an hour!"

Steph and Mari erupt in a chorus of cheers, and Annabel rolls her eyes. Carrie, across the table, smiles into her wine, her eyes following Steph and Mari.

I lower my voice to speak to Annabel. "It's only an hour."

She shakes her head. "I love you guys. And I love our nights out. But god, Charlie's been sending me spicy texts since we sat down and I'm just too horny for an hour."

A beat of silence washes over the table as we process Annabel's admission before we all start cackling.

"It's not funny!"

"I know, honey, but other people have to get laid too," Mari says, wrapping an arm around her shoulder and pulling her in for a hug. "I promise we won't keep you out late."

Annabel huffs and takes another sip of wine.

We finish our meals and our wine and head into the brisk November air. The bar is within walking distance, so we pull our coats tight and set off with our heads ducked to the wind.

When we get there, we're pleasantly surprised to see there's no line.

Until we get to the hostess, who informs us there's a significant cover.

I let the news sink over the group, hoping this is the nail in the coffin that'll let us go home. But instead, Steph and Mari start rummaging through their bags for cash.

"Here!" Mari says, handing over a twenty.

"Fuck, I don't have any cash!" Steph says.

"Me neither," Annabel says, and I can tell from her tone that she's hoping this is the end of the dancing idea, too.

Steph looks at me, eyes wide.

If there is one person in this world I can't say no to, it's her. And she knows it.

I huff as I reach into my bag and grab enough cash to cover everyone who doesn't have enough. "One hour," I remind her.

Inside, the music is too loud to talk, so Annabel and Carrie and I stake out a table and drink, waiting for Steph and Mari to be done. They're having the time of their lives, dancing and drinking and being general hooligans. There's a small part of me that's glad we came, considering how much fun they're having, but the larger part of me craves home.

Or maybe I'm just craving my walk with Zeke.

When they've had their fill, we head back outside. Annabel grabs a few pretzels from a cart on the street and passes them out to us to soak up the alcohol. Mari is still dancing to the music we can hear on the street, and—

Shit, where's Stephanie?

I whirl in place, searching for her blonde hair, and see her across the street, talking to a guy who's entirely too young for her while he hands her a cigarette and helps her light it. She waves over her shoulder as she walks back toward us, the lit cigarette held loosely between her fingers.

"Steph, what are you doing?"

"It's a Friday." She shrugs, taking a drag. Annabel hands her a pretzel and Steph's eyes light up as she takes a bite. "Oh shit, thanks."

"Steph," I scold, and even I hate the way I'm talking right now.

I'm tired and I don't want to be here and although I want my sister to have fun, she's annoying the daylights out of me. *Is this who I am now? A fun-killer?*

I want Steph to have fun.

But I also want her to live a full life.

Sure, one cigarette isn't going to kill her early.

But for fuck's sake, Steph, seriously? Sometimes I wonder if she does these things just to get on my nerves.

I swallow it, even as her gaze bores into me like she's daring me to say something.

It's one night, Gabi. One night.

I redirect my attention to the rest of the group, ignoring her pointed stare. "Shall we head back?"

"Yes!" Annabel shouts, already on the move and leading us toward her apartment.

Relief pounds through my veins as the rest of the girls follow her.

We're on our way.

The walk is short but the steps are long. I'm aching to take off my shoes and jacket and sit on a crowded couch with a bunch of boys playing a nerdy game.

There was a time in my life where going out dancing would have been my ideal Friday night, but I'm just not there anymore. I want to be comfortable, to chat with good friends and have a couple lazy drinks in a place where I don't have to watch my back or make sure my friends get home safe.

Until we reach Annabel's apartment, I'm the only one who'll make sure we don't lose anybody, that nobody gets hit by a car or targeted by someone with bad intentions. But once we're there, I can take a breath. Charlie will watch over Annabel, and Steph will get sucked into one of Oliver's never-ending stories. Mari will try to insert herself in the game even though she has no idea how to play. Carrie will watch it all happen with a little smile on her face like she always does.

And Zeke will lock eyes with me above it all, just as entertained as I am by our crazy friends.

Except, by the time we get there and head up the elevator to their floor, it seems that all chaos has broken out on the other side of the door. We hear their raised voices from all the way down the hall.

Annabel's eyebrows shoot up as she slips the key into the lock and gently pushes inside.

"Hey guys," she says hesitantly.

Oliver's face is bright red, and he and Kick are towering over a scribbled game board that's been torn clean in two. Henry sits in a chair by the window, looking out over the city lights, one hand absently scrolling through his phone as his attention turns toward us, and Charlie and Zeke lean on the kitchen counter, observing whatever was happening on the couch with full glasses of amber liquid in front of them.

"Steph," Oliver gasps, the color draining from his face.

"What's going on?" She takes a step toward them and looks down at the map.

Oliver and Kick glance at each other. "He said my story line doesn't make sense," Oliver says quickly, like he's tattling.

"It doesn't!" Kick insists. "And we went over this and agreed to a change and then you backpedaled!"

"Why are you being so overbearing? It's a freaking *story*!"

"There's no reason for action! Why would we put our characters' lives in danger if the bad thing isn't going to happen for another three thousand years? There's no immediacy!"

"We're putting our characters in danger because it's a game and that's what you do!"

"Not mine. I'm not sacrificing Delvin Pendergast on your stupid storyline without reason. Last time I did that, you killed him."

Mari's lips twitch, a smile threatening to break out. Steph holds her hand over her mouth, delight dancing in her eyes as they slide to mine.

"I didn't kill him, you took a gamble in combat and *lost*."

Kick takes a step toward him. "Because if I didn't, Henry's character would have *died*! You put us in an impossible position! This is why we don't let you dungeon master!"

"That's rude! I'm the only one with any sense of creativity here!"

Annabel moves into the kitchen, coming up on Charlie's other side and weaving an arm around his waist. He leans down to kiss her, one hand weaving into her hair.

For a moment, I'm jealous of what they have.

And then I notice Zeke looking at me, and my cheeks heat.

Steph picks up the pieces of the game board from the coffee table, holding them together.

"Oliver, did you draw this?" she asks.

Huffing, he breaks his gaze away from Kick and looks down at the pieces she's holding together. "Yeah, I did."

"Wow, you're so talented. Look at these mountain ranges," she comments, turning the map to Kick, who mutters something noncommittal under his breath. "I can't believe you did all this in pen. It's incredible."

Oliver shrugs. "I used to draw cartoons when I was in high school."

"Oh my god, and this dragon!"

And just like that, the tension in the room dissolves. Steph peppers in a few more questions about Oliver's map, and Henry meanders over, pulling Kick into a different conversation while putting a fresh drink in his hand.

I follow Mari and Carrie into the kitchen, where they promptly pour themselves wine from the box on the counter. Charlie is hunched over Annabel, talking close, and I feel almost like I'm infringing on one of their intimate moments even in the crowd of people surrounding them.

I lean on the counter on Zeke's other side.

"Are game nights always this interesting?"

He shakes his head, turning toward me. "Definitely not."

"I thought for a second we'd be walking in on a fistfight."

"I thought for a second I'd be breaking one up. Luckily Steph is a good distraction."

The eye roll that passes over my face is unintentional.

"What?" he asks.

I shake my head. I don't want to rehash the whole night right now. "Just, sisters. You know."

He nods. "Oh yes, I know."

He stands up straight, crossing his arms and leaning one hip on the counter.

"How is Kelly?" I ask, momentarily struck by his tall frame, the full height of him when he stands up straight. I'm used to being eye level with most guys—I'm on the tall side, too, after all. But he towers over even me.

"She's at home for the night," he says, seemingly relieved. He holds up his drink. "So I can sit back and enjoy the show." He nods to where Oliver and Steph are still chatting over his game board.

"Oh good," I say. I know how much he worries about her. It's sweet.

"Can I get you a drink?" he asks.

I wasn't going to have another, but what the hell. "Sure."

"I think Charlie only has wine and whiskey. And kiwi martinis, but—"

"Wine is perfect."

Zeke turns and weaves between where Mari and Carrie are chatting next to the box of wine. With him gone, I get an uninterrupted view of Charlie and Annabel making out.

I reach out and poke them both on the shoulders, and they turn to me, looking a little surprised. "Get a room."

Annabel glances around. "But everybody is here."

"We won't miss you."

They're quiet for a moment. "I have to get changed," Annabel says, and I can't help but laugh that she's even *trying* to play it cool. She takes a step away, nodding first at me, and then pointedly at Charlie.

He waits only a few seconds before following her. "I should help her."

Zeke places a glass of wine in my hand. "Finally. That was getting uncomfortable."

"They're new," I say. "New and fresh in love."

Zeke grins at me. "I didn't take you for a romantic."

I laugh. "I wouldn't go that far. I'm just happy for them."

"Me too. Not everybody gets that."

"Do you think you'll get that?" The question slips out before I have time to think about it. It's too personal, too intimate for our burgeoning friendship, and way too suggestive. I take a desperate sip of wine, hoping to hide the color leaching into my cheeks.

He blinks and then shrugs. "I think I already had it, and, uh, it wasn't all it's cracked up to be." He shrugs, uncrossing his arms. "What about you Gabriel*l*a, do you think you'll find a great love one day?" I don't miss the inflection in his voice when he says my name. He takes a sip of his whiskey, watching my face, and I struggle to find the right answer.

"I don't know. Probably not."

His eyebrows furrow. "Why not?"

I shrug. "When I was little, my dad told me that all great love really is, is great timing. It kinda took the wind out of love's sails, you know? Not that love doesn't exist. It just all comes down to these external factors that have to line up in the perfect way. I guess it just made me realize that—sure, it can be magic if that's what you're looking for—but all *great love* really is, is a bunch of things you can't control happening at the right time. And I don't see that happening for me."

I've never told anyone this before, and it feels weird to voice it right now over a glass of wine at someone else's apartment with Carrie and Mari chatting loudly behind us and a group of people on the couch drunkenly playing some game where you have to hold your phone on your forehead while everyone shouts terrible clues about what's on the screen.

"Maybe you just haven't let it happen for you because you choose to believe a cynic's definition of love instead of finding out for yourself."

"Or maybe it's saved me from countless terrible relationships that I would have stayed in if I believed in a fool's definition of love."

Zeke is quiet for a beat, his expression unreadable. "Has it?"

My heart catches.

It has not.

And this whole time I kind of thought it would, like knowing the truth about love would save me from the worst bits of it. I tried on different guys like they might be in the right place, at the right time for me, and they were all just wrong, wrong, wrong.

"No," I say, slightly dumbfounded.

Zeke shakes his head. "Hey, I'm sorry. That came off kind of harsh."

I laugh. "No, you're totally right. I just never thought about it that way."

Frankie, Dustin, Greg who I dated for two years but refused to introduce me to his parents, Cameron before him who showed up half an hour late to every date smelling of beer and weed because hanging out with his buddies was more important than doing anything with me.

I shake my head. "I've dated some real losers."

Zeke laughs. "At least now you know what to avoid."

"So, men?"

He laughs. "Probably a good start." He reaches out with his free hand and touches my arm, sending a little shiver down my spine. "For real though, I didn't mean to be an asshole. Charlie told me about Dustin tonight and it was fresh on my mind."

I snort. "Is that what boy talk is these days?"

He nods. "All night we sat around wondering what the girls were doing, what the girls were thinking, and then once you were on your way back we staged an elaborate fight scene in the living room to draw your attention to our manliness. Steph stepped in before we could start the sword fighting though."

I can't help but laugh. "Sword fighting, huh?"

He grins. "It's all part of the gameplay."

"Well next time I'll make sure she doesn't interrupt."

He crosses his arms again, a smug look crossing his face. "If you want to see it so badly, you can just ask, you know."

My jaw drops. "Zeke!"

"Zeke, are you saying something uncouth to the lady?" Kick asks, and our attention jumps to the couch, where Mari has the phone pinned to her forehead.

"She was upset she missed the sword fighting!"

"Oh no!" Carrie says in her mousey little voice, and the group busts out laughing.

Zeke grins at me and I shake my head, taking another sip of my wine. My face flushes at the thought of his *sword*, but I can't let it show. We have such a good friendship going.

Although, he's the one that offered.

His words send the flush rushing up my neck again. *You can just ask, you know*.

Jesus.

We refill our glasses and join our friends on the couch. I'm grateful to hold the silly phone on my forehead when it's my turn, but I can't escape his voice; it cuts through all of the other noise as everyone shouts at me. Even though I know he's trying to give me clues about the word on my forehead, all I can hear are the words he said earlier.

If you want to see it so badly, you can just ask, you know.

As if he wouldn't hesitate.

6

ZEKE

By the time we leave Charlie's, we've each had one too many drinks, and Gabi is a blonde blur in front of me. She saunters along in her tight little jeans with her jacket that doesn't keep her nearly warm enough, and I have to fight the thoughts of her that keep popping up in my head.

Until tonight, I hadn't seen Gabi in jeans, and—well, the yoga does her good. She keeps looking behind her like she's wondering why I'm not walking next to her, and I have to keep reminding myself that she's not there to be ogled.

And while the now-familiar flashes of Gabi in my bed, wearing my clothes, dance around in the back of my mind, there are new scenes there now too. The glide of her jeans down her legs, my thumb on her pouty bottom lip, trailing down her chin.

A Friday night movie. Breakfast at my kitchen table. Her yoga mat across my floor.

Wait.

I nearly trip over my feet as my body catches up to my mind.

Tonight has been confusing—I'm sure the alcohol doesn't help—and I keep seeing flashes of moments that aren't sexual in nature at all, but tender moments of laughter, or comfort.

And that's very strange.

It must have been her revelation tonight that love doesn't exist. That it's all just planning and convenience. She's been giving her life to timing rather than searching for something real and meaningful.

I had that once, even if it didn't turn out the way I wanted it to. Marissa wasn't my person, but I'm not about to say that some part of our relationship wasn't genuine love. Especially toward the beginning, at least.

And this girl who deserves nothing but the best of humankind has spent her life waiting for the universe to serve her the right person on a platter "when the time is right."

Gabi deserves better than that.

I fall into step beside her, my confused thoughts subsiding with the cool air on my face. She tugs her jacket tight around her shoulders and I feel the urge to tuck her under my arm, rub my hands along her skin to warm her up. But that doesn't seem like a good idea.

I shake my head in an effort to stop the overthinking.

I have one job to do: make sure Gabi gets home safe.

"You're quiet tonight," she says, knocking gently into me.

And the thoughts start again.

I shake my head. "Too much whiskey."

"Whiskey dick but in your other head?"

I let out a surprised laugh—there's something unique and erotic about the word 'dick' from Gabi's mouth. Like she's too proper for it.

But it's also comforting, like my stupid joke about

showing her mine backfired in a good way, and suddenly we can discuss things like dicks.

I cringe, thinking back on it. I was deflecting, my discomfort talking about love and feelings and stuff rearing its ugly head and deciding the appropriate moment to insert an inappropriate joke was immediately after Gabi confessed that she doesn't believe in love.

Even though I'm not sure I believe that.

The way she talked about it was almost wistful, like she thought some people could have it but she specifically couldn't.

And I wanted to insist that she's wrong, because if there's someone in this world deserving of true love, it's her.

So I made a dick joke.

"Yeah, something like that." I try to wipe the night from my mind but her words keep playing over and over, that love is nothing more than timing. There's something about that sentiment that I can't reckon with. "Hey, are your parents still together?"

Her eyebrows crinkle when she looks over at me.

She nods. "Yeah, they're together."

"Are they happy?"

She shrugs. "As far as I can tell, yes. They have their fights like anybody else but, yeah, I think they're happy."

I nod.

"Why?"

I shake my head. I don't want to say it, but it all seems so obvious to me.

But I guess obvious things become forgotten things when you're busy paying attention to all of the *other* things.

She cocks her head to the side, waiting for me to speak.

"It's just funny to me that you have this notion that love is all about timing despite watching your parents for, what, thirty-some years? You make this grand declaration that love isn't really *love*, but timing, yet the sole reason for that belief isn't living a lonely hermit lifestyle, but actively proving you *and* himself wrong."

She blinks, taking a breath as her attention turns to the sidewalk in front of her.

"I guess I never really thought about it that way."

"I mean, I could be wrong. I don't know you or your parents well enough to say that, but thirty years is a hell of a lot of life to hinge on timing."

Her eyes narrow. "You make an interesting argument."

I shrug. "Don't worry, we're reaching that point in conversation where I'll feel the need to make a dick joke soon."

She grins at me. "Is that what happened?"

"Maybe I just like keeping you on your toes."

Her apartment looms ahead of us, and I slow my steps, extending this limited alone time we have.

There's something about our walks that I've really been enjoying.

Just Gabi and me, walking and talking.

I watch her fingers as she steps up to the gate and punches in the code. It's the same one I punched in when Annabel called and told me to get my ass back to Gabi's in no uncertain terms.

She looks at me out of the corner of her eye.

"Gabi."

"I know."

"Email them."

"I will."

I grab her arm as she pushes through the gate and she pauses, looking up at me. "What if it was Stephanie?"

"Breaking in?" she asks, laughing. "She breaks in once a

month to water my plants. Well, they're her plants, really. I never wanted them and I'm pretty sure she just ran out of space to store them at her apartment."

I raise an eyebrow at her.

She sighs. "Yeah, I would be upset. It's just—" She turns to me as she leans up against the gate. "With Steph, I barely trust her to take care of herself sometimes. If some guy showed up, I'd have no doubt in my mind he had bad intentions. Zero doubt. But with me? I'm scared of Dustin because of the things he said, not the things he did. He was never violent. Never even outwardly mean, really. He was just a manipulative jerk whose words I was never able to unwind. It was me being weak, honestly. It was me not being able to differentiate between the sweet words and the constant cuts which he wove together *brilliantly*. I just couldn't figure out what he was really *saying* until hours later and by then, the moment had passed and if I brought it up, it would only make things worse. But he was never *dangerous*. I was just dumb."

She rolls her eyes as she continues along the pavement, waiting for me to follow. I shut the gate, trying to swallow the range of emotions that pulses through me.

I'd really like to cave in Dustin's face if I ever get the chance.

"You realize you're describing emotional abuse, right?"

She shoots me a glare over her shoulder. "I'm not a victim."

Her voice is icy cold. I must have hit a nerve.

She walks ahead of me, her arms crossed over her chest. I take a few quick steps to catch up with her.

"I'm sorry, Gabs," I say, knocking her arm.

She softens, letting out a long breath. "I'm sorry, I must have had too much wine tonight."

I follow her up the stairwell to her apartment door and take a moment to wrap my arms around her. Only weeks ago, I would drop her at the gate and continue on my way with a wave over the shoulder, and now we've progressed to a hug at her door.

It's nice.

Not that it means anything. But it's nice.

She releases a breath into my chest, the warmth spreading outwards, and once I see that the hallway is empty aside from us, I close my eyes, holding her against me a little longer than I normally would.

"If you can't do it for yourself, can you please request a code change so I don't have to worry in the same way that you would if it was Steph who had random men showing up outside her door?"

She stiffens in my arms, but I hold her there an extra second until she relaxes again.

A few strands of blonde hair fall across her face when she looks up at me, and my fingers twitch with the urge to brush them behind her ear. But I don't. That would be too much.

She nods, almost imperceptibly. "I'll request a code change."

"Thank you." As soon as I let her go, I miss her warmth.

"But I just want to make it clear that it's for you. So if somebody misses their cousin's daughter's best friend's barbecue, it's your fault, okay?"

I smile and nod. "They can file a complaint straight to my shredder."

She grins. "Thanks for being my scapegoat."

"Anytime, babe."

I stiffen. I didn't mean to call her babe. It just slipped

out. She cocks her head to the side, her eyebrows crinkled and a slight smile on her face.

That's weird. To her, I'm either a cocky asshole who calls all girls babe, or someone who read *way* too much into that hug.

Not that it wasn't nice, though.

Power through it, Zeke.

She inserts her key in the lock, turning it and propping the door open.

I bite my lip as she turns back to me.

"Thanks for walking me," she says, as she always does, but it feels almost like she's baiting me to say it again.

Anytime, babe. "Sure thing."

The moment feels unfinished, but I'm not about to stand around and wait to accidentally call her babe again—or god forbid, do something worse—so I turn on my heel and head back down the stairs.

"Hey Zeke?"

I stop, peering through the railing at her, the light from her apartment escaping into the hallway from behind her.

"Yeah?"

"If it wasn't all it was cracked up to be, I don't think it was really love—or, whatever *your* definition of love is."

I blink, and she shuts the door.

7

GABI

I read through the email as we take our seats at the bar down the street from Corinne's studio. It's only a few short lines detailing an update to the new gate combination that all residents should take note of. And it doesn't feel as scary as I thought it would.

A sense of relief floats through my body—a sense of accomplishment too, although now is when the hard part starts. Now is when I start holding my breath every time I run into someone in the courtyard or while unlocking the gate, just in case they make a stink about the new code.

But there's also a release in my shoulders and my chest that can't be attributed to yoga or our impending drink with Corinne. I realize that I've been treating the courtyard and the stairwell to my apartment like a little kid avoiding the monster under the bed, like the danger isn't really there as long as I get from the street to my apartment as quickly as I can—and god forbid I linger long enough in the courtyard for the monster to grab my ankles.

With one measly email, my safe places expand a little bit.

GABI

Some floozy requested a new gate
code: 2753

ZEKE

Sounds like a smart floozy. Text me when
you're done.

"You can't leave us," Gemma says as the server drops off our drinks.

Corinne levels her with a look. "Gemma, do you not realize what you have right in front of you?" Corinne asks, motioning to Natalie and me. I watch Corinne's expression, unsure where she's going with this. "You have two girls who can do these classes in their sleep, just *like* you. I understand you're upset, but use your resources, girl. You don't need me anymore."

Gemma looks up at her. "But you lead us."

Corinne shakes her head. "I have seen each one of you stop listening to me during class. Don't think I don't notice when your mind wanders—I see your body moving on its own accord, finding the next pose with muscle memory. You don't need me anymore."

I gulp. She's not wrong.

Corinne repositions herself so she's looking at all of us.

"You're not helpless," Corinne says. "Help each other. Guide each other. Yoga is meant to be what it *needs* to be." She takes a deep breath and looks each of us in the eyes. "The studio is closing, but you've all learned enough to continue on your own. Continue your practice with each other." She takes a sip of her wine. "Of course, if you want to continue with me, you're welcome at teacher training, as I said before."

Gemma rolls her eyes, huffing from her nose.

"That might work," Natalie says as if the idea is just occurring to her and wasn't Corinne's all along. "I mean—Gemma, I know you need your time to unwind right now—but Gabi and I—" She looks to me for confirmation and I nod. "I think maybe we can lead for now. At least until we find a more permanent solution."

"I'd be happy to send you a couple guides and my notes," Corinne offers.

We all look at Gemma, the holdout.

She shakes her head and then shrugs. "I guess we can try it."

Corinne nods. "You girls will do great," she says and squeezes Gemma's hand.

I let out a breath I didn't realize I was holding, and catch Natalie's eye as Corinne asks Gemma about the baby. I nod, just enough to let Natalie know I approve of the plan. She clinks her glass to mine and turns her attention to Gemma's parenting woes—she's been having trouble getting her daughter to eat anything other than mac and cheese and tasteless pasta for weeks now, and it's wearing on her.

She lets out a long breath. "It's like this impossible challenge. We are the only people who can make her eat food. The only people who are watching her and keeping her alive, and she won't *let* us! Have you ever tried reasoning with a baby whose favorite thing to do is defy you? It doesn't work." She takes a flustered sip of her wine as Corinne rubs her back. Her voice lowers as she leaves her wine on the table in front of her. "I feel like I'm failing her."

Natalie reaches across the table and grabs her hand. "It's just a phase, Gem. You'll figure it out. Have patience with yourself. You are *not* failing her."

Natalie's son is old enough that he can stay home alone when she goes to yoga. Feeling woefully unprepared to help

Gemma through the trials of parenthood, I let Natalie lead those conversations.

She shakes her head. "I could be home right now, trying again with some berries. She'll eat berries."

Natalie lets out a long breath. "Gem, how many hours have you put into feeding her this week?"

Gemma blinks. "I'm not sure."

"How many hours have you put into yourself this week?"

Gemma sighs. "Pretty much just these two and yoga on Tuesday. I could argue for shower time and the book I read before bed, but even in those moments I'm listening for her."

"You're never going to get rid of the mom guilt, but you can allow yourself a few hours of relaxation."

Gemma sighs. "I know. Maybe one day I'll figure out how to do that. I'm sorry––I feel like every time we do this, I end up commandeering the conversation to complain."

Natalie shakes her head. "You're fine. It's all part of the process."

We spend the next hour jumping between topics––yoga, Corinne's new program, Gemma's trouble getting her kid to eat.

And when we finally get the check, I let Zeke know we're just about done. A little jolt of excitement runs through me at the prospect of seeing him.

Outside the restaurant, I exchange tight hugs with the girls and promises to see each other soon.

As soon as we part, I scan the street for that dark shadow and spot him two doors down, a grin breaking out over his face as he falls into step beside me. "How was your drink?"

He's wearing sweatpants tonight. I've seen him in all manner of clothing at this point—jeans, shorts, dress pants —but never sweatpants. He looks like he just rolled out of bed, and he looks so comfortable, so at ease with his hands tucked into his pockets, that I'm a little jealous.

Not that I want to be in *his* pants.

I mean—

Well...

Oh jeez.

He looks so good my brain has stopped functioning.

"It was good," I say, hiking my bag up a little higher on my shoulder. "We're going to try leading each other a bit, like rather than private classes, the three of us will get together and switch off. I think it might actually work—I can't believe we didn't think of it before."

He shrugs. "Sometimes, in the heat of the moment, you don't think, you just react."

"Well, I'm optimistic."

"I'm glad to hear it," he says, and runs a hand through his hair. It sticks up a little bit, looking all mussed and morning-after.

I shake the thought from my mind, but I can't help my eyes returning to his sweatpants.

"What?"

He's looking at me looking at him.

I shake my head. "I didn't realize you were a sweatpants kind of guy."

His eyebrows furrow. "I mean, who *isn't* a sweatpants kind of person?"

"Touché. I don't know, there's always something surprising about seeing someone in something different than you normally do."

He smiles, but we both know I'm not making much sense.

"Well, if you must know, I have a deadline looming at the end of the week. This website is giving me a bit of a run for my money. It's a little more complicated than I thought so I'm spending my nights in my office. Sweatpants are my work from home uniform."

"I'm surprised you bother wearing any at all."

He laughs. "Well, it depends on the weather but it's getting cold out now, so sweatpants it is."

When we reach the gate to the courtyard, he eyes the soon-to-be outdated code I punch in.

"When does the new code go into effect?"

"First of the month." I push the gate open and hold it for him. He closes it gently after himself, and follows me through the courtyard to my stairwell.

"I'm honored to have been granted future access."

I shrug. "Well, I figured, just in case, you know? Someone besides me should know the gate code."

I should tell Steph the gate code too, I realize. She actually needs it for whenever she comes over to water the plants. I don't know why Zeke was my first text. *Maybe because of Dustin?* Except the change in gate code essentially nullifies that risk.

Maybe I just want him to have it. For some reason.

His footsteps trail after mine on the stairs, and my heart rate ticks faster as his arms weave around me, heavy on my shoulders. He pulls me into him, his scent now familiar and oddly comforting.

"Good night, Gabriell*a*."

"Good night, Zeke."

His footsteps echo on the stairwell, and he flashes me a quick grin through the railing before he disappears to the first floor, the stairwell door clanging loudly behind him.

I shut my apartment door and drop my bag on the kitchen floor, a certain optimism flowing through my veins.

8

ZEKE

I'm not sure I've ever been so relieved to finish a website. I love The Corner Deli. I love Rob and Della, the sweet old couple who own it. I even love the design and branding of the website.

But their daughter set the whole thing up years ago, and despite looking nice, it's a pain in the ass to make any changes to. Lots of fitting square pegs into round holes.

But now I'm done. And if I'm allowed to say so myself, I think it looks pretty damn good.

So I head down to the deli for dinner.

I order food and a six-pack and pull out my computer at one of the tables near the back. I wrote up a little how-to doc for them, and I'm sure they'll be calling and texting to ask a myriad of questions, but the design is honestly really simple.

It's always the simplest things that demand the most complicated work.

I feel a little flutter in my heart when Della eyes me over the counter. She gives me a quick wave before turning her attention to the customer walking in the door. Her dimples flash as she smiles at him and tucks a strand of gray hair behind her ear.

A few minutes later, when I'm most of the way through my sandwich and halfway through a stout, she stops by, her grin matching mine as she sits next to me at the table.

"Judging by the look on your face, you have something to show me."

I nod. "It's done."

She turns to the counter, eyeing her husband. "Rob, come here!"

He hands off a sandwich to one of their employees and washes his hands, drying them on his shirt before taking a seat at the table.

I walk them through the website, front end and back, and do a quick run-through of the documents I wrote up for them. They ask a few questions about how to edit orders and mark them as complete, and where they can find past orders, and I walk them through every scenario I imagined as I put the website together. My presentation culminates with a handoff of their login information.

"Zeke, thank you so much."

"I'm glad you like it. I know you'll have questions. Don't hesitate to call me, okay?"

She nods.

Rob takes his glasses off and wipes them on his shirt, still staring at the screen. He shakes his head. "I don't know why I'm surprised," he remarks, scrolling through it again. "I knew you were talented, but I guess it's just really cool to see The Corner Deli with a website that rivals—I don't know —Amazon."

I laugh. "I wouldn't go that far, but I think it looks good too. Your daughter had a really good start."

They smile at each other.

"So are we good to start taking orders this weekend?"

I nod. "I'll hang out here for a few hours over the weekend to help with the first couple."

"Oh, you don't need to do that."

I shrug. "It's a lot easier for me to hang out here than run back and forth when you inevitably call me."

She rolls her eyes. "I suppose you're right. We'll feed you on the house this weekend."

I grin. "Don't tell me that. I can eat *a lot*."

"Give us your worst," she dares.

"Della!" One of the employees motions to her, unable to juggle the phone ringing and the customers walking in the door.

"We should go. Thank you, Zeke. We'll read your guides tonight."

"Call me with any questions. I mean it."

Della squeezes my arm as she stands from the table, Rob following close behind her. When he gets to the counter, he stops to give one of the customers a quick handshake, their smiles wide as they greet each other.

I close my laptop, the handover complete.

This feels good. I haven't had a challenge in a long time. Even though this one was a struggle at times, and seemingly impossible at others, it feels good to have done it.

Mostly because I like Della and Rob, and they desperately needed to upgrade their technology.

I finish my sandwich and beer and take the rest of my six-pack home. As I walk, I realize I haven't heard from Gabi tonight, probably because I was so concerned with finishing the website that I forgot to ask her if she had yoga.

I'm mildly annoyed that she didn't text me first, but if I know Gabi, she doesn't want to impose on my night. I pull out my phone and text her.

Hey. Yoga tonight?

By the time I push into my apartment and throw my beer in the fridge, I have a text back from her.

GABI

Heading in now!

I refrain from opening another drink and instead take a quick shower. I throw on real clothes instead of the sweats I've been working in for the past week and head out the door to meet Gabi.

I can't imagine any other way I'd rather celebrate.

Her words have been worming their way into my mind since last weekend. With all of the website work I had to do, I didn't really have time or head space to give it a second thought—that if it wasn't all it's cracked up to be, it probably wasn't love.

But there's something optimistic about that. My mind runs in circles around the idea, wondering what exactly it was that Marissa and I had, if not love. *Infatuation? Mutual admiration?*

Does it really even have to be named?

Maybe I can write off Marissa as one big, six-year mistake.

Maybe she doesn't have to take up so much of my mind, when she already took up so much of my life.

I shake it off as I spot the yoga studio, the dimmed lights on the second floor like a beacon shouting, "Gabi's in here bending over!"

It'll be a few minutes before she comes down, so I scroll through my phone while I wait.

And for a moment I wish Gabi and I were closer. The

kind of close where I could pick up a bottle of champagne and invite myself in for a celebration.

But Gabi is delicate, even if she insists otherwise. And being yet another guy who presumes permission rather than asking for it seems like a great way to put myself squarely on her shit list.

So for now, I'll settle for a walk home.

9

GABI

Yoga isn't working for me tonight.

Probably because today has been a long freaking day.

It was supposed to start with a meeting at the Marigold Beauty office, but once we got there, we realized their CEO's assistant had double-booked us.

We've been trying to get a meeting with them for *months*, and I thought we were going to finally close the deal.

Not today, apparently.

Charlie was nice enough to take me and Mariah, our Outreach Coordinator, out for a breakfast on the corporate card instead. I wouldn't call it a win, exactly, but it was better than being upset over all the materials we prepared.

I'm not sure if that's the reason yoga isn't working for me tonight or if it's something else. But I'm distracted.

Corinne gave us some of her notes, and I've been doing my best to follow along. I did an hour of yoga before leaving the house today to see if I could match what Corinne does, and I did reasonably well. She's right—I do know the motions. But it didn't calm my mind like it usually does.

I volunteered to lead our first group session. Natalie and Gemma seem wary but willing to try it.

I guess I am too, but more than I'm nervous, I know that I need this. I know that Natalie and Gemma need this, and I could be the one to bring a little bit of peace to their busy lives.

As much as it pains me that Corinne is leaving, I'm starting to see this as an opportunity. Maybe what Corinne does for me, I can now do for other people.

Her suggestion to come to teacher training echoes in my mind.

I say a quick goodbye to Natalie and Corinne before I leave, and my heart rate kicks up a bit when I realize the one thing I've been looking forward to all day is waiting for me only a few minutes away. I can slosh through being stood up by Marigold Beauty; I can force myself through a yoga class that doesn't feel right; I can brush off the thought of Frankie Carver.

As long as I get to walk home with Zeke.

He emerges from the shadows with a grin on his face, his normal glower melting into a smile. He stuffs his hands into his pockets as he starts walking with me.

"Hey Gabriella."

"Hey Zeke."

"How was yoga?"

I glance up at him and he catches my eye, his eyebrows rising.

"It wasn't working for me tonight." I shrug. "I did an hour of yoga before leaving because I wanted to practice some notes Corinne sent me, for when we do our little group sessions, and that felt only okay, and I thought the class would bring me out of it, but it didn't. Unfortunately."

He crinkles his eyebrows at me. "Did you maybe do too much?"

"Too much yoga?"

He nods.

I answer immediately. "No."

He raises his eyebrows.

"Maybe."

He grins again, and his smile is so contagious that my mood lifts a notch or two purely from looking at him. "You seem happy tonight."

He shrugs. "I finished that website."

"Oh, that's great! That was bothering you, right?"

He nods. "Yeah, I handed over the keys tonight. They have all the login information and I wrote up a couple guides for them too. They're older, not all that technologically savvy. I'm sure I'll still get some follow-ups, but yeah. It's done."

"Well, congratulations."

"Thanks, Gabi. They seemed really happy about it." He takes a few steps in silence, seemingly reflecting on this. "I was pretty frustrated for a while there, but when I saw how pleased they were with it, all the frustration melted away. That really does make it all worth it."

"Worth it," I repeat.

He grins again and knocks my arm with his. "Are you making fun of me?"

I hold up two fingers. "Maybe a little."

"Alright, Ms. Yoga-Every-Goddamn-Night."

"It helps me relax! And I've only gone three nights this week!"

"Yeah, but two hours tonight counts as two nights."

"That's not fair, those rules weren't made clear beforehand."

We push through the gate, into the courtyard, and walk along the path that leads to my apartment. Zeke's departure looms ahead of us, and I find myself searching for a reason for him to stay.

We head up the stairs, my disappointment growing as the seconds tick down.

He wraps his arms around my shoulders and pulls me into him, his scent familiar now, the warmth of his body calming me. We sway back and forth like that for a second and I savor it, unwilling to be the first to let go.

And then he pulls away, taking a step toward the stairs behind him.

I swallow and turn toward my door, inserting the key and turning, pushing it open.

"Good night, Gabi."

He turns to the stairs, ready to make his exit.

"Hey," I say, and he pauses. My breath catches in my throat. "Do you want to come in?" I stumble for an explanation. "Have a celebratory drink since you finished that project?"

He pauses and nods, the grin returning to his face.

"That sounds great."

10

ZEKE

Gabi's apartment fits her. Her door opens to a small kitchen with a dark wood table in the center, with granite countertops lining one wall. A few steps beyond, there's a cozy living space with a modern gray sofa, covered in woven blankets in various neutrals, with a small coffee table in front, her remotes lined up neatly on a tray. Succulents cover a side table that's pressed up against one side of the couch.

Beyond the living area is a large window that looks out over the courtyard—dark now, aside from the lights lining the walkway. To one side of the living room, I catch a glimpse through the door of her bedroom—more neutrals and more blankets folded on the edge of her bed. A bathroom sits at the juncture of her bedroom and the space between the kitchen and the living room.

"I only have white wine," she says, peering into the fridge and pulling out a bottle. "Is that okay with you?"

I nod. I couldn't care less about the wine. "Sounds great."

She pulls out two glasses and pours us each a generous serving before slipping the cork back in the bottle and placing it back in the fridge. She hands one to me and holds hers up to cheers.

"Congratulations on completing your website." We clink.

"Congratulations on embracing yogi leadership." She pauses for a second, her glass halfway to her mouth, and starts laughing.

We take a sip.

She gestures to the couch. "Do you want to sit?"

"Sure."

I follow her over, taking a seat gently next to her. She grabs a blanket from the arm and unfolds it, pulling it over her legs. "It's always colder by the window," she explains sheepishly, as if I'm judging her for using a blanket in her own apartment. She offers the opposite edge of it to me, and I pull it over into my lap even though I'm not particularly cold.

"So can I see it?" She tucks her feet underneath her and leans toward me, her elbow balanced on the couch behind us.

"The website?"

"Well, yeah, I want to know what we're celebrating." Her eyes are wide, her smile genuine.

I'm suddenly self-conscious. "Sure."

I grab my phone from where I dropped it on the coffee table and navigate to the tab that's still open to The Corner Deli.

"The bones of the website were already there. Their daughter made them a pretty simple one years ago, but they wanted to start taking catering orders on the weekends, so that interface is really what I worked on." I click through to the menu and give my phone to Gabi. "It doesn't look like much from the front. A lot of it was backend work, lots of fiddling to get the admin side to a place where two senior citizens can easily work with it."

She scrolls through the website and starts clicking through things that I can't see from this angle.

"This place looks really freaking cute." She turns the phone to me to show me a landing page I know all too well, a picture of the make-your-own six-pack station front and center. "This is near you?"

I nod. "It's just a little mom-and-pop shop but it's a great place. Best hoagies in Philly, and the owners are just *nice* people. I go there for dinner a couple times a week."

"You'll have to take me sometime," she says offhandedly, and my breath catches in my throat.

Gabi wants to hang out with me.

Or maybe she's just really that interested in The Corner Deli. Maybe she's a deli girl, the insides of her brain filled with good hoagie places and dreams of sliced meat.

"Anytime," I say.

She smiles as she takes a sip of her wine, resting it on the side table next to her after. "The website looks really nice. I can't speak to the backend but it's easy to navigate, loads fast, and it's a great balance of function versus beauty. Their daughter did the branding work?"

I nod. "Photos, color scheme, the About Us page. I just did the catering part and the admin interface that they'll see."

"It's really seamless—you can't tell that there were two different visions for it. I didn't actually place an order, but I went through to the submit button and it felt very easy, very intuitive. Nice job, Zeke."

Why is there a warmth spreading in my chest? It must be the wine. I take another sip.

"Thanks."

"So what's next on the freelance list?"

I shrug. "A friend of a friend has talked about putting together a website for his business. Plumber, should be pretty easy––get a nice template and throw on his logo and phone number, something like that. Henry also asked about a few updates to his website a while ago, but they're pretty minor; he just doesn't know how to do it himself."

I built the current website for Henry's T-shirt shop a little over five years ago. It started as a side hustle but has since grown to encompass a factory out in the suburbs, and every few months Henry asks me about some change or another to optimize speed or checkout flow. I make on-the-fly updates with no set timeline, and he compensates me with food, booze, and overstock T-shirts.

Gabi nods, her eyebrows knitting together. "How do you get your clients?"

"Mostly word of mouth. That's why I like doing the mom-and-pop stuff. They always have friends or relatives or are members of a church or something like that. It keeps things personal. I like doing things for other people, and too much selling without enough connection makes it feel like —well—work."

She nods. "God, that sounds nice."

I forgot Gabi is a sales rep. I hope I didn't offend her. "I could probably make a hell of a lot more if I *did* want to work at it."

"But would it be worth it?" she asks, and I can tell she already knows the answer.

I shake my head. "No, probably not."

"All I do is the not-fun part," Gabi laments. "Constantly reaching out to people who want nothing to do with me. Constantly scouring for leads." She takes another sip of wine. "And that's not even my job really. I'm supposed to be crafting an outreach strategy, figuring out the best way to close people and then sending Charlie out to do the dirty work, but the girl on my team who is supposed to do all that just got back from maternity leave and we're still transitioning stuff back over to her."

"Yeah, unfortunately those things take time."

She takes a sip of her wine. "Honestly—this doesn't help *me* at all—but I'm kind of hoping she quits to stay home with her baby. Not for, like, corporate reasons. For baby reasons. She was showing us pictures today and I wanted to squeeze that little baby so bad."

"Extra cute baby?"

Gabi's eyes roll back in her head. "Oh my god, those little pink cheeks. I love her. I haven't even met her but I love her just from her pictures."

She squirms excitedly in her seat, and there's something so adorable about it that I can't help but smile. She says she believes love is nothing but timing, yet she falls head over heels in love with someone else's baby. "Must be one cute baby."

"They're all cute." She takes a sip of her wine, brushing me off. "Even the ugly ones."

I laugh. "My sister was an ugly baby."

Gabi's mouth falls open and she whacks me lightly on the arm. All of my nerves seem to zero in on that spot, the ghost of her touch lingering long after she's taken her hand back. "Zeke! No she wasn't!"

"I'll show you one of the pictures she hasn't burned at some point and you'll change your mind. She knows it, the whole family knows it. Luckily—or unluckily, if you're me— she just got prettier and prettier as she got older. Big green eyes, big red hair, just like our mom's. Really cute little freckles across the bridge of her nose."

Gabi narrows her eyes at me. "I'm sure she was a beautiful baby."

"Well, I'll let the two of you duke that one out."

Kelly was not a cute baby. She was beautiful because she was ours, but she was not an objectively cute baby.

Gabi adjusts her position, sinking further into the couch in a little cocoon beneath the blanket, and as she moves, her knee grazes my leg, resting there. For a moment, I expect her to move it, and when she doesn't, I let out a long breath.

"What's she like?" Gabi asks.

"My sister?"

She nods, leaning her head back against the couch. She holds her wine against her chest, peering up at me from underneath thick lashes.

God, I do not feel like talking about my sister right now.

"She's twenty, in college at Temple. A little wild but surprisingly responsible considering her age. Smart as shit but will do just about anything for a Bloody Mary, at any time of the day."

Gabi grins. "She sounds fun."

"Too much fun," I agree. "But she's young and exploring the world. It's all part of the experience."

"You seem like a good brother."

I shrug. "I don't know. I could be better."

"Well, if you treat her anything like you treat me, you're a good brother."

I scrunch up my face, a little opposed to the idea of treating Gabi the same way I treat my sister. "I mean, I kind of hope I don't," I say, before realizing what I'm alluding to.

In my defense, her knee is resting on my leg and every time I turn my head, I catch another whiff of whatever perfume she uses—something girly and delicate and so very Gabi. She's pressed into the couch next to me, her face turned up toward mine and her lips so soft and pink and distracting.

"You hope you don't?" Her eyes are locked on mine, and —*is it just me, or is she moving closer to me?*

"Well, yeah," I start, but I don't know how to continue, because I feel like she just check-mated our conversation. I can either tell her that she gives me fuzzy feelings that make me kind of want to kiss her.

Or I can just do it.

She's close enough now that I can just dip my head.

My lips brush against hers lightly, and she sucks in a breath. She puts her hand on my chest, sliding up to my neck as she pulls me closer, each individual fingertip sending jolts of electricity from her skin straight to my groin.

I lean forward, putting my wine on the coffee table, and rest a hand on her waist, pulling her into me. I've fantasized about this more than I'd like to admit. The warmth of her hip underneath my palm. The silkiness of her hair wrapped in my fingers. The press of her chest against mine.

The blanket is suffocatingly hot and I push it away from us, my hand running lower on her hip and dipping underneath the fabric of her sweatshirt as she pushes her body up against mine, her arms wrapping around my shoulders, fisting my hair.

And then my fingers graze the skin of her back, hot and smooth on my hands.

I'm straining at my pants, and I have a wild urge to tear her out of every bit of clothing and fill her repeatedly until the sun comes up.

I haven't felt this way about anyone in years. This merciless, full-bodied desire to pleasure her.

I reach down and grab a handful of ass, squeezing as she lets out a little noise of delight.

And that little noise only compounds my desire. *God, is this actually going to happen?*

I run a finger along her waistband, testing the waters, and when she only leans further into me, I slip my thumb beneath the lycra.

And then she tenses.

No no no no no no no.

I take my hands off her, a sudden fear that I pushed her too far commingling with my breathless need for her.

But instead of moving away from me, she slows our kiss, the desperate need it started with melding into lazy lips and tongues and teeth. She nips at my lower lip, my anxiety easing, and I place a hesitant hand on her hip, keeping her close but staying solidly above her clothes.

When I finally pull away from her, I feel the absence of her warmth against me like a weight, heavy on my chest. Her cheeks are pink, her breathing shallow, and I can't help but search her eyes for any lingering discomfort. *Is she upset with me? Was she just looking for a good old fashioned make out?*

It occurs to me that *I* kissed *her*. *Was she looking for anything at all? Did I misread this whole situation?*

She nods. "I think I'd have to agree with you, there."

"Agree with me?"

"I really hope that's not how you treat your sister."

The wine rises up my esophagus. "Oh god, Gabi, ew!"

She laughs, and all of the tension leaves my body. She leans back into the sofa again, except this time she's tucked underneath my arm, and the weight of her pressing into me feels so good that I can almost ignore the uncomfortable tightness of my pants.

She's halfway in my lap, her knees tucked together in

front of me, my hand resting on them possessively, and the warmth of her skin is intoxicating.

I leave a gentle kiss on her head. She sighs, her body expanding and contracting as she wiggles closer to me.

This is nice.

This is *too* nice.

We sit on the couch like that for a long time. I don't know how long because somewhere in the fury of our kiss, my phone disappeared into the couch or somewhere on the floor, and I'll be damned if I untangle our limbs just to check the time. She tells me about Steph's escapades and her yoga friends who sound a little bit like trainwrecks. Her happily married parents that she looks up to so much.

Despite their whole family being the result of "good timing."

But I don't bring that up. She'll have to reckon with her screwed-up definition of love in her own time.

Or maybe...

No.

Nope.

Not having those thoughts.

Eventually Gabi yawns and leans further into the couch —into me—and honestly, I would sit here all night if she wanted to fall asleep like this. But she has work in the morning, and I can't imagine sleeping like this would actually be restful.

I want to claw my heart out of my chest as I sit up, moving away from her.

"I should probably head home."

She nods, sitting up straighter and pushing her arms above her head in a stretch. I can't help my eyes as they dip to the sliver of skin that's revealed at the bottom of her sweatshirt, as they linger on her rudely hidden curves.

We stand, and I grab my phone from where it had been hiding underneath the blanket.

She walks me to the door, running a hand through her mussed hair and rubbing at her eyes.

God, she's attractive. Drop dead fucking gorgeous.

I knew this before. She's objectively beautiful. Tall and blonde with the kind of rack that starts wars, but there's something about her rubbing the sleepiness out of her eyes and tugging the sleeves of her sweatshirt down over her hands that is both X-rated erotic and absolutely adorable at the same time.

She touches my arm as we reach her front door, her face turning up toward mine. I'm flabbergasted that this girl is asking me to kiss her right now.

I weave an arm around her waist, pulling her close, and dip my head to hers.

Her lips are perfect—soft and delicate but full of desire. Visions dance in my head of her sweatshirt on the floor, the slide of her leggings down her skin, those lips widening around me.

Lord have mercy.

It takes everything in me to step outside her door and reorient myself with the outside world.

I let out a long breath as I listen for the gentle click of the door locking behind me.

I glance around the empty stairwell, trying to slow my thoughts as I start my walk home. The entire world is a little more vibrant tonight. The cars are faster, the voices louder, the store lights brighter.

And there is an incredibly strong tug deep in my abdomen that refuses to lessen even as the brisk air hits my face. I try to will it away but the thoughts running through my head do the opposite. The feel of Gabi's skin on my hands; the smell of her perfume that must be stuck to my sweater because if I turn my head the right way I catch the tiniest whiff; the elastic of her waistband.

The waistband.

The heat building in my abdomen wanes a bit as I remember her tensing up. I hate that I pushed her too far.

In my defense, that kiss was *hot*.

When I get home, I strip and get in bed. The website took a lot out of me today, and I was almost certain I'd fall asleep as soon as my head hit the pillow.

But I find myself thinking of Gabi. I check my phone to see if she texted.

> GABI
>
> Get home okay?

God. She's sweet too.

> ZEKE
>
> I did. Good night Gabriella.

I hit the lights and burrow under the sheets, but after only a few moments I see my phone light up again, and I can't resist checking it.

> GABI
>
> Good night Zeke. :)

11

GABI

I spend the next several days obsessively running my fingers underneath my waistband like I can convince myself out of thinking about Frankie Carver.

Am I driving myself mad? Probably.

But next time Zeke's fingers skirt the waistband of my pants, I want to be confident that the only man on my mind is him. I hate that during what should have been a moment of excitement, I clammed up. I don't know how much further things might have progressed, but I didn't want them to stop because stupid Frankie Carver decided to pop into my mind again.

By the time the weekend rolls around, and thus Thanksgiving, my waistband slapping has turned into a nervous tic which—for better or for worse—has replaced my habit of picking at my nails. My manicure has never lasted so long.

I run my thumb underneath the waistband of my leggings as I wait for Steph to come down from her apartment. She lives in an old converted townhouse in South Philly with an incredibly charming roof deck garden and unfortunately poor water pressure.

Since we don't have much extended family in the area, it'll be just us and our parents for dinner. We do that regularly, though, so the only thing different about tonight will be the addition of mashed potatoes and a rotisserie chicken instead of a turkey because my mom—wonderful woman she is—can't cook for her life.

Steph flies out the door in leggings and an old sweatshirt I recognize from our dad's closet circa twenty years ago, her hair in a messy bun high on her head and an iced coffee in her hand. She throws her purse over her shoulder as she double checks the door is locked and runs the last few steps to where I'm idling.

"Hey, thanks for driving," she says, throwing her purse in the back seat and setting her coffee in one of the cup holders.

I slide my thumb underneath my waistband before pulling away from the curb and heading for 95.

"No problem. How was the tailgate?"

She sighs. "It was great. We didn't really tailgate, though. We kind of just went to the bar and closed it down. Almost got kicked out though because Kay and I were dancing on a table and accidentally might have broken it."

I shake my head. *My sister.*

"Was it that rodeo-themed bar? I thought dancing on the tables was kind of the point."

She pauses. "I didn't know there was a bar where you were *supposed* to dance on the table."

I laugh. "I guess any bar *you* go to is a table-dancing kind of bar."

"Yeah, pretty much. I mean, if I am, there are probably five guys watching and buying more drinks than they would be otherwise, so I consider it a small service to help out local businesses."

"You should charge for that."

She considers this for a moment. "That would take the fun out of it, I think."

Zeke pops into my mind. He said the same thing about web design.

That's been happening over the past few days. Something in everyday life will remind me of him, and he gets stuck there.

I haven't texted him since that night. I don't know if I'm nervous or scared or some combination of both. He hasn't texted me either though, which is simultaneously a relief and a *huge* concern.

I run my finger underneath my waistband again.

When we get to our parents' house, my mom is microwaving a bag of vegetables and stirring up instant potatoes. My dad sets the table, his smile easily reaching his eyes when we walk in. Steph throws her purse on the ground by the door, and I place mine gently next to it. Her iced coffee is quickly abandoned on a bookshelf, and I slip a coaster underneath it so it doesn't ruin the wood.

My sister.

"Hi Dad," she says, giving him a quick hug before hovering over our mom's food, dipping her finger into the mashed potatoes and licking it.

"*Stephanie*," she scolds.

"Yummy."

My dad gives me a big hug, his gray beard scratching against my head, and I can't help feeling like our little family *must* be the result of something more than timing.

There's love here—a lot of it. I can feel it in the way my mom slaps Steph's hands away from the food; my dad's hand on my mom's hip as he reaches around her for a serving spoon; my mom's gentle kiss on my forehead in greeting and the subsequent tucking of a strand of hair behind my ear; the laughter and the family photos and the eye rolls when Steph regales us with last night's adventure.

Maybe Zeke was right. Maybe that one thing my dad said to me so many years ago isn't worth holding onto when everything he says and does contradicts it.

Maybe love is more than timing.

God, I'm turning into a sap.

Midway through dinner, Steph puts her fork down. "I have an announcement."

I uncharacteristically speak through a bite of mashed potatoes to seize this opportunity. "I thought you weren't going to say anything until you were further along."

"Oh, fuck off, Gabi."

"Stephanie." My mom gives her a look. "We're at the fucking dinner table."

My dad snorts, and Steph rolls her eyes.

"As I was saying." She shoots me a glare. "My company is putting out a new policy for the coming year. Starting in January, I'll be fully remote, so I will be moving." She grins, looking around the table for reactions.

"To where?" my dad asks.

"I don't know yet."

My parents glance at each other. "Okay, well, we look forward to seeing the place once you're there."

"Are you moving, like, across the city or, like, across the state?" I ask.

She looks disappointed by this question. "I was thinking another country."

My mom raises her eyebrows. "What country?"

"Well, I haven't thought that far. I just thought it would be fun to travel for a bit and see what place speaks to me, you know?"

"Be safe," my dad says.

She rolls her eyes. "I'm always safe."

"I'm your dad, I have to say that."

"Thank you, Dad."

My parents move on easily from this conversation—Steph has plenty of big ideas, but most of them don't exactly shake out. She was going to move to Europe after high school, and to Greece when she graduated. In her defense, she did make it to Spain for a semester abroad.

"Any big birthday plans?" my mom asks Steph.

She turns to me, grinning. "We're going dancing."

"Great," I say dryly.

I swear I'm not a Debbie Downer—I just know that the entire night is going to be spent looking out for Stephanie and her friends. I *like* dancing, when I get to go out and listen to the music and just *move*. I don't like babysitting.

I weave a thumb underneath my waistband and notice Steph's eyes tracking the movement. I quickly drop my hand.

WHEN WE HEAD BACK to my car, thoroughly stuffed, I feel a tug on the back of my pants.

"God, Steph," I say, stumbling backward a step with her pull.

"What's with the waistband?"

"What do you mean?" I throw my purse in the back seat, next to Steph's, and start the car.

"You keep pulling on it. It looks like you're feeling the baby."

I make a face as I throw the car in reverse. "It does not."

She shrugs. "I mean, you'd have to have sex to have a baby, but that's what it looks like."

I roll my eyes.

I pull out of the driveway, my eyes on the reverse camera.

"Are you?"

"Am I what?"

"Having sex."

I really, really want to be having sex with a certain blue-eyed member of our friend group.

But I don't say that. "No."

"Not with Zeke?"

My breath catches in my throat. I can't control my eyes as they flash to hers. *What does she know?* "No."

Her eyes narrow, and I struggle to keep mine on the road.

"Do you want to?"

This is the problem with being interested in a friend. Whatever Zeke and I are, it's not enough to be telling anyone about it.

But Steph is my sister, and although sometimes I feel the need to keep things from her, this seems like something worth sharing. A fun thing that we can both be excited about.

I bite my lip, debating. *Will saying it out loud jinx it?* "Desperately."

She squeals, the sound harsh and entirely too loud for the confined space.

"God, Steph. Come on. You're going to blast out my eardrums."

"Oh my god, I knew it! Oh, Mari's going to be so upset. She bet there was nothing going on but I mean, come on. Zeke doesn't live *that* close to you to be walking you home every other day."

I glance at her out of the corner of my eye as I merge onto the highway. "Steph, you can't tell anyone, okay? We haven't, like, talked about anything. It's just a crush, okay? Keep it quiet."

"Okay, okay, okay. I will continue to pretend like I'm a sore loser. I won't tell Mari. But Gabi, come on. Spill."

My cheeks turn pink. This conversation is usually the other way around, Steph filling me in on whatever wild romp she had over the weekend. She's been oddly chaste recently, I realize.

"We made out."

She's quiet for a few seconds. "That's it?"

"Yes, that's it, but that's a hell of a lot more than *not* making out."

"Gabi," she says, my name sharp on her tongue. "You *have* to fuck him."

I shake my head. "I mean, I'm not opposed to it. It's just new! It only happened two days ago, okay?"

She's bouncing in her seat. "Oh my god, Gabi, please just call him when you get home and *do it*. You *so* need it. And he's got that, like, dangerous vibe to him without actually being dangerous, you know?"

"I'm not going to call him tonight. But I will take your approval to heart and maybe in the coming weeks, I will."

"Oh Gabi, what's the problem? Drop your pants and have some fun. Life doesn't always have to be so serious."

The *problem* is that I'm terrified that in the moment we've been leaning toward, I'll be thinking of Frankie Carver rather than Zeke Morgan. And *that's* a pretty damn big one.

But Frankie Carver is one of those things I never figured out how to talk about, even to Steph—and how the hell do I explain that in the twenty minutes it takes to get to her apartment?

Although, it hits me that Steph snapped my waistband only a few minutes ago, and it took until now for Frankie Carver to pop into my mind. *Is my new nervous tic actually helping me?*

"I have to do things in my own time. You know that."

She sighs, turning her attention to the highway flying by us. "I know, Gabi. Just don't let time steal your happiness."

My heart jumps at her words. I glance over at her, her head resting against the window as she stares out. She doesn't even know what she said, the internal debate that's been looping in my head ever since Zeke told me I believe in a cynic's definition of love.

My dad, the cynic, and my sister, his equal opposite.

"Did Dad ever tell you, when you were little, that love is nothing more than timing?"

Her face scrunches up. "No, I don't think so. But it sounds like something he would say. One of a million misanthropic platitudes he's thrown our way over the years. I wouldn't listen to him, Gabi. He was probably just having a bad day. Besides, what dad doesn't want his daughter to find love?"

I bite my lip. "Yeah, I think I agree with you. I guess it just got stuck in my head and now I'm having trouble unraveling it."

She doesn't speak for a few moments. "Gabi, are you in love with Zeke?"

"No," I scoff. "Steph, we made out two days ago. I'm not in love with Zeke."

"You don't have to be physical with someone to love them."

I give her a look. "I'm not in love with Zeke."

She nods, her attention returning to the highway. "Okay."

When I drop her off at her apartment, she waves over her shoulder as she unlocks her door and steps inside.

I pull away from the curb and head home, finding a parking spot only a block away from my apartment. I carry my pepper spray in one hand as I walk and try to ignore the absence I feel that can probably be attributed to the lack of Zeke walking next to me.

When I get home, I change into my jammies and sit on the couch, annoyingly aware of my phone on the cushion next to me.

I tidy up the blankets and choose a silly show on Netflix to binge, eyeing my phone as I do.

I grab a glass of water and clean some old food from the fridge, my phone black and unperturbed.

I get my slippers from my bedroom and tie my hair up. I turn the show off, knowing I'll fall asleep on the couch if I sit down for too long.

I head into my bedroom, flipping off lights as I go.

And before I climb in bed, I text him.

12

ZEKE

GABI

How was your Thanksgiving?

I tried to leave her alone over the past few days because I don't want to be another Dustin to her.

I take a sip of whiskey, wondering where to start. My sister, sneakily drinking a bottle of wine at dinner *herself* before falling asleep in her mashed potatoes? My mom awkwardly excusing herself from at least five different conversations with *those* cousins that you desperately try to avoid? My dad trying and failing to get everyone to sit down at the same time and eventually giving up and eating Thanksgiving dinner by himself, only to later get berated by my mom for having the audacity to cut the turkey without her?

I call her instead.

"Hey Zeke."

"Happy Thanksgiving, Gabriell*a*."

"Happy Thanksgiving."

"I hope it's okay that I called."

"Oh, totally fine. I was just getting in bed and realized I hadn't talked to you in a few days."

I miss you.

There's movement in the background, the sound of sheets being adjusted. I can feel her body in my hands so viscerally that if I closed my eyes, I'd believe I was right there next to her, her silky blonde hair scattered over her pillows, her body warm and pliable and tucked right up against mine.

"Yeah, I'm glad you texted me. I've been a little swamped with work this week but—" *But what?* I didn't think this sentence through. "I've been thinking about you."

Oh god, that was worse than I expected.

I mean, it's true, but way too direct.

"I've been thinking about you too," she says, and I can hear a smile in her voice.

I take another large gulp of my drink.

"So how was your Thanksgiving?" she asks, her voice low and calm.

I can imagine her lying in bed—probably with speaker-phone on so she doesn't have to hold her phone up—with her sheets bunched up around her and an array of extra blankets surrounding her because she's always cold. The phone lying only a few inches from her mouth as she closes her eyes. My voice the last she'll hear before she falls asleep.

I launch into the many laughable moments from my day, and she giggles and gasps and reacts at all the right moments. I finish my drink while we're on the phone and make my way into my bedroom, shutting off the lights on my way.

When I get in bed, I mimic what I imagine she's doing—blankets up to her chin in a dark room, phone only a few inches away.

When I close my eyes, I try to filter out the grainy quality of the call so it's like she's right next to me.

Eventually her words give way to gentle breathing, but rather than hang up the phone, I just listen, letting her little breaths lull me to sleep.

I WAKE up more refreshed than I have in a long time. I check my phone as I roll over to see that sometime in the middle of the night, we were disconnected. *Did she hang up the phone? Did I?*

Does it matter, really? I fell asleep to the sound of her breathing and slept like a baby.

I don't know whether to be excited about that or concerned.

I *like* Gabi. And I haven't felt that way about someone since Marissa, who very nearly had me giving up everything I wanted in life for the sake of being a part of *her* dream.

Something tells me Gabi wouldn't expect the same of me.

Or maybe I'm just delusional, reading too far into feelings that have barely had a chance to take hold yet.

I shake off my thoughts and run through my morning routine—coffee, gym, shower, and a light breakfast—and sign onto my computer. I have a conference call with Rob, Della, and their daughter this morning to go over the website. I'm not sure what their questions are yet but hopefully they're easy.

Rob and Della are early, their computer set up at one of The Corner Deli tables. They're wearing their typical uniforms—branded T-shirts and jeans, Rob's glasses sliding halfway down his nose as usual.

"Hi, Zeke," Della shouts, waving.

"You don't have to shout, dear. He can hear you fine if you speak normally."

"I know," she shouts, and then, realizing what she's doing, lowers her voice. "I know, I just never trust the microphone to pick up what we're saying."

"How about I let you know if I can't hear you?"

"Well what if *we* can't hear *you*?"

"I'll start directing flights," I say, waving my hands above my head.

She grins. "Okay, I guess that works."

Leanne signs on, quickly flipping on her camera and microphone. She's at work, a blazer covering her shoulders and corporate artwork on the wall behind her. She's probably a few years older than me, with light brown hair and sharp eyes. "Hi Mom, Dad. Hi Zeke, nice to e-meet you."

"Nice to e-meet you too," I say. "So what do you have for me? What can I help with?"

"Did my parents fill you in on what we're looking for at all?"

I shrug. "No, but I'm sure I can figure it out as I go."

"She wants a website," Della shouts.

Leanne presses her lips together. "Thank you, Mom."

Della gives her a thumbs up before leaning back in her chair.

"This isn't about The Corner Deli website?"

Leanne pauses. "Mom, Dad, did you tell him *anything*?"

Della leans forward again. "No, we were going to do that now."

Leanne shakes her head, laughing. "Okay. So I guess I'll start by saying my husband and I run a vertically integrated interior design firm––we do everything from mockups to installation to woodworking. We've been working off kind of an old website for the past five or so years. I built the original, very similar to my parents' website, and we hired a guy to come in and get it integrated with some of our systems. That didn't work out very well, so for the past five years, we've been bending over backward catering to a website that kind of works, but not really. We don't really care about preserving the *look*, per se—we want to preserve the branding, of course—but ultimately we want something functional. We have too many systems that are reliant on the right orders getting routed to the right places to continue with a website that doesn't serve those needs."

My mind trips over itself as I stare at Leanne. I get the feeling she paused to get my initial reaction, but I'm still absorbing her first sentence.

I run through Leanne's explanation again in my head. "So you're looking for integration work? Not just website stuff?"

"Essentially, yes. We want to refresh everything, but mostly we want everything to work right."

"Gotcha. I mean, I'll have to take a look and see what's what. This sounds a little more complicated than a mom-and-pop deli."

She nods. "I know. The last guy was a consultant we found online somewhere who didn't give a shit and left us high and dry. We've been working with a broken system for five years now, so while it's not ideal, it does mean that you can take all the time you need. We just want somebody who cares enough to do it right. And judging from what you did for my parents, I think that's you."

Somebody who cares.

Leanne knows just the right buttons to press.

"Okay. Well, I'll see what I can do."

13

GABI

Today is the day. Corinne's studio has closed, and Gemma is having a nervous breakdown.

We sit at my kitchen table, water bottles and phones strewn across the surface. Gemma's husband keeps calling her because he can't get the baby to stop crying, and his panic is leaching into her through the phone.

"She's been crying for three days straight," Gemma says, her eyes bloodshot as she stares at another text coming through the phone. "She's not sick. She's not uncomfortable. She's not hungry or constipated. I don't know what to do."

Natalie grabs her hand. "It happens sometimes," she says. "When Parker was a baby, he once cried for a whole week."

"How did you get him to stop?"

"Time."

Time. The answer is always time.

"So here's what you're gonna do. We're going to get on our mats and go through the flow Gabi prepared, and for that hour you're going to trust that even if the baby is unhappy right now, your husband will keep her alive. Then you're going to go home, request an appointment with a new pediatrician, just in case—and I don't even care which, just Google and pick the first one with a solid star rating—and then you're going to take your husband and baby on a walk around the neighborhood and not even care that she's screaming because you and Luke need to touch some grass and hold hands for a bit."

Gemma swallows. "Okay."

Natalie turns to me. "Alright Gabi, you're up."

My heart jumps into my throat. Of course the day I'm supposed to lead us through is the day when Gemma seriously needs Corinne.

We roll out our mats in the area between my kitchen and the living room, and with Corinne's notes splayed out in front of mine, I run us through our progression.

My first few movements are a little jilted. But as I repeat Corinne's cues and do my best impression of her, my nerves recede, and the next poses come naturally. Gemma's eyes close, her chest filling and emptying at an even pace. Natalie follows along silently, her movements graceful as always.

And while the beginning of our session is a little slow and uncomfortable, the end is smooth and natural.

"Namaste."

Natalie smiles, her eyes fixed on Gemma as she lets out one last big breath.

"I feel better," she says, and all of the relaxation I searched for during our session immediately morphs into excitement.

I did it. I scramble over and hug her, thrilled that I was actually able to help.

"Thanks, Gabi," she says into my shoulder. "I really appreciate you leading us through. I could feel you channeling Corinne there."

"I channeled her so hard."

"Sounds naughty," Natalie comments and our cackles fill the stillness of my apartment. We roll up our mats and Natalie and Gemma gather their things from the kitchen table. I walk them outside to the gate and wave as they head off in their respective directions.

"Now go touch grass with your husband and remember that babies are tough—but you're tougher!" Natalie calls over her shoulder to Gemma. "And thanks again, Gabi, you did great!"

I can't help the glow of pride that warms my body.

When I get back upstairs, I fall onto my couch and text Zeke about my win.

> ZEKE
>
> Who needs teacher training when Gabi's around? ;)

I smile at the text.

This feels too good. First Gemma, actually relaxing into herself for a moment. Natalie, telling me I did great. Zeke, suggesting I'm already good enough to be a teacher.

This is intoxicating.

I can't help googling Corinne's program.

Almost three months of training—weekdays, weekends.

I'd have no time for Zeke.

I shake my head, the concern taking me by surprise. *Thousands of dollars and two hundred hours of my time, and the first thought in my head is Zeke?*

14

GABI

By the time Steph's birthday rolls around, Zeke and I have been texting almost daily.

And thank god, because without going to the studio several times a week, I haven't found a good reason to invite him over. We haven't talked about our kiss—what it means, whether we want to do it again—and I'm itching to ask, but I don't want to do it over the phone.

He said he's been thinking about me.

That *has* to mean something.

If all goes well, I might see him tonight. He and Henry are at Charlie's for a non-game night hangout, and if I drop enough suggestive hints toward Annabel, I'm sure she'll lead the charge back to her apartment.

Once Steph has had her fun, of course. It might be two in the morning by that time, but there's a little ball of hope in my stomach that Zeke will still be there.

Steph's girl gang meets up outside the club before heading in together. She looks like a disco ball, like usual, and eyes are drawn to her as she secures drinks for the group and leads us to the dance floor. At some point, someone throws a lei around her neck, and beach balls start flying over our heads. Steph makes friends with a few shirt-less men who easily meld into our group as the music pumps around us, the crowd thickening.

And eventually Steph points to the back room, where we order another round of drinks and stake out table space as people leave their seats. She manages to make friends with someone across the rope, in the bottle service section.

When she returns, she has a wild look in her eye.

"Guys, I found straight men and they invited us over to their booth," she says, doing a little dance. She glances at her phone before continuing. "And they're hot."

Great.

But I diligently follow the group over and stand in an awkward semi-circle around their booth because it's not nearly large enough to accommodate seven extra people. But they pour us shots and pass them around, and Stephanie, the liquor goblin she is, instantaneously throws it back, Kay and Leilani not far behind. I probably would have stopped them if I didn't see that the bottle was sealed before he poured—but it's Steph, and if she wants to get plastered for her birthday, she's more than welcome to.

She holds a shot out to me, but I refuse it.

"Oh come on, Gabi. It's one shot."

"I don't do tequila."

"Sure you do."

Time stands still as I process the voice I'm hearing. A chill runs down my spine as my eyes find the speaker.

Frankie Carver.

His face is partially obscured by the darkness of the booth, but his wide grin is unmistakable. A sharp chin, strong build, cocky stance, one arm thrown lazily over the back of the booth. His eyes burrow into mine, my face probably conveying all of my inner thoughts, a restless monologue of *no no no no no.*

My breath catches in my throat as I turn my gaze from him to the bright eyes of my sister, the shot held out between us.

"Everybody does tequila," Steph says, playing along.

I take a step back. And another, and another, until I turn and remove myself from the VIP section altogether. I don't stop until I'm surrounded by the group on the dance floor that Stephanie befriended, who—although I haven't said a word to them—I've adopted as part of our group.

They're at the bar, and I wedge myself on their other side, like I'm hiding.

God, I'm *hiding* from Frankie Carver.

It takes my mind a second to catch up, to realize just how cocky an asshole he is.

I have a restraining order against him, yet he has the audacity to grin at me like that. To taunt me.

And now I'm mad at *myself* for getting spooked by it. It's Steph's birthday, and I just ran away from her without explanation.

I shake my head, as if I can just forget the last ten minutes ever happened. My mind kicks into overdrive trying to determine the best way to not ruin Steph's birthday while simultaneously removing myself from Frankie's presence.

I'm about to swallow down the anxiety pumping through my veins and rejoin Stephanie in the bottle service section when one of the shirtless men turns to me.

"Hun, are you alright?"

I nod. "No, I'm fine."

"No? But you're fine?"

He leans over the bar and flags down the bartender. "Can we get some water over here?"

"Just… this guy."

He raises his eyebrows, slapping his suspenders against his bare chest. He hands me the water the bartender places on the bar in front of us and waits pointedly for me to take a sip.

"I hate it when straight men come here. This place is just… not meant for straight guys. Do you want to hang out with us until your friends get back?"

It takes me a second to process his words, but I nod when I do. "Thanks."

He smiles and returns to the conversation he was having before I showed up. I take a few deep breaths, willing my heart to slow. They don't focus on me at all, but I do notice his hand weaving to the small of my back as someone passes behind us.

They place another drink order, with the addition of a vodka cranberry for me. I don't usually go for a fourth, but there's a buzzing in my head I'm anxious to quell and alcohol seems like the perfect antidote.

As I take a sip, his eyes connect with someone over my shoulder. "Hey, birthday girl!" I turn to see my sister approaching.

"Gabi!" she yells, her eyes flaming. *Oh fuck, she's mad.* "Where the fuck have you been? We've been looking for you for twenty minutes! Why aren't you answering your phone?"

Oh, Jesus. I reach into my bag and pull my phone out to see at least five missed calls from her—I must not have felt the vibrations. "I'm sorry, I didn't feel it."

Her shoulders relax, and she lets out a long breath. Annabel is behind her, her eyebrows furrowed. "Are you okay? What was that?"

"I just—"

"Did you know him?" Annabel asks, taking a step into

our circle. Her eyes narrow, and I can only imagine she's putting together the pieces of what she just witnessed. The night Frankie Carver cornered me in a bathroom, she was supposed to be meeting Charlie, but instead, he was talking to the police with me. Taking me home and putting me on the couch with a cup of tea.

I can only imagine Annabel knows the story—and now she has a face to put to the name.

Except I never told my sister what happened. I never told anyone, really, aside from the cops. Charlie only knows because he was there.

And now doesn't feel like the time to start talking.

I nod and watch as Steph's eyes search mine. "From where?"

"Just a long time ago."

I can see the confusion in her eyes—she knows everything about me.

Or at least, she thought she did.

Steph shakes her head, crossing her arms over her chest. "Well, now that I know you're not *dead*, are you ready to head to the next place?"

My heart drops. *The next place? There's more to this night?*

"Where are we going?" I start guzzling my drink in preparation.

Steph smiles knowingly at me. "Annabel's."

My sister may not *know*, but she knows when I need a safe space. And she's delivering, even on her birthday.

A flood of relief gusts through me, and she rolls her eyes as she leans down, saying something only Annabel can hear. She hugs the shirtless men quickly, and I realize she must have already known them somehow—she tells Kev, the one in the suspenders, that they'll do lunch again soon.

Maybe Steph doesn't tell me everything, either.

I down the rest of my drink as I follow them to the door, where the other girls are waiting.

The cold air is like a shock to the system. I wouldn't say I'm sober, but the weight of what I'm walking away from hits me like a truck. Frankie Carver behind me, a smug smile on his face after months of trying to forget him. My sister, forgoing her birthday festivities because she knows the best place to put me is Annabel's apartment. With Zeke.

The streets are crowded with late night partiers, and we have to weave between other groups as we walk. After a few blocks, Steph pauses, staring down at her phone for the millionth time tonight.

"What's wrong?" I ask, coming up behind her. My words are slow, like they're not coming out totally right, and I realize my drunkenness is probably showing through.

"Rod texted me." She holds the phone out to me, and the message is blurry but the meaning clear: despite telling Stephanie he'd show up tonight, he's flaking out. Again.

I search her face for signs she's upset. Tonight isn't going exactly how she'd planned.

My heart sinks. I ruined her night of dancing, and now her long-term, on-again-off-again boyfriend is ditching her.

She shakes her head. "Fuck him. I've had about enough."

"I didn't realize he was back. Wasn't he in Colombia?"

"He's not back for good, he's just visiting. Ugh, I just feel so stupid. I need a drink."

She continues walking, her heels slapping the ground with staccato determination.

She gets ahead of me easily, but I catch up to her. She shouldn't be annoyed on her birthday. "Do you want to go to another bar? We don't have to go home right away." I catch her hand so she'll pay attention to me. "I know what you're doing and although I appreciate it, it's your birthday. I want you to have fun."

She gives me a small smile and wraps her arm around my shoulders. "I always have fun, Gabi. You know that. I think going back to Annabel's is the right move tonight. But thank you for making sure I'm having a fun birthday."

"Can I do anything? To—you know—make sure it's still fun?"

She shakes her head, sidestepping a group of guys who make no effort to hide their ogling.

"No, but thanks, Gabi." She takes her phone out again, a look of brazen determination on her face. "But you know what? If Rod ditches me on my birthday, that's fine. He's not the only person in this world who wants to fuck me, and I bet I'll have a lot more fun with someone else." She texts as she walks, her legs moving inordinately fast as I struggle to see what she's typing over her shoulder.

But the vodka is really hitting me now, and her quick movements and rapid-fire texting are making it difficult for me to see whose presence she's requesting.

15

ZEKE

We hear them before we see them, like the rumble of a stadium in the distance.

Voices, elevator dings, squeals, heels on wood.

And what sounds like male voices?

I close the laptop, having gone over all of the updates I made to Henry's website already. I slip it into my bag and tuck it underneath the island, unsure of what's about to blast into the apartment. Henry's across from me, leaning on the counter, and I take up one of the few bar stools on the other side.

Charlie weaves back into the kitchen, topping up his drink. He offers me some but I politely decline; Kelly's at a frat formal tonight, and I'm planning on picking her up from wherever it is she lands.

The noise outside the door reaches a crescendo as a key slides in, and the three of us turn toward it, waiting.

And then they're inside, in a blur of party dresses and hair and perfume.

"Hey man," Oliver says, clapping me on the back when he sees me. "I didn't know you'd be here."

Where did the girls find Oliver? And Kick?

"We didn't know you'd be here, either."

Oliver shrugs. "I was summoned by the birthday girl. Gotta show up if you're summoned by the birthday girl. Kick just happened to be at my house."

Henry, transfixed by the multitude of little dresses that just entered the apartment, joins them in the living room.

Bringing up the rear of the group, I spy Gabi, shutting the door behind her and turning with a look of bewilderment to the noise preceding her.

She takes a few steps forward, blinking as if trying to get her bearings, and then her eyes connect with mine.

And there's something so absolutely gut-wrenchingly adorable at the breath she lets out when she sees me, her shoulders relaxing as she beelines straight for me.

She's wearing monster heels and a slinky purple dress that's riding just a little too high on her thigh. Her hair is long and straight down her back, and she drops her jacket on the back of the couch as she walks, the thin strap of her dress falling down her shoulder without the jacket to hold it in place.

"Hey Gabs."

She ignores the greeting, instead wrapping her arms around my neck, her body winding into the space between my legs.

She stays there, her body relaxing into mine, and I don't mean to, but I catch Charlie's eye over her shoulder. His eyebrows are raised.

"You alright there, Gabi?"

She steps away from me, and I'm torn because I want to

strangle Charlie for asking the question and causing her to move away from me, but also—she doesn't really look okay.

She nods, pushing her hair over her shoulder. I pull her strap up, and while I'm there I gently tug on the hem of her dress, bringing it down an inch or two. I can feel Charlie's eyes on me but I don't really care—if this is enough to cause an issue, he's got his priorities wrong.

"Yeah, it was just a long night."

"You seem drunk," Charlie says.

Is that abnormal? Does Gabi not drink enough to be drunk? Should I have already known this?

"I might be a little drunk," she admits. My hands are still on her hips, one of her arms resting on my shoulder, and although I want to savor in this moment, touching her, there's also a part of me that has kicked into overdrive, my concern for her growing with every passing second.

Annabel appears next to Charlie like a little polka dot sprite, pulling him down to whisper something in his ear. His face blanches. She disappears as quickly as she came, gliding past Gabi and squeezing her arm gently as she goes.

"Are you sure you're alright?" Charlie asks.

"Is there something I should know?" I ask both of them, sensing a change in the atmosphere.

Charlie's eyes bore into Gabi's, and she shakes her head. "Gabi."

She flinches. "Frankie." Charlie shuts his eyes, shaking his head. "Wait, wait, wait, but I'm fine! One of Steph's friends saved me—-he was so sweet. I'm really fine."

"Who is Frankie?" I don't like Charlie's reaction *at all*.

"Gabi, why didn't you say something?"

Say something? Something about what? I thought Dustin was Gabi's only problem. Now there's some guy named Frankie too?

"I just didn't want to ruin Steph's birthday. And I panicked, and I ran away, and now I'm drunk but I'm also *fine*."

So Gabi doesn't really get this drunk—and some guy named Frankie caused her to run away from her friends and her sister, who I know from experience she watches with a hawk eye.

"Can somebody please tell me who Frankie is?"

Charlie shakes his head, ignoring me. "What happened?"

She shrugs. "Nothing. He made friends with Steph and they wanted to drink tequila and I—" She looks over her shoulder as if one of the drunken buffoons behind us is actually taking the time to listen. "I panicked and I ran away, but that's okay! It's like a self-preservation response and I self-preserved." She stumbles over her words.

"Who the fuck is Frankie?" My voice is stronger than I mean it to be, but I'm getting a little pissed off here that some guy is scaring Gabi.

She closes her eyes, and for a second, I think she's about to cry. My heart drops into my gut because that's the *last* thing I want to do. I just want somebody to tell me who the fuck Frankie is so I can tear his throat clear out of his body.

But she opens them again and sighs. "Just an asshole."

Charlie turns to me, finally. "He assaulted her a few months ago. She got away with a swift kick to his groin. She has a restraining order against him but apparently failed to take advantage of it."

"Shh, Charlie, god."

"Gabi, don't you think he deserves to know?"

And there it is. An assumption of Us. She's still tucked between my legs, and my hands are still on her hips, but it's the first time we've been alluded to as anything more than friends, despite how obvious it might be from our current state.

Her eyes find mine. "Just don't think less of me, okay?"

My heart shatters into a million little pieces. "I wouldn't dare."

She falls into me again, and I grab onto the counter so she can't push my chair over. I wind an arm around her waist, and with a pointed glance in my direction, Charlie steps around to our side of the island.

He squeezes Gabi's shoulder as he passes. "Let me know if I can help, okay?" I hear him murmur to her, his words loud enough that only the two of us can hear.

She nods but her face is buried in my shoulder, and I feel incredibly guilty that it feels so good to have her so close, wildly furious that some guy is upsetting her, and downright murderous that I didn't know about him until tonight.

"Gabi, do you want me to take you home?"

She looks up at me with her big brown eyes. She smiles and nods and immediately grabs her jacket from the back of the couch. A few seconds later, she has her arms around Stephanie's shoulders, saying something into her ear as they sway back and forth. Steph kisses her on the cheek, brushing her hair out of her face, and Gabi waves a lazy goodbye to the rest of the group.

Annabel swoops in just before she winds her arms around me again, but they speak in voices too low for me to hear. And then Charlie's there too, saying something to her, and she waves them off easily, giving them each a big hug before turning back to me.

"Ready?"

"Very ready."

When the apartment door closes on the noise behind us, she lets out a big breath.

"Are you sure you're alright, Gabi?"

She nods, smiling up at me. "I'm okay."

But then I notice a little shiver run down her arm as she pushes her hair over her shoulder. She's breathing heavily and running a hand along her waist almost obsessively. She adjusts her jacket, her hair, the hem of her dress.

I press the button for the elevator and we wait a few moments for the doors to open, Gabi a blur of movement in the corner of my eye.

When we step into the elevator, I wrap an arm around her shoulders, pulling her into me.

Her face hits my chest and only a moment later she starts shaking, the most delicate little sobs escaping her throat. She wraps her arms around me, clinging to me, and I have to fight the urge to start destroying things because the only thing I can get my hands on right now is the one thing I need to touch gently.

She pulls away from me and wipes her eyes before we step out of the elevator.

"Gabi, what can I do?"

She shakes her head, leading the way across the wide lobby to the street. "Nothing. I'm sorry. I don't know what came over me. I'm fine."

I saw the way she talked to Annabel, to Charlie, when they tried to help. I remember the way she snapped at me when I told her Dustin emotionally abused her. I feel helpless, words apparently useless to her.

But maybe I can make her laugh.

I eye her as I speak. "You're a tough bitch, aren't you?"

Her eyes snap to mine, wide, and her mouth ticks up

into a hesitant smile. She laughs, and I can breathe again. "I can't believe you just said that."

I pull her in for a hug before we reach the street, hesitantly optimistic that now that she got a little cry and a little laugh, she'll be okay. I check her face for smudged makeup and wipe a black mark from the corner of her eye. She stares up at me, her mouth slightly agape, and leans into my touch.

I open the car door for her and make sure she's fully inside before closing it. I run around to the driver's side and get in, the engine roaring to life. The radio blasts at full volume and she jumps—I reach forward to turn it down before putting the car in gear. "Sorry."

"You *would* drive a muscle car blasting—what was that—Motley Crue?"

I flash her a grin. "I absolutely would."

She laughs, the sound like wind chimes on a summer day.

But just before I pull away from the curb, my phone rings. Kelly.

Fuck.

I answer through the Bluetooth connected to my car.

"Hey Kell."

"Hey Zeke." I can't tell if she's drunk.

"What's up?"

"Can you come get me?" *Fuck.*

"Where are you?"

"At a bar off Columbus. They were drinking a *lot* and the one guy wanted to drive, and"––She huffs into the phone––"they left me here because I wanted to get an Uber, but now it's saying there are none available."

I lean my head back, looking at Gabi, who's listening silently and playing with the hem of her dress.

"Send me a location pin. I'll be there in a few."

"Thanks, Sneak."

Gabi's eyebrows furrow as I end the call. "Sneak?"

I pull away from the curb, winding around Charlie's apartment building and heading east, to Kelly, instead of north, to Gabi's.

"When she was three or four and I was in high school, she caught me sneaking out to make out with a girl. I thought I could bribe her with a cookie—which worked for a couple weeks—but eventually my mom picked up on all the missing cookies and confronted us. She thought it would be a simple lesson. A don't-steal-cookies-from-the-cookie-jar type of thing. Except apparently Kelly had more of a conscience than I thought. She started crying and confessed the whole thing. But what stuck was the way my mom confirmed the story. She honestly wasn't that mad—she just said, 'Zeke, you little sneak!' and Kelly thought that was just the funniest thing in the world. So I got grounded for two weeks, and Kelly got a cookie for telling the truth."

There are drunk people all over, and I take a side street to avoid any areas packed with nightlife.

"That doesn't sound fair. She was part of the whole plan."

I shrug. "She was the baby. She didn't really face consequences until she was a teenager. Even then, she got away with a ton of shit."

Gabi's quiet for a second, nodding.

"I called her Tattle until she was about thirteen and got upset because apparently snitches get stitches."

She laughs, turning her attention to the dark streets outside.

"Is this okay? I know you wanted to go home. I just can't leave Kelly standing on a street corner by herself."

She turns back to me, smiling. "Of course it's okay. I would do the same for Steph."

She angles the vents toward her, pulling her jacket tighter. I tick the temperature on her side up a bit, and she smiles at me in thanks. She wiggles down in her seat, her crossed legs leaning up against the center console. I can't help reaching forward and squeezing her knee.

When we reach Columbus, I'm a little angry to see that Kelly's standing completely alone on the side of the road. There are groups of people around her, so she's not *isolated*, but I'm ticked off that she went with a group and the group left her behind.

I pull up to the curb and get out, calling her name to get her attention before she accidentally sits in Gabi's lap.

"In my side!" I tell her, beckoning her over as I pull the seat forward. Her eyebrows crinkle as she peers in the car, realizing only now that I have someone with me. She raises her eyebrows, watching the road as she rounds the car and climbs in back.

Once she's in, I throw the seat back and sit down.

Gabi grins at me and then turns to Kelly. "Hey, Tattle."

There's a moment of silence in the car that stretches to eternity before Kelly's face turns up into a smile and she starts cackling. "Don't tell me we're bringing that back."

Gabi turns in her seat so she can see my sister. "I'm Gabi, your unfortunate stowaway this evening."

"Not unfortunate," I correct her, glancing in the rearview to see Kelly's eyes darting from me, to Gabi, and back again.

"It's nice to meet you, Gabi." Kelly seems far too happy about this. "Actually, it's an absolute delight to meet you. I didn't think Zeke had a dick anymore, honestly."

"Kelly," I scold as the girls burst into laughter.

But I will gladly be the butt of their jokes if it means Gabi isn't crying anymore.

I pull back onto the road and head toward her apartment.

"So how did you meet?" Kelly asks, leaning forward so she's between us. I check the mirror to make sure she has her seat belt on, and she does, so I don't say anything about her prying.

And then I glance at Gabi, worried this conversation is headed in too serious a direction. "It's been a long night, Kell. Why don't we leave this for another time?"

Gabi raises an eyebrow at me. "We met through friends. His best friend is my best friend."

"Charlie? Really?" She sounds like she doesn't believe this, probably because she hasn't met the new version of Charlie who only has eyes for Annabel. She met him *back then*, when he had eyes for anything with two tits and a grab-able ass, and he certainly wasn't ashamed of it. "You're too hot to be friends with Charlie."

Okay, so my sister is drunk and hitting on Gabi.

Gabi's eyebrows shoot up, and she turns in her seat. "I think I love you."

They giggle, and although I'm not upset that they're getting along, my relationship with Gabi is far too young to be throwing Kelly into the mix. As much as I love my sister, she's a live wire waiting to implode something, and putting her in a confined space with someone I'm interested in for too long sounds like a disaster waiting to happen.

We turn into Gabi's neighborhood, taking the main strip down to Gabi's more residential street.

"Oh god, that yoga studio is the *best*," Kelly mutters.

Oh no.

"Oh my god, you go there?"

"Um yeah, Corinne is, like, my spirit animal."

"No, she's *my* spirit animal! I'm so sad it closed."

Kelly's quiet for a second. "It did *not*," she says in disbelief.

Gabi nods. "It is closed, closed, closed."

"No!"

"Yep. Corinne's done with it."

We pull up to Gabi's apartment, and the three of us spill out. Gabi punches in the gate code and we wind through the courtyard, the girls walking ahead of me. Gabi points out the different flowering bushes and reminds Kelly every few steps that since it's cold out none of them will have flowers for a few months yet.

I've been forgotten. Despite being everyone's ride and the only sober one tonight, I have been rendered secondary.

We get up to Gabi's apartment, and I'm about to hug her goodbye and promise to text her tomorrow when she pauses, her eyes narrowing and a smile blooming across her face.

"Hey, do you guys want to come in and watch a movie?"

A movie? In the middle of a night on a Friday when the majority of participants are drunk.

"That sounds great!" Kelly exclaims, eagerly following her inside.

How the hell am I going to extricate myself from this?

Gabi makes popcorn and pours four glasses of water because she's drunk and can't count. Kelly grabs a blanket and makes herself comfortable on one end of the couch, and I take the other, Gabi filling in the middle. She puts the popcorn and the water on the table.

"Drink water," she says, to no one in particular, as she guzzles down one of the glasses.

She puts on some '80s movie that Mari's been gabbing

about for far too long. I think I've seen it but I'm not sure I care either way; I'm so tired I'll probably be asleep in ten minutes and wake up in an hour with a crick in my neck that'll last into next month.

But then she leans into me, tucking her legs up underneath her.

Okay, maybe this isn't so bad after all.

She pulls a blanket over her legs and my hand finds its way to her thigh. She sighs, leaning her head on my shoulder, and I'm suddenly so glad that the two of them hit it off.

But after a few minutes, giggles turn to the heavy breaths of sleep.

And I'm left awake, alone, and watching an '80s movie I don't care to see.

I jostle my shoulder a little, testing just how deeply Gabi is asleep, and her nose crinkles but she doesn't wake up. I slip an arm under her shoulders, the other under her knees, and pull her up off the couch, blanket and all. I take her into her bedroom and place her gently on top of the covers, pulling another of her many blankets on top of her so she doesn't get cold.

When I get back into the living room, Kelly has stretched herself out over the couch, her legs reaching past the spot I had been sitting in before. She's snoring lightly, one arm dangling off the couch.

I flip off the TV, take a few sips of my water, and settle down into the only open seat remaining—an armchair about the size of a toddler.

Okay, maybe it's bigger than toddler-sized, but in the middle of the night when I'm searching for a place to sleep, that's about what it feels like.

I cross my arms, trying to fold myself into a position where my head has some support as well as my legs. Eventually I get *almost* comfortable, my feet propped up on the coffee table and my arms crossed over my chest, but it's a far cry from my cave, my silk sheets and blackout curtains.

All I know is, after tonight, these girls *better* buy me breakfast in the morning.

16

GABI

My head is pounding.

I open my eyes to a dark room. I feel like I am literally about to die.

My night flashes through my mind—the club, Steph's concern, Charlie's anger, Zeke's boiling rage, my tears in his shoulder.

A cringe rolls through me.

I sit up, remembering Kelly. The movie that I don't recall finishing.

I'm covered in blankets, but my bed is still made underneath me. I'm wearing my dress from last night, but it's not exactly covering much at this point.

I push the blankets off and tiptoe to the door to see if they're still here—and they are. I pull out a pair of jammies as quietly as I can and slip my dress off, throwing it on the ground until morning, and replace it with a navy-blue silk button-down and matching shorts.

I move silently into the living room. Kelly is spread across the length of my sofa, and Zeke is folded into my armchair, a pinched expression on his face even in his sleep.

The water I poured is still on the coffee table, and I grab one, eagerly downing the entirety of it in a few seconds. I count four on the table and snicker a little to myself. Kelly must have been drunker than I thought and poured herself a glass, not realizing I already got her one.

She's cute.

But Kelly seems fine right now.

It's Zeke that I'm more worried about. Zeke the responsible one, taking care of both of us on his Friday night.

I run my hand down his arm, trying to wake him gently, but he jerks at my touch.

He blinks up at me, sleep in his eyes, and stretches out his neck as he sits up, like he can already feel a pain building there.

I grab one of the full glasses of water and take his hand, tilting my head toward my bedroom. He runs a hand through his hair, standing from his chair, and follows me in.

He seems a little stunned, or maybe he's just half asleep. I chug some more water and leave the rest on my nightstand, then reach down to untie his sneakers. He kicks them off easily and then waits, as if expecting further direction. I consider taking his shirt off too, assuming he doesn't sleep fully clothed, but I'm not sure I trust myself to do that without kissing him, without pushing him down on my bed. With the pounding in my head, I don't think I can do that right now.

Although if it happens, it happens. Having him in my bedroom has some less than savory thoughts running through my mind.

But rather than follow through on them, I pull my covers back and get in, grabbing his hand and pulling him in after me.

The mattress moves as he gets comfortable. He wraps

his arm around my waist and pulls me into him, my back warm with his body heat. He leaves a kiss on my neck before letting his head drop to the pillow.

After only a minute or so, his breathing deepens. I close my eyes and relax into him.

17

ZEKE

I wake up alone, which is not in itself surprising, but after only a second, I realize it should be. I feel satin around me, a scent of something warm and sweet in my nostrils. I roll over, trying to avoid the blinding sunlight across my face, but there's no escape.

I open my eyes, holding a hand up to block the offensive sunlight.

I'm in Gabi's bed, her gray sheets strewn haphazardly around my legs. The door is closed, and I take a second to sit up, the events of last night sinking in slowly. I spy Gabi's dress on the floor and something stirs deep in my abdomen, inspired by the thought of her slipping it off at some point in the night. *Was I here, only a few feet away when she changed?*

I only vaguely remember her hand in mine, dragging me into bed with her. I was half asleep, and although a small jolt of electricity pulsed through me at the thought of being in bed with her, it became dormant as soon as my head hit the pillow.

I stand and stretch, wiping the sleep from my eyes as I open the bedroom door.

And there they are, whispering to each other at the kitchen table. Gabi glances up as I take a step toward them, her smile widening when she sees me.

"Good morning." She stands up and then pauses, as if she's not entirely certain what she was planning to do. I can't help but clock her long legs, the silky shorts that only barely cover the ass I can still feel so viscerally in my palm. Her nipples strain against her shirt, and I have to force myself to look away.

I'm suddenly very angry that Kelly is here. The first time Gabi and I wake up together should be an intimate moment. Even if nothing happened last night.

I also kind of want a moment to make sure Gabi is, in fact, okay. Her breakdown in the elevator might have been brief, but I'm not stupid enough to think that that means it wasn't real. She kept it together for everyone else—even her sister—yet she trusted me enough to let it out.

That has to mean something, and I'll be damned if I let her think I've forgotten about it.

"Good morning," Kelly parrots, her grin wide and annoying.

Gabi swallows. "I have yogurt and oatmeal, and I cut up some fruit and made some mini-pancakes. What do you usually eat?"

"Um. Coffee?"

She pulls a mug out of a cabinet over the sink, her shirt exposing just a sliver of skin above her shorts. I wonder how mad Kelly would be if I told her to skedaddle herself on home.

Fuck, I can't do that.

She pours me a full mug, and I sit down across from her at the table, Kelly between us. She picks at some fruit, a little grin on her face, as Gabi takes her seat, stirring a few more pieces of fruit into her oatmeal.

The smell of pancakes is stuck in my nose, and although I'm not one for sweets in the morning, I can't help but grab one. They're tiny, so I just hold it in my hand and take a bite.

And my god, that's good.

"You made these?"

"God, Zeke, swallow before you speak."

I ignore my sister, putting the rest in my mouth.

Gabi shrugs. "I don't usually make pancakes but I thought it might be nice since there are three of us. Usually I just have oatmeal," she says, lifting her bowl. "So eat up. I certainly can't finish everything off myself."

I take another pancake, shooting Kelly a look before she has a chance to speak. She fights a smile as she turns her attention back to her plate.

"The pancakes are good," I say, and I can just *feel* Kelly's amusement, despite her intense focus on her own breakfast. I take a sip of my coffee as she pops a piece of fruit into her mouth.

"Thanks," Gabi says, smiling genuinely at me as she takes another bite.

What I wouldn't give to slide my chair over next to hers, steal a little bit of her oatmeal and rest my hand on her thigh. Throw my arm along the back of her chair without an audience and joke with her like we always do. Ask if she's okay and watch her nod and sigh and tell me that she's fine, that she just got a little spooked but now that I'm here, she feels better.

But with Kelly here, we're back to being just friends.

Or is that just what we are?

I take a sip of my coffee.

Does making out with a friend automatically make you something other than friends?

Gabi's eyes find mine across the table, and she smiles. I grab another pancake—she made them for us, after all, and they're *delicious*.

I slept in her bed last night.

That's not something friends do.

Well, some do. Right? Girls do that all the time.

But not with guys. But if you sleep with someone of the opposite sex, you're usually *doing something* before the sleeping part. Which we didn't.

I drink more coffee, my brain going one further than just waking up and deciding to tick into overdrive instead. Maybe it's because I'm not at home and can't go through my normal routine. I'm wearing last night's clothes and I need to wash my face. I can't get the feel of Gabi's skin out of my mind, and it's driving me insane that I can't see whatever's happening inside her head.

When we're done eating, Gabi gathers our plates and throws them into the sink. She packs up the pancakes and puts them in a baggy to go for me, insisting that she won't eat them herself and they'll just go bad in the fridge. Warmth spreads through me as she hands them to me, her fingers grazing mine as she smiles up at me.

"We should probably get you home," I say to Kelly.

She grins as she grabs her purse from where it's draped over the kitchen chair and slips her shoes onto her feet. She looks like she's paying attention to the clasps around her ankles but I know better, so instead of kissing Gabi like I want to, I wrap an arm around her shoulder and pull her into a hug.

"You doing alright?" I murmur into her ear while she's close.

She pulls away from me just enough to see my face. "Please just ignore all of that. I'm totally good," she says, her voice equally low.

"You sure?"

She nods, rolling her eyes. "One vodka cranberry too many."

I squeeze her to me once more, savoring the press of each of her curves into my body.

It physically pains me to let her go, to take what's left of her mini-pancakes instead of taking her on the kitchen table.

Fucking Kelly.

Gabi gives her a hug, too, before we head out the door, and in that moment I'm jealous of my sister getting to be close to her.

As soon as Gabi closes the door on us, I beeline for the door at the bottom of the stairs. I can see in Kelly's face that she's ready to talk about this, but I don't think I am. At least, not with my sister.

But it turns out much worse—Kelly's ready to *sing* about it.

"Zeke and Gabi, sitting in a tree..."

"Kelly, stop."

"You are *so* in love with her." Her voice is high and squeaky.

"I am not."

Even if there was something going on there, it's far too early for love. I'd be lying if I said I didn't care about her—but that doesn't equate to love.

"You are *obsessed* with her."

"I am not."

I hold open the door for her, even though she's pissing me off a little bit, and it clangs shut behind us.

"Oh Zeke, I saw the way you looked at her. You could hardly take your eyes off her." Kelly clacks ahead of me, pulling her jacket over her shoulders as she walks. "I didn't even know you were dating anyone! What's up with that, dude?"

"Kelly, seriously. We're not dating."

"You want to, though."

I mean, yeah. But I don't say anything—too much information in Kelly's hands could be dangerous. She might tell our mom. Or try too hard to befriend Gabi and turn herself unwittingly into a Trojan horse that destroys us from the inside out.

"I think she wants to, too," she says, her voice a little softer.

"Look," I say, deciding to give her just enough information to satisfy her but not enough that she can start embarrassing me at family meals. "I like her, okay? But we're not dating. So don't go blabbing. The only reason you even met her is because both of you happened to need me on the same night."

"Don't worry, I won't tell Mom you're in *love*." Her eyes flash over the word.

"You don't exactly have the best track record."

She rolls her eyes. "I was *four* and you had me lying about necking with a girl." I push through the gate at the end of the courtyard, letting Kelly through before pulling it shut behind me.

"I gave you so many cookies."

"Even from a young age, I knew honesty was tastier than a cookie."

I laugh. "Tattle," I tease.

Her eyes flash. Her old nickname has been resurrected.

"Kitten," she calls me.

"Kitten?"

She grins. "As in smitten?"

I roll my eyes, and she cackles as she clambers into my car.

Kelly and I can tease each other all day—and I would never admit it to her—but a little part of me is scared that she's right.

I think about Gabi constantly—her body, her mind, her happiness. I wonder what she's doing and thinking and what sort of position her body is in when she's at yoga. I wonder if Charlie is nice enough to her at work, and I wonder what she's eating and when and whether she likes it.

Before Gabi, I was certain I had experienced love and that it just wasn't all that great.

Gabi took that assumption and crumbled it to pieces with one sentence.

If it wasn't all it was cracked up to be, I don't think it was really love—or, whatever your definition of love is.

And ever since then I've been fumbling my way through feelings I don't think I've ever had for someone before. Is it love? No. At least, not yet.

But it could be.

DECEMBER

18

GABI

I'm doing it.

I'm going to teacher training.

After several nights fraught with indecision and a healthy dose of skepticism, I invited Gemma and Natalie over again for another yoga session. This time, I put myself fully in the teacher mindset.

Gemma was more relaxed this time, although I could still see some tension in her shoulders. Natalie breezed into my apartment with an air of belonging that made me feel like, for an hour or so, my personal little space wasn't just my home but a safe space for the people I care about to find a little bit of peace.

I liked that. A lot.

And even though I moved through the poses with the girls and took the same deep breaths I encouraged them to, there was something rewarding about not just taking a moment for myself, but giving one to someone else.

After that session, where I embraced this role rather than shunned it, I realized teacher training was the place for me to be. I don't know how I'll use my certification yet, but there's a part of me that thinks it will be to replicate those moments exactly. Maybe I'll just do private sessions for friends and family, find students by word of mouth only. Just like Zeke finds his clients.

Zeke crosses my mind again as I push through the doors to the yoga studio. He's been doing that frequently, popping up at the most random times of day as if the thought of him sits in the back of my mind waiting for a craft beer or a dark sweater to bring him swarming into the forefront.

I was nervous about not seeing him with the amount of time teacher training is going to take up over the next couple of months. I'm still nervous about it, if I'm being honest, because there's a little part of me that craves the feeling of him against me, but also his words and thoughts and existence.

That feeling is quelled partially by the vibration of my phone in my bag, which—when I finally find it between all of the yoga crap I have stuffed in there—shows a text from him wishing me good luck on my first day of class.

He's in Virginia, meeting with a new client before agreeing to work on their website. He left only a few days after my fateful drunk night, and we haven't spoken of it since.

I take it as a good sign that he hasn't started ignoring my texts. He seems like the same Zeke as before—if anything, maybe a little more talkative.

But I still want to crawl into a hole and die every time I think about crying into his shoulder.

Over a big, fat *nothing*.

I wonder if he's in his hotel room right now, fingers flying over his keyboard as he sorts through everything he has to do. Maybe he's at the bar, having a drink after a long day of logistics, planning, and discovery. Maybe he's having dinner with his client, the daughter of the couple who owns his favorite deli.

She better not be hot.

I create a version of her in my mind that's happily married with three kids and an attractive husband she wouldn't dare leave, even for the dark and mysterious freelancer she's hired.

I wave at Corinne when she catches my eye, and she smiles, nodding as I lay my mat out along one wall, copying what everyone else has done. It's my first class, but everyone else has been here for a few days already. Corinne agreed to sneak me in as long as I promised to do a few extra sessions with Gemma and Natalie to make up for the missed time.

She introduces me at the beginning of class, and after an awkward wave and a few friendly smiles, she dives right into her lesson.

It's not anything like going to a yoga class, but I didn't expect it to be. We move through some poses but most of the time is spent listening to Corinne share her experience.

I'm certain there's no other teacher in the world who's better to learn from, and although the true meaning of yoga is not what makes me enjoy it so much, I find myself drawn to the history, to the *why*.

By the time class is over, I'm exhausted from paying attention in a way that I haven't since college, but I'm also a little exhilarated.

I have zero plans for this. I have absolutely no idea how a certificate is truly going to help me in life, but I'm enjoying it.

And that is something I haven't felt in a long time.

Maybe some things don't need a reason.

And there's Zeke again, popping into my head as I gather my things back into my bag.

Maybe some people don't need a reason either.

On the way out, Corinne waves me down, asking if I'd like to grab a drink with her at the bar across the street.

And of course I say yes, because I love Corinne and wouldn't dare give up the rare opportunity to hang out with her.

So we walk over together and pick two seats at the bar. Behind us is a row of booths tucked against the opposite wall, complete with ragged red vinyl seating and dog pictures lining the walls.

We order two white wines from a gruff bartender who doesn't say anything to us but promptly brings two generous pours.

"So how did you like your first class?"

I let out a long breath. "I liked it a lot. It's not the same as, you know, going to a class, but I enjoyed it for other reasons. Honestly I'm just kind of looking forward to leading Gemma and Natalie again. It's nerve-racking but really rewarding."

Corinne nods as she takes a sip of wine, waving me off. "Oh, it's always a little nerve-racking in the beginning, but you get the hang of it. The teacher training is great but it's a whole different beast than actually leading a class. I'm so thrilled to hear you're enjoying that part of it though. So many people get through teacher training and realize they don't actually want to teach."

I shrug. "I'll be honest, it's not that I really want to *teach*," I say, watching her expression carefully—the last thing I want to do is offend Corinne. "I guess I just know the feeling I get from yoga, and seeing Gemma, especially—even Natalie too—just follow along and *get* something from it, is nice."

"Spoken like a true teacher," she says, clinking her wine-glass to mine.

"When you first suggested this, I almost thought it was a bad idea, because of how much I used it as an outlet. I thought teaching might take that away, but in a way, it makes it stronger. I have to focus on bringing everyone through with me. Before, I searched for the outlet for myself, but now, I kind of feel like I'm searching for it for everyone else, and that makes it all the more powerful."

Corinne nods. "I always thought of it like an empathetic response. You take a little bit of what your class can't carry and help them squash it. Whether it's a physical need or an emotional one."

"Exactly," I say, taking an overzealous sip of my wine and choking on it.

"Well don't get too excited there," Corinne says.

I take another sip to soothe my throat, shaking my head.

The bartender places two waters in front of us, and I blink back the tears in my eyes.

Zeke, pulling me into his chest.

"Well I'm glad you're enjoying it," Corinne says, moving her wine in small circles along the wood of the bar. She's pensive, quiet for a moment, before she turns to me. "You know, they're looking for a new tenant for the studio."

"Oh?"

She nods. "I've been friends with the owners for years now. They said if I can find someone to take over the lease, they'll prolong the rate. It's a good deal."

"Is it going to be another yoga studio?"

She turns to me. "If you want it to be."

"What does that mean?"

"Why don't you take over the lease? It's the cheapest you'll find, and I know you love the space. You can teach

Natalie and Gemma in a space made for it. You can hire some other teachers and make a real go of it. Better than I ever could. You have that attention to detail. That drive that I never had. You could make something really great out of it."

My first instinct is to laugh, then sputter, then take another daringly large sip of wine. "Corinne, I can't take over a studio. I'm not even qualified to teach yet, let alone run a studio."

She shakes her head. "You don't need a cert to run a studio. If you're uncomfortable, coordinate some other teachers to come in until you're done with training. But you have the thing you need that so many people don't, long before and long after they go through training. You have the passion for it."

I swallow. These are strong words, coming from Corinne.

"I'd be happy to help you as much as I can. Even teach, if you want me to."

"Why did you leave in the first place if you're so willing to come back?"

"Gabi, I love yoga. Everything about it. But the business of it? Not so much. The insurance, the scheduling, the instructors who ghost you, the students who leave bad reviews. It's all too much for me. I just want to teach, and I get to do that now, without the headache of everything else."

"I wouldn't know the first thing about running a business."

She shrugs. "You can learn. Just think about it," she says, taking another sip of wine. "And give me an answer in three weeks, okay? That's when the rent gets jacked up and shopped around to the highest bidder."

"Okay," I say, slightly winded. I take another sip of wine

as Corinne delves into one of the concepts we went over in class today.

But I'm not really listening. I'm *definitely* not considering taking over the studio. I'm a little flabbergasted that she asked me in the first place. More than anything, I'm floored that she thinks I would be *good* at it.

Gabi Pierce, businesswoman?

I certainly couldn't have come up with that idea.

Just the thought of it makes me want to laugh.

When Corinne and I finish our drink, we part with a hug on the sidewalk. And as soon as we walk away from each other, I furiously text Zeke to see if he's still awake.

It's gone from chilly to straight-up cold over the past few weeks, so I wrap my coat tighter around me and duck my head to the wind. It's not a long walk home, but it feels like it tonight.

And after only a few minutes, my phone rings.

"How was your first day of school?" I ignore the note of mockery in his voice.

"It was really good. I mean, it's different, but good."

"You sound happy." And *he* sounds happy that *I* sound happy, and the whole thing kicks up a little flutter of butterflies in my stomach.

"I am happy. And kind of amused."

"Amused?"

I cross the road, careful to look both ways and switch my phone to the other ear. "Corinne wants me to take over the studio."

"Like, run it?"

"Like, own it. Her studio is done, but she said the owner of the building asked if she knows anyone who'd be willing to take it over. And she thought of *me*," I say, laughing.

He's quiet for a moment. "Why *wouldn't* she think of you?"

"Okay, we all know you're sweet. But I can't just up and decide one day to start running an entire business."

He laughs. "People have done crazier things."

"Yeah, but I have a full-time job. And like, I don't know how to do that stuff."

"I can help you."

"Zeke, not to be an asshole here, but what do you know about running a yoga studio?"

"Not much about the yoga part, but I *am* technically a business."

I pause, this little piece of the puzzle settling differently than it did before. I always thought of Zeke as a freelancer, but I guess that is *technically* a business. He has clients and pays taxes—or so I hope—and coordinates meetings just like other people who own businesses.

"I guess I never really put that together," I say.

"Yeah, well, I don't really love all the business-y parts of it. But it's necessary."

Just like Corinne.

"Well," I start, a little stumped, "I mean, I can't just, like, *open* a yoga studio."

He makes a noise that sounds suspiciously like a laugh. "Gabi, you can do whatever the hell you want to do. You just have to make up your mind and do it."

"I'm not opening a yoga studio."

"Okay. But if you wanted to, you could."

"Yeah. If I wanted to, I guess I could."

"So do you want to?"

I scoff. "I mean—no."

He snickers. "Okay, Gabi. You wouldn't have brought it up unless you were considering it."

I cross into what I consider to be the start of Fairmount, where the streets get a little quieter and the bars become just a little bit cuter.

"What are you doing?" I ask, feeling like a subject change is necessary.

"I'm in bed," he says. "Had a long day. Lots of meetings, lots of people, lots of everything."

He sounds a little resigned, and I feel a pull toward him, wishing I could curl up next to him and feel his breathing turn deeper.

"I hope I didn't wake you."

"You didn't. But for what it's worth, I'd be happy if you did."

My breath catches in my throat. Even when he's had a long day, he makes a point to make me feel good.

"Hey Zeke?"

"Hey Gabi."

"When you're back, will you take me to The Corner Deli?"

He lets out a long breath. "Yeah. And I can't even tell you how much I'm looking forward to it."

By the time I reach my apartment, I can hear the sleepiness in his voice. I close the gate gently so he won't hear over the phone—something tells me he wouldn't be pleased with me walking around the city at ten at night—and tell him he should get some rest.

I hear him adjusting as he admits that he probably won't make it much longer.

"Good night Zeke. You're doing a good job."

He exhales a raspy noise through the phone. "Good night Gabriella." He sucks in a breath like he's going to say something else and decides against it. "You're something special."

When he hangs up, his words echo in my head. *You're something special.*

When I get into my apartment, I see a rogue shelf has fallen in my coat closet, the pristine organizational system that used to exist in there lost in a pile of coats, shoes, and purses.

I shut the door on the mess and decide to deal with it later.

I head to bed with a fresh mug of tea and a smile on my face.

Zeke thinks I'm something special.

19

ZEKE

"So tell me," she says, eyeing me over a dirty martini, "how bad is it?"

We're at a restaurant down the street from Leanne's office and my hotel, and judging from the friendly way she greeted the hostess, she comes here frequently. There's a long bar with a variety of glasses hanging overhead, and a little yellow candle on every table. Soft piano music plays through the speakers.

I shake my head. "It's not *bad*, per se," I start. "But it's a lot."

"A lot, how?"

She takes a bite of her Caesar salad, and I pick at the sandwich I ordered, my hunger having evaporated over the past two days. I take a sip of whiskey instead.

And then I launch into everything I found that would need to be fixed or changed. I pull up the list I created on my phone and explain the different side projects that would develop from this project, and I outline the things that need to be fixed with or without me there to do it.

She listens intently, her eyes on the white tablecloth in

front of us. She swirls her martini, nodding at some parts, shrugging at others.

At this point I'm daring her to call the whole thing off. I eye her, trying to gauge what exactly she's thinking, but by the time I'm done, it seems almost blank.

She purses her lips. "So what you're saying is, this is going to be tedious and expensive?"

I wince at her words. "At the very least. And honestly, I'm not totally sure I can make it happen. This seems like something you need a whole team for, if you want it done in any reasonable time frame."

She takes another sip of her drink, and then levels me with her eyes. "What if I told you I don't care if it's done in a reasonable time frame? That you can lean on any of my employees and we'll redistribute their responsibilities elsewhere, temporarily?"

That's not where I expected her to go. I thought she'd give up, ask for my notes and move on to the next sucker who sees her as a fat paycheck.

"I would ask you why."

She sighs. "Because I've been burned before. This isn't something we can half-ass, and honestly, your stress level right now kind of makes me think we need you. The last guy took one look at us, threw some cut-and-paste code into our systems, and billed us down to hell and back."

I nod. "You definitely need a little more than cut and paste. You need a prescriptive process, really, and a system that supports that process." I take a sip of my whiskey. "It's probably going to get harder before it gets easier. The way these systems are set up, there's a good chance you'll end up doing more manual work in the short term while security vulnerabilities are patched up. Employees don't like that. Not to mention the connection between your accounting software and your inventory is shoddy at best. Arguably no better than physically sending someone into the warehouse to account for things themselves."

She laughs, her brown hair falling over her shoulder as she tips her head back. "Yeah, we already do that. I think Carlisle was just pretending we have our shit together when he walked you through it."

Great, now I have to figure out what else they're trying to hide.

"So Zeke, tell me. If we want you to continue, how long will it take and how much will it cost?"

She smiles at me, but I can't help feeling like I'm being sized up by a cougar.

I drew up a plan and an estimate this afternoon. With the number of unknowns and the sheer size of the knowns, I came up with a quote that—even in my world of computers and APIs and code that I write in my sleep—would make anyone with a modicum of sense balk.

And at this moment, something in my gut tells me it's still not enough, so when I recite it to her, I make a last-minute decision to double it—both the cost and the timeline.

She swirls her drink again, thinking on it.

And then she nods. "Okay."

"Okay?"

"That sounds reasonable considering the amount of work that's needed."

My blood freezes in my veins.

Did she actually just agree to that?

My initial estimate was a number I was cautiously comfortable with, considering the amount of time and thought that would go into this project. It took into consideration the loss of my other projects and my free time. It was a number that would hopefully make it worth it in the end, assuming nothing goes horribly wrong.

But doubled? If I don't think too hard about how much work this is going to be, I might actually be excited for it.

I text Gabi when I get back to the hotel, feeling like a celebration is in order.

ZEKE

Can I take you to The Corner Deli tomorrow night?

20

GABI

I take the trolley to Zeke's apartment, very aware that despite living in Philadelphia for over ten years, it's the one mode of transportation I've managed to avoid thus far. The car is cramped and the steps are steeper than I thought they'd be, so I trip on my way up and just barely catch myself before landing a palm in years of SEPTA grease lining the floor.

But Zeke takes the trolley to me, so it seems like something I should be familiar with.

The ride is short and thankfully quiet, and when I step down the too-steep stairs to the asphalt of the road, I take a second to orient myself before continuing on my way. I looked up the street view of the trolley stop before leaving so I know without looking at my phone that I need to cross the street and head north.

I text him when I'm a block away and a second before I raise my fist to knock on the door, it opens. Zeke's grin is contagious as he takes in my pink cheeks, my hunched shoulders.

"My god, I didn't realize it was that cold out," he says,

shutting the door behind me. He turns to me, his hands cupping my freezing cheeks, and his eyes land on mine.

I had been so consumed by the trek here—by the cold—that I forgot what today was.

A date with Zeke.

And he already has his hands on me, his skin touching mine in a way that's so gentle yet mildly possessive. His hands wrap around to the back of my neck, and he leans forward slowly, his lips pressing against mine with delicate precision.

A wave of heat rushes through me and I'm suddenly too hot, overdressed for the warmth of his apartment.

"I've been waiting to do that a long time," he says, and a wave of relief crashes over me that I wasn't the only one. His strong arms weave around my neck, pulling me in for a hug.

I think this might be the absolute best way to start a first date.

I unwind my scarf from my neck, letting in some air, and follow him into his apartment. It's larger than I expected, and I realize that he must have two floors, judging from the staircase along one wall. His kitchen area is homey, a dark wood table along one side with bench seating and Edison bulbs over a dark granite countertop.

In the living room is a brown leather couch—only one blanket, but I can fix that—situated across from a large TV, the blinds of the windows open just enough to let in the last of the day's sun.

The whole place is cozy, like I could curl up in a ball on one end of the couch in some thick socks with a mug of tea while he works on his laptop on the other, his hand resting on my leg when he isn't typing. I can see us splitting a bottle of red wine, two glasses on the dark coffee table. Climbing the stairs at the far end of the room, his hand in mine, and falling into his sheets, his arms snaking around my waist.

"I hope the trolley wasn't too bad." He grabs his jacket from a closet a few feet from the door, checks that his wallet is in the pocket, and pulls it over his sweater.

"No, not bad at all."

This moment feels so intimate, probably because I haven't seen it before. He's been to my apartment a handful of times and been inside twice now. He's seen me sleepy and barely put together. Yet I haven't even seen him so much as put his shoes on.

"You ready? Or do you need a few minutes in the warmth?" He takes a step toward me, his fingers grazing my cheek, and my body alights from the inside out.

"I think I'll be okay."

"It's only a block away if that's any consolation."

"Just enough time to turn me into an ice cube. Hope you're bringing your ice pick."

He grins, and my heart thrums in response.

"Would you like a heavier jacket?"

I glance down at the one I'm wearing, a pink bomber jacket I wear each year until winter dictates I can't any longer. I try to avoid my knee-length puffy coat as long as possible—usually until January—but this December's unseasonable cold is making that difficult.

Zeke sees my internal debate and reaches back into the coat closet without waiting for an answer.

"It's not as stylish, but hopefully it'll do the trick." He hands me a thick black jacket with a fleece lining, and I trade him my bomber jacket. Pulling it on, I can smell him all around me, some combination of laundry detergent and soap and *him*, that I nearly ask if we can skip the deli altogether and just continue trading items of clothing until there's nothing left to trade.

But I know he loves this place, and I'm pretty hungry, so I let his too-big jacket swallow me up, zipping it all the way with a smile. "How do I look?"

He raises his eyebrows. "Really good."

Something about the way his eyes travel down to my legs and back up again makes me think he really means that.

The walk over is much warmer, the jacket providing a nice buffer between the biting wind and my ass, which I now realize was also frozen.

The deli is just as charming as in the pictures. There's a small array of flowers in a refrigerator by the entrance, ranging from roses to lilies to daisies to tulips. Next to that is a rack of puzzle books—sudoku and crosswords. Further in is a scattering of mismatched tables and chairs, set up cafeteria style, with a long deli counter along one side that has a line of five people waiting. In the back are refrigerators that boast a mix-your-own-six deal.

Zeke grabs my hand and heads to the back. "Want to split a six-pack with me?"

I nod as he grabs one of the cardboard carriers tucked on a countertop to the side of the fridges.

"What do you like?"

I had been nervous he'd ask me this question. "I don't know. I'm not really a big beer drinker." I scrunch up my nose, hoping this isn't a deal breaker.

He pauses. "Well, shit."

"I'm happy to try it though. Maybe you can suggest a couple that are kind of mild? Maybe that taste like cake? Or wine?"

He laughs. "How about I pick the mildest ones that I like, and you can try it, and if you don't like it, I'll drink it?"

"Perfect."

He gathers an array of bottles, tapping his chin a few times as he makes final decisions. Then he leads me to the counter, where I'm instantly overwhelmed by the sheer number of choices laid out on the menus on the wall above us.

"So cheat sheet: the hoagies are bang, the salads are above average, the chili is the best I've ever had, the pizza is about what you'd expect getting pizza from a deli, and anything considered an entrée will make you see God."

I laugh and decide on pad thai, intrigued by the fact that it's made from spaghetti squash instead of noodles. And the possibility of seeing God.

"Ooh, good choice," he says, ordering a hoagie for himself.

When we sit down at a table toward the back, he sets each of the bottles in a line between us.

"So," he starts, his finger on the cap of the first one. "Cream soda." He moves to the next one. "Coffee stout. Cake, as requested." He grins at me, and I can't help but return it. "Crème brûlée. Regular cider. And a pear cider."

"Hmm. Cream soda."

"Really?"

I furrow my eyebrows. "Did you expect me to pick something else?"

"Honestly I thought for sure you'd go for the pear cider. Maybe the cake."

He opens the bottle and slides it toward me, watching as I take a sip. "So what do you think?"

I shrug. "It tastes like cream soda that's gone bad."

His eyebrows furrow. "Okay, let's try the next one then." He takes the cream soda from me and takes a sip, moving it to the side. "Which one?"

"Cake?" I say, going with my original request.

"Cake it is," he says, popping the cap off and sliding it across the table. He watches my face again and makes the determination before I do that the cake beer is not for me, either. "What is it you don't like about it?" he asks, his eyes narrowing.

"They all just kind of feel like an assault."

He raises his eyebrows, the hint of a laugh behind his smile. "An assault?"

"Like the taste is so sharp—almost overwhelming—you know?"

He thinks for a second, and then hesitantly reaches for the coffee stout, popping the cap off and sliding it toward me once again. "Try that."

I take a sip, and I'm pleasantly surprised by the smoothness. It's not my favorite flavor in the world, but it's nice, kind of like an iced coffee with a bit of a kick.

"Have you found The One?"

If that isn't a loaded question. I nod. "This is The One."

"Whew! For a second there I thought I'd be chugging a six-pack by myself. Are you sure you like it?"

I take another sip and let out an overenthusiastic "yum" afterward.

He grins again, and I continue to melt.

"Gabriell*a* is a stout girl," he says, taking a sip of the cream soda beer I had rejected. "Who woulda thunk it?"

Our food arrives on trays a few minutes later, courtesy of an older woman with wispy gray hair tucked into a bun on her head.

"Zeke, dear," she says in greeting.

"Thank you, Della.

"You brought a friend," she says, turning to smile at me as she places my tray in front of me.

"This is Gabi. Gabi, Della."

"Nice to meet you, Gabi."

"Nice to meet you too, I've heard many good things."

"Oh, I'm sure most of them have to do with me being unable to change my Wi-Fi password or charge my mouse."

"In your defense, Della, each of those things only happened once."

She shrugs. "What can I say? Your generation was born with a computer at the end of your fingertips." She turns to Zeke. "I hear Virginia went well with Leanne?"

He nods. "Well enough. It's a lot of work, but I think it's doable."

"Good, dear, good." She pats him on the shoulder. "Well, I'll let you get to your food. Enjoy, kids!"

"The famous Della," I say once she's out of earshot. "I feel touched by greatness."

Zeke grins. "She's a great lady."

We dig into our food—and wow, Zeke wasn't kidding about it being a spiritual experience. "I don't think I'll ever be able to eat normal pad thai again after this."

He grins, taking a bite of his hoagie. "I'm glad you like it."

"I might be addicted to it."

Whatever lingering apprehension he had about finding a beer I liked was zapped with my enjoyment of the food. We relax into our seats, settling into conversation so comfortable I nearly forget I'm on a date.

With Zeke.

The realization kickstarts my heart and I get a little self-conscious, reminding myself to chew with my mouth closed, to not overeat or burp when the carbonation of the beer inevitably catches up to me.

"So Virginia went well?" He hasn't told me any details yet.

He nods, leaning back in his chair. "I think I'm going to do it."

"That's great."

He shrugs. "It's the sort of project that I know I'll be pulling my hair out over, so I'm a little apprehensive about it." He sighs, leaning forward to wrap up the rest of his sandwich. "It's a lot bigger than I thought it would be."

I swallow, resisting the urge to make a dirty joke. "Like, more complicated?"

"More complicated and just messier in general." He takes a sip of his drink. "And I'm probably going to have to go down there a lot, probably at least once a month, if not more than that, until it's done. There are just so many moving parts that I don't think I'll feel confident doing the whole thing from home."

I nod. "Well luckily, it's not too far. And we're not in the Middle Ages, so it's not like you'll be disconnected from everyone. You'll just be, you know, a little farther away."

And now I'm speaking in riddles because the only thing I'm thinking about is having to listen to his voice over the phone instead of against my skin.

"Yeah. I'll miss game nights, though. Especially when they coincide with girls' nights."

A blush creeps up my neck. "They won't be the same without you."

We're silent for a beat, our eyes connected across the table.

"I think we should get you a bottle of wine."

"Only if you'll have some with me."

"Deal."

We take our trays to the drop-off counter toward the

door, and Zeke packs up what's left of our six-pack. He downs the cake beer quickly, chucking the empty bottle into the recycling bin. He shouts a hasty goodbye over his shoulder as he leads me to the door, his hand on the small of my back.

"Wait a second, Gabi," he says, tugging on my arm to stop me. We're in the entryway, about to push out to the street, and he takes a deep breath, closing his eyes for a second. "How good does it smell right here?"

The scent hit me a few feet ago—a mingling of roses and lilies, if I know my flowers as well as I think I do.

"Zeke Morgan, you like lilies, don't you? Or is it the roses you're into?"

He shakes his head. "I can't tell the difference. Probably both. It just smells so fresh, you know? Pretty."

"Why don't you buy some flowers for your apartment? The lilies would work nice in there, a little bit of cream against your leather couches."

He seems to consider it, then wrinkles his eyebrows, shaking his head. "No, I can't buy flowers for myself. That's weird."

I roll my eyes. "You're too manly for flowers, huh?"

"I mean, no. Not if I was buying them for someone, but just for myself? That's weird."

"You're missing out," I tell him as he holds the door open for me. I wrap his jacket tighter around me, tucking my nose into the neck and breathing him in. My scarf is stacked up around my ears as he leads me in the opposite direction of his house to the liquor store, where I grab my favorite bottle of white, and we continue back to his apartment.

The sun is setting when we get back inside, the whole place bathed in a warm yellow glow, and I just want to sink into it—the warmth, the coziness, him. He stows the rest of his sandwich and beer in the fridge and grabs two wine-glasses, pouring us each a glass and placing them on the coffee table in front of the couch.

He pulls out two coasters from the sliding drawer beneath, and I grab one for a closer look.

They're thick and heavy, not like the flimsy cocktail coasters you get at bars or the cheap stacks you get from box stores. They're stone, it seems, with different pictures on each one. A London phone booth. Amsterdam tulips.

"Oliver and I went backpacking through Europe one summer in college," he explains, leaning back into the couch next to me and taking a sip of his wine.

I'm suddenly blindingly jealous of Oliver.

"I love these," I say, putting them back on the table and resting my wineglass on top of the London one.

He shrugs. "They're looking a little raggedy these days —I have a bunch, but most of them are missing half their paint at this point. I'll probably need to replace them soon."

Visions of European adventures with Zeke dance in my head. "They're charming."

He laughs. "You know, Gabi, I had a feeling you'd be into coasters."

"Gotta protect your wood," I joke, and he snorts in response.

I tuck my feet up under me and the movement brings me closer to him, my knee touching his. A little electric jolt runs from the warmth of his touch, straight up my spine. He rests his forearm on my knee, and I can't help but stare at it, marvel at the weight of it on my leg.

He draws little circles on my skin that have me inching closer until I find myself leaning in to him, so enamored by his hands on me and the warmth of his skin. When I glance up at him, he takes the opportunity to gently press his lips to mine.

And when he pulls away, I want more.

I push toward him, my hand landing on the back of his neck and bringing us closer.

The hand on my knee stops those little circles and squeezes, moving higher on my thigh to my hip. His tongue slips past mine, tangling with me, and my hands move to his chest, his neck, his hair.

I'm nearly in his lap now, so desperate to be closer to him.

"Gabi," he says into my neck, like a warning.

"Zeke."

"Maybe we should slow down?"

My heart jumps into my throat as I pull away from him. *Am I going too fast for him?* "You don't want to?"

"Oh god, Gabi, I do," he says, running a hand through his hair. He has one arm behind me, keeping me close. "I really do, believe me. But we're friends, you know?"

Now I'm confused. Is he friend-zoning me? "Well, maybe a little more than friends?"

He scrunches up his face. "I didn't mean it like that. Yeah of course, but I just don't want to mess up by going too fast."

"Is it because I froze up last time?"

There's a beat of silence between us.

"Because it really seemed like you wanted to before I froze up."

He lets out a breath. "It's not *just* because you froze up, but yeah, I don't want to push you."

I take a deep breath. "I froze up because the last time a hand skirted the inside of my waistband, it wasn't welcome."

His eyes bore into mine, a hint of pity in them.

"Gabi..."

I take his hand, separating his fingers, and slip two underneath the edge of my jeans. He follows my movement, his fingers hooking there and moving gently along the edge, winding around to my back.

"It just took me a minute to get used to the feeling, to disassociate *that* with this," I say, moving toward him again, his fingers still tucked between my skin and my jeans. I kiss him, relishing in the way he fists my waistband, pulling me closer, the way his other hand moves into my hair, deepening our kiss.

"Gabi, it's not just that," he says, one arm clamped around my back. He runs a hand through his hair, breathing out heavily. "I like you, Gabi. Maybe more than I should."

"I like you too." *Not seeing the problem here.*

"I can't just sleep with someone casually."

It takes me a second to realize what he's saying. He's asking me to *be something* with him.

"Then we won't sleep together casually."

"You're sure?"

I nod, subconsciously biting my lip.

He accepts my answer.

His eyes darken, his arm tightening around me, pulling me to him. His kisses turn deliberate, his hands grabbing at my ass and pulling me into his lap so I straddle him. He's thick beneath me, his length rubbing me through our jeans and teasing at just how intoxicating it will feel to have him slip slowly into me and fill me.

He palms my ass, and I grind against him.

"Gabi," he mutters into my cheek, the warning in his voice changing into something more gruff, primal. He kisses down my neck to my collarbone, his hands winding up underneath my shirt, wrapping tight around me and sinking my body into his.

He grabs my hips, lifting and pushing me down into him. I let out an involuntary moan.

"Lift your arms."

I do, and he drags my shirt up over my head by the hem. His eyes are transfixed on my chest as his hands move up my torso. He reaches behind me, undoing the clasp, and watches with rapt attention as my bra falls between us.

"Jesus, Gabi," he says, one hand flat on my abdomen and slowly raising higher, leaving a trail of goose bumps along my skin as one thumb flicks at my nipple, drawing another moan out of me. "You are so beautiful." He dips his head and takes one in his mouth, his thumb still playing with the other. His tongue dances around, sucking at it.

I throw my head back, barely able to hold on to myself with his tongue on my nipple and his hardness rubbing me through our jeans.

"Gabi," he says, drawing my attention back to him. He kisses up my chest to my neck. "You're about to come with your jeans still on, aren't you?"

I pause, slowing my grinding but not willing to stop. "Maybe."

"We can't have that. Stand up."

He stops touching me, waiting for me to move.

So I stand, bare to him from the waist up, and his eyes lazily appraise me.

When he comes to his feet in front of me, his hands find my waist, leaning down to kiss me gently, as if we weren't just fucking with our clothes on.

I weave my hands underneath his sweater, my fingers running across his chest. I push his sweater up, and he pulls it over his head.

I can't help but stare at him, all muscle and warmth, with just a little bit of chest hair that presses against me when he pulls me in for another kiss. His hand weaves into my hair as mine move desperately across his skin, aching to memorize every slope of his skin, every taut muscle.

"God, you're sexy," I mutter, still taken by his body.

"You're one to talk." His hands reach lower, finding the clasp of my jeans.

He lowers to his knees in front of me, pressing a kiss to my stomach. He undoes the button and slides the zipper down slowly, peeling back that flap of denim and pressing a kiss on the triangle of my underwear.

His eyes lock on mine as he gently tugs my jeans down. As they hit the ground, he holds a hand out, helping me step away from them.

His thumbs loop underneath my thong, pulling and then releasing so the strings snap back against my body. I'm so energized that just the movement of the fabric nearly sends me over the edge.

"Jesus, Zeke."

He does it again, a wicked grin on his face as he presses his mouth to my underwear, just slightly above where I'm desperate for him.

He runs a thumb down my center and I shiver.

"Gabi, you are soaked through your underwear."

"Might as well take them off, then."

His eyes flash, and he hooks his fingers into the sides again, slowly pulling down and exposing me.

"God, Gabi." My underwear leaves a trail of wetness against my thigh—I can only imagine the mess he's looking at.

He leans forward, pressing a kiss to the sensitive skin there. His tongue slips forward, just barely hitting that sensitive bundle of nerves, and I cry out.

He stands, pushing me backward until my knees hit the

couch. His hand nudges between my knees, creating space for him as he settles between my legs. With one hand on my hip, he kisses me, his tongue winding into my mouth as my hips start bucking up at him.

He leaves a trail of kisses from my chin to my collarbone, to my nipples, to my stomach. His lips brush the skin at the corner of my thigh before licking a delicate line along my center.

"Soak my face, Gabi." He pushes my thighs wide and buries his face in me.

His tongue circles my clit as his fingers trail up my leg, skirting the corner of my hip. I take a sharp breath in as his fingers push inside me, pulsing slowly at first and then picking up speed.

I can't control the noises I'm making at this point, the feel of his tongue flicking and sucking at me totally overwhelming any sense of self-consciousness I had before. He pushes another finger inside me, and I feel like I'm about to burst.

"Zeke," I pant.

He grunts in response.

"I'm going to..."

He presses down on my hip, holding me in place, as his tongue continues against my clit and his fingers pulse rhythmically into me. His eyes lock on mine as my orgasm crashes around me, his lips tilting into a smile as he watches me.

As I slowly stop shaking, he kisses up my thigh, my hip, my stomach.

"That was the tastiest dessert I've ever had."

I groan at his words, simultaneously spent from my orgasm while also feeling my body responding to his mouth as his tongue licks a circle around my nipple.

"Zeke, that was..." *I have no words.*

"I know," he murmurs into my skin. He kisses my neck softly, his nose grazing the sensitive skin just beneath my ear as he settles between my legs. He kisses my cheeks, my neck, my collarbone. His hands are in my hair, his hips moving against mine.

I reach between us, undoing his pants and pushing them down over his hips, and he groans into my shoulder.

"Zeke, I want you."

"Fuck, Gabi," he says, as I push his underwear down and take him in my hand. *And holy fuck, he fits this in his pants?* My mouth goes dry at his size. I pump him as his breathing ticks faster in my ear, his muscles tightening.

"Are you on birth control?" he asks, his lips brushing across my cheek.

I nod. "Yeah, I am."

One hand weaves behind my neck as he presses his mouth roughly to mine, his breath running hot over my cheek. I can tell by the way he grabs me that he's ready to be inside me, and I position him at my entrance, running the tip along my core. He watches the movement, his head resting on my shoulder, and looks up at me as he slowly sinks inside me.

"You okay?" he asks, leaving a kiss on my cheek.

I nod. "Are you?"

"Barely hanging on," he jokes, as he pushes deeper with a groan. He curses as he settles in deep, his hips straining against mine.

He moves slowly as I adjust to him, and then faster, setting a pace that has my insides clenching, release so close already. I pull him close to me, desperate to feel his chest against me, and he rocks into me harder, every muscle tense as he wraps an arm around my waist.

My nails tear at his back as he fists my hair, his pace increasing. I arch into him, and as he moves, he hits that perfect spot. The pressure grows as he pinches a nipple, a gasp rasping from my throat. "Zeke, I'm going to come."

He thrusts into me harder, and I clench my muscles, eliciting a groan from him.

"Come with me," he says.

And I break apart around him, his grunts heavy in my ear as I'm filled with his warmth.

His breaths are ragged on my neck as he collapses into me, skin on sweaty skin.

"Gabriella," he whispers, leaving a loud kiss on my ear afterward. "You feel so good."

I wrap my arms and legs around him, holding him as close as I can.

"I can't wait to do that again."

21

ZEKE

Gabriella Pierce is in my bed.

Gabriella Pierce is in *my bed*.

What sort of alternate reality did I land myself in? Because I refuse to go back.

Her silky blonde hair is splayed across my sheets, the contrast startling. She's wearing one of my old T-shirts while we wash her clothes, and a pair of old boxer shorts that certainly never looked anywhere near as sexy on me as they do on her right now.

She smiles sleepily at me, reaching for me. I place the water I got for her on the nightstand and crawl into bed next to her. She snuggles up against me, pressing her butt into me, and my body has a lot of ideas based on that one small movement.

I think I've had this daydream before, but it does not compare to reality one bit—her warm body smelling like flowers and vanilla. I run a hand down her hip, excited just to feel her curves, and she turns toward me, pressing a kiss into my bare shoulder.

"Again?" she asks, her knees falling open between scattered sheets.

Fuck yes.

I dip my hand underneath the boxers she's wearing, drawing one finger along her slick center, and she shudders closer to me, her hips bucking in my direction.

"You are insatiable," I whisper into her ear, slipping a finger inside of her, keeping my thumb pressed on that bundle of nerves.

"*You're* insatiable. I was ready to fall asleep."

"Please. You're too wet to be thinking about sleeping," I say, slipping in another finger and upping my tempo.

She starts moaning into my shoulder, and I take my hand back, tugging the boxers down. I grab her by the hips and move her onto my chest, pushing my own underwear down just low enough to expose myself, and she settles on top of me.

She grinds her hips into mine in lazy circles, sleep still in her eyes as she places her hands on my stomach, rocking into me.

When she comes, I roll on top of her and take my turn, thrusting into her with everything I have left in me, which— granted—isn't much at this point of the night.

She smiles up at me as I empty myself inside her, and I can't help but wonder what I wouldn't do to see her smile at me like that, full of carnal satisfaction and comfort and safety.

She stumbles into the bathroom to clean herself up, and tucks herself in next to me a few minutes later, her head on my shoulder.

Before long, she's breathing deeply, her breath brushing gently across my bare skin.

I kiss her temple, the scent of her shampoo intoxicating, and close my eyes.

Gabriella Pierce is in my bed.

And she is mine.

I WAKE UP DISCOMBOBULATED, my mind replaying images of Gabi's naked body riding me—but I'm alone.

I panic, running through my night again. *Did I take any strange substances? Drink too much? Hit my head?*

No, no, and no.

I get out of bed, scanning the room, and see no evidence that she was ever here. My sheets are twisted, but that's not unusual. I don't see the T-shirt she borrowed or the boxers.

I pull on a pair of sweatpants and head downstairs, my heartbeat calming as I smell the coffee brewing.

"Good morning, sunshine," she says, her smile wide as she looks up at me from the kitchen table. She's halfway through a mug of coffee, her cup balanced on one of my Europe coasters. She puts her phone down on the kitchen table as I approach, leaning into me when I press a kiss to her forehead.

"Good morning," I say, pouring myself a cup of coffee. "You're up early."

She sighs, smiling sadly at me. "I have yoga today. I have to get going soon."

"No," I say, sitting down on the bench next to her and wrapping an arm around her to pull her close. "We can do yoga here. Just get naked and bend over; call it a lesson."

Her laughter is everything.

"Corinne will be upset with me if I miss any more class. She gave me a pass on the first couple I missed because she's known me so long, but if I miss any more she won't be able to sign my certificate." She licks her lips and presses them to my shoulder. "But I don't hate the sound of that if you'll take a rain check."

"When will you be done?"

"I think around eight tonight."

"What? That's like twelve hours of yoga."

She nods. "I told you it was an investment."

"You're going to spend twelve hours doing yoga? How does that not break you?"

"It's not all physical. There's a classroom component, and we take turns teaching each other and cuing, and we take breaks and stuff, too."

I sigh, taking a sip of my coffee as she runs her hand over my bare back. *God that feels good.*

"Well, you're welcome to cue me anytime," I say, shivering at her touch.

"And you're welcome to stretch me out and tell me I'm doing a good job anytime."

My dick throbs at her words. "Jesus, Gabi."

She smiles at me wickedly. "I figured I should give you something to think about when I'm not around."

"Well, that plus however many times we did it last night. I'm not going to be able to *stop* thinking about you."

She rests her head on my shoulder. "I *so* don't want to go to yoga today."

I put my arm around her. "You'll be happy you did."

"Will I, though?"

I give her a look.

"You're right."

"How are you getting home?"

"I'll probably walk."

It's a new studio, and further from her house than the

one before. I hate the thought of her walking that alone. "Do you need some company?"

She grins at me, nodding.

When I close the door behind her, I'm thrilled that last night happened but simultaneously terribly depressed that it has to end.

I spend the day wading through pages and pages of documentation, doing my best to throw my energy into something productive.

I count the minutes until eight, desperate to see her again, to undress her and take her to bed in her little gray apartment that smells just like her.

Because Gabriella Pierce is mine.

22

GABI

Yoga is exceedingly difficult today.

Physically, I'm sore, and I could really use a rest day or two.

Mentally, I'm distracted, the thought of seeing Zeke at the end of all this causing me to check the time far more frequently than I would otherwise. *And is it just me, or is time moving slower today?*

One of my fellow students is running us through a lesson, and she's harping on downward dog. That's fine with me—it's a comfortable pose—but it also reminds me of Zeke, of his offer this morning to bend me over and *teach* me, and that's making this pose slightly more difficult, considering each time we return to it I can feel his thighs behind mine, his thickness rubbing against me. I can feel the burn of his hand slapping my ass, his fingers digging into my hips as he holds me steady, rocking into me.

Keep focused, Gabi.

I breathe in the smell of the mat, the ever-present scent of body odor and lemon cleaner that permeates this studio. I listen to my cues, following directions like a good girl.

Oh Gabi, stop.

I direct my energy into my arms, flexing my muscles to take away from the pressure building deep in my abdomen.

And then I think of his arms on either side of my head, flexing as he buries himself inside me, and I nearly lose my balance and topple over with the sheer need that shoots like fire through my body.

I should have just skipped today. I'm not paying attention at all.

I resort to counting to keep my mind occupied, like I'm counting sheep trying to fall asleep but instead I'm counting breaths—counting the number of fantasies I hold at bay in my mind until I'm finally released from yoga and into Zeke's arms.

When we're done, I'm sore and tired and jittery. I throw everything haphazardly into my bag, channeling Natalie's chaotic energy in my haste to leave the studio, and text Zeke that I'm heading out.

I wrap his jacket tight around me, my parting gift when I left his apartment early this morning, and throw my bag over my shoulder. I'm about to be the first person out of the studio when Corinne calls me back.

"Gabi, hold on a second!" She's rolling up her mat at the front of the room, making sure it's perfectly wound before she velcros the straps on. She has a wide array of accessories that she brings with her, ranging from blocks to straps to cushions to candles to grippy socks. She takes her time organizing and packing everything away.

I take a step toward her, wondering if she's going to make me wait until she's all packed up to tell me the reason she called me over.

"I just wanted to ask if you've thought about taking over

the studio at all." Her voice is hushed, like she doesn't want her other students to hear her.

My heart drops. *No, Corinne, I have not thought about taking over your studio!*

"No, I haven't really. I'm not sure it's great timing for me —I mean, I have a full-time job and this teacher training is so much already. I won't have time for months."

She nods, carefully adding her blocks to her oversized yoga bag. "I know the timing is awkward, but I can't help but think how wonderful it would be for you to run things. Especially now that you're in teacher training. And you have such experience with the minutiae of the behind-the-scenes work." She rolls a strap into a small ball like a party streamer, securing it with an old hair tie.

"Right, but I'm not qualified. And I don't have the money."

Corinne shrugs. "It's not as expensive as you think. You could probably lean on the regulars I had coming in, even the girls in this class. All you'd have to do is find money for the first month or two of rent—the rest you'll make up for in class passes."

I fight the urge to ask her, again, why she's so opposed to running the studio if it's that easy. That cheap.

The last of the students mill out of the studio, and it's just Corinne and me. She rolls up her grippy socks, tucking them in a side pocket of her bag.

"Why do you think I can just decide, one day, to run a yoga studio?" I ask her, the question coming out a little brasher than I intended.

She rears back a little and cocks her head to one side, studying my face.

"It has nothing to do with what you *can* do. It's your passion, Gabi. You're a yogi at heart, and where there's a will, there's a way. This studio is small and already has a customer base—all you have to do is assume the responsibility for it. You don't have to change your lifestyle or your desires, or learn a new skill beyond what you're already doing. It's not that you *can* just decide to run a studio, it's that I see the passion it takes as well as the attention to detail it takes, coming from my years of experience in *not* having the latter of the two." She stands, throwing her gigantic bag over her shoulder. "I'm not suggesting it because I think you *can*, I'm suggesting it because I think it will be fulfilling to you. Otherwise I wouldn't have said anything at all."

I gulp. "I didn't realize."

"All that being said"––She turns to the main doors, and I walk with her––"if you're not interested, it's no skin off my back. I've already released myself from that life, but I know a good deal when I see one. That studio is already set up for you, and the owner is a kind old man who's more interested in spending time with his kids at the beach than he is in searching for a new tenant at market rate."

She pushes through the doors, holding them open for me to pass through after her.

"No, you're right. I should think about it. I shouldn't just balk at the idea of it because it's new."

She smiles. "Like I said, think about it or don't. I loved that studio, but that doesn't mean you have to, too. But the owner wants an answer by the new year, so if you want it, you better figure it out."

I nod. "I'll think about it. I'm sorry, I didn't mean to be rude about it. I appreciate you thinking of me, and I'll consider it."

She waves me off. "You did twelve hours of yoga today—it's understandable. These classes are tough."

We reach the sidewalk and pause, knowing we're both going different directions.

"I appreciate you pushing me," I tell her.

She reaches forward, rubbing my arm in my too-large coat.

"It's an invitation, not a push." A familiar refrain.

"Thanks, Corinne."

She nods, and she looks like she's about to turn to continue on her way home when she speaks again. "Are you alright today? You seemed a little distracted. You can talk to me, you know."

Oh god, she knows. She knows I spent last night fucking my brains out instead of taking these classes seriously.

I nod. "I'm really fine, Corinne. I mean, I was a little distracted today, but really, you don't need to worry about me."

Leave it to me to piss off the most levelheaded woman I know and then get called out on an all-night fuck session within the space of two minutes.

"Are you sure?"

"Hey," he says behind me, and my face immediately turns bright red.

Corinne's eyebrows raise, and I close my eyes, wishing I didn't have to see the pieces falling into place. A look of understanding washes across her face, as she looks from my bright red face to Zeke behind me.

"I take it this is the distraction," she says, and embarrassment runs rampant through my veins. A small smile appears on her face.

I nod, wishing I was anywhere else.

"Well, I'm glad the distraction is nothing more than tall, dark, and handsome." She holds a hand out to shake his. "Corinne. Nice to meet you."

"Oh, Corinne. I've heard so much about you," he says. "Zeke."

"Well, I better be on my way," she says, nodding to us before turning in the other direction. "Get some rest for tomorrow, Gabi," she throws over her shoulder.

Bury me. "Yeah, see you tomorrow, Corinne!"

"Nice to meet you!"

I shake my head as Zeke's arm lands around my shoulder. "Oh god, she knows what we did last night."

"She does?"

"Didn't you hear her? You're the distraction."

"Happy to be of service." He kisses my cheek, his breath hot on my skin. "Reporting for duty in T-minus twenty minutes." His tongue flicks at my earlobe and I feel another burst of heat in my core.

We walk home quickly, his arm around me or his hand in mine, and by the time we get to the stairs up to my apartment, his hands are underneath my jacket, grabbing my ass and pulling me into him, my cold hands snaking under his sweater so that he shivers into me but tells me not to stop touching him.

I unlock the door with his hands on my hips, his mouth nibbling at the space between my neck and my collarbone.

We explode into my apartment in a fury, clothes dropping to the floor in quick succession as we stumble our way into my bedroom. He pulls my leggings off in one graceful movement, and then pauses, waiting for me to pull my overly tight sports bra over my head.

I sit on the edge of my bed to pull it up, my breasts falling heavy against my chest as they're released, and lower my arms to his astonished face.

"Jesus, Gabi, can you please do that again?"

"Take my bra off?"

"I swear, I will never ask you to put on clothes ever again, but that might have been the hottest thing I've ever seen."

So I pull my sports bra back on, settling my boobs in like they were before, and repeat the movement.

"Gabi," he says, grabbing my hand and pressing it to his erection so I can feel how hard he is.

I tear at the clasp to his pants, unzipping him and pulling him down on top of me. He rests his weight on me easily, lining himself up with my entrance and thrusting into me. He grunts into my ear as my nails tear into his back, his fingers digging into the skin of my hips. I cry out as he pushes me over the edge, and moments later, his breathing goes ragged in my ear as he releases into me.

After we extricate ourselves, I slink out of bed to the bathroom, grabbing his shirt along the way, and see that one of my—or Steph's, more accurately—succulents has been knocked over, dirt scattered across the floor.

My first thought is that we knocked it over in our haste to undress, but it's quite a distance from my bed.

"Did you knock over a plant?"

"Me? No. Did you?" He leans back in bed, his head resting on his hands.

"Maybe Steph did. She probably stopped by to water the plants."

I grab my phone off the nightstand and take a quick picture of the leftover dirt on the ground to send to Stephanie.

I clean myself up and we order Chinese food to eat on the couch in our underwear. I flip through Netflix until I find something dumb and funny to watch, and lean into him as he picks at the last of his food, one arm thrown over my shoulder.

"Corinne asked me about the studio again today," I say, toeing the blanket over me from the arm of the couch.

"And did you say yes?"

I glance up at him. He waits for my answer with raised eyebrows.

"No. But she said some nice things about me. That I'm passionate and uniquely able to run it. It was really nice. And it kind of made me consider it."

"You *should* consider it. At least think about it a bit."

"That's pretty much what she said, too."

"What's stopping you, Gabs?"

I shrug. "Time. Money. Crippling self-doubt."

He settles into the couch, leaving a kiss on my shoulder. "You have time. Plenty of it. It's not like teacher training is forever—it's a lot *now*, but once it's over, you'll be kicking yourself for ignoring this opportunity. And don't even get me started on that self-doubt shit. You need to cut that out because you're too incredible not to think you can do this. If it's what you want."

How did I get so lucky?

"And I mean," he starts, "if money is an issue, I can float you for a bit. This contract is pretty big. And it almost seems like kismet, that I get this project right when you need a little extra seed money."

I nearly scoff at the idea. "Zeke, that's so sweet, but I can't take your money for something like this."

"Why not?"

I sit up, looking into his eyes. "Because it's not right. This would be like a hobby project, you know? I don't know when I would start making a profit, or even *if* I'll start making a profit, and I can't take your money on something that's essentially a crap shoot."

He shrugs. "I think that's your self-doubt talking.

Investors take bets on less sure things every day. And it wouldn't have to be anything formal. It could even just be a line of credit. Or the security deposit on the space, you know? If that's something that's stopping you, let me take the concern off the table."

We've been together less than twenty-four hours, and he's trying to give me insane chunks of money. *What?*

"Zeke, why would you offer me that?"

He looks at me sheepishly. "Because I like you."

"But we've just barely started dating."

"I consider myself a good judge of character."

I give him a look.

"I'll always try to help someone I care about. No matter the cost. It makes me feel good."

There's something so genuine in his words that I stop before telling him he shouldn't offer so much of himself. "You're sweet." I push myself up to kiss him.

"Think about it," he says as I settle back into the crook of his arm.

A laugh track plays on the TV, and I snuggle in closer to him, pulling the blanket higher over myself.

At some point, my eyes drift closed, and the next thing I know, I'm being carried into my bedroom, tucked under my covers, and cuddled from behind.

"Good night, Gabi," he whispers into my ear, one hand resting possessively on my hip.

I WAKE UP EARLY, feeling refreshed, my body pressed against his.

In the early moments of the morning, his deep breathing becomes the soundtrack for a different kind of fantasy, one where I climb those familiar old stairs to Corinne's studio and pull my mat out from the supply closet tucked in the corner. I lead a yin yoga class in the morning, the light from the sunrise leaking in through the windows over an array of mats in front of me.

In the haze of sleep, I grab for my phone to check the time, and it takes me a moment to remember what Steph is replying to when I see her text on my phone.

STEPH

??? Wasn't me!

I sit up, rubbing sleep from my eyes as I scan the room.

Zeke's underwear *is* in the general vicinity of the knocked over plant.

It must have been our frantic undressing that knocked the poor succulent to the floor.

23

ZEKE

Kelly tumbles into the car in a wave of cinnamon and presents. She wears a sweater with a reindeer on it, and her hair falls over her shoulder in a frizzy braid that I have no doubt will match our mom's perfectly.

She looks down at my clothes in disdain once she's situated in the car. "What, you couldn't give up the Grim Reaper act even for Christmas Eve?"

"I don't do Christmas sweaters."

"You did once."

"You were eight and crying because I was the only one who didn't match. So sure, if you're going to blubber all Christmas long and ruin that makeup I know you spent at least half an hour on, then yeah, I'll put on a Christmas sweater."

She huffs, clicking her seat belt. "I bet if Gabi asked, you'd wear a Christmas sweater."

I try to stop the smile from taking over my face at just the mention of her name and focus on pulling away from the curb. But in doing so, I take too long to answer.

"Oh my god, you would!" I keep my eyes on the road but I can see her shaking her head in my peripheral vision. "I bet you'd even wear one that lights up if Gabi asked you to."

"I would not." *I definitely would.*

She reaches behind her neck for a moment, and suddenly her sweater comes to life, the nose of the reindeer blinking red. "Zeke, look how stylish I am. Don't you want to be like me?"

I laugh. "Kelly, turn that off. It's a hazard."

When we arrive, the house smells like pie and there are string lights hung everywhere. My mom has decked out the living room in Christmas paraphernalia and moved around the furniture to create more seating. We're a popular flyby stop on Christmas, relatives and friends stopping by on their way to or from other places, an honor my mom takes very seriously.

She has on a snowman sweater with buttons that light up. My dad has managed to avoid electronic clothing, but not Christmas attire altogether—his sweater depicts a hundred falling snowflakes.

We throw our presents under the tree and obey my mom's barked commands as she coordinates the food, the timing of visitors, and the Christmas playlist. Kelly got her chaos bug from her and slips easily into my mom's brain, predicting what she's going to need and when.

Whereas my dad and I seem to be getting in the way more than we're helping.

"Just sit, Zeke," my dad says eventually, pulling me out of the way as Kelly, eyes aflame, tells me to move. "They'll tell you when they need you."

I sit at the dining room table with my dad, nibbling at the desserts laid out there. I don't touch the pies, of course, but the cookies are fair game—they can easily be rearranged to hide the missing ones. My dad does the same, eventually reaching for a bottle of whiskey and pouring us each a glass.

I text Gabi while I have a spare moment.

ZEKE

I've been shunned by order of Chaos Kelly.

I take a sip of my drink, listening to the sounds of Christmas. My mom, talking on the phone to some relative or another and easily putting on a calm air, as if she didn't snap at my dad ten minutes ago for putting the mashed potatoes in the oven five minutes too long. Kelly, deciding she doesn't like my mom's playlist and changing the song every twenty seconds.

My phone buzzes as Kelly whirls around the corner with another plate of cookies in her hand. I lean over to see what kind they are as I unlock my phone. Snickerdoodle, it looks like.

GABI

Steph and my parents are drunk dancing to Carol of the Bells.

I can't help the smile that comes to my face at the thought.

ZEKE

Okay, you win. And how do you drunk dance to Carol of the Bells?

"God Zeke, can't you go two days without her?"

My face reddens. I thought Kelly was moving too fast to pay attention to what I'm doing. "God Kelly, mind your own business."

She raises her eyebrows. "Mind my own business? Good comeback, that one must have really taken some thought."

"Who's the girl?" my mom asks, suddenly appearing in the doorway as if she has nowhere better to be. She takes the seat next to me, grabbing a cookie from the plate and rearranging them so it still looks full.

Kelly has the decency to look sheepish as she opens the bottle of whiskey and tops me up in apology.

"Gabi," I say, her name suddenly sounding foreign on my tongue.

Kelly urges me on. "Gabi, who's friends with Charlie. She does yoga and makes really good pancakes," she starts, and then pauses, as if waiting for me to take over.

My mom is staring at me with wide eyes, waiting for me to expand on Kelly's description of her.

"She's smart," I start, feeling like I'm learning to speak again. I haven't talked to my parents about a girl since Marissa, but I suppose now is as good a time as ever to tell them about Gabi. "And caring. Wildly attentive." My mom's smile turns into a grin, and my dad watches me speak with the same contented interest with which he does most things. "Polished. Pretty."

"She's hot," Kelly interrupts.

"*Kelly*," I scold.

"You're underselling, Zeke."

"I'm trying to be respectful."

"When do we get to meet her?" my mom asks, ignoring our bickering.

I shrug. "Whenever you want, I guess."

My mom claps, holding her hands at her chest, and Kelly's eyes go wide. "Bring her for dinner after the holidays?"

"Okay."

My mom returns to the kitchen, and I shoot Kelly a look that she quickly skirts away from, following in my mom's footsteps.

My dad waits until the girls are gone to speak. "I'm happy for you. You know, it's really important in life to find someone hot." I nearly spray whiskey out my nose, and he laughs into his.

I check my phone again, now that the cat is out of the bag, and see a video pop up of three people in a dimly lit room with Christmas lights strung up behind them, dancing.

GABI

Like this.

24

GABI

When I get to my parents' house, Steph and my mom are already on their second bottle of wine. Christmas Eve dinner is a very chill affair for us—we order an inordinate amount of Chinese food and eat what we want, when we're hungry. Steph has YouTube up on the living room TV, and she's playing some alternative, off-key version of "All I Want For Christmas Is You" and singing equally off-key with it. My dad sits on the couch across from her, a plate of fried rice and lo mein in front of him.

My mom walks out of the kitchen as I drop my bag by the door, her long hair piled high on her head and a fresh bottle of wine in her hand.

"Oh honey, let me get you a glass," she says, leaning forward to hug me and kiss my cheek before disappearing back into the kitchen.

Steph sits up, taking another sip of her wine, and I catch a glimpse of something bright and colorful behind her head. I move closer, trying to get a better look.

"Steph," I say, reaching forward and picking up her hair,

which is suddenly a myriad of colors—purples, blues, greens. The top half is still her yellow-blonde color, but the bottom is an array of mermaid colors. "Holy shit."

My mom places an overly full wineglass in my hand.

"Your office doesn't mind that? Don't you have to meet with clients?"

She shrugs. "I don't think clients will care, and my boss made it a point to say how much she liked it, so I'm not too worried." She takes a large gulp from her own glass. "But I'm glad to hear *you* like it so much."

Oh, fuck. How do I manage to do this every goddamn time? Steph lives a different life than me, and though I know my office would care, she's more than capable of making the determination of whether her own would.

Sometimes I forget my little sister is a grown woman now.

"I love it, Steph. The colors are so pretty."

She continues, stuck on my comment. "We're basically remote already. The only times I'll even see anyone from the office are for client meetings and that'll essentially be my boss and Annabel, who don't give a flying shit."

I bite my lip. I've stepped in it.

"It's not my job to worry about your office. You're right. It really does look pretty, Steph."

My mom must not have been paying attention, because she swoops in at that moment and lifts the top portion of Steph's hair. "Doesn't it?" she asks. "I just love these colors, and it makes so much sense for you, Stephy, with how much of a little beach baby you were. My little mermaid." She presses a kiss to Steph's forehead.

"It looks really nice," I repeat, but I can tell from Steph's flat expression that she doesn't believe me.

So rather than dig myself in deeper, I leave my mom and

sister to fight over YouTube and make myself a plate of Chinese food in the kitchen. I sit down next to my dad and curl up under one of the many blankets, listening to my mom and Steph singing far too loudly and far too terribly to the same ten Christmas songs done in different styles, over and over and over again.

Zeke texts me through the night, little updates about his Christmas Eve, and I can't help but smile into my phone at each one.

Eventually, Christmas Eve turns into a full-blown karaoke night. The Chinese food is abandoned in the fridge and another bottle of wine is uncorked on the coffee table in the living room. My mom and Steph goad me into glass number three, and eventually glass number four, and before I know it, Steph and I are singing the Disney songs we grew up with, though I notice she deftly steers us away from *The Little Mermaid*.

At some point she ties the top half of her hair up, and all I can see is glimmering blues and greens in front of me, and I reach out, weaving her hair into my fingers, but she pulls away from me, twirling her hair over her shoulder.

Yep, I've really stepped in it.

Later, when we're irresponsibly opening windows to let in a little breeze, my dad starts corralling us all to our respective rooms. Steph, with overindulgent hugs for both my parents and a curt nod for me, falls easily into her old pink and yellow bedroom. I stay up a little while longer, chugging water over the sink to avoid the headache tomorrow.

"Come on Helena, time for bed," I hear my dad's voice in the living room, coaxing my mom away from the music.

"Oh just one more song, please?"

He grumbles, sighing loudly. "Okay, one more song."

When I move into the living room, another full glass of water in my hand, the beginning notes of "All I Want for Christmas," leak from the stereo *again*, my mom's eyes closed as she leans into my dad, her fingers peppering the syllables of the song into his shoulder.

He wraps an arm around her, pulling her close, and in that moment, I can't help but wonder what must have been going through his mind when he told me, more than twenty years ago, that love is nothing more than timing.

Because watching them—even just experiencing the moment from the sidelines when neither of them are even aware I'm there—I feel something more than happenstance. Something more than being in the right place at the right time.

I turn and head upstairs to my old bedroom, the muted purple greeting me like an old friend as I shut the door behind me. I change into a pair of silky jammies that feel out of place in this bedroom, and text Zeke good night before falling easily asleep in a bed so familiar I could map the lumps in my dreams.

25

ZEKE

Christmas passes in a blur of extended family and chaotic Morgan girls.

The day after, Kelly and I load our presents into my car and head back into the city, exhausted from ever-present people and food and *cheer*. I drop her at her apartment, slightly concerned by the stunning lack of cars around what's otherwise a bustling part of campus, and remind her that she can always come stay at my apartment if she gets lonely—or freaked out. I make sure she still has a key and she rolls her eyes at me, but there's something creepy to me about an empty college campus.

I text Gabi when I'm home, and she shows up on my doorstep an hour later, her hair windblown and her cheeks rosy red. She carries a gigantic bag over her shoulder, and I notice little red ribbons peaking out one side of it.

Thank god I thought to get her something.

"Hey Zeke," she says, a grin on her face as she steps into my apartment and lands a cold kiss on my cheek. She breezes past me, throwing her jacket into the coat closet and dropping her bag next to it. From it, she pulls a red gift bag the size of a wine bottle and a squishy thing wrapped in candy cane paper.

She grins at me as if waiting for an invitation to sit down.

"Did you get me a Christmas present?"

She shrugs noncommittally. "Maybe."

I grab her hand, dragging her to the couch, where I already set hers out on the coffee table. She freezes when she sees them.

"Zeke!" She sets the presents down on the table. "But—"

"But what?"

"Well, I don't think I got you enough." She glances hesitantly at the presents in her hands.

"My presents are pretty self-serving if I have to be honest."

She wrinkles her eyebrows. "Promise?"

"Promise."

She goes first, ripping the wrapping paper carefully along the seams.

"Zeke," she says, running her fingers over the fabric underneath. "You didn't."

"Well, you keep complaining about me only having one small blanket—I figured it's about time I listen," I say as she pulls the rest of the paper off and tears the blanket out of the cardboard sheath.

"Oh my god, it's so soft," she says, pulling the fabric up to her face.

She shakes her head. "Open that one," she says, pointing to a similarly sized present that she brought.

When I tear off the paper, I realize she bought me a blanket, too.

"Okay, so do the presents cancel out if we buy each other the same thing?"

She grins. "No, that just means they're double special."

She pulls over the next present, giving me a look when she hears the clink of glass bottles beneath the paper. "Zeke, did you buy me milk?"

I laugh. "Yes, you got me."

She pulls the paper off, revealing a *mostly* cold six-pack of stouts from The Corner Deli. "I thought, since you liked the java stout, that you might want to try a few others. But if you don't, there's also a bottle of white wine in the fridge for you."

"That's so sweet, Zeke, thank you." She starts laughing again. "But uh, why don't you open that one now."

I pull over the liquor bag and open it to see a bottle of white wine. I can't help but laugh. "Okay, so are we on the same page, or are we on the same page?"

I throw the last small present into her lap. "Technically not from me," I tell her, as she unwinds the delicate string around the top. "Sent from my parents, who Kelly decided to tell all about us. They're excited to meet you—when you're ready."

She smiles at me, the grin on her face so intoxicating, and unwinds the package, exposing an array of homemade Christmas cookies.

"Your family is adorable," she says, leaning forward and kissing me. "I can't wait to meet them."

My insides glow, thinking of Gabi in my childhood home. She's already met Kelly, which is an obstacle unto itself, but something tells me she and my mom will get along famously.

She takes a cookie out of the cellophane wrapper, biting into it, and spins the bottles in the cardboard holder. "Can you open?" she asks, holding one out to me.

The vanilla bean stout. I twist the cap off and give it back to her, watching her face as she tries it.

"Definitely a stout girl," she says, nodding as she pulls a coaster from the drawer underneath the coffee table and sets it on top. "I'd ask if you want one, but someone special bought them for me, and I think I'd like to try them all for myself," she teases, leaning over and kissing me, her scent billowing around me and causing a blood rush down south.

"Well, luckily I have a chilled bottle of white wine for myself," I tease back, and she pouts, clearly torn between my gift and her preferred drink. I wait a second before continuing. "But maybe I'll save that for later."

She nods. "Yeah, save that for later."

We settle into the couch, some silly sitcom playing as she snuggles into me.

At some point through the night, our clothes hit the floor, and I relish in the sight of Gabi's soft skin tucked underneath the blanket I bought her, the way she leans forward to take a sip of her beer and the blanket falls down a bit—just enough to send a jolt down to my dick.

I leave a kiss on her forehead and she scooches in closer to me, sighing into my shoulder.

Only minutes later, her breathing turns deeper.

And then my phone starts buzzing.

Why is Leanne calling me right now?

A deeply unpleasant feeling thrums in my gut, and I debate sending it to voicemail and calling her tomorrow morning—but something tells me she's calling me this late for a reason.

So I extricate myself from Gabi's arms, leaving a little piece of myself on the couch as I head upstairs. I answer once I'm out of earshot but keep my voice low until I can shut myself in my office.

"Hey Leanne."

"Zeke, hey. I'm sorry for calling so late but we're having a bit of an issue and no one here is able to figure out what's going on."

"What's the issue?"

She describes a variety of things that sound unconnected to me, so I offer what sounds like the stupidest suggestion but it's the first thing that comes to my mind.

"Have you tried turning your router off and turning it on again?"

She grumbles, and I hear her moving around in the office, shouting at who I can only assume is her husband. *What are they doing at the office this late?*

A few minutes later, they're able to remotely operate their machines again, and the weight sitting on my chest slowly releases.

"Oh thank god that was an easy fix." She's moving around again, doors closing and chairs squeaking. "Now the reason I called you..."

My heart drops. *That wasn't the reason she called me?*

She launches into a long rant, the weight growing even heavier than before on my chest.

They can't take orders on the website.

And thanks to the contract I signed only a couple weeks ago, I'm first in line to fix this issue.

Fuck.

A sinking feeling leaching into my bones, I agree to head down to Virginia in the morning and see what's happening.

When I hang up, the only thing I can think of is Gabi on my couch, sleeping naked underneath a fuzzy blanket. Gabi in my bed, my silky sheets tangled up around her legs. Gabi in the morning, sleep in her eyes and her body soft and warm and *mine*.

I can't believe I have to leave her.

I feel like a teenager again, ready to throw a hormone-fueled tantrum because I'm not allowed to stay out late and try to get lucky with a girl who's so far out of my league it's a wonder she even recognizes my existence.

But I don't have to leave until tomorrow.

So I go back downstairs and intertwine her limbs with mine again, pulling her into my side and carefully staying awake, savoring the moments we have. I weave her silky hair between my fingers. Draw little circles on her bare shoulders. Rest my head on hers so her scent fills my nostrils.

I can't believe I have to leave all of this.

26

GABI

I wake to the sound of someone moving around, drawers opening and closing and the sound of the shower running somewhere in the background. It's early, I think—I can't really tell with Zeke's blackout curtains. It *feels* early.

I pull his sheets up around me, the silk warm and soft and the bed so comfortable that I'm not sure I'm even willing to leave it in the first place. It's the kind of soft that pulls you in, zaps your energy and holds you hostage.

When he comes out of the bathroom he's wearing only jeans, his hair wet and mussed as he runs a towel haphazardly over it.

"You're awake." His voice is soft as he leans over and kisses me gently, brushing my hair out of my face. He turns and pulls a shirt out of the bureau behind him, tugging it quickly over his head.

"What's the rush?" I sit up, moving to the edge of the bed and catching him by the pocket before he can breeze past me again. I pull him into me, the zipper of his jeans scratching against my chest.

He looks down at me, playing with my hair, and shakes his head. "I have to go to Virginia."

My heart drops. "What?"

"Leanne called last night. They can't take orders and I'm not set up in their systems yet to work from home. I have to go down there for a few days and see what I can do."

I lean my head against him, his strong muscles flexing against my cheek. "No."

I sound like a petulant child.

He wraps his arms around my neck, holding me close. "God, Gabi, I know. There's nothing I'd rather do than crawl into bed with you. But we'll have more days like this. We have nothing but time."

I glance up at him, the sentiment surprising me. He tucks my hair behind my ear, his touch so delicate.

"Stay as long as you want, okay?"

I let out a groan into his stomach.

"I know."

When I look behind him, I see his duffel bag is already packed by the door.

"This sucks."

"Yeah, it does. But I'll be back by New Year's, okay?"

He unwinds my arms from his waist and plants one knee on the bed so he can bend down and kiss me, his arms weaving around my waist and pulling me up into him. "Call me, okay?"

I nod, missing his touch as he moves toward the door.

"And really, stay as long as you want. The thought of you in my bed will probably motivate me to get shit done in half the time I would otherwise."

I sigh, falling back into his sheets. "Maybe I'll just stay until you're back, have every meal at The Corner Deli and hang out in your bed naked under my new blanket, drinking my stouts."

He pauses at the door. "Now that's just cruel."

"Hurry back."

"There's a spare key next to the coffee pot if you need it." He grabs his bag off the ground. "Bye, Gabs."

And then he's gone.

I SPEND my morning puttering around Zeke's apartment. I get a shower and wash my clothes from last night. Make coffee and eye the key on the counter next to it. He texts me when he gets to Virginia, and I send him a picture of my coffee mug on his table.

GABI

Would be better with you.

When lunchtime rolls around, I slip the key into my pocket and head down the street for a salad. I pick up another six-pack—two stouts and a couple bottles I've noticed Zeke likes—and throw them in the fridge for when he gets back.

When I'm done eating, I trail my fingers along the countertop, debating going all in and just crashing here while he's gone.

Is that weird?

I like the warmth of his apartment. The darkness of his bedroom and the smell of him surrounding me. I could steal a pair of sweatpants and watch Netflix and eat at The Corner Deli like my life depends on it.

I could be here when he gets back, and we could pick up right where we left off this morning.

Something tells me he wouldn't mind that.

But as I head upstairs, grappling with the idea of rooting around in his drawers while he's not here, Gemma texts me.

> GEMMA
>
> Are you around? My MIL won't leave. Need to get out ASAP.

I don't want to leave Zeke's, but if Gemma needs me, I really should go.

And I can always come back, right?

I slip his key into my pocket as I leave, locking the door behind me, and the warmth of his apartment is immediately extinguished with the biting cold of the December air.

I take the trolley home, my bag thrown over my shoulder and my new blanket tucked underneath my arm. I resist the urge to wrap myself in it as I walk; I'm not sure it's cold enough to be *that* girl.

As I walk the last block to my apartment, the wind stills and the sun shines on my face. For a moment I relish in the feeling, this temporary halting of the elements.

Until I feel eyes on me, a little prickling sensation on the back of my neck that tells me to turn around.

And when I do, I see him across the street.

Dustin. Walking in the opposite direction from me. He's not looking at me now but he must have been. I refuse to believe my body just *sensed* that someone I know was walking behind me.

But it's just a coincidence. He *does* live near here, and I'm only a block away from the main strip of bars and restaurants. It's not totally inconceivable that he'd have to walk by every once in a while, and the fact that he didn't say anything could mean that I'm now off his radar.

When I turn back to my apartment, Gemma is in front of the gate, waving at me animatedly. I glance back in Dustin's direction but he's walking quickly away from me, his face turned in the other direction.

Maybe last time—when he showed up unannounced—he finally got it through his head that I'm done with him.

"Hi Gem," I say, and she leans in to give me a quick hug.

She gives me a once over, her eyes narrowing as she motions to what I'm wearing. "It's giving '90s grunge. Did I catch you on a walk of shame?"

I snort, pulling Zeke's jacket tighter around me. In the past, I might not have taken this question so well, but something about slinking home after my night with Zeke kind of turns me on instead. "Yes."

She raises her eyebrows. "I hope I didn't interrupt anything."

I shake my head. "He had to go to work."

"Sad."

"Works out well for you."

"That's true. Do you have alcohol?"

I laugh, pressing in the gate code and letting us in. "I have white wine."

"Perfect. Can I have all of it?"

"Sure."

We climb up to my apartment and I sit Gemma down at my kitchen table, throwing my blanket over onto the couch and leaving Zeke's jacket on the back of a chair. I pour us each a glass, and Gemma regales me with Christmas stories of backhanded compliments and snide side-eyes.

"Everything is just so *interesting* to her. *Interesting* that I chose to feed Taylor orange food—she won't eat anything else, so yeah, I'm going to feed her orange food. *Interesting* that I unwind with yoga rather than 'traditional cardio,' whatever that hell that means," she says, holding up air quotes. She takes a sip of wine. "Everything is *interesting*, and I'm about to turn around and scream at her that she's fucking interesting, but of course if *I* were to do that, I'd suddenly be just that much more fucking *interesting*."

"So you and your mother-in-law are getting along well, it seems."

She rolls her eyes at me. "It's been days of this. I can deal with it at a distance, but in a house that size, every corner I turn, she's scrutinizing *something* that is just freaking interesting." She shakes her head. "And how much do you want to bet that when I go back there tonight, she's going to make a comment about how interesting it is that my breath smells like wine."

"She'll be gone soon, Gemma. Just a few more days."

She leans forward and rests her forehead on the table. "I don't think I have it in me."

"Then come here when you need a break. I'm off this week—we can do yoga and drink wine whenever it's too much for you."

"Really?" She looks up at me, her arms still splayed across the table.

I nod. "Really."

"You're too nice to me," she says, reaching out and grabbing my hand. "I'm a mess. I'm needy. I'm over the top. And you're always so nice to me. I don't know why."

"Everybody has it tough sometimes. You're going through a rough patch with Taylor and need some support. That's okay. Maybe one day you can return the favor."

She lets out a deep breath. "Well, until then, I'm going to make sure you never run out of wine."

"I'll take that deal."

Gemma stays for another hour and another drink, spouting story after story about her family's Christmas, before deciding she should probably head back home. We make a plan to drag Natalie out to do some yoga together this week, and with a tight hug at the gate, she takes a deep breath and heads home to face her mother-in-law.

27

GABI

J ust as I sit down on my couch, tea in hand, Zeke calls me. We've talked every night since he's been gone, me in my jammies under a pile of blankets and him in his hotel room, propped up in bed.

"Hey," I say, muting the TV and balancing my phone on the arm of the sofa.

"Hey Gabriell*a*," he says. I hear the ruffling of his sheets in the background. "What are we watching tonight?"

I blow on my tea. "Same channel as last night."

"Making it easy for me tonight, huh?"

I laugh. "Well, after last night's debacle, I figured I'd save us both the time and keep things simple."

"I don't know what you're talking about. Twenty minutes is very fast for figuring out how to change the channel."

"You're right. You really should get an award for that." I take a hesitant sip of my tea that burns my tongue. "So how was today?"

He sighs into the phone. "The same as yesterday. Long. Lots of annoying things that don't make sense. Lots of cubicle-sitting and that weird corporate office smell." I make a face at his words. "But on the bright side, I'm just about done. Everything is up and running again, so I'm just making sure I have access to everything I need to access and then hopefully—*hopefully*—I won't have to come back down until this project is over."

"You'll be able to do everything from home, then?"

"I think so. It sucks that this happened right now, you know? When you actually have some free time, of course I get tapped to fix stupid shit that should never have broken in the first place. But I would have needed to come down here soon anyway so I'm trying to look at it as a jumpstart rather than an inconvenience."

I nod. "I like that you can think about things like that."

He exhales into the phone. "It's either that or being upset about it and screwing something up trying to just get it over with. I hate that only a few days ago I finally had you in my bed and I just had to leave like that."

"Finally, huh?"

He snorts. "Finally. I've been waiting patiently since that night outside your apartment when you casually dispelled everything I thought I knew about relationships."

Is that what we're doing? A relationship?

I struggle to remember which night he's talking about. He's walked me home so many times now that they're all starting to blend together. "What night was that?"

"Ah," he starts, clearing his throat. "You told me that if I thought love wasn't all it's cracked up to be, then it probably wasn't love."

My heart stutters. "Oh. Yeah, I remember that."

He pauses for a moment. "And ever since then, I've just really wanted to see your tits."

I laugh, the tightness in my chest giving way to ease.

"Zeke, you can't deflect with dirty jokes if I know now that that's what you're doing."

"I'll stop when it's not effective anymore."

I bite my lip. "I like you, Zeke."

"I like you too, Gabi. A lot." He's quiet for a moment. "You're a big part of why I'm doing this."

"I am?"

He makes a noncommittal noise. "I mean, if you do decide you want the studio, I feel like I can help. I know if you do it, you want to do it yourself and I respect that. But I can't help thinking that this timing is for a reason, you know? This isn't the kind of contract I just *take*. A big part of that is Rob and Della. Leanne is their family, you know? But it's still more than I normally take on. Especially with how much I have to learn as I go." He sighs, the sound heavy through the phone. "I just have this feeling in my gut like it'll all be worth it at some point, and I can't help but think that part of that feeling is you."

"I can't take your money for the studio," I say, but it comes out sounding like a rejection of him rather than his money. "But I really love how supportive you are. It's nice to be believed in."

"Gabi, you're so freaking smart. So dedicated. You're the only person who doesn't seem to believe in you." He scoffs. "If you're not into the studio, I understand. But I think you'd crash through even your own expectations."

I twirl my teabag above my mug. "You make me feel way more capable than I am."

He doesn't skip a beat. "Good. That's how your person should make you feel."

"Are you my person?" I can't help the smile spreading on my face.

He's quiet for a second. "Don't make me crack another dirty joke."

"I'll let it pass. But just know that I'm grinning like an idiot."

He laughs. "Me too." I hear shuffling from his end, and a deep exhale that I imagine accompanies his head hitting his pillow. "Gabi, can I ask you something?"

"Anything."

"What is it that really makes you nervous about the studio? I mean, you've listed the usual culprits. Money, time, security. But it seems like something you want. Do you ever imagine what it would be like? To get up in the morning and go to yoga all day instead of your job? To connect with students instead of people you're trying to sell to?"

I take a sip of my tea, letting the chamomile slosh around my mouth before swallowing. "I don't ever really get that far. I pretty much think about the lack of a steady paycheck and my head starts buzzing."

"Buzzing?"

I sigh. I don't usually tell people how bad my anxiety gets. "Whenever I get really anxious, my whole body goes into overdrive. I get tense and I can't really think straight and it's like TV static in my brain. I love the idea of a studio, but there are so many unknowns. I'm good at my job and it pays well. Even if it's not everything I'm passionate about, I'm lucky to have that."

He hums. "Maybe you should talk to someone about that, Gabs. Everybody has *some* anxiety, right? But it sounds like yours might be bigger than that. Like it might be holding you back. I mean, you're not even letting yourself *dream* a little."

"I dream plenty."

"Gabi, I don't think you let yourself dream at all."

I pout at the phone. "How would you even know that?"

"The same night you dispelled everything I thought I knew about relationships, you told me that love is nothing more than timing. You've taken the exciting things in life and turned them into formulas. Love equals timing plus a reasonably attractive person. Fulfillment equals steady paycheck plus competence."

"You're way more than reasonably attractive." My breath catches when I realize we're circling around *love* again. "You're at least panty-dropper attractive."

He laughs. "Deflecting, are we?"

My face reddens. "Maybe a little bit."

"Seriously, Gabi. Let yourself imagine it a bit. Figure out a way to get past the anxiety, whether it's yoga or talking to someone. You might realize you want it more than you think."

I take a slurping sip of tea that dribbles down my chin and wipe it away before I speak again. "Why are you so intent on me considering it?"

He lets out a long breath. "That's a long story."

"I have time."

I hear him shuffling in bed again and imagine him turning over, his eyes on the ceiling and his arm thrown over his head in the same way he did at his apartment. "Remember when I said I had love and it wasn't all it's cracked up to be?"

I laugh. "Like two minutes ago? Yes, I remember that."

"Well, I chose my dreams over my girlfriend because she didn't want me to have any."

"She didn't want you to dream?"

"No. She wanted me to be an accountant."

I can't help the laugh that escapes me.

He laughs lightly with me. "It's funny now, but it wasn't

at the time. Back then, I thought I was choosing between my person and what I wanted to do with my life. Did you know I have a degree in accounting?"

"I think you said you worked in accounting. But I didn't know you had a degree in it." It's hard to picture Zeke dealing with people's taxes, filling out the same forms over and over again and managing people whose lives he has no interest in.

"Well, I have it because my girlfriend at the time wanted me to start working at her family's firm. We started dating in high school, ended up at the same college, and she convinced me to follow in her family's footsteps rather than doing what I wanted to do. Web design or software engineering or something else techy." He lets out a long breath. "After I graduated and figured out I hate accounting—at least, the daily practice of it—I told her I wanted to try my hand at web design. And we ended up breaking up over it."

"She broke up with you because of that?"

He lets out a frustrated sigh. "I don't know. Honestly, I went over it so many times in my mind that I don't know whose fault it is anymore. Her, for always telling me what she wanted and expected, or me, for hearing it and thinking that we'd still be fine if I decided to blow up the life plan she'd created for herself? If someone tells you what they want over and over again, is it really their fault if things don't go to plan when you choose a different path?"

"Maybe it wasn't either of your faults. Maybe it just wasn't meant to be."

He's quiet for a beat. "I don't like believing in fate."

"You made your own fate."

"I guess you could call it that." I hear a muffled grumble in the background. "All I'm saying is that I've been in your shoes right now, struggling with what's been handed to me versus what I want. You're incredible, Gabi. You can do whatever you want in life. I want to be the person you look back on and see as an ally, not a detriment. I don't mean to be pushy about it. I just want you to see what I see when I look at you."

"Zeke, stop. My ego's getting too big."

He laughs. "Maybe a bit of an ego would do you some good. Maybe seeing the potential in yourself would let you take what life's offering."

I can't help the thoughts that fly through my head. The urge to tell him that I love him pops into my mind, but our relationship is too new. We're just getting to know each other, and I know I only feel this way right now because he's building me up so much.

Or do I?

"And Gabi?"

"Yes, Zeke?"

"Penis."

I snort into my tea to the sound of his laughter through the phone.

28

ZEKE

I manage to get home from Virginia a little earlier than I thought I would, so I take my time showering and getting dressed. I ask Gabi if she's hungry, and then head over to The Corner Deli and manage to sneak in just before they close for the day to grab a sandwich for me, the salad Gabi told me she likes, and a bouquet of lilies flecked with little silver sparkles for the holiday.

When I get to her door, her wet hair is tied in a bun on top of her head, her lips a bright red but her eyes devoid of their usual black rims.

"I would have been ready earlier if you gave me more of a heads up," she says, motioning to her face.

"I'd rather see you like this." I step inside and wrap an arm around her waist, planting a kiss on those deep red lines.

"Oh Zeke, now I'm going to have to redo my lipstick too."

I shut the door as I step inside, debating throwing our food on the floor so I can pick her up and take her straight into the bedroom. She's wearing this little dress—a *little* dress—that showcases her long legs and amplifies her already generous chest. It's a dark blue but it sparkles all over, shimmering like the ocean at night.

I pull the flowers out of our food bag and hand them to her, leaving the food on the kitchen table. "I saw you eyeing them last time."

She tries to limit her grin, biting her bottom lip even as her face explodes in delight.

And that face right there is exactly why I bought them.

I can't help but smile as she takes them from me. "You bought me flowers?"

"Maybe you'll forgive me for screwing up your lipstick again." My hands now free, I grab her hips and pull them into me. Her free arm wraps around my neck, her chest pressing into mine. I kiss those red lips, her freshly perfumed neck, her perfect collarbone.

When I pull away from her, she stares up at me, smiling. "I think I might start over with some lip gloss," she says, reaching up and wiping lipstick off my mouth.

"I like that idea. I was hoping for a kiss at midnight, after all."

She grins. "Maybe before then, too?" She leaves a kiss on my chin and then takes a step back just as I move to pull her closer. "Because holy hell, Zeke, you look *good*." She looks me up and down, and something about her gaze on me creates a little pool of fire in my abdomen.

I didn't do anything special, really—I wore dark slacks instead of jeans and a black button-up since I was told this would be a fancy party.

"*You* look good." I reach out, grabbing her hands and pulling them around my neck. I reach down, fingering the hem of her skirt. "So good I kind of want to skip the party and just celebrate you."

"Oh, Charlie would kill us."

You have no idea. I leave a kiss on her temple.

"But we'll have all night to celebrate," she says, her teeth raking against my neck and sending a jolt of electricity through me.

"If I make it."

She grins. "If you make it."

She steps away from me, releasing her hair from the bun. I'm overwhelmed by the scent of her shampoo. "I just want to get my makeup done real quick. Should only take me fifteen minutes but go ahead and start eating if you're hungry."

"I can wait."

I follow her into the bathroom and lean against the doorframe as she smears on cream after cream.

"How were Natalie and Gemma?" The two of them have been here consistently over the past week to run through routines with Gabi.

She sighs, smiling at me in the mirror. "They are *so* on board with me taking over the studio."

"Are *you*?" *That would be news to me.*

She shakes her head. "I don't think they realize how much work it would be."

"I don't think you realize how much you'll like it."

She shrugs noncommittally and then catches my eye in the mirror. "I do think I'd like it."

"There's my girl."

She smiles at me, biting her lip, and then continues applying stuff to her face. "It's weird to think about, though —doing something that I might actually be good at. Like I'm good at my job—or at least I hope I am—but there's something different about being good at something that you can

—I don't know—share with other people? Like it's something you do together for mutual benefit?"

"That sounds like a great place to be."

She sighs. "I'm thinking about it." She catches my eye as if to say she followed through with our conversation the other day, that she's daring to dream a little. "But am I just thinking about it because Natalie and Gemma were building me up so much earlier? I know me, and telling me I'm good at something is a surefire way to make me keep doing it. I mean, god, Dustin figured that out and used it against me."

"It's not being used against you, though. It's being used to your benefit. You're focusing on the wrong side of things."

She shrugs. "Well. I'm thinking about it."

"Good for you. And the offer still stands, if you need money to float a month or two," I say, taking a step forward and kissing her cheek while she's not busy putting stuff on it. I put my hands on her hips and she leans back into me, wet hair against my shoulder. "I think you would be the best yoga studio owner I've ever met."

She turns to me, weaving her arms around my shoulders, and I'm struck by the *view*—her ass in the mirror, just peeking up over the countertop, and her chest pressed against mine, a long line of cleavage just outside of tasting distance.

"I'd be the *only* yoga studio owner you've ever met." She runs a hand down my cheek. "And thank you."

"Let me know what you need. And also, not true—I've met Corinne."

She huffs, beaten. "You're just telling me what I want to hear."

"What you *want* to hear is how good you would be at it,"

I say, gauging her expression, and I think I see a hint of a smile on her face. She sighs into me. "How you would lead a class with love because your passion for it oozes from you just when you talk about it."

I push her wet hair over her shoulder, letting my hand run down her arm to her hip.

"Why are you so nice to me?"

I scoff. "Because you deserve it."

She lets out another breath into my neck, and then I feel her lips there.

Man, this girl likes being praised.

The realization that my words might lead to less clothing makes my dick throb. She presses into me, the friction urging me forward as I reach behind her, slipping a hand underneath her dress and grabbing a handful of that yoga ass.

She moans into my shoulder, and I'm gone.

I push her up onto the vanity, sliding between her legs, and pull her hips forward so she can feel just how hard she makes me. I steal a kiss from her, and she matches my urgency, reaching for my belt and pulling it loose, unbuttoning my pants and setting me free.

I run a finger underneath the edge of her underwear, testing the waters, and find her soaking for me. She throws her head back as I slip one finger inside her.

"Gabi, you are so beautiful."

She clenches around me tighter, and I feel like I've found the Easter egg in a video game.

Words of affirmation are Gabi's love language—and *love* language.

I slip another finger inside her, my dick absolutely aching with need but desperate to explore this further. Her eyes are closed as I kiss her forehead, trailing down to that place under her ear I know she likes so much.

"I need you to take the dress off."

She pushes off the counter, turning away from me. "Unzip me."

I pull the zipper down and she grabs at her sleeves, letting it fall to the floor. I watch in the mirror as her tits are exposed, and pull her hair over her shoulder so they're not covered. She leans back into me, eyes heavy with desire.

I reach around her, palming her breast, and her head hits my shoulder, her eyes shutting.

"Gabi, open your eyes."

She looks at me expectantly.

"Look how beautiful you are."

She rolls her eyes, turning toward me. "I don't want to look at *myself*."

I take a step away from her. "Turn around."

She pauses a second as if waiting to see if I'm joking—and then does as she's told.

I press against her, thumbing the lace of her underwear and slowly pulling them down, her thighs soaked. She squirms against me as if trying to cover herself, but I hold her steady by her hips.

"You are so wet," I say into her ear, reaching down and spreading her with one finger. She moans into me, and I'm not sure just how much longer I can wait to bury myself inside her. I slip a finger inside her again. "And fucking gorgeous. Do you know how good that makes me feel? This beautiful, smart, caring, passionate girl, dripping for *me*?"

She clenches around my fingers, and I can't wait any longer.

She turns then, quickly, and I'm about to tell her to stop

it, to turn around and watch herself, when she drops to her knees in front of me.

Fuck.

Her lips wrap around my cock and I see *stars*. She licks a delicate path along the underside and I start trembling, holding onto the vanity so I don't keel over with the feeling of her mouth on me. I weave one hand into her hair, torn between being gentle with her and fucking her face.

"Fuck, you suck me so well."

She looks up at me, those eyes so big and brown—and I'm already close to losing it. When I hit the back of her throat and she gags just a little, I know we need to stop or I'm going to blow my load before she has a chance to get off.

"Gabi, I need to fuck you," I say, reaching forward and pulling her up by her arms. I push her against the counter, bending her over, and line myself up with her entrance. I move up and down, teasing her a little, and then slip inside slowly.

And she tenses up.

I pull back out. "Are you okay?"

She nods quickly, her eyes flicking up to mine in the mirror. "Yes. Don't stop!"

"You tensed up." I run my dick hesitantly along her center.

She shakes her head. "I'm fine, I'm fine. Honestly, I just got a little nervous because—"

"Because why?"

"Because I don't have much control in this position and—"

I wait for her to continue. "And what?"

"You're really big," she says, her face sheepish. "But I don't want you to *stop*!"

I shake my head, unable to stop the grin from spreading

across my face. Some things are just *always* nice to hear. Even if it does mean I have to be gentler with her than I want to.

Leaning my head down against hers, I run my dick along the wetness pooling between her legs, nudging that little bundle of nerves that has her pushing her ass back into me. I kiss the place beneath her ear that always makes her squirm, and relish in the way she moves against me.

"How about this?" I ask, pushing inside her just a little bit. The little moan that escapes her sends a jolt through me. I run my hands along her arms, pulling her shoulders back and down. I trail my fingers along her neck, leaning her back against my chest. "We'll go really slow. And you're going to relax into me and trust that I'm not going to push you too far, okay?"

"I trust you," she says automatically, and I see in her heavy breaths that she's at least *trying*. But the fact that she tensed up at all tells me just how important it is not to hurt her. She closes her eyes, leaning into me.

I push inside her further, pulsing slowly so she can adjust to me. She shivers back into me. "How does that feel?" I ask, even though I have a good idea from the expression on her face.

Her eyes pop open. "It feels like I can take more of you."

I nip at the bottom of her earlobe, eliciting a note of pleasure from her throat, and push further into her. She's almost taking all of me now, so I go slow.

"You're taking me so well," I say, my voice low in her ear.

"I want all of you," she says.

I shake my head, still pulsing slowly. "I don't want to hurt you."

She pushes her ass into me.

"You won't hurt me," she insists. She grabs my hand and

puts it on her breast, squeezing hard, and I *really* want to let loose on her.

But she was nervous.

"I'll be really upset if I hurt you," I say. "I promised I wouldn't."

"Zeke, I can take you," she insists.

I continue the pace I was going before, even as she presses her ass back into me, clawing at my hips to urge me deeper.

"Zeke, fuck me harder!" she finally says, a look of determination on her face as she leans further over the vanity.

And I obey.

As I build up speed and bury myself fully in her, again and again, she reaches up, clamping a hand around the back of my neck.

"Zeke," she pants, and my name from her mouth sends me close to the edge.

I go faster, fisting her hair in my hand, pressing her hips hard into the vanity. She tugs on my neck, her lips finding my cheek, her teeth grazing my skin.

I clamp my arm across her chest, her tits spilling over my arm, and I can hear in her breathing just how close she is to coming.

Me too.

But her eyes are closed again.

"Gabi, open your eyes. I want you to see just how beautiful you look when you come."

She does as she's told.

"Good girl."

And she explodes, coming with a cry, her nails digging into the skin of my neck as I thrust into her, holding on to my own climax just long enough to know that she's finished hers.

When we're done, I kiss her neck, her ears, her cheeks, her hands. Anything I can get my mouth on.

She sighs into me, her eyes closed again, but I'm not going to force them open again—she looks too peaceful right now, sexually satisfied and leaning against me so heavily. Her chest rises and falls with each breath and I don't want to let her go. I don't want to disentangle our limbs and continue past this moment into a night with anyone other than her, and her alone.

But I begrudgingly do.

She turns, winding her arms around my waist and resting her head on my shoulder. I run my hands up and down her naked body, savoring the feel of her skin underneath my fingertips. The curve of her hips and her delicate shoulders. Her grab-able ass and smooth legs.

"I'm not going to have time to get ready."

"Go like that, you look hot."

She laughs into me and the sound is like music.

I help her back into her dress, enamored by her languid, lazy movements.

I did that.

I zip her back up, leaving little kisses along her neck. She checks the time on her phone and shakes her head.

"Okay, I'm going to just finish my makeup and hope for the best with my hair. I don't think I'll be able to eat *and* do it." She shakes her head. "I knew I should have dried it earlier and instead I played on my phone like a dummy."

"Do you want me to dry it while you do your makeup?"

She raises an eyebrow at me. "Do you know how to do that?"

I shrug. "I don't know. I have a mom and a sister, isn't it mostly just point-and-shoot? Twirl it a bit with one of those prickly brushes?"

She pulls open the top drawer. "This kind of prickly brush?"

I nod. "Yeah, that looks like it."

She hands it over to me. "You're up, rookie. Make me pretty."

29

GABI

Zeke's movements are jilted and unpracticed as he pulls the brush through my hair. He concentrates too hard on what he's doing, and it's kind of adorable, the way his eyebrows wrinkle together and he accidentally tugs too hard once or twice.

So different from the commanding man he was only a few minutes ago, instructing me to watch myself come.

Good girl.

Another rush of heat runs through my body at the thought, but he doesn't notice. He's too concerned with drying my hair.

I take another moment to watch him before smudging on my eye shadow. I don't trust many people with my hair, but I trust him—and within a few moments, his movements become background noise.

I swipe on mascara and see him cock his head behind me. "Is that waterproof?"

I pause. "What?"

"Your mascara. Is it waterproof?"

"Yeah. My eyes get watery in winter so I don't bother with the non-waterproof stuff."

He nods, seemingly satisfied with this answer.

"Why?"

"Just curious."

"Are you planning some midnight swimming?"

He shakes his head. "No, just visions of spraying champagne."

"Oh. Ollie?"

He nods. "It's always Ollie."

By the time I'm done with my makeup, my hair is dry, with a gentle face-framing curve.

I don't think I've ever felt so close to someone—sexually, but intimately, too, in that way that has nothing to do with sex but trust.

"How did I do?"

I turn to him, wrapping my arms around his waist and looking up at him. I plant a kiss on his chin. "You did perfect. You're hired."

"Really? I passed?"

"With flying colors."

We head back out to the kitchen and I put the lilies in a vase while he throws our food on the table. I take a whiff before joining him, absolutely intoxicated by the smell of them and the fact that Zeke bought them for me.

Zeke bought me flowers.

Zeke called me a *good girl*.

My body is overwhelmed by the sensations—this brightening in my chest that makes it hard to breathe while at the same time a little pool of fire builds in my abdomen.

"Do you want a drink at all?" I ask, peeking into the fridge to see if I have anything other than white wine and the champagne we were asked to bring to the party.

He shakes his head. "I'll probably go easy on the booze until Kelly texts me she's home."

Before I sit down, he pulls me into his side, kissing my temple.

"I meant everything I said, you know."

I glance up at him. "I didn't doubt you."

"You asked why I'm so nice to you. And I don't want you to think I'm nice to you just to get in your pants. Not that I didn't *really* enjoy the outcome."

"I know, Zeke."

He pulls me in closer. "It does concern me a little, though, that you think I'm being particularly nice to you. I mean, telling you nice things about yourself is, like, a basic requirement of dating someone."

I shrug. "Maybe I dated Dustin far longer than I should have. He only ever said nice things if he wanted something, and it worked until I figured out what his game was. Even after, it still worked for quite a while, honestly." Zeke runs his fingers through my hair and I lean into his touch. "But when you do it, it seems genuine. Not like you're trying to get something from me. You just want me to be happy. To feel good about myself."

"You stole the words right out of my mouth."

He kisses me lightly, and when he pulls away from me, we sit down at the table to eat. "Do you ever talk to your sister about this stuff?"

I raise my eyebrows. "Not really. She's got enough going on. And I'm not all that sure she'd even understand."

He unwraps his sandwich and then pauses. "Maybe you should. I mean, at Charlie's party it seemed like she didn't even know about Frankie. Don't you think you could lean on her a little? You shouldn't be surprised that someone is nice to you, particularly me, and it makes me nervous that instead of recognizing these bad experiences for what they were and chalking Dustin and Frankie up to bad dudes, you're internalizing it and thinking of yourself poorly instead."

I'm a little stunned at his words. *Has this been bothering him?* "I don't think poorly of myself."

"That was so not the point."

I shrug. "I guess I've been dealing with it in my own way."

I think about all the waistband slapping I was doing after I flinched with Zeke.

In hindsight, it does feel a little deranged.

Zeke takes a bite of his sandwich, unbothered. "Well, it's just a suggestion. Kelly grinds my gears constantly but I lean on her if I have to."

"Do you?"

He nods. "She's super empathetic. She'll slap me and say I'm being a pussy for not running a yellow light but if something's bothering me, she's happy to sit and listen. I bet Steph would do the same for you. Just like you'd do for her."

I stab a piece of lettuce.

I can just imagine Steph's eyebrows rising, her eyes flashing as I ask her to comfort me about things that happened months and years ago. The moment of understanding when she realizes why I was being a psycho at her birthday party and asking me why I didn't just say something then.

"Yeah. Maybe. I guess I just feel dumb talking to her. She's my younger sister. She's got this brightness to her. This ability to blow past the shit that happens to her and come out smiling on the other hand. And I just get stuck." I think about Christmas, about how angry she was with me when my first question about her hair was whether work approved. "She's sunshine, and I'm the clouds that dull her."

He moves his chair closer to mine, taking my hand, and his eyes find mine.

"Gabi, you're moonlight." My breath catches in my throat. "You're subtle and calm and protective. Thoughtful and resilient. Sure, Stephanie shines bright. No one's going to argue that. But Gabi, you glow."

I can hardly catch my breath as his thumb runs along my knuckles. "Zeke..."

There are no words.

I push my chair back and round the table to him, his eyes following me as I move. I sink down into his lap and wrap my arms around his neck, taking a moment to press my face into his skin. He squeezes me tight, his lips brushing across my temple as his breath runs past my ear.

We stay like that for a long minute, quiet aside from our breaths.

When I pull away from him, taking a second to truly look at him, he raises his eyebrows.

"How did I get so lucky?"

He rolls his eyes, pulling me back against him. "I could say the same thing."

He kisses my cheek and then breaks the moment by slapping my ass. "Now go eat your salad."

I disentangle myself from him, sliding back onto my own seat and stabbing at a few pieces of lettuce I'm wholly uninterested in, with Zeke sitting right next to me. He turns back to his sandwich but pauses when he sees me looking at him.

"Are you alright? Why aren't you eating?"

I shake my head, swallowing down an overload of

emotions running through my body. "I don't know. I thought I was hungry but I guess I'm not."

He sets his sandwich down, his eyes boring into mine, and I realize I'm creating an issue where there isn't one. "Gabi."

I shake my head. "I'm fine. I think I just need a glass of water."

"I'll get it for you." He gets up before I have a chance to, pouring me a glass from the pitcher in the fridge. He puts it in my hands and then waits expectantly for me to take a sip.

"Thank you." He's still standing there. "Can you please eat your sandwich?"

He sits down, his eyes still on me, and I make a show of spearing a piece of lettuce on my fork.

"I'm not some breakable thing, you know. I won't die if I don't eat."

"We're going to a New Year's party. You might."

I laugh, and as he reaches over to squeeze my hand, every nerve in my body focuses on that spot. I can hardly breathe, his words still running through my mind. *Gabi, you're moonlight.*

For the first time, I don't feel like the cloud that dulls my sister's sparkle. Or a burden on someone else's fun time.

I'm just me. And Zeke sees it.

Before we leave, he kisses me deeply, wrapping an arm around my waist and pulling me against him.

"You look beautiful," he says, leaving a kiss on my forehead, and that bursting feeling in my chest comes back with a vengeance.

WE HEAR the party before we see it.

When we get off the elevator, Zeke and I look at each other.

"Is that coming from their apartment?" I ask.

Zeke nods. "Sure seems like it."

We don't bother knocking when we get to the door at the end of the hall.

Inside, there is a smattering of people—most I recognize, but some I don't. I thought this was going to be a friends party, but I recognize the neighbors from the other apartment on this floor. Charlie's mom, brother, sister-in-law, and nephew. Annabel's parents, judging from their resemblance to her.

And of course, our loud group of friends standing around the island, sparkly girls and whiskey men, chatting animatedly. Steph brought along Kay and Leilani, and from the decibel of their voices, all three of them are already drunk. Kick brought a friend with him, who—just like Kick—looks like he played college football. He stares unapologetically at Leilani's ass as Kick says something he pays no attention to.

Charlie pops out of nowhere, smothering first me, then Zeke, in overzealous hugs.

"For a minute there I thought you guys weren't gonna show."

"We wouldn't do that," Zeke says, sounding unnecessarily solemn about a party that wouldn't miss us one bit if we weren't here.

"So serious," I joke. A look passes between Charlie and Zeke.

Before I can ask what all *that* was about, Charlie turns on his heel and disappears back into the party. "Thanks for coming!" he calls over his shoulder. "Booze is on the island!"

My eyes narrow as he walks away. "Why is he so serious about this party?"

Zeke shrugs. "My bet is on the family. It's always different when you've got parents and kids at a party."

I glance to where Charlie's family is chatting in one corner around a makeshift table covered in a sparkly table-cloth. "Yeah, you're probably right. His mom doesn't get out much."

Zeke nods sadly.

Charlie's mom is in a years-long battle with dementia. He and his brother spend a lot of time with her at her apartment, but this is the first time I've seen her out in years. She watches the party with a small smile on her face, present but reserved.

Zeke pours me a glass of wine and we say a quick hello to Charlie's family—who both of us have met multiple times but never together. Annabel introduces us to her parents, who seem happy to be here but overwhelmed by the size of the party.

I am a little bit, too, to be honest.

When we make our way to our friends, still happily chatting around the island, I'm absorbed in Steph's conversation with Kay and Leilani. Zeke accepts a small glass of whiskey from Charlie, pacing himself so he can have champagne at midnight and still be available to Kelly if need be.

As he and Charlie talk, he catches my eye and smiles at me, and I can't remember having a connection so strong with someone that I can have a full conversation with them across a crowd of people that feels just as intimate as the words he whispered into my ear earlier.

Gabi, you're moonlight.

And then Steph destroys our moment.

"Are you fucking him yet?"

"What?"

"Are you?"

My moment of hesitation is enough for her to put the pieces together, and her eyes go wide. "Oh my god, you are! How dare you not tell me as soon as it happened!"

"What, do you want me to call you during the cigarette?"

She pauses, her eyes wide. "Did you have a cigarette?"

"No, of course not!"

I look back at Zeke, but his attention has moved on to Charlie.

Steph's moving toward me, her arms wrapping around me. "I'm so happy for you. You really needed a good lay."

I laugh. "Alright, Steph. That's not all he is, you know."

"It's not?" Her smile ticks wider.

Kay and Leilani are uncharacteristically quiet, waiting for my answer.

"I like him." I sound like a grade-schooler with her first crush.

Steph's jaw drops, and she starts jumping.

Jesus Christ, Stephanie.

"Oh my god!" she shouts.

"Steph, play it cool." I glance back over toward him, and now Zeke and Charlie are both looking at us, their attention drawn by Stephanie The Disco Ball bouncing next to me. He sees me looking and a little wrinkle appears above his eyes. I shake my head quickly and turn back to Steph. "You're drawing attention!"

"What are we jumping for?" Annabel weaves into our group, holding a green drink. She jumps with Steph, but not as enthusiastically.

"Gabi's in love!"

"Stephanie!" *Why did I tell her this? Just, why?*

"Oh, Zeke? Is this news? I thought this was going on for a while."

I cock my head to the side, picking up on movement from Zeke's corner of the kitchen.

I guess out of the two of us, Zeke has looser lips.

"He told you?"

Annabel shakes her head. "Charlie told me, but I guess that would have had to come from Zeke if it didn't come from you."

"What are we jumping for?" His voice is warm over my shoulder.

Steph grins, and Annabel bites her lip, looking between us. Where there was jumping and shouting only a moment ago, there is now silence.

And then I feel Zeke's hands on my hips, so natural there yet so perfectly timed for this conversation. He pulls me back, into his chest, and kisses my cheek—nothing sexual about it, just a greeting—and it's enough to elicit squeals from Steph and Annabel.

"Did you know what you were doing?" I ask over my shoulder, so only he can hear.

"I had an idea."

"Mari, you owe me fifty dollars!" Steph shouts, grabbing her attention from the other side of the island. Mari looks confused for a moment and then flips Steph off when she sees Zeke's hand on my waist.

"I like this a lot," Annabel says, leaving her drink on the counter so she can wrap us both in a hug. "This is a good thing."

I eye Charlie as he surreptitiously switches out Annabel's green drink for water, and he rolls his eyes when he catches me looking. Annabel sees my side of the exchange and turns on him. "Charlie! Can you stop? We're hosting a gigantic party and I've had the equivalent of three sips at this point!"

He shrugs. "It's going to be a long night—I'm just making sure you're hydrated."

She takes the green drink from him, thinks about it for a second, and then takes the water too.

"Thank you," she says begrudgingly.

The girls fall back into conversation, and I turn to Zeke, leaning into him.

"Have you heard from Kelly yet?"

He nods. "She's at a campus party. Hopefully that means getting home will be quick and easy."

"GabiGabiGabi." Steph taps my arm, and I turn to her. "Sorry," she says quickly, more to Zeke than me. "Do you want to get tattoos with us next weekend?"

"What?"

Steph nods. "Me and maybe Leilani and Oliver and Henry are going to go to the tattoo convention next weekend, wanna come?"

"What are you getting a tattoo of?"

She shrugs. "I don't know yet. I might not even get one, or maybe I'll get something small that I can cover up if I need to."

"Steph," I start, about to tell her she shouldn't be getting a tattoo if her primary concern is needing to cover it up— but before I continue I feel a little nudge in my side from Zeke. "I don't want a tattoo, but thanks for the invite."

She rolls her eyes at me. "Fine, just thought I'd ask."

I grab her arm before she flits off back to her friends. "Thank you, though, for thinking of me."

She smiles. "You're welcome."

And then she rejoins Kay and Leilani, looking at tattoos on their phones.

I lean back into Zeke as he wraps his arms around me, and I think I could be absolutely anywhere in the world and be happy as long as I had him right behind me, nudging me in the right direction.

"You'd look hot with a tattoo, by the way."

I laugh. "Come on, I couldn't pull that off."

He shrugs, leaving a kiss on the nape of my neck. "I could see something delicate for you. Maybe like the outline of a girl doing yoga or something. Or a flower."

"And where would I put it?"

He twists my hips so I turn to face him, and he takes his time looking me up and down. I feel a heat building in between my legs again.

"You could put it here," he says, drawing a delicate line down the inside of my arm. "Or here." He reaches behind me, his fingers trailing down my neck. "Here." He grazes my hip. "Or here." His thumb runs underneath my breast, sending a little chill down my spine. "You have many options."

"I might get a tattoo just so you'll run your fingers over it like that."

He grins and then leans forward so his lips are pressed against my ear. "Only if you're a good girl."

Warmth turns to liquid fire as I bunch his shirt in my fists.

"You can't say that in a crowd full of people."

He kisses the space just beneath my ear. "I don't know, I kind of like the effect."

He takes my mouth with his, his tongue pushing inside and filling me with the taste of whiskey. He grabs my ass with one hand, the other winding around my waist and clamping me to him.

"God, get a room!"

I ignore the shout, so intensely focused on Zeke that he could probably undress me right here and I wouldn't even mind. I feel him hardening against my hip and lean into him further. When he pulls away, I fix him with a grin; he's stuck with me for the next few minutes.

He shakes his head. "Whew, Gabi."

I stand on my tip toes and whisper into his ear. "Don't call me a good girl unless you're prepared to do something about it."

30

ZEKE

As midnight approaches, Charlie and Annabel start popping champagne and passing out plastic flutes. Most of the party is plastered—aside from the parents—and I keep an eye on my phone in case Kelly texts me. I don't like that she's at a campus party when campus is all but deserted.

I fill up a flute for Gabi and one for me, and we find a spot by the windows where we can see the midnight fireworks going off.

The countdown is *loud*. Gabi stands in front of me and I wrap my arms around her neck, pulling her close.

The sliding door that leads to the balcony at the far end of the windows opens, and my attention snaps to it, just in time to see Charlie walk outside, Annabel trailing behind him. They've asked everyone to stay inside, claiming they want to avoid any drunk falls.

I know the real reason.

Shouts of "Happy New Year!" ring out around us, and I pull Gabi into me by the hips and kiss her with all I've got. Noisemakers sound and friends hug and couples kiss, and in the corner of my eye, I see Charlie getting down on one knee.

I spin Gabi around quickly and point, resting my hands on her shoulders. "Look."

"What?"

And then she stiffens. "Oh my god."

A wave of energy rolls through her, and she takes a step toward the window like she's about to bang on it, but I grab her before she can.

"Oh my god, oh my god, oh my god," she says, her body taut in my arms, her hands over her mouth for what seems like the longest moment in history.

Annabel turns toward him, her arms crossed over her little polka dot dress and the cold January air whipping her hair around her face.

And her eyes go wide as she leans toward him. I can read the words on her lips as I hear Gabi still muttering them in front of me.

"Oh my god, oh my god, oh my god."

The party has silenced now, a collective breath held as he asks her.

And then she's crying, and nodding, and kneeling down with him as he slides a ring on her finger, fireworks booming out above them. They share a kiss there, kneeling together, and then he slowly pulls her up to her feet, wrapping her up in his arms and guiding her inside where they're met with cheers loud enough to pop eardrums.

Gabi's off like a rocket the second they step inside, one of the first people to accost them, wrapping her arms around both of them so tight that I'm afraid one of them might stop breathing. Annabel's crying happy tears, and despite the multitude of people congratulating them and hugging them, Charlie keeps one arm around her, refusing to be separated.

In that moment a little bloom of jealousy arises in my stomach.

I want that.

I want to make Gabi cry happy tears.

I want our friends and family to surround us, wishing us a happy life together.

The person who pours every glass of champagne for her.

The person who cares for her, loves her, dotes on her, carries her when she can't carry herself.

I want Gabi. In a bigger way than I ever thought I would.

When the chaos has settled and they've been sufficiently swarmed, she finds me.

"You knew!" she accuses, even as she wraps her arms around me.

"I did." I kiss her head, folding her into me, and hug her tight.

"And you didn't tell me!"

"I was under strict orders not to."

She grumbles. "Oh, I'm going to kill Charlie!"

"Gabi, be real. Could you have made it through this whole night without tipping off Annabel?"

She leans back, looking up at me. "I can keep a secret."

"You'd either be grinning like the Cheshire Cat all night or you'd ask to see her manicure or you'd have been like Charlie all night, constantly taking her drinks."

She swallows. "No, I wouldn't have."

I give her a look.

"Okay fine!" Her little fist hits my shoulder. "You know what? I don't even care! I'm just so happy for them! I'm so happy I was here to see it, I can't believe Charlie—"

"I know, right? Manwhore Charlie gets the girl."

"If you'd told me this time last year that Charlie would be proposing, I would have called a psych ward."

She has her arms around my neck and I love that we can have a conversation like this, two people standing close in a crowded room. She looks up at me, and her eyes are so big and brown and her makeup is still as perfect as it was when we got here, her dress scratchy on my hands but her body warm and soft underneath it.

"Where do you think we'll be in a year?"

She sighs, her fingers threading through my hair.

"I don't know. As long as I'm with you, we'll be somewhere good." She bites her lip, smiling at me.

I lean down and kiss her, and when I pull away, she has her lip in her mouth again, like she wants to say something else.

"I think I'm going to take the studio."

I raise my eyebrows. "You are?"

She nods, the excitement showing on her face. "I mean, when else would I do it? It's being dropped in my lap and it's *weird* timing, but when does this sort of opportunity show up?"

"That's awesome, Gabi. I'm so proud of you."

She glows, pressing her lips to mine. "Thank you, Zeke." She shakes her head. "I have to go text Corinne." She steps away from me and weaves through the party to where her purse hangs on the back of a chair in the kitchen.

She pulls my heart farther with every step she takes, her absence like a weight.

I follow her, checking my own phone while I go, and see that Kelly's texted me.

I find it decidedly not funny that she opens with telling me not to worry and then lets me know her party got shut down by the police. I text her a Happy New Year back and decide to just tease her about it later.

She's home safe—that's all that matters.

And Gabi is here with me, texting Corinne with a smile on her face. I can't stop touching her, pulling her close, wanting her next to me and all around me. I pour us both more champagne and she smiles over the rim of her flute as we cheers to Charlie and Annabel. To her future studio.

And all I can think about is the way she holds my heart in one of those delicate, manicured hands, completely oblivious to just how easily she could break it.

I kiss her ravenously at each and every chance I get, and when we finally head back to her apartment, buzzed from champagne and good news, I tell her to take off her dress, to get on top of me, to ride me.

And she obeys, like the good girl she is.

JANUARY

31

GABI

I wake to a pounding in my head.

"Oh god."

Zeke's arm is around my waist, and he pulls me in tighter to him. My dress is on the floor, my sheets tangled between our legs.

"We don't have to be awake yet," he mumbles into my neck, his breath hot on my skin.

Last night comes tumbling back to me—champagne, Charlie and Annabel, the studio, Zeke...

Zeke, needy and demanding and relentlessly calling me a *good girl*. His hands in my hair, running along every inch of my body. Heat pools in my abdomen, warring with the pounding in my head.

I turn toward him, fighting against the sheets. His skin is warm and so welcoming, his chest strong underneath my palms. I run my leg up his and find that he's naked too—and I notch my knee around his waist.

One eye pops open underneath mussed hair.

"You better be careful," he warns, his voice low and gravelly. He reaches one hand down to my ass, moving us closer.

"Or what?" I dare, and he raises an eyebrow.

He grumbles. "I'm not awake enough for a clever response to that, but here." He grabs my hand and puts my hand on his rock-hard erection. "That's 'or what.'"

I start stroking him and he groans into the pillow.

"Gabi, what are you?"

I raise my eyebrows. "What am I?"

"You're unreal. Sexy as fuck. Goddamn adorable at the same time." He brushes my hair out of my face, his hand reaching around to the back of my head and winding into my hair as I pump him harder. "Fucking smartest woman I've ever met, not to mention *talented*." He groans into my neck as I feel wetness pooling between my legs. "I don't deserve you."

His hand moves up my leg, drawing a slick line at my core, and my breath catches.

"I don't deserve any of this." He pushes me onto my back, climbing on top of me and resting his weight on me. He kisses me deeply as one hand trails down my hip, the other slipping under my back.

He moves downward, leaving a trail of kisses down my stomach, his fingers slipping inside me as his mouth lands on that bundle of nerves. He moves slowly, lazily pulsing into me.

"I don't deserve this beautiful pussy so soaked for me." He takes a moment to kiss my thigh, his fingers still pumping, and a shiver runs down my spine. One hand moves to my knee, grabbing hold of my thigh. "These strong legs." He takes a handful of ass. "This delightfully grab-able ass."

I laugh as he starts moving back up, his fingers continuing their lazy motion, bringing me *so close*. "This stomach." He licks my belly button and I arch into him, the urge to laugh fighting against the urge to beg him to fuck me already. "These tits that are just—I mean, these tits could start wars." He takes a nipple in his mouth and I suck in a breath. He pinches the other with his free hand.

"This perfect neck," he says, nibbling my skin. He leans down and kisses me, shoving his tongue in my mouth. "This mouth that can suck my soul right out of my cock." I moan, his words and his fingers nearly sending me over the edge.

He pulls away from me for a second, looking me in the eyes. "This big, beautiful brain." He kisses me on the temple, and there's something so tender about it that I feel my chest swell. His kisses move down my collarbone. "This big, big heart."

He rests his head in the crook of my neck as he maneuvers himself to my entrance.

"This everything of yours." He pushes inside me with a grunt.

He kisses me while thrusting inside me, his weight heavy, our chests grazing as he moves. He leans down into me, kissing my neck and my collarbone, his tongue drawing big lazy circles across my skin.

He groans into my neck as he sends me over the edge, my nails raking down his back and my legs clamping around his waist. I arch up into his chest as he pushes into me harder, his orgasm just over the horizon.

After he comes, he collapses into me again. "Gabi, you are everything."

I find his mouth with mine. "You're my everything."

He runs his fingers through my hair, his eyes on mine. He lets out a long breath and then lets his head drop to my shoulder, laughing. "Jesus, Gabi."

"What?" I ask, unable to hold my own laughter at bay.

He only shakes his head, kissing me lightly.

When we finally get out of bed, I steal the shirt he wore

last night and start making pancakes. He sits at my kitchen table drinking his coffee and watching me, his hands reaching for me every time I pass by him, grabbing my waist or my butt or pulling me in for a kiss.

I nearly laugh when he pulls my chair next to his so he can rest an arm around my shoulder while we eat. He peppers me with kisses between pancake bites, and afterward, we fall into bed again, our New Year's Day a collection of orgasms spread across my apartment.

But as the sun sets, the reality of the upcoming week hits.

Tomorrow, I have to be at work. Then teacher training for three hours afterward.

And on days like tomorrow, I'll have to somehow fit in running a studio too.

My chest tightens at the thought, and I catch Zeke looking at me.

I'm sprawled out on the couch and he sits on the other side, my legs propped up on his. He cocks his head to the side, squeezing my knee.

"What's with the tension, Gabi?"

I sit up, folding my legs underneath me. I pulled on some silky jammies a while ago, but the air still feels cold without his skin against mine and I tug the blanket over me.

"I think I might be in over my head."

He sighs. "I was worried that was going to get you."

"What was going to get me?"

He shrugs, searching for the words. "Your anxiety."

I huff. "It isn't *getting* me. I think it's telling me to hold up a bit because what I'm doing is a big thing."

"A big, *exciting* thing," he corrects.

"I don't know if I'm ready for this."

He turns toward me, grabbing my hand. "Gabi,

remember what you said to me that night at Charlie's months ago?" I shake my head. "You said that love being nothing more than timing has saved you from countless bad relationships—and then you realized what a hoax your brain had you believing."

"Yikes. Yes." The memory hits me like a brick, an instant shattering of a belief I never questioned before.

"This is the same thing. A hoax your brain is stuck on. Being nervous is fine, but tell me this: when you said last night that in a year you wanted to be running your own studio, were you lying?"

I don't have to think about my answer. "No."

"Do you still think this is a good opportunity?"

"Well, objectively, yes."

"Then just jump, Gabi. Stop letting your brain slow you down. You want this; it's right here for the taking. If you keep letting fear govern your life, you won't have that studio next year. You won't have it the year after, either. Some things you don't get to be ready for. Some things just happen and you have to embrace them."

I want to believe in his words, but that nervousness in my chest is still there.

If the studio was up for grabs in a few months, after I was done with teacher training, it would feel like kismet. If I could get a few months of actually teaching under my belt, that would be even better. If I hadn't missed the first few teacher training classes. If I didn't suddenly meet Zeke and want to spend time with him too. If I didn't have to work eight hours a day.

My head is filled with all ifs and no answers, just a wild indecision fueled by too many things happening at once and no reliable picture of the outcome.

"The timing just feels so wrong."

Zeke's jaw clenches. "Gabi, tell whatever part of your brain is insisting that timing matters to kindly fuck off." He sighs. "It's a yes or a no, Gabi. Yes means now, and no means never—because if timing really matters, you'll never do it. Do you want it or not?"

I swallow. "I want it."

He leans over and kisses me tenderly, his hand on the back of my neck.

"Now hold on to that."

32

ZEKE

My heart beats wildly.

I had thought that maybe a night of sleep and a sober morning would bring me back to my senses. I had thought maybe the swelling of my heart last night was temporary, fueled by too much champagne and happiness for my best friend and his new fiancée.

I had thought, I had thought, I had thought...

But today, waking up to Gabi pumping me, to her body so ready and willing for me, the feelings came rushing back again.

And then I thought they'd go away throughout the day. Maybe it's too much to expect them to wane overnight, especially with someone like Gabi in bed next to me. But if anything, they grew stronger.

I feel this need to have her close to me at all times, to touch her, to hold her in my arms, to please her and pleasure her constantly.

And then she starts talking about timing, and I want to blame this sickening crunch in my chest on her anxiety, like it's contagious or something, but just like Gabi's ignoring her wants out of fear, I'm ignoring my feelings for the same reason.

I'm in love with Gabi Pierce.

Head over heels, ready to wife her up and move her in with me and promise she's my only one.

And all she can talk about is timing.

Timing of a goddamn yoga studio that's honestly not all that expensive and comes on a month-to-month lease.

I want to scream at her that it's so beside the point—but her fears are real, just as mine are.

She's afraid of failure. She's afraid of enlisting the help of her friends. Afraid of leaning on me if and when she needs to.

Even though I'd take contracts that are too big for me if it meant giving her everything.

I'd burn down cities to be needed by her.

I'd do just about anything to hear her say *fuck timing*.

Because as long as she thinks timing has absolutely anything to do with it, I'm one of two things: I'm either the guy who showed up at the right place and the right time, and I'm *good enough*, or I'm the guy she leaves when time dictates she finds her real person.

I'm too far gone for either option.

I want her to take this studio and make it the massive success it will surely be in her hands, and then I want her to turn to me and say, "God, what was I thinking with all that timing bullshit?"

And then I want her to choose me.

33

GABI

"I'm overwhelmed."

I push my computer away from me, getting up and grabbing a glass of water from Zeke's fridge. I only got here an hour ago, but it's already dark out, his apartment melding into shadows and silence.

He looks up at me over his computer screen as I sit down again. I only started my list a few minutes ago, but I already know I'm in over my head.

There are small things that I can check off pretty easily, like paying the landlord and signing up for the same discount websites Corinne was on. Then there are things that will take research, like business insurance. Where the hell do I get that? And how do I know if it's the kind I need? Branding—did Corinne have a brand, or did she have a hodgepodge of a studio that happened to work?

I can handle buying spare mats in case of newbies or someone forgetting theirs. I can handle scheduling and outreach to local yogis to ask them about teaching a few classes. I can do advertising in my sleep, and I can make lists of all the things a yoga studio needs to have on hand.

But what about paying teachers? And taxes? Not to mention, how do I get paid? Do I need a separate bank account?

"What's overwhelming you?"

Zeke closes his laptop and walks around the counter to where I'm sitting, pulling over a stool next to me and looking at the list I've typed out on my computer.

"Yeah, I can see how this might be overwhelming." He copies my list over to a spreadsheet and starts rearranging all of my notes. "But part of that is because big lists are, by nature, overwhelming." He creates a flow chart, rearranging everything I have written into prerequisites and desired outcomes.

"I didn't know you were a spreadsheet whisperer."

He smirks at me. "I'm not, but it seems to be expected of you if you have more than the most basic knowledge of computers, so I've picked up a few tricks. This is how I plan out my work, actually."

He adds another item to the end of the flowchart—a website—and adds an assignee column with his name in it. He glances at me. "Learn to lean on people, Gabi. I can spin up a website for you in hours."

When he's done, he pushes the laptop in front of me. He's added a few more things to do, but he's grouped everything into categories and separated some big tasks into more bite-sized chunks. He has himself listed on several rows, including taxes and a lesson on paying contractors along with the website. Under business insurance, he listed Henry —which boggles my mind a bit because last I checked, he sells T-shirts online—and Annabel under branding. Corinne has a few lines, too, mostly stuff pertaining to the studio that I might be able to handle myself, but her expertise would probably give me more confidence.

"How did you make my brain dump make sense?"

He wraps an arm around my shoulders and presses a kiss to my temple.

"Welcome to web development. I hope this is the closest you'll ever get."

I arrow through the different boxes, and although there are no timelines on any of the tasks, it's clear which things Zeke has highlighted as a priority.

"So it looks like I need to choose colors. And pick a name." I crinkle my eyebrows. "There's no way that's the most important thing for me to focus on right now."

"It's not the most important—it's a blocker. If you don't have a name and colors, I can't make you a website, Annabel can't design something for you—if she agrees to, of course—and you can't sign up for a bank account or get insurance. So it might not be the most important, but it's what you need to do first."

I nod. "Okay. Yellow and gray."

He raises his eyebrows at me, and he reaches forward to check off the colors line. "Good job, Gabi. You already crossed something off the list. You should do a mood board or something, too, though, now that I'm thinking about it. I could probably guess what shade you're looking for, but a mood board would help me, probably Annabel too."

He adds that as another task after the colors.

"Well hey, that's not fair, I get another task when I complete one?"

He shrugs. "That's how it goes. You'll be happy with how much you've accomplished once you've checked off three-quarters of these and it's double what you originally expected to do."

I huff. "Fine."

"Go make a mood board and think about your name."

"I'm pretty sure it's Gabi."

"Gabriel*la*," he's quick to correct, grinning at me as he winds around to the other side of the counter again.

He sinks into his work again, and I envy his focus. He can switch from one task to the other with such ease—something I can do easily, *usually*, but not when I have absolutely no idea what I'm doing.

I have to learn *everything*.

"Henry's already going to be in the city on Friday so he'll come here first for dinner if that works for you," Zeke says, still looking at his computer.

"What?"

He glances up at me. "He's going out with Oliver and Kick, but he said he can stop by beforehand."

"You already talked to him?"

He shrugs. "Why do tomorrow what you can do today?"

"Jesus, I better get started on that mood board."

"I don't think Henry needs your mood board." I fix him with a look, and he bites his lip, holding back a smile. "But I'm sure he'll indulge you if you want to show it off."

"You're such a problem," I tell him, and he grins.

"Happy to be of service." He turns his attention back to his computer. "You should ask Annabel sooner rather than later, too. You don't know what she's got going on with planning a wedding and everything now."

"Should I even be asking her? I don't want to impose."

"She can say no if she wants. Offer her whatever the going rate is for freelance graphic design. She might want the extra money for the wedding."

I raise my eyebrows at him; he's not paying attention to what he's saying. A second later, he looks up at me, shaking his head. "Actually, Annabel is probably going to have a pretty lavish wedding with or without your money, but it's still courteous to offer, I think."

I laugh. "Yeah, okay. I'll ask her."

I send her a quick text as I navigate over to Pinterest and start throwing pictures together. She calls me a second later.

"Gabi."

"Annabel."

"This is exciting."

I laugh. "I guess. It mostly just feels overwhelming."

"Can we, like, barter?"

"Barter?" I look up at Zeke, wondering if I'm missing something, but he seems as confused as I am.

"Yeah. Like I'll make you a logo. I'll make you a fucking *fire* logo, but I don't want your money. How about the first month of my membership is free?"

"Aw, you want to join the studio? That's so sweet."

She laughs. "Of course I do! But does that work for you? Logo in exchange for a month?"

"Yeah, absolutely, that sounds more than fair. Thanks, Annabel."

"What's the name of the studio? Do you have any ideas of what you want it to look like? Or any logos you like that I can emulate?"

"Um, I don't know about a name yet. But Zeke is making me make a mood board so I can send you that."

"Oh yeah, that'll work. Is he there with you?"

"Yeah, he's here."

Zeke looks up at me again, his eyebrows raised.

Annabel lowers her voice. "Are you naked?"

I laugh. "Not currently, no."

"Oh god, I wouldn't blame you if you were. He's so hot."

I hear Charlie's voice in the background. "Who's hot?"

"Oh fuck," she mutters. "Steve Carell! And this doesn't concern you."

"Steve Carell? That's the first name you can think of?"

She pauses for a moment. "Steve Carell is *hot*."

"You're so weird."

"It's all part of my charm." She sighs. "Send me your mood board and your name when you have it, and I'll put something together for you."

"Thanks, Annabel."

When we hang up, Zeke is grinning at me. "Steve Carell?"

I shake my head. "You don't want to know."

34

ZEKE

Gabi is adorable.

She clicks around on her laptop, biting her lip. Her brow is furrowed and she narrows her eyes at something on her screen. She has such intense focus, and I can't help smiling, knowing she's trying to aggregate the perfect photos to represent what she wants from her studio.

Her eyes flick up as if she's trying to think of something, and they land on mine in surprise.

"What?"

I shake my head. "You're cute when you think too hard."

Her eyes narrow, a smile playing at her lips. "Don't you be looking at me while I'm thinking."

"I'm sorry, I'll keep my eyes to myself."

I grin at her, and focus on the block of HTML I've been editing. When I glance back up at her a few seconds later, she's returned to her screen too, her lips pursed as she types something out. Probably adding more to her monstrosity of a list.

She groans, dropping her head into her hands. "Nothing sounds right."

I get up, rounding the island to where she's propped up, and lean over her, just enough that my chest grazes her shoulder. I can smell her perfume and—wow, there's nothing I want to do more than drag her off her barstool and lay her down on the couch. Or in my bed. Hell, I'll accept the floor.

When I'm able to rein in my thoughts enough to see what's on her screen, I realize she's moved on from her mood board to her name. She has a jumble of words on the screen, as well as thesaurus results for a number of words including *peace, sanctuary,* and *balance.*

"I just want it to be what I want it to be without it not being what someone else needs it to be."

I narrow my eyes, trying to decipher her words. "I don't know what that means."

She sighs. "Like for me, I go to yoga to find my peace. For the most part. But sometimes I also go to sweat, and those two opposites are not easily encompassed in one word. I don't want people to think it's a meditation studio, but I also don't want people to think I only offer power yoga. You know?"

"Ah. You want to make it clear it's yogi's choice."

She pauses, staring at me. "How did you do that?"

"Do what?"

"Yogi's Choice Studio." She types it out on her screen and stares at it for a few seconds. "Is my brain fried, or is that the name?"

"If you like it, then I'd say that's the name."

She stares at it for a few more seconds. "I think I like it."

"I want credit for coming up with it on all marketing materials. Any signage, too."

She grins at me, her hand landing on my chest as she kisses my cheek. "All credit will go to Zeke Morgan, who can't even touch his toes."

"Hey, I wasn't warmed up!"

"I think you were pretty warmed up."

We had been in bed for a good hour or two by then, so she's absolutely right.

"Yeah, well, you can't touch your toes either."

She raises her eyebrows at me, slipping off her stool and easily resting her palms on the floor in front her.

I was hoping she'd do that.

"I don't know, can't really tell with your shoes on," I say, taking the opportunity to palm her ass and run my hand up along her spine. She goes to stand up straight again and I hold my hand firm, keeping her there.

"I can't stay bent over forever."

I slap her ass, just enough to make a sharp sound, but not enough to hurt her.

"You will if you want to be a good girl."

I take her hand and drag her up to my bedroom.

In the morning, I slip out of bed early to put on coffee, only to see that it's already been made.

I just left Gabi upstairs, delightfully exposed beneath the covers and snoring softly, so my only conclusion is that there must be someone else here.

Kelly clears her throat from behind me.

She's sitting on my couch in sweatpants and a T-shirt, her phone plugged into the wall next to her. Her hair is wild, as usual, and pulled into a haphazard bun on her head.

"Good morning," she says, poorly disguising a smile.

Fuck.

"How long have you been here?"

"Long enough."

Which means she probably heard round two in the middle of the night and round three somewhere around dawn.

I can't help it—Gabi is *really* hot, and she slept naked last night.

I nod. "Let me get a shirt."

When I get upstairs, I lean over her, one hand on her hip to gently wake her. She rolls toward me, her tits on full display, and I kind of want to completely ignore Kelly and bury myself in this woman one more time.

I can't believe this girl is in my bed.

"Kelly is here," I murmur into her ear.

Her face scrunches up in confusion. "Kelly?"

"She must have let herself in late last night."

It takes a few beats for Gabi to understand. "She probably heard us fucking."

I nod. "I'd bet good money on that." I rub her hip, struggling to take my eyes off her chest. "I just wanted to let you know so you didn't come downstairs naked. You're welcome to, if you still want to, but I figured it'd be better to let you know."

She giggles into the pillow. "I'll get dressed."

"You don't have to get up now. Sleep. It's one of your few days off."

She shakes her head. "Last time I saw Kelly, I was drunk. It's about time I redeem myself."

"She was drunk too, and she's twenty years old. You don't need to redeem yourself one bit."

She grabs the hem of my sweatpants and pulls. My knees hit the edge of the bed frame, and I catch myself around her, her hands snaking up around my neck. I lean down and kiss her, winding one arm beneath her waist and pulling her in close to me, the brush of her chest against mine sending fire down my spine.

"We probably shouldn't," she whispers.

"Probably not."

"But maybe a little wouldn't hurt," she says, pushing my sweatpants down as I pull the sheets from between us, her naked body ready and willing underneath.

We're quiet this time, aware of the visitor downstairs, and take turns shushing one another as our pace waxes and wanes and finally builds to an aching crescendo.

Afterward, we take a quick shower, water running in rivulets down Gabi's naked body. At this point, I have to look away. I just can't resist.

She throws on a pair of leggings and one of my T-shirts, and she looks so good it's unfair. I do the same—sweatpants, though, instead of leggings—and follow her downstairs.

"Kelly!" Her voice is bright, full of energy that she definitely didn't have twenty minutes ago.

"Gabi!"

"When did you get here?"

Kelly smiles. "A little past two."

Gabi nods, no doubt doing the same math that I did.

Whatever. It's been years since I've been into someone like I'm into Gabi. If Kelly wants to show up in the middle of the night without warning, she can deal with the consequences.

"How was your night?" Kelly asks knowingly.

Gabi glances at me and shrugs. "It was great. Fucked like animals."

My jaw drops and Kelly sputters into laughter. "Oh my god, I *so* did not need to hear that about my brother!"

"You asked!"

"I have learned my lesson and will never dare ask again."

She gets up from the couch as Gabi heads for the coffee machine.

"Mom and Dad texted," she says, her voice lowering as Gabi takes out two mugs, having already clocked Kelly's on the coffee table. "They're coming for breakfast if you're interested."

I hear the bluff in Kelly's voice, like she's daring me to either decline the invitation or not bring Gabi. I don't know what her reasoning is, but something in the way her wide eyes follow mine to where Gabi is pouring coffee makes me think she's just curious.

Meddlesome, yes, but curious.

"I'll see if Gabi's up for it."

Kelly's lips twitch into a smile, and as much as I don't need her watching the moment, I walk up behind Gabi as she pours a second cup of coffee, sliding it across the counter toward me. I kiss her temple, sliding one hand to her opposite hip.

"Kelly has invited us to breakfast with my parents," I say, watching her reaction carefully.

I am without a doubt *there*, but I don't know if Gabi is yet.

She turns to me, her eyes wide. "When?"

I shrug. "Like now. Or half an hour. Ish."

She nods and glances over her shoulder to where Kelly is no doubt eyeing us. "I would love to, but I *look* like I just spent my night fucking you."

"They're not all that formal. And besides, look at Kelly."

Gabi gives me a look and then nods. She bites her lip as she thinks. "You know what? I can wear yesterday's work shirt with the jeans I brought for tonight."

"Is that a yes?"

She nods, moving her hands in a circular motion like I'm going too slow for her. "Yes, that's a yes. But I need to get ready ASAP. Do you have a blow dryer?"

"Um, I think Kelly might have brought one here at some point."

She nods. "Okay. I need it, if you can find it. I'm just going to do some quick makeup and see if I can tame my hair before it dries in a rat's nest."

She takes a large sip of coffee and heads toward the stairs, on a mission.

And I end up rooting through my bathroom closet for a hair dryer my sister has probably only used once.

My sister, who sits smugly on the couch in her sweatpants with smudged makeup while my girlfriend is thrown into an early morning whirl trying to prepare for the breakfast my sister sprung on us last minute.

When I manage to find it, I hand it over to Gabi, who has it plugged in half a second later and directed toward her hair with one hand while trying and failing to do her makeup with the other.

"Here," I say, reaching for the hair dryer so I can take over. She gives me a small smile in the mirror as I run my fingers through her hair, doing my best to make up for the fact that I lack one of those prickly brushes.

When she's done with her makeup, she turns to leave a kiss on my chin. I turn off the hair dryer and leave it on the sink so I can wrap my arms around her.

"You look great," I say, leaving a kiss on her neck in that spot right below her ear.

She shivers at the touch. "Don't turn me on right now! I actually look halfway decent for meeting your parents."

"A little bit of sweat and mussed hair never hurt

anyone." I press into her, conveying to her *just* how good she looks.

She whirls away from me, pointing at me. "You stop." She rubs her hand over the spot I had my mouth on, her eyes closing for a second. "Or at least pause until afterward, okay?"

"Not fair. You get all dressed up and I can't even touch."

She smiles. "It's called patience, darling."

"Darling? Am I your darling now?"

She takes a step toward me, her hands on my waist as she leaves a kiss right on my chin.

"You're my everything."

Her words hit me like a punch straight to the gut.

You're my everything.

I lean down and kiss her, my heart swelling and a chill running down my spine when I feel her hands on my chest.

When my parents arrive, Kelly runs out to meet them at the car and no doubt announce that not only do I have company this morning, but I'm bringing my date to breakfast.

I can't wait to meddle in her life when she starts dating someone seriously. She gets to play the cute little sister role, but I bet all the meddling will ring differently when I get to play the scary older brother role.

Kelly brings them inside, my mom's red curls bouncing along after my sister's and my dad pushing his glasses up on his nose as he closes the door behind them. My mom unravels the scarf around her neck and my dad pulls his hat off, stuffing it into his pocket. They smile politely at us, waiting for introductions.

"Mom, Dad. This is Gabi," I say, the words so odd and unfamiliar on my tongue. I don't know if I've ever introduced a girl to my parents before. In high school, Marissa just kind of started hanging around one day.

After her, there wasn't anyone else to introduce.

"Nice to meet you," she says, shaking my dad's hand first, since he's closest.

He nods. "Pleased to meet you, Gabi."

My mom swoops in next. "Gabi, can I hug you?"

She laughs. "Of course."

"Don't overwhelm her, Stace."

My mom keeps Gabi in a hug a second longer than socially acceptable. "Oh she's fine, Pat."

"I'm fine!" Gabi agrees, but I make sure to double-check as we leave my apartment all bundled up like marshmallows against the January cold. We bring up the rear so I can lock up on my way out, and I take a moment to pull her close.

"You good?"

She nods, her scarf covering her mouth but her smile showing in her eyes nonetheless. "I like your family."

"Well, we'll see how you feel after breakfast."

She stands on her tiptoes to press a kiss to my cheek, and it's mostly scarf but nice regardless.

We walk down the street to the diner and slide into the same booth as last time, a large display case of pies towering over one side. Kelly has taken hold of the conversation, regaling us with the many ideas she has for her birthday in a few weeks. We'll do a family dinner that night, of course, but afterward she'll be out with her friends hitting the bars as a newly minted twenty-one-year-old. And I remind my dad when he fidgets uncomfortably across from me that I'll be around just in case.

"Be careful, okay?" he says to her.

She rolls her eyes. "I'm always careful. And when I'm not, I tell Zeke."

My mom snorts. "Just make sure you're respectful, Kelly. It's a new relationship."

Kelly scoffs. "I was pretty respectful last night."

"Kelly!" I scold as Gabi bursts into laughter. My dad's jaw drops as he turns his attention to the pies next to us and tries to hide his reaction. My mom grins, chewing on her lip, and I can so easily see the laughter she's suppressing for my benefit.

"I'm just saying, I came over looking to actually get some sleep."

"Kelly, so help me god, when you start dating someone, you're going to wish you knew how to keep your mouth shut."

"Oh, scary threat," she taunts.

The waitress comes over at that moment, searching for drink orders, and I order a Bloody Mary that I plan on not drinking and not sharing with Kelly.

My mom disentangles our conversation, asking Gabi what she does, who then launches into a full explanation of her day job. I gently remind her that she's opening a studio, and, cheeks pink, she adds that to her resume. My mom's eyebrows rise as she tacks on all of the things she's doing—working full time, opening the studio, 200-hour teacher training.

"How do you have time to sleep?"

"I don't think she does," Kelly quips, and I have to resist the urge to kick her under the table.

But breakfast goes on without a hiccup. Gabi fits easily within our family, like there was always a place for her. And afterward, when we're finally alone in my apartment, she's still smiling, like she feels it too.

35

ZEKE

G abi sits across from me at my kitchen island, our de facto assigned seats over the past few weeks. She frowns over something, her bottom lip caught between her teeth.

"What the fuck," she murmurs.

"What?"

"My insurance premium is due in a lump sum? I thought it was a monthly payment." She clicks around a few more times, shaking her head.

I close my laptop, focusing on the concerned expression on her face.

Gabi's refused my help every time I've offered, but this seems like a new level of panic.

She rests her head in her hands, breathing deeply.

"Gabi, can I please cover your premium?"

She lifts her head, glaring at me. "I can't run a business if I can't pay for insurance."

"And a lot of businesses don't magically have enough money to start with. You're essentially prepaying for a year of insurance, not just one month. I don't think it's that unreasonable to take a little help."

She shakes her head, her eyes stuck to her screen. "I'm already so far in, I can't back out now."

I pause. "You're not seriously considering abandoning all the work you've done because you have to pay a normal cost of operating a business, right?"

She shoots me a look. "Well when you say it that way, it sounds stupid. But in my head, this is an unforeseen expense that drastically alters every financial projection I've made."

I reach toward her and grab her hand, drawing her attention to me, and her face softens.

"I don't take handouts," she explains, her voice smaller. She shakes her head. "I mean, god, Dustin used to just hold *dinner* over my head—I can't be beholden to you. It's too much."

Her words inspire a nauseous feeling in my stomach. "Just when I thought I couldn't hate the guy more."

She winces. "He was not my best choice."

I stand and move around to the other side of the counter, pulling her into my chest.

"I get that what Dustin did has you hesitant. And I'm kind of relieved that you told me because I've been wondering why you're so anal about switching off who pays for food, but I won't ask you for anything in return. You can pay me back over time if you want, but I'd really like to help, you know? This contract I'm working on is a lot of money, and sometimes I wonder why I bother with it. It's a pain in the ass. But something like this, helping you get started? It's all worth it if I can do that."

Worth it a thousand times over.

She looks up at me, her face still filled with apprehension. "It makes me nervous."

"Everything makes you nervous."

She rolls her eyes at me. "I mean, you're not wrong. I just like you, you know? I don't want this to change things."

I shrug. "It won't change a thing for me. It might make me a little more grateful for Leanne, but it won't change anything for us."

"Are you sure?"

"Gabi, I've never had to beg someone to *give* them money."

She scrunches up her face. "I'm going to pay you back."

I raise an eyebrow. "Is that a yes?"

She nods. "Thank you, Zeke." She presses a kiss to my jaw and a sweeping sense of relief settles over me.

I write her a check and stuff it in her bag before she can protest. And then I treat her to dinner, accepting no objections.

FEBRUARY

36

GABI

January passes in a blur of checklists and working dates with Zeke.

The day before the studio opens, we split a bottle of wine on my couch, sharing the blanket he got me for Christmas, and watch the snow falling through the over-sized window. I snuggle into his shoulder, grateful for the bit of warmth he lends me. He keeps one hand on my knee, the other balancing his wineglass above the blanket. He leaves tomorrow, right after the opening, to finish up the last leg of his project in Virginia. He pushed it off as long as he could, but he'll start missing contracted deadlines if he waits any longer.

"So how does it feel?" His voice is low, the snow quieting my already calm apartment.

"How does what feel?"

"Running a yoga studio," he says, like it's the most obvious thing in the world.

We hadn't been talking about it. Rather, it was one of the few nights we *weren't* talking about it. Probably because there's nothing left to talk about.

All that's left is the doing—the walking to the studio tomorrow and the teaching and the kickoff of this thing I've been busting my ass for over the past two months.

"Overwhelming."

He squeezes me tighter, leaving a kiss on my temple. "Before you know it, it'll be second nature."

"A girl can dream," I say, pushing myself up so I can kiss him.

He pushes his tongue into my mouth, one arm weaving around my back and pulling me closer to him. "Mm, I've missed you," he says into my neck, nibbling on my skin. He sets his wineglass down on the table and turns back to me, his other arm weaving up into my hair as he leaves little kisses along my collarbone.

I run my hand up his arm, his muscles clenching beneath my touch, and I realize how distracted I've been lately, how removed I've been from our relationship despite being with Zeke all the time.

I've missed him, too. His kisses, the way he holds me, his lips on my neck and the way his body moves so perfectly with mine.

I pull on the hem of his shirt, lifting it above his head, and he throws it on the ground next to us. I run my hands over his strong chest, relishing in his warmth, in the way he grabs my hips, pressing us together.

He stands, lifting me with him, and my breath catches with the movement.

"I need you," he says, his voice low and his breath blowing hot against my neck as he carries me into my bedroom, throwing me down on top of the sheets and climbing on top of me.

I pull his mouth to mine, desperate for his kiss.

He complies, his body settling between my legs, his thick

length pressing into me as he pushes my shirt up, over my head. As he reaches behind me to pop the clasp of my bra. As he claws wildly at my leggings, throwing them to the ground.

"God, Gabi, I need you." He pulls away from me so I can undo the clasp of his jeans and push them down over his hips. He kisses me, then, while running his fingers along the edges of my underwear, slipping underneath just enough to feel the wetness pooling there and groaning in approval. He pulls them down, discarding them on the floor, and draws a slick line down my center, sending a shiver down my spine.

"Cold?" He has a wicked grin on his face.

"Just a little needy." I push his underwear down, pumping him, and he buries his face in the pillow over my shoulder, his breathing growing heavier.

"Fuck Gabi," he says, his voice low in my ear. He kisses my neck, his tongue leaving little spots of moisture along my skin that cool with his breath.

He palms my breast, rubbing my nipple between his fingers, and I arch up into him, pumping him faster as his hand trails down my stomach and pushes inside me. He moves languorously, providing friction on that sensitive spot in just the perfect way.

If he's not careful I'm going to come before he's even inside me.

"Zeke," I moan, as he leans into me, taking a nipple into his mouth.

"Hmm?"

"I need you to fuck me."

He groans, snapping to attention and settling himself between my legs. He positions himself at my entrance and moves slowly up and down, teasing me.

"Zeke," I moan, shimmying my hips down in an attempt to get him inside me faster.

"Yes, Gabi?" He circles my clit and my hips rock up, desperate for him.

"Zeke, fuck me."

"Your wish," he says, finally pushing inside me, and causing a gasp to jump from my throat, "is my command."

He kisses me as he moves, his tongue tangling with mine as he buries himself inside me again and again. He slips his arm behind me, pulling my chest to his. He grunts into my neck, and my hands roam his body, desperate for more of him. I kiss his neck, his chest, his mouth, as he thrusts into me harder and harder.

"Fuck, Gabi, you feel unreal."

"Zeke, I'm going to…"

"Wait for me, Gabi. Come with me."

But I'm unraveling beneath him as he picks up speed, his arm clamping me to him as he pushes deeper, harder, and I go over the edge.

"Fuck, Gabi, I love you."

He jerks into me as I process his words, the weight of them only hitting me after a few seconds. I watch him in surprise as he collapses into me.

Surprise, but not fear.

I think I've loved him for a long time.

"Fuck, Gabi," he mutters, as he finishes and relaxes into my neck. "Jesus, I'm sorry, you don't have to say it back. I got swept up." He shakes his head. "Oh man, just keep swimming."

I grab his face with my hands, looking into his eyes, and he looks away, embarrassed.

"I love you too."

He kisses me lightly, his hand weaving up into my hair again.

"And uh, did you just quote Dory?"

He scrunches up his face. "Yeah, that happened. Like I said, swept up."

I laugh, kissing his cheeks and his forehead and his mouth.

"I love you," I repeat.

"Gabi, I love you *so* much. And god, I've been waiting to say that for so long."

"Aw, Zeke." I press another kiss to his cheek before he rolls gently away from me, and I head into the bathroom to clean up.

When I come back out, he pulls me back down into bed.

"You are something else, Gabi," he says, pulling me in close and wrapping his arms around me. "You are absolutely perfect."

He kisses my neck, my cheek, my shoulder, and I turn to him, burying myself in his chest. He holds me there, and I don't think there's a place in this world I'd rather be than right here in his arms.

We lie like that for a long time, bodies intertwined, and just when I'm about to nod off, he speaks.

"I love you, Gabi. You're going to do so well tomorrow."

I WAKE up with an odd mix of emotions—elation, love, apprehension. Zeke snores gently next to me, and I sneak out of bed early to make pancakes before my big day.

I start the coffee and while it's brewing, I look out the window at the snow.

... And it's still falling.

Wasn't that supposed to stop last night?

I grab my phone and check the weather, and see that they extended the expected duration of this storm for the rest of the day.

Fuck. Is this going to impact my opening?

I'm counting on money from drop-ins today, from monthly pass sign-ups.

I can't get snowed out today.

I eye the check sitting on my kitchen table. *I will not use you.* I managed to cover my insurance premium without using it, but I'm toeing a dangerous line. I *need* people to buy monthly passes today or I'll have no choice but to deposit that money.

I take a deep breath and stir the batter for the pancakes. This has to be a good morning. Zeke told me he loved me last night. I can't let apprehension over the studio affect our relationship. I can't let snow fuck up my opening.

Power through, Gabi. All will work out.

My body buzzes as I cook.

Zeke loves me.

The snow is falling.

The pancakes are... *fuck, burning!*

I grab the pan and slide them off, giving my heartbeat a second to calm down. I shake my head and start over, taking a few deep breaths and trying to focus myself.

If there's ever a day I need yoga, it's today.

I stand in front of the stove this time, watching them with a hawk eye. When they're perfectly golden brown, I slide them off onto a plate and throw them on the kitchen table. I wash some fruit and pour two mugs of coffee when I hear Zeke stirring in the bedroom.

He's wearing only sweatpants when he joins me in the kitchen, and for a moment I totally forget about my nerves. He looks so good—his abs on display, his pants hanging low on his hips, the sleep still in his eyes. He shuffles toward me and, with one hand on my hip, kisses my cheek.

"Smells delicious," he says, his eyes wandering over the food I set out. I hand him his coffee, knowing that's what he really wants, and we sit at the table, that check taking up an inordinate amount of space for something that's ultimately a third of a piece of paper.

I notice him eyeing the window.

"Snow's a bit heavy," he mentions, pulling his phone out of his pocket and, no doubt, checking the weather. He looks up at me, concern in his eyes. "It's supposed to snow all day."

I nod. "I know."

He swallows, and I can hear the words he's about to say before they're out of his mouth. "Should you reschedule the opening?"

I'm shaking my head before he finishes speaking. "I can't. I have teacher training next weekend—I have to at least do the first couple of classes myself before handing it over to another teacher."

He glances at the big window again. "I guess most people are going to be local, right?"

Today is mostly friends, really. Gemma, Natalie, Annabel, Steph, Kelly, Corinne, and a couple of their friends. All are coming from within the city, most from this neighborhood.

"Yeah, they're almost all local."

He nods, but his face betrays some lingering uncertainty. "I wouldn't be surprised if you got some cancellations."

I hold my hand up. "Do *not* will it into existence."

He raises his eyebrows. "I just want you to be prepared if it happens."

I nod. "If something goes wrong, I'll deal with it when it happens. I don't need to be thinking of worst-case scenarios all morning."

He bites his lip, nodding. "Okay."

I hand him a pancake, and he bites into it ravenously, holding it like a heathen with one hand.

He leans over, the pancake nearly flopping over to the table as he kisses my cheek. "You're going to do great today."

"Thank you."

Throughout the course of the morning, Zeke sets up his laptop at the kitchen table and works, and I run through an accelerated version of the class I'm teaching. The snow is unrelenting, and I have to fight to keep ahold of my anxiety.

An hour before I have to leave, I check my phone.

Steph can't make it because the buses have stopped running.

Corinne, for the same reason.

But that's okay—if it's just the two of them who can't make it, that's still a full class. And everyone else is closer—walking distance, really. And where buses can't drive, a city girl can walk.

I take a shower and put on my favorite pair of black leggings and a cutoff shirt. Zeke grins when I step into the kitchen, looking me up and down.

"You look good," he says as I gather my bag and start layering on all of the clothes I'll need to make it through the snow.

"Thank you."

I check my phone again before leaving.

Annabel can't make it now, either. I guess that's to be expected, though, since she's coming from Center City.

But the girls in the neighborhood will still be there—Gemma, Natalie, Kelly.

I take a deep breath before heading out into the cold.

"I'll come pick you up in an hour," Zeke says, planting a kiss on my cheek.

I shake my head. "Stay here. It's cold out. I'll be fine getting home."

He raises his eyebrows. "I kinda wanted to see you after your first day."

I stand on my tiptoes to kiss his cheek. "That's sweet of you, but I was hoping maybe you'd warm me up after my walk and that won't really be possible if you're freezing, too."

He considers this. "Okay, I'll wait here and have a hot cup of tea ready for you. Does that sound good?"

I nod. "Thank you, Zeke."

The snow falls in thick flakes as I walk out into the courtyard. It sticks to my jacket and my hat, and after only a short distance, my feet are freezing cold.

But I have a studio to run.

I trudge down street after street, one of only a few people trekking out in the snow. I pass a group of kids throwing snowballs at each other a few blocks beyond my apartment and ignore the one that narrowly misses my face.

When I get to the studio, I wipe my feet on the mat outside the door and head up to the second-floor space.

I spent some time up here cleaning over the past few days, and the lavender scent of the product I used lingers. I tuck my snowy shoes into a cubby by the door and throw my coat on the rack. I pull the curtain from the window and eye the storm.

The snow is still heavy.

I check my phone. Gemma won't be able to make it.

My chest grows tighter. This is going to be a class of four

or five people. Natalie is bringing her sister, who's visiting for a few days so their sons can hang out. Kelly is bringing a couple of her friends, though I'm not sure how many since we've been communicating through Zeke.

But a class of four or five is still solid. It's intimate. Caring. If anything, they'll leave feeling like they were given individual attention.

I can work with that.

But as it gets closer to class time, I start getting worried.

Natalie is usually early since her timekeeping is a little chaotic and she chooses to be a little too early rather than a little too late. And Kelly—well, she's in college. Maybe she's on college time.

But when I check my phone again, I see a text from Zeke.

> ZEKE
>
> Hey, Kelly said she can't make it. She and her roommate got halfway down the block before her roommate slipped and landed pretty hard on her tailbone.

But did she die?

I might die if Natalie and her sister don't show up.

What was I thinking, trying to proceed with this grand opening while the weather is so blustery?

I was thinking I've sunk a hell of a lot of time and money into this and there's no way I'm pushing it another two weeks if that means having to deposit Zeke's check.

> GABI
>
> Okay

Start time creeps closer, and I begin hoping that Natalie and her sister *don't* show up. A class of two people? I don't know if I can do that. I can with Natalie and Gemma, in the confines of my apartment, but boasting a grand opening to the world and then only leading two people?

I'll be a laughingstock.

Better for everyone to think they were the only ones who canceled, that this whole thing went on without a hitch regardless of their absence.

Maybe I'll just take out another credit card this week and make Zeke think the same.

Maybe this is for the best. Maybe this is just an indication that this isn't going to work out.

Maybe this is the universe telling me to cut my losses while I can.

I look around at all the hard work I put in, at the invisible lists hidden within the walls of this studio. The cleaning supplies and the brand-new mats and the logo Annabel designed for me. The website Zeke created.

I'm about to start packing up my things when the door bursts open.

"Sorry we're late! Man, that snow." Natalie walks in, her voice quiet, followed by a woman who looks just like her, if not a couple years older. They both have that big, curly hair and wide smile.

I swallow over the lump in my throat.

"No problem!" I say, heading across the room to my mat.

"Is it just us?" Natalie asks, eyeing the room.

I nod. "Just a soft launch today. Thanks, Snow, you asshole," I joke.

Natalie laughs, but I see her eyeing me as she and her sister get situated, taking off layers of clothing and rolling out their mats.

I focus all of my energy on the anxiety pulsing through

my veins, on quieting the voices in my head telling me to stop and back away from the yoga mat.

Two people.

Two people.

What a fucking joke.

37

ZEKE

I can tell she's upset by her terse texts. I *knew* she was going to be upset the second I saw the snow through the window this morning. The moment she loudly exclaimed "fuck!" and threw what I could only imagine–judging by the delicious smell–were her signature pancakes in the trash.

I told her to cancel, and she insisted on going through with it.

But where there's snow, there are cancellations. Delays. People get crabby and traffic gets slow and nothing goes quite as you'd expect it to.

So when I have to tell her that Kelly can't make it, I'm sure it only rubs salt in the wound. I hate that it's coming from me and not Kelly, but they never got a chance to trade numbers, so I get to be the bad guy who has to inform Gabi that her grand opening will be smaller than expected.

I settle into Gabi's couch, my feet on the coffee table in front of me and my computer propped in my lap. I'm going through my materials for this week, making sure I have all of my ducks in a row before going down to Virginia so I can zip through my plan, get everyone trained in every way that I need to, and get the hell back here as quickly as possible.

It's not ideal that my final week in Virginia happens to fall during Gabi's first week of running the studio, but it's the only timing that made sense. I've pushed this week as long as I possibly could so I could help Gabi with whatever setup stuff she needs. I know she can run shit. She can do the yoga and coordinate and take all of the pieces she's created and turn them into a functioning business, but the process was hard on her. She doubted herself and I wanted to be there for her until the moment the switch flipped. Until she could click into the part of it that she knows and loves and doesn't have to focus on the stressful *before* stage any longer.

But I guess I didn't prepare for snow either, because until now, I was fully expecting Gabi to come back from her very first class elated.

Now I'm not so sure. Her short response has me spiraling. *Did people show up? Is she okay? Does the lack of a period at the end of her text mean she's waiting for me to say something to close out the thought?*

I put my phone down. She needs to concentrate, and she's *probably* not mad at me.

Probably.

But just as I get back into my project plan, I hear a key in the door. It jiggles a bit, like whoever is on the other side isn't as familiar with the door as Gabi.

It takes me a second to realize it's probably Steph, coming to water the plants.

But... Steph should be at yoga.

I push my laptop onto the coffee table and stand, my eyes on the door as I take a hesitant step forward.

When the door swings open, it's someone I don't recognize.

Red, puffy coat. Sunken, foggy eyes. He doesn't seem to notice me standing across the room from him.

An intense sort of rage pulses through me as I realize this must be Dustin, and this is not the first time he's done this. That night when Annabel called me and told me to rush back here—he was never after Gabi at all, but her money. The collapsed shelf in her coat closet that had me thinking all of her purses and coats were really *that* heavy. The knocked over plant that we so willingly attributed to hastily removed clothing.

It was all Dustin. Breaking in here and stealing from her.

"What the fuck do you think you're doing?" The timbre of my voice surprises even me.

He jumps, his attention snapping toward me.

"I just left something," he says, motioning to the coat closet.

"I don't think you fucking did."

He has the audacity to ignore me, to continue toward the coat closet, where he rips open the door and starts pawing through her shit.

"What the fuck, man. Get out." I'm across the apartment in seconds and grab ahold of his collar, tugging him back.

And he's surprisingly light. The puffy jacket makes him look bulky, but I feel like I'm tugging on nothing but air. The glassy look in his eye as he swings around and struggles to land a punch on my cheek has me thinking that whatever he's on right now is probably the reason he's so skinny. The reason he's breaking into Gabi's apartment like a fucking lunatic.

I ignore the ghost of a punch and drag him into the hallway, only realizing then that kicking him out doesn't exactly do much if he has a copy of the key.

"Give me your key," I say, pausing at the top of the stairs and vaguely considering throwing him down them.

But the last thing Gabi needs right now is a dead ex and a murderer boyfriend.

Morally, though, I'd be delighted to see his skull explode along the staircase.

"Fuck off," he spits, trying to twist away from me, but I still have that iron grip on his collar.

"Give me your key or I'll take it from your broken body after you hit the last stair."

I fix him with a scowl.

He shakes his head, still struggling to pull out of my grasp. But his movements are slow, and instead of waiting for him to make the right decision, I reach into his pocket and grab the key myself.

I just hope this is the only copy he made.

I'm about to threaten him again when a door opens behind me. "Everything okay?"

No, buddy, everything is not okay.

I ignore the voice and instead turn to Dustin. "If I ever fucking see you again, you're dead. Got it?"

He only glares back at me, and a second later when I finally let go of his collar, he scrambles down the stairs, the door at the bottom clanging shut behind him.

I take a deep breath, running my hands over my face and turning back to Gabi's open door.

Her neighbor, a slightly older man with a graying mustache and a large stomach hidden behind a velvety gray robe, eyes me. "Are you okay?"

I nod. "Do you have the number for building management? Fucker copied her key."

"Gabi's?"

I nod.

He shakes his head. "She's a nice girl. She doesn't deserve that." He lets out a long breath. "I'll get you that number."

38

GABI

Natalie and her sister give me quick hugs before they leave, bundling up in their coats and snow boots and gliding down the stairs without a care in the world. Natalie makes a point to tell me I fixed the place up nicely, and her sister thanks me profusely for extending the invitation to her.

And all of it feels so contrived.

This isn't a grand opening—it's a death march.

I clean up, putting the candle back in the closet and running the Swiffer over the wet footprints. I hit the lights, lock the doors, and head down to the street.

The courtyard is empty, but of course now it's stopped snowing.

A bus blazes by on the street outside the fence.

I shake my head, stomping through the snow to the gate.

I nearly scream out into the quiet white abyss.

Fuck you, snow, you bitch.

I unlatch the gate and step out onto the sidewalk. Someone has shoveled, and I hate them for it.

I relish the cold while I walk, desperate for something

just as bitter and angry as I am. I dare the snow to bite my toes, to jump higher than my boots and soak my leggings just so I have something to be angrier about, just so that fiery rage inside of me has something to melt.

It's all my fault, really. I put myself in an impossible position. I made bad financial decisions. I pushed through this thing that I wasn't ready for, and I created a mess out of everything I cared about in life.

Will I ever be able to do yoga again without thinking of this day?

I put in all of the work to make this dream a reality, and the universe swooped in and said, "nah, we're going with bad luck today."

Because no matter how hard I try, and no matter how much thought and strategy I put into this, it really all just comes down to luck.

I shake my head as I push through the gate of my apartment. My toes are numb and my fingers—despite being shoved deep into my pockets—are following suit. My face hurts and I can't tell if it's the cold that's inspiring tears to drip from my eyes or if it's emotions, but either way it's happening, and I swear they're turning to icicles on my cheeks.

I don't know what to say to Zeke when I get back. I haven't cashed his check yet, but after today, I'll probably need to. I have another class tomorrow that I'm expecting will be no better, and after that I'll be paying instructors to come in and teach classes that don't even pay for an hour of the instructors' time until I'm done with teacher training and can do them all myself.

Which I'll have to, if today is any indication of the level of demand for these classes. If only two people are showing up, this thing is destined to fail. There's no amount of strategy that can dig me out of this hole.

And Zeke put just as much into this as I did. And I took the end product and made a fucking mockery of all of our work. All of *his* work.

I don't know if I can tell him how terribly I failed.

I don't know if I can take the embarrassment.

Maybe I can find a way to float for a few months, surreptitiously make some deal with the landlord to get out of the lease. Maybe I'll look back on this time in a few years and laugh at how disastrous it was.

Maybe one day it will just be a silly story.

Right now, it feels like I'm dying.

Which I know is my anxiety talking, but it doesn't make this feeling any less real.

I can hardly catch my breath as I scale the stairs to the second floor, and I have to quiet the part of me that's saying it's because I'm having a heart attack. More than likely, it's because I power walked home during a blizzard and my lungs are just a little overworked.

I take a deep breath at my door, still unsure what I'm going to tell Zeke, and push inside my apartment.

Only to see four people sitting around my kitchen table—Zeke, two police officers, and Brian from next door, dressed in his typical uniform of a bathrobe and slippers.

I stop in my tracks, searching their faces for an answer as each of them turns toward me.

Zeke is standing a second later, rushing around the table and immediately wrapping me in a gigantic hug.

"How did it go?" he asks.

"Uh, fine," I say, unzipping my jacket and dropping my bag on the floor next to the door. "What's going on?"

"Hi Gabi, nice to see you," Brian says, giving me a small wave.

"Hi," I say, copying his movement and feeling incredibly weird about it. "Nice to see you, too."

Zeke puts his hands on my shoulders, and only then do I see the cuts on his face. I reach up, running my thumb over his cheek. "What happened?"

His eyebrows crinkle, and his hands follow the path mine took across his skin.

"Zeke," I say, my anxiety increasing exponentially as I put together one piece after another.

Did he get in a fight with Bathrobe Brian?

No, no, no. They wouldn't be sitting so civilly across the table from one another if they got in a fight.

But *something* must have happened.

"What's going on?" I ask, as Zeke directs me to the chair he was sitting in. The movement only makes my heart thump faster.

"Dustin broke in," he says, kneeling on the ground next to me like I'm a toddler he's breaking bad news to. Like I'm some delicate thing that might crack into pieces. He grips my hand as he speaks. "And you can tell me if I'm wrong about this, but I'm pretty sure the broken shelving in your coat closet was his doing. The knocked over plant, too. And I'm fairly certain that night when he was outside your apartment, he wasn't looking for you. He was hoping to slip into your apartment and steal from you unnoticed. But you interrupted him."

I blink at him, and then turn to the rest of the people at my kitchen table.

A mix of emotions flows through me. A minute ago, I was falling apart over my professional failures.

But this is something totally different. My safe space has been forever compromised.

I've been walking around my apartment without concern for so long, just puttering about life thinking no one could touch me here.

And all of that is suddenly shattered.

I swallow over the lump building in my throat. "What happened to your face, though?"

Zeke shakes his head. "He punched me. Twice. I honestly didn't think it was hard enough to leave a mark but maybe I was running on a little more adrenaline than I thought."

"He punched you?"

Now the anger is flowing. *How dare he. How dare he do that to someone so good. How dare he break in here and attack someone like Zeke.*

I don't realize I'm saying these things aloud until Zeke wraps his arms around me. He kisses my temple and holds me tight, and after a second I start feeling guilty for not only ruining the thing we've both worked so hard for over the last few months, but also being the reason he got punched.

I am the reason all of these bad things happen to Zeke Morgan.

"Gabi, it's okay," he says, and now I feel guilty for being the one needing comfort when *he's* the one who got punched.

"It is so *not* okay."

He brushes my hair behind my ear. "Look, they want me to come down to the police station so they can take pictures of--" He gestures to his face. "If you can come with me, I'll get you all set up at my apartment afterward, okay?"

I nod. "Yeah, okay."

But in my head, I'm asking him what happens after that.

What happens when he leaves for Virginia? Do I just stay at his apartment indefinitely?

I don't think I'm ready for that. Especially since he doesn't know just how miserably today went. I'll feel like I'm squeezing him for all he's worth, taking what I can get from him and leaving him high and dry when I can't give anything back. I'm running on fumes right now, financially and emotionally.

Bathrobe Brian clears his throat. "I'll keep an eye on your apartment while you're not here. I got a good look at him, so I'll let you know if he tries anything further. I'm happy to poke my head in every once in a while if you'd like, but you let me know what you're comfortable with."

Zeke smiles at him. "Thank you."

"Thank you," I say, but the words feel meaningless as I say them.

Zeke shows the three of them out after getting Brian's phone number and promising the police officers he'll meet them at the station shortly.

And then he pulls up a chair next to me, gathering my hands in his. "Are you okay?"

I nod. "I think I'm a little dumbstruck."

"I figured you would be. And I hate to pile it all on you today, of all days, but I did something that you might be a little angry with me for before I called the cops."

I blink. *There's more to this?* "What?"

He watches my face as he speaks, the little slice of blood on his chin distracting me. "I called your landlord and broke your lease."

I pause. "You what?"

He shrugs. "And I'm sorry. I'm really sorry because I know I stepped out of bounds, but Gabi, you can't stay here. And I was scared that you would come up with some reasoning in your head where it's okay to stay here because Dustin isn't a *threat* or he's not *violent* or something. But Gabi, he thinks of this apartment as fair game, and as long as he's on whatever he's on, and as long as he thinks he can get away with it, he will continue doing this. And I can't handle the thought of you getting hurt in the process."

"You––" I shake my head, not fully believing what he's telling me. "You can't *do* that."

"I know. And I wanted to tell you now in case you wanted to punch me too because it might make me feel a little better, honestly, and it'll just create more evidence for the police report."

I stare at him. "I mean, yes, you overstepped, but how did you even do it? You can't break my lease––you're not on it."

He shrugs. "Money."

"You paid off my landlord to break my lease early?"

"Yup. Sent it to him with Venmo already so it's not negotiable. Which––if I'm being honest––I did because I knew you could convince me not to and I felt very strongly at the time that the only possible response to this is to get you out of here. Now I'm questioning it, because you're more important to me than anything and I'm terrified you're going to tell me to kick rocks because of it, but I do still feel a little right in doing it because even if you *do* tell me to kick rocks, at least you still have to leave your apartment."

"Zeke," I say flatly.

He winces. "I'm sorry," he repeats.

I stare at him.

"Gabi, I'm really sorry."

I shake my head. "I just don't know where I'm going to live."

I don't have money. The studio is a failure. And now I'm homeless.

What the fuck.

"With me," he says automatically, and my heart starts thumping again.

I shake my head. "Zeke, we haven't known each other long enough."

"Temporarily," he corrects. "We don't even have to call it living. You'll stay with me until you find a place to live. Crash with me, even. Hell, you can stay in Kelly's room if you want, and she can have my bed if and when she needs it, and I'll go sleep on the couch, if that makes it easier for you. I'm not trying to trick you into living with me––that will come in time, if and when we decide to do that. I'm just trying to keep you safe."

Fuck, why is this man so sweet?

I shake my head. "Okay," I say, this one little word holding so much meaning that it's kind of hard to process what I'm agreeing to.

He takes a deep breath. "Alright, this is your last chance." He motions to his face. "Wanna take a hit? Give me all you've got. Thumb out, though––I don't need to add an emergency room trip to this day."

I give him a look. "I'm not going to punch you."

"You'd be justified."

I lean forward and kiss his cheek. "No, I wouldn't."

He lets out a long breath and scoots his chair closer so he can hug me. "I'm sorry," he says into my ear, his voice low.

"You can stop saying sorry now," I say, leaning into his warmth, the comfort of his hug.

"Not for the breaking your lease thing. Just for... all of today. I'm sorry."

It feels like he knows how terribly yoga went. How upset I was before I even got to my apartment.

"Thank you for being here."

He shakes his head, his skin warm against my neck. "I'm so fucking thankful that I was the one who was here and not you. I just... I can't even imagine."

"I'm kind of terrified that you were here without me."

He pulls away from me, a smile coming to his face for the first time since I got back. "You were scared that I was here alone?"

I nod. "Well, of course."

"Were you going to break out some of those sick yoga moves on him, protect your man?"

I roll my eyes. "I don't know if I could have helped but I would have tried."

He grins at me. "*You* probably wouldn't have hesitated to throw him down the stairs."

"You almost threw him down the stairs?"

He grimaces. "I was fucking *angry*. But something in my gut told me that was the wrong move." He sighs. "I don't know. He seemed delicate. Like that might actually end him. And as much as I wanted to, it wasn't worth not being here for you."

"Aw, you chose not to commit murder for me? How sweet."

Now it's his turn to roll his eyes.

"Come on, Gabs." He stands, holding his hand out to me. "I already packed you a bag. Let's get out of here."

39

ZEKE

abi seems remarkably fine considering the events of the day. I thought for sure there'd be tears, or at least some nervous shaking or something that could be considered a freakout.

But she sits with me in the police station where they walk us through filing a police report, which is kind of ridiculous because while I endured two punches from the guy, Gabi took years of emotional abuse and likely has some sort of PTSD because of it. But because she doesn't have a stupid mark on her face, she gets swept under the rug and forgotten. Again.

When we get back to my apartment, we fight to take care of each other. I want her to sit down on the couch and have a cup of tea, but she wants me to sit on the edge of the bathtub so she can rub Neosporin on two cuts that aren't really deep enough to warrant it.

Eventually, we settle on the couch, me holding her tea while she dabs at my face. I wrap her in every blanket I own, but she still looks cold.

Or maybe I'm just feeling inadequate for her right now and anything I try to do or give her won't be enough.

Maybe I'm expecting emotion from her where there is none. Maybe this is the unfortunate aftermath of her relationship with Dustin, that even when he ultimately breaks into her apartment, it doesn't affect her as much as I expect it to because to her, that's just *him*. Maybe she still doesn't believe that he's capable of violence. Maybe she still thinks of him as an annoyance rather than a big fucking problem.

But maybe that's a good thing. Sure, she could call the landlord and reverse everything if she wanted to, but that would mean I'm out that money. And I know how she feels about taking my money, and I would bet loads more of it that she wouldn't do that.

Am I a manipulative asshole? Possibly. Is she safer because of my manipulative assholery? Definitely.

So I'm not going to bring it up. I'm not going to make her think that her emotional response isn't enough or that she's being too calm about a situation that she should be freaking out about. I'm going to follow her lead. I already took the action that needed to be taken, so it really doesn't matter how she processes today's events.

All that matters is that she's okay. She's safe here.

I pull her into my chest, pushing her tea into her hands. I realized when we got here that I don't have one of those electric kettle things, so I heated up water for her in the microwave while ordering one off Amazon that'll get here tomorrow. I feel bad that she's drinking subpar tea, but it's the best I can do for her right now.

She doesn't seem to mind though. She sips it daintily, leaving it on one of my Europe coasters after she winces at the temperature.

"Hey, don't you have to leave soon?" she asks.

I shake my head, pulling the blanket higher over her. "No, I'll cancel it. Or go next week or something."

"Zeke," she says, looking at me.

"Gabi," I parrot.

"You have to do your job."

I laugh. "I'm literally my own boss. I can do what I want."

She huffs. "You know that's not really true. You have to finish out this contract."

"I will. Just... another time."

She turns toward me, resting a hand on my abdomen. All of my brain power focuses on her touch. "I don't want you to push this off for me. I'll be fine."

"Gabi, your ex broke into your apartment today. I'm not about to just *leave* you."

She takes another hesitant sip of her tea. "But I'm okay. And I don't want to fuck up your work for you. I'll feel bad."

"Don't feel bad. You're more important."

She lets out a long breath, biting her lip. "I want you to go."

I narrow my eyes. "You want me to go, like, you want me to go to work as planned and finish out the contract or you want me to... not be *here*?"

She looks away, and for a second I wonder if I actually did push her too far.

"Both."

I shake my head. "What?"

"My anxiety is at a high level right now, and you being here is going to––one––make me more anxious because I feel like I'm negatively impacting your life, and––two––I can't always process things when people are around. Like my attention goes to them instead of what's going on in my head, and I know that it's not the most healthy coping mechanism but I think I need to be alone for a little bit. Not to mention, I'm all up in your space and that's going to make me more anxious too. Like, this isn't just me staying the night––this is me *staying*. And I'm suddenly self-conscious about everything. About where I leave my shoes and my hair in the drain and leaving too many blankets on your couch. And a couple days to get used to the space alone will give me time to get used to it. And clean, before you're back." She shakes her head. "Like a cat, you know? You're supposed to leave them alone in one room for a week and eventually, once they're comfortable, their curiosity drives them out."

I stare at her.

I don't know what to make of any of this.

"Are you making things up just to get me to leave?"

She presses her lips together. "I'm trying to be very honest about the way my mind works and what I need after a stressful day. Your coping mechanisms are different than mine, and that's okay. I'm advocating for myself right now. Advocating for what I need." She sighs. "And I need things to continue as if today didn't happen. So I can feel like I'm clicking back into my life rather than spiraling. And part of that is not feeling like a disruption to your life, because I care about you and what you want." She swallows. "I don't want to be another person who stands in the way of your dreams."

I pause, a little piece of the puzzle clicking together. "Gabi, I already have the dream."

"And it can all fall apart at any second."

I search her face for some hidden meaning.

"How did yoga go today?"

She shrugs, reaching for her tea again. "It went fine. It was like any other class."

"How do you feel about it?"

She takes another small sip and then rests the mug back on the coaster. "Honestly, Zeke? Yoga is the last thing on my mind right now." She won't look at me.

"I can't tell whether you're deflecting because you had a stressful day or because it didn't go well."

"Zeke. It went fine. Okay?"

"Why won't you talk to me?"

"Zeke! Please. Can you just sit with me?"

"Can't you see why I wouldn't want to leave you when you say things like that?"

She runs her hand over her face, and when it drops to her lap, I see a glisten in her eyes.

Fuuuuuuck. Nonononono.

"Gabi," I say, instantly mad at myself for pushing her. I wrap my arms around her and tug her into my chest again, and a second later, the most delicate sob escapes her.

Fuck, this one's all my fault.

"Gabi, I'm sorry. I'm really, really sorry. Whatever you want. You want me to leave? I'll leave. You want me to sign over my apartment to you? Sure. You want to come to Virginia with me and spend all week eating shitty room service while I work? That's fine too. I don't know what to do in this situation but you're right––I should listen to you when you tell me what you need."

"I'm sorry," she grumbles into my chest. She lifts her head, and I immediately wipe the tears away. The tears that were my fault. *Fuck.*

She was doing fine until I started poking at her.

"Don't be sorry. I'm sorry. Tell me what you need and I'll do it."

"I want you to continue as if nothing happened."

I swallow over the lump in my throat and let out a long breath. "Okay."

40

GABI

"Every particle of my being is telling me not to leave right now," he says, his duffel bag hanging from one hand, his computer bag from the other. "I'm fine. I promise."

He swallows. "You're not scared to be alone? You're not waiting for me to leave so you can go hide in my closet?"

I give him a look. "If I decide that I'd like to hide in your closet, I reserve the right to do so."

He's quiet for a second. "I put the laundry basket in the bathroom and threw a spare pillow on the ground where it was. Just in case."

Why are you so sweet when I'm so crazy?

The edge of his mouth ticks into the most hesitant smile, and it nearly makes my whole strong facade crumble in a second.

"Thank you."

"But don't stay in there all night, okay? Call me if you're scared and I'll be back here as fast as my car can drive."

"I know, Zeke. Thank you." I stand on my toes to kiss his

cheek, and he takes the opportunity to wrap an arm around me and press his lips against mine.

"Are you sure you don't want me to stay?"

"I want you to go finish out your contract so you can come back to me."

He nods, letting out a long breath as he turns toward the door. "Okay. I will go close everything out, but please––please, Gabi––let me know the second you might need me. It's a long drive but I'm happy to make it. At any time, okay?"

"I know. Thank you, Zeke."

He looks at me once more, his eyes filled with uncertainty and maybe a hint of longing, before turning on his heel and disappearing through the front door.

And I am suddenly alone.

I let out a long breath as I round the counter to Zeke's fridge and pull out a bottle of white wine. I pour myself a tall glass and bring the bottle with me to the couch. I flip on the TV and throw my feet on the coffee table, but I don't bother changing the channel. I know I won't be paying any attention to it anyway.

I suck down half the glass when I sit and top it off afterward. If I don't finish the glass, it doesn't count as one, right?

Right, Gabi.

The last twelve hours have been a whirlwind, and I'm not sure how to make sense of it in my mind.

My dream, cut off below the knees.

My apartment and my sense of safety, *poof* in a cloud of smoke.

Zeke, gone to Virginia. By my own insistence.

But I can't think when he's around. I want to be near him and talk to him and lean on him, but I don't even know how I feel about *him* right now. I mean, breaking my lease *is* overstepping a boundary, even if it's one that makes total sense. I agree with the sentiment, but I'm not sure I agree with the execution.

But it's better than being at my apartment. It's not like Dustin knows where I am now, and as much as I'd like to think the latch on my door would keep him out, it doesn't mean I'd feel *safe* if he showed up. Here, there's a long hallway outside Zeke's door that leads to the front entrance. Fewer people coming and going, and almost all of the neighbors familiar, if not friendly.

I take another thirsty sip of wine.

When I check my phone, I see Zeke texted me before he left.

ZEKE

I love you Gabi. And I'll be back as fast as I can. Let me know if you need me.

GABI

I love you too. I'm fine. Thank you for everything you've done for me.

I guzzle more wine, topping off my glass as I navigate into my email to see what my sign-ups are looking like for tomorrow and the couple of classes through the week. I'm not expecting much, considering I just opened and I was expecting to tell people in person to sign up online to ensure they have a spot.

But it looks like overfilled classes won't be an issue. No one has signed up at all.

I go ahead and cancel the class.

I shake my head, downing more wine and sinking further into the couch.

It's only when I throw my phone to the other end of the couch and stare directly into my wine that I let the tears fall. Zeke caught a few of them, probably not realizing they were mostly for the studio and not because I was scared. He thinks I'm scared of everything. Afraid to exist in my own space.

I guess in some ways, I am. But I could care less about my apartment. About Dustin, even if he is a problem.

I take big gulping sips of wine as I try continually to swallow over the lump in my throat.

Am I being self-destructive? Yes. But no one can see me so it's not really happening.

Except after two glasses... ish, and what has to have been two or three dumb sitcoms I've paid absolutely no attention to, I hear a key in Zeke's door.

My heart drops, and I instantly go into panic mode. My eyes roam the living room, searching for places to hide or weapons to throw, but I find myself painfully still. Like I have the urge to move, but I can't make any of the normal muscle movements happen.

And then I clock the red hair coming through the door.

"Fuck," I say, instantly collapsing back into the couch and throwing my arm over my face.

"Jeez, what are you doing sitting in the dark like this?" Kelly asks, throwing the lights on as she passes through the kitchen to the living room. Her eyes pause as they land on the wine, and then flick to my face. "You're sad," she deadpans.

I shake my head. "I'm fine."

"You're literally crying."

"You scared me."

She pops a hip, raising one eyebrow, and then gestures vaguely in my direction. "I'm not an idiot, Gabi. That's a blubber sort of cry. And for Christ's sake, you need a tissue." She grabs the roll of paper towels from the kitchen island and winds her way around the coffee table, sitting down on the couch next to me. She rips one off and hands it to me. Her voice is softer when she speaks again. "What's going on?"

I shake my head. I will not lose my shit to Zeke's little sister. "I just had a bad day."

She nods. "Zeke told me."

"He told you?"

"Yeah, he asked if I could pretend I was drunk and stumble in later tonight to make sure you were okay. I told him to shove it and let me handle it."

I snort as I wipe the tears away on a very uncomfortable paper towel. "Very on brand, for both of you."

"Gabi, you're obviously having a tough time. Why'd you send him away?"

I give her a look. "Because I need processing time."

"Processing time to sit in the dark, guzzling wine by yourself?"

"He has work. He shouldn't be babysitting me. Especially when it's so important to him. He gets clients through word of mouth. This is everything he's ever wanted in life. I can't be the reason he fucks it all up. The reason he has to forgo his dream."

She grabs the bottle of wine and takes a sip. "Maybe you're his dream."

"That's a nice sentiment, but it's not reality."

She shrugs. "Why not?"

"Kell, he *had* love. Love that already made him make this choice, and he chose his work. Sure, I had a bad day, but I'll get through it. *We* might not, though, if I'm the reason the thing he's worked so hard for goes belly up."

"I'm assuming we're talking about Marissa here, right?"

I shrug. "Sounds familiar," I grumble, taking another long sip of wine.

She lets out a long breath. "Look, I'm not one to meddle in other people's relationships, but I'll tell you something about Marissa. She was entitled, and I could see it even at four years old. She had Zeke wrapped around her little finger, got him to go to the same college as her, managed to control just about every aspect of his life because he thought that was what love was––a sacrifice, by definition." She refills my glass when I set it down on the coffee table. "But I think with you, he sees someone like himself. Someone who wants big things that she wants for *herself*, not for status or for the sake of the family accounting business." She rolls her eyes. "Gabi, when they split up he told me that love isn't worth it, that I'd do better to be independent and find fulfill-ment in being alone––which is not a *bad* thing, but it certainly showed me what a cynic he'd become." She takes another sip straight from the bottle. "And the fact that he found you and he's so head over heels ready to do anything for you tells me that he gets something out of your relation-ship that he's never gotten out of a relationship before. That he's never gotten out of a *job* before. Sure, he's generally a happy person. He likes his life. But with you in it? I've never seen him so happy."

I can tell she's waiting for me to say something by the expectant lift of her eyebrows.

"I love that he's happy. And I am too. But my one bad day isn't enough to wreck everything he's worked for."

She waves me off. "This is what you'd call a family emer-gency, and it warrants time off work."

I snort.

She eyes me. "I'm not kidding."

"I mean, family? Kelly, come on. We've only been dating for a few months."

"When you know, you know."

"Are you saying that you know or that he knows?"

"I take my cues from him. He knows, so I know."

I shake my head. "He *knows?*"

She nods. "He knows." She glances down at her phone, shooting off a quick text. "And I understand that you want your alone time, but your vote has been discounted for tonight by reason of too much wine and sitting in the dark crying. Zeke will be back in an hour or two, and your sister and Charlie have already been mobilized. FYI, if you want to"––she gestures to my face––"get rid of the snot and stuff."

I grab another paper towel and wipe my nose self-consciously. "Please don't let him come back."

She glances down at her phone again. "He's agreed to leave in the middle of the night so he won't miss any work, but he'll still be here with you while it doesn't affect 'his dreams.'" She air quotes and rolls her eyes. She holds my gaze for a second, as if challenging me. "Is that okay with you?"

I nod. "It's okay with me." And then I think about it for a second. "Wait, what did you mean by 'my sister and Charlie have been mobilized'?"

She smiles. "They're bringing you some more stuff from your apartment. And if I had to guess, more wine." She reaches forward and takes another long sip from the bottle. "Or at least, I told Zeke that you asked him to ask them to."

I snort. "For me or for you?"

She shrugs, a mischievous smile falling across her face. "You'll never know."

TWENTY MINUTES and another glass of wine later, there's a knock at the door. Kelly jumps up from the sofa, gesturing for me to stay seated, and crosses the kitchen to the front door.

Steph barges in first, her eyes scanning the space until they land on me. She trudges forward, two bottles of wine in her hands that she rests on the coffee table in front of me, and then collapses into the couch next to me, wrapping me in a full-bodied Stephanie hug that's both awkward and so full of love at the same time.

Behind her, Charlie has his arms full of blankets, one of my duffel bags thrown over his shoulder. Annabel comes in last, closing the door gently behind her and immediately taking the place on the couch next to me, on the opposite side of Stephanie. She wraps her limbs around me in a similar way, the two of them squeezing me so tight that I can hardly breathe.

"Need. Air."

They break apart by an inch as Kelly distributes glasses to each of us, taking it upon herself to pour everyone—— including her not-quite-twenty-one-year-old self——a generous serving. She sits on the floor on the other side of the coffee table as Charlie takes the armchair next to us.

"Gabi," Steph says, pulling my attention toward her. She takes a sip from the bottle just like Kelly. "Tell us what happened."

I shrug, taking another sip even though at this point I know I'm pushing my limit. "Dustin broke in."

She narrows her eyes. "And you're scared?"

"I don't know about *scared*. I just feel kind of... tired of it all."

Steph squishes closer to me, winding her arms easily around my waist. "I get it, Gabs. You've been working your-self to the bone and just when you think you finally get to relax, this happens. It must be frustrating."

I shrug. "I guess."

"Tonight should have been a celebration."

I shrug again, not really wanting to think too hard about yoga.

"I have to go to the bathroom," I say, mostly to avoid the conversation but also because I kinda had to pee when Kelly got there but I didn't have the energy to actually make it happen.

I wind between everyone, Annabel reaching out to squeeze my elbow as I pass by her, and climb the stairs to the second floor. I shut myself in, pee, and take a look at the mess that is my face before leaving. I swipe away bits of smudged makeup and pat some cold water in my face in an effort to hide the blubbery skin.

It's not great, but it's an improvement. With a sigh, I let myself out of the bathroom and walk back downstairs. Charlie grabs at the edge of the blanket so I can sit, and then throws it over me once I'm settled. When I reach for another sip of wine, I realize that everyone is quiet, watching me. I put my glass back down on the coffee table. "What?"

"Gabi, how was yoga today?" Steph asks again, her eyes on mine.

"It was fine," I say, even though I can feel their eyes on me now. I know where this line of questioning is going, and it's nowhere good. It's Blubber Town, and I'm trying my hardest to avoid that while other people are here.

Steph's eyes narrow, and I know I'm not going to get out of this. "How was yoga *really*?"

The tears come before the words, my face scrunching up together as I sink into the couch and bury it in the leather. Steph and Annabel are on me in a second, both of them a tangle of limbs caging me in.

"Alright, make room," Charlie says, squeezing in on

Annabel's other side and hugging me around her. Not one to be left out, Kelly rounds the coffee table and piles up behind Steph.

"I'm Kelly, by the way," she says, as she leans her full body weight into Stephanie. Her voice is low since all of our faces are squished close together. Steph starts giggling, which starts Annabel off a second later, and even though the tears are still streaming down my face, I can't help but let out a little laugh along with them. A hiccup jumps from my throat, the weird mix of emotions combining with the wine to confuse my body.

"Gabi," Steph groans, squeezing me even harder before pulling away. Our hug disintegrates slowly, everyone taking back their seats and drinking wine. "What happened?"

Annabel forcefully wipes the tears from my face with the cuffs of her sweater.

"It was only Natalie and her sister," I say, pressing my lips tight together since they're a little wobbly.

Annabel's shoulders drop, and I swear I feel Steph's heartbeat come to a halt.

"Gabi, I'm sorry," Annabel says. "The snow was *so* heavy––I just couldn't imagine walking all the way to the studio and back in *that*."

I nod, waving her off. "I know, that makes total sense. You don't need to apologize."

"I'm sorry, too," Kelly says. "My roommate slipped on the way there and hurt herself and I didn't feel right leaving her at the time. But I had every intention of going––today was just really rough for getting *anywhere*."

"Kelly, seriously. That makes total sense. There's no need to apologize."

Steph lets out a long breath, and my eyes snap to her face. She bites her bottom lip. "Gabi, I know you're upset.

And I'm really sorry, too. If I had known how much our presence meant to you today, I would have found a way there. I thought I would be one of the few who couldn't make it. But Gabi, why didn't you cancel? I mean, they were comparing this storm to the snow storm of '96. Do you remember the snow storm of '96?"

"Well, not really."

"Exactly. It was a weather event that happened so long ago we were too small to even notice it, but it's a freaking *weather event* from thirty years ago that they still reference today. Meaning this snow storm was a big fucking snow storm."

I shrug. "If I waited any longer to open, there's a chance I would run out of money. And there's still a good chance, but Zeke broke my lease at my apartment so I guess I can probably float for a bit now. But it just... it doesn't feel good." My voice cracks, but I swallow over the lump building in my throat.

Steph pulls me in for another hug. "You realize you can ask for help, right? I'd be happy to give you money."

"What? I can't take your money. You're my little sister."

She rolls her eyes. "I have some extra." She catches my eye, a slightly sheepish look on her face. "I, uh, broke my lease this week, too. So I'll actually have quite a bit extra over the next few months."

"You broke your lease? Why?"

She waves me off. "Look, it's a long story, but I'm going to Costa Rica for an indefinite amount of time. And where I'm going, rooms are super cheap."

My jaw drops. "By yourself?"

She waves me off. "Yes, by myself, and FYI, you're taking a few of my plants while I'm gone—you just have to water them on the first of the month since they're all succulents."

She turns to Charlie and Annabel. "You guys are, too." She pauses as she looks at Kelly. "Do you like plants?" Kelly nods. "Then you are, too." She turns back to me. "But this isn't about me, it's about you. I'm in a position where I can actually help you for once. Please let me!"

"You can't go to Costa Rica by yourself," I say. "Why?"

She sighs. "Well, I won't really *be* by myself."

I raise my eyebrows.

"Rod will be there."

A fiery anger rushes up through my chest, spurred on by Annabel's groan. Steph shoots her a look. "You're going to Costa Rica for Rod? Steph, he can hardly make a dinner reservation on time, let alone be there for you in Costa Rica."

"He's gotten better with time management."

"And what about everything else? Are you guys, like, officially back together?"

"Well, no. But we're going to meet up in Costa Rica and talk. Spend time together just the two of us, and I think it'll be really good for us! We can reconnect away from all this," she says, gesturing vaguely to the city outside the window. "It's only an hour time difference and it's *so* beautiful. And I know the language so it's not like it'll be difficult getting around."

"Steph, I love you, but that's a stretch to say you can speak Spanish."

She gives me a look. "I know enough." She holds up a hand to stop me from going on. "I'm going to Costa Rica," she says with finality. "And I would really like to make sure my sister is okay with the extra money in my bank account that can be paid back at any time in the future."

I bite my lip, considering her offer. "I pushed through today because I was feeling the squeeze financially. But now that I don't have a lease, I think I'll be okay." I squeeze her hand. "But I love that you offered, and if I didn't think I'd be okay, I would accept."

"Would you really? Will you tell me if that stops being the case?"

I nod. "Unless I can use it for a little reverse manipulation? Like I take your money *and* guilt you into not going to Costa Rica?"

She reaches over to give me a hug. "Nope. My mind is made up."

I let out a long breath. "Well, in that case, I will not be taking any of your money."

She rolls her eyes. "Look, just because you're a big shot studio owner now, doesn't mean it's not still a learning experience, okay? Don't let one bad day––where you probably should have canceled class––color this experience. Your lesson today is to freaking cancel if somebody mentions the snow storm of '96."

I sigh, taking another sip of my wine. "I know. It's just hard to convince myself that today isn't one big red flag about how things are going to go."

"It's one day," Annabel repeats.

"It's one hundred percent of my experience running a studio," I counter.

"And the next day you teach, it will be fifty percent," Charlie interjects, leaning forward in his chair. "And then thirty-three percent, and then twenty-five percent, and then twenty percent, until it's the tiniest little sliver of experience that can be explained away by snow. Come on, Gabi, you don't give up this easily. I've seen you take on a hell of a lot worse. And you know what? This might not be what you need to hear, but it kind of can't get any worse. You really only have a positive trajectory here to look forward to."

"I mean, zero people could have shown up," I snap back.

Charlie gives me a look before leaning back in his seat. "One day you're going to look back on everything you've done and realize what a fucking rockstar you are. You just have to not let your brain derail you first."

I suddenly realize my anxiety must be a little more obvious than I thought. "Char, that's sweet," I say, begrudgingly accepting his compliment and leaning forward to knock his knee.

He lets out a long breath. "Annabel told me I can't try to influence you to stay on the team, but just know that I'm really upset you'll be leaving."

I tense up. "Uh, I'm not quitting."

He rolls his eyes. "I know you're not quitting *now*. But as the only person who knows you professionally, I think I can say with certainty that it's only a matter of time. I mean, you're fucking great at your job. Like really fucking great. And focusing all that on something you really want—that you're passionate about—is only going to bring good things. It's going to take a couple months for the studio to kick into high gear, but once it does, you're going to be strapped for time again, and I, for one, know what choice you're going to make."

"You think?"

He nods. "Yeah, and I'm dreading it as far as work is concerned, but I'm excited for you. For where this could go."

I smile into my wine. "You really think I'm that good at my job?"

"I wouldn't be where I am without you."

"Charlie, you're being so sweet." I knock Annabel's elbow. "Is that your doing?"

She snorts. "He has gotten sappier recently, hasn't he?"

He shrugs. "I'm happy," he says, as if that explains *everything*.

Although, judging by the wistful expression on his face as he gazes at Annabel, I think it actually might.

"Wow, that was bizarre," Kelly mutters, her eyes wide as she stares at the two of them.

Charlie gives her a look. "Comment from the peanut gallery?"

She shakes her head. "Nope. No comment. Just... happy you're happy."

Annabel narrows her eyes. "Oh, you knew slutty Charlie, didn't you?" she asks.

Kelly presses her lips together.

Charlie points at her. "No stories. I don't need to be getting into trouble for things that happened years ago."

Annabel waves him off. "Oh, like you'd get in trouble for things that happened in the past." She turns to Kelly. "What stories is he referring to?"

Charlie looks at Kelly, who remains silent.

"There are no stories," Charlie says.

Kelly clears her throat and takes a sip of her wine.

I take the pause in conversation as an opportunity to stand. "I'm just going to throw the wine in the fridge," I say, gathering the spare bottles in my arms and stepping around Steph's legs. I find a place for each bottle in the fridge and turn around to join everyone on the couch again, when I realize Steph is right behind me.

She puts her hands on my shoulders. "Are you doing okay? For real? I can't help but think that there was a lot more going on with Dustin than any of us saw. I'm really sorry that I missed what was going on with you."

I shake my head. "Steph, don't let yourself feel guilty over that. There's no way you could have known. That's kind of the game he played: how far he could push me until he met resistance."

She grimaces as she winds her arms around my waist. "I hate that you went through that. I noticed when you were dating him that you were a little more withdrawn, but I figured you were just living your life. I thought you were happy, honestly. That you found your person and all you wanted to do was spend time with him." She shakes her head, letting out a long breath. "Meanwhile you were dealing with a fucking nutjob. You're just always so put together, it never occurred to me that you might need help once in a while, too."

I kiss her cheek. "For what it's worth, you give the best help."

She gives me a look. "It's too little, too late."

"It's just what I need, right when I need it."

She gives me another quick squeeze.

"I'm sorry for causing an emergency phone train," I say.

She shakes her head. "I literally only care that you're okay." She leans against the kitchen island, her eyes finding mine. "You've seemed off, recently. Even before the studio. And I just wanted to check in, make sure everything is alright."

I nod. "I'm okay."

She nods, quiet for a second, and then reaches out and tugs on the waistband of my leggings.

I blink at her, this one small movement communicating more than words ever could.

She waits silently for me to speak. Meanwhile, Kelly seems to have gotten permission to tell slutty Charlie stories from long before Annabel. They're giggling together, Annabel seemingly delighted to hear about the many entertaining times Charlie's gotten turned down.

Thankfully, Kelly's only selecting stories that seem to poke fun at Charlie rather than highlight just how much he got around. Probably for Annabel's sake.

I turn back to Steph, feeling like telling this story is a now-or-never moment.

And I think I can lean on her with this.

"Do you remember that guy you were talking to when we went out for your birthday?"

She nods. "The one who spooked you?"

"I know him. *Knew* him. Last year he cornered me in a bathroom and tried to... well, you know." I slap my waistband against my skin. "The only thing that stopped him was my fucking skirt. So many buttons and clasps that it would have taken a bomb squad to get it off." I shake my head. "And it was fine. I got over it. Or so I thought, until I straight up flinched when Zeke touched me. And I just—I don't know—I was trying to desensitize myself, and it turned into a nervous tic."

"Oh, Gabi," she says.

"But it's fine now—I got over it."

She narrows her eyes at me and then reaches forward to snap my waistband. "I don't think this," she says, doing it again, "is an appropriate way to *get over* being assaulted."

I shake my head. "It worked, though."

"Have you talked to Zeke about it?"

I nod. "Yeah. He was really sweet about it. Really kind."

His lips leaving small kisses on my stomach, his movements gentle.

Steph nods and pulls me in for another hug, our hips leaning against the kitchen island next to us. Her voice is softer when she speaks again. "I'm sad you didn't feel like you could tell me."

The tears prickle behind my eyes again.

"I didn't want to burden you. It doesn't need to be your problem. I can handle it."

"Just because you *can* doesn't mean you *should*. You've seemed on edge lately—for a long time, actually. And I'm your sister—I can't help but feel like I should have figured it out. I should have figured out a way to be there for you even if I didn't know what was going on."

"Don't blame yourself. You can't know what I didn't tell you." I take a deep breath, swallowing down the lump. "For what it's worth, it feels good to have told you now. Like you're on my side."

She hugs me tighter. "I'm *always* on your side."

I breathe into her shoulder and we rock side to side. "I love you, Steph."

"Love you too, Gabs. You can always talk to me."

At that moment, the front door opens, and my heart leaps out of my chest as I turn toward it.

Zeke drops his bag by the door, his eyes roaming the apartment full of people until he finds me. He raises his eyebrows, like he's waiting for permission to come inside.

I let go of Steph with a quick kiss on her cheek and run to him.

41

ZEKE

The way she lets her breath out when she sees me is everything. She crashes into my chest, her arms winding tight around my waist. I wrap my arms around her shoulders and squeeze, so relieved that she's happy to see me. She's not letting go, so I close my eyes and tug her closer, my cheek pressing into the top of her head.

She's the one who had a rough day, but I feel like I was the one who really needed this hug.

"Thank you for letting me come back."

She shakes her head, pushing away from me for a second. "I'm sorry for pushing you away. I just... I don't know, it felt like I needed to cry alone in the dark, but now that everyone is here, it kind of feels like maybe I needed a hug or two and I was just too scared to ask."

I tug her back into my chest, letting out a long breath in her ear. "I will give you as many hugs as you'll let me."

She shakes her head. "I'm sorry."

"You don't have to apologize to me after a day like today. I know your brain is scrambled. I know you're just trying to do what's best for you given the situation."

She glances up at me. "Promise you won't miss work for me."

"I promise."

Kelly already read me the riot act via text. I didn't realize it meant that much to Gabi, that I continue doing what I'm doing. I just wanted to be there for her––and fuck work–– but rather than seeing just how much I care about *her*, Gabi saw just how similar she was to Marissa.

Even though she's *nothing* like Marissa.

I thought what I had with Marissa was love, that everything I gave her was necessary for us to be happy. But I shortchanged myself instead, giving everything I had to someone who wanted a walking checklist.

No shade, if that makes her happy. But it wasn't *me*.

Meanwhile Gabi saw everything I was doing to try to help her and cared more that it was detrimental to my life. This whole time I was worried about her not living her dreams, yet when the rug was swept out from under her, she only cared that I lived mine.

I'm annoyed with her for not vocalizing it, but way more than that, I love her for caring so much about what I want.

But we can work on vocalizing stuff later. Tonight, my girl just needs hugs.

And I will *deliver*.

WHEN OUR FRIENDS LEAVE, I tug her upstairs and throw her in my shower. I turn the water up until the heat is nearly unbearable and position her under the water while I strip down and step in behind her. I massage her shampoo through her hair and scrub her down from head to toe, and when I take a second to clean myself, she only turns around, pressing her body against mine like she can't take two seconds away from me.

A stark contrast from earlier.

She winds her arms around my waist, resting her head on my chest as I struggle to divert sudsy water away from her eyes.

When I'm done, I just wrap my arms around her, letting the water fall around us, and leave a kiss on her forehead.

"I know that I'm being ridiculous," she mumbles.

I shake my head. "You're not ridiculous. You're allowed to have human emotions, you know."

She pulls away to give me a look. "I *feel* ridiculous. I feel out of control and upset and like I'm having this little explosion inside me that's disrupting *everyone* despite trying my hardest to keep it contained."

"Gabi, somebody broke into your apartment. It's okay to be upset."

She pauses, blinking up at me, and then bites her lip. "Only two people came to my class."

And all of the pieces click into place.

She sniffs. "Honestly, I could kind of care less about my apartment. About Dustin. I'll probably give you shit about breaking my lease without consulting me, but even that I don't care about very much." Her lip trembles. "It just feels like I put everything on the line here and... it didn't pay off. I offered up the one thing that quiets the static in my mind, and now every time I even think about yoga, I'm going to think about this day."

I tug her close again, brushing her hair out of her face as the water runs through it. "Gabi, this isn't the end. I'm telling you, power through just another week. You're going to see a change. You can't fight the weather, though out of everyone

I've ever met, you're the only person I think is a worthy opponent."

She laughs, a quick exhale into my chest.

"Seriously, Gabi." I push her away from me, holding her by the upper arms. "This is not the time to give up. It's time to double down and power through."

She lets out a long breath. "Why can't it just for once not be about timing? Maybe it's time for *nothing*. Time to just exist." She grumbles as she turns to let the water run through her hair. "It feels like it's never the right time for anything you really want when you want it."

I blink, my mind struggling to catch up with what she's saying.

She sighs. "I guess you're right. I just have to wait. And wait and wait. And maybe one day the studio will magically be successful. I just hope it hasn't driven me into the ground by the time it is."

A second later, she opens the shower door and steps out, stubbing her toe as she grabs the towel from the rack on the other side of the door.

She's just drunk, right?

She's not having doubts about... us.

Right?

But by the time I rinse the rest of the soap from my body and follow her out to my bedroom, she's already fast asleep in my bed, her wet hair splayed out across the pillow.

I SPEND two hours tossing and turning while Gabi snores peacefully next to me.

And when I check my phone and see that it's three, I give up and sit up in bed.

My thoughts have overpowered me. I didn't sleep a wink, thanks to adrenaline, and if I have to be on the road by four anyway, it doesn't make sense to just twist my sheets for the next hour.

I know most of it is because of the events of yesterday. Even knowing Gabi's safe next to me, I hate that that fucker was creeping around her apartment for so long. I feel like I failed her, and it was only some weird twist of luck that landed me in her apartment instead of her when Dustin broke in.

But it's also the fact that Gabi's still talking about timing. I *feel* like we have something special here. And I think she does too. *But if there's any small part of her that thinks everything we have is just timing... doesn't it make this whole relationship a sham?*

I know I'm overthinking–it happens when I don't sleep enough.

I turn to her, running my fingers along her arm to wake her gently.

"What time is it?" she asks, sitting up almost immediately.

"It's early," I say. "Lie down. I just wanted to say goodbye before I head out."

"Oh," she says, settling back in and moving closer to me. She pulls the sheets up as she buries her face in my side. "Man, I forgot that you going to work requires you to leave."

I run my fingers through her hair. Along the back of the T-shirt she stole from me last night.

I wait a second before I speak, willing myself not to do it. Not to let the overthinking demons show. "Do you still believe in timing?"

She turns her head, popping one eye open to look at me. "Timing?"

"Last night, you said everything was about timing."

She shakes her head. "I drank too much wine last night. Don't listen to me."

"But do you?"

She sits up, the covers falling to her lap as she eyes me. "You mean the timing of us?"

I nod.

She runs her hands through my hair and pulls my arm around her so she can snuggle in closer. "Maybe timing is just what you make it. Maybe love is nothing more than an agreement to say 'fuck timing' altogether."

I pull her in closer, leaving a kiss on her head. "Do you mean that?"

She turns to look up at me. "I want *you,* Zeke. I'm not going to let timing, or fate, or whatever it is I used to believe get in the way of that."

42

GABI

Tonight is our last dinner with our parents for the foreseeable future, and for the first—and last—time in quite a while, Steph offered to drive.

I try to not think too hard about why or I'll start the pity party back up again.

While we eat, my mom and Steph fight over what music to put on, Steph winning by pulling a puppy dog face and reminding everyone she's leaving for Costa Rica for an indefinite amount of time. My mom shakes her head, surrendering the remote to her.

"Fine, you win," she says, and Steph grins. "I don't understand why you *have* to go to Costa Rica."

Steph shrugs. "It's not that I *have* to go to Costa Rica. Rod will be there for a while, and on the long list of places he goes, it's pretty safe. Comparatively."

"I know, honey, but you're going to be by yourself flying and driving, and ugh..." She wraps Stephanie in a hug, her hair flying in Steph's face. "I just hate the thought of you doing all of that alone."

"Mom, I won't be *alone* for most of it."

I catch a look between my parents that I can feel in my soul. We all know Stephanie is going to be alone for most of her trip. Rod doesn't exactly have the best track record.

"Just don't stay to prove a point, okay? Come home whenever. Your bedroom here is always ready for you."

"I'm not proving a point, Mom. I'm giving my relationship with Rod a shot. He just happens to be in Costa Rica right now, but he might not be there long so I *have* to go while I have the chance."

My mouth goes dry. I always knew this trip was about Rod, but I don't think I realized how serious it was to her. She's not just going to Costa Rica for sloths and a suntan—she's pulling a hail mary on her relationship and seeing if things can work when they're both in the same place at the same time.

My little sister, who's so much more courageous than me. So much more willing to take a risk and love and be hurt.

My mom sighs. "I know, I know. Just be safe."

"I will, Mom," Steph says, rolling her eyes at me. She finally picks a music station, and *of course* it's because Alanis Morrissette is playing.

I take the moment of distraction as an opportunity to ask my dad the question that's been burning in the back of my mind for days now.

"Hey Dad?" I push my plate onto the side table next to me.

"Hey Gabi," he mocks, a smile coming to his face. He turns to me, giving me his full attention.

"Do you remember when we were little, you said something about love being nothing more than good timing?"

He thinks for a moment, running his hand over his thinning hair. "Yeah. Yeah, I think I remember that. You must have been, what, eight or so?"

"I think so." I play with the hem of my blanket. "Do you still believe that?"

He sighs. "There was a long, long time I believed that. When you girls were little, I—well—your mom adjusted really quickly to being your mom. She popped you out and was off like a shot, ready to be whatever you needed her to be." Steph's nose crinkles in my peripheral vision.

"I didn't know what to do with myself. I didn't know how to fold laundry correctly. I didn't know what way to cut your sandwiches. I didn't know which Barbie was the right one to buy. In hindsight, none of that really mattered. But for a long time I thought I must have just shown up at the right time in your mom's life because there was no reason for her to pick me, this helpless idiot who doesn't even know how many times to cut a grape so his daughter won't choke on it." He sighs, smiling at my mom.

"I felt really undeserving of this"—he waves in my mom's general direction—"perfect woman who not only popped out two babies but took care of them in a way I could never dream to."

"Aw, Pete," she says, moving from her couch to ours and nudging me out of the way so she can hug my dad.

He takes a kiss from her and then continues. "All that to say, I'm not sure I believe in timing anymore. All this..." He gestures vaguely at us, at the house we grew up in. "All this is a product of hard work. A refusal to let the hard days win. You could argue that timing, or fate—or whatever mumbo-jumbo is popular these days—is what made all of this possible, but I think it was just two people who saw the best in each other and helped each other grow."

"Aw Dad," Steph says, and she's in my lap now, layering

another hug onto my parents. I rest my head on her back and we sit there for a second in the world's most awkward family hug.

My dad grumbles and shifts under us. "Alright. I love my girls, but this is a really bad position for my back."

Steph cackles as she extricates herself, and my mom plants a kiss on his cheek before falling back into the other couch with Steph.

My dad reaches over and pats my knee. "I'm sorry if I gave you the wrong idea of what love is supposed to be."

I glance over at my mom and Steph, who have returned to scouring music stations.

I think of my mom's kiss on his cheek, the way he had no qualms saying just how highly he thinks of her, so many years later. The years of laughter, family vacations, loud music and our own unique traditions.

And I get a little mad at myself for letting one small sentence deconstruct all of the love our family has.

I shake my head. "I think you gave me the best idea of what love is."

"You know I wasn't totally sure what to expect when you offered to drive today. I thought for sure you had a sneaky plan of some sort."

Steph gives me a look as she pulls out of my parents' driveway. "Well, to be fair, I *do* have an ulterior motive."

I raise my eyebrows. "Which is?"

She gives me a small smile as we exit the neighborhood. "I'm whisking you away."

I narrow my eyes. "To where?"

"You'll see."

After a few minutes we merge onto the highway, and although we're still heading in the direction of the city, we're definitely not going the *fastest* way back.

But as I start considering potential destinations, she exits, pulling onto a side street and stopping in front of what looks like an old converted single-family home. She stops the car and then looks at me.

"Where are we?"

She sighs. "We're at my therapist's office."

I wrinkle my eyebrows. "What?" *Steph is in therapy?*

"I am gifting you my appointment."

"Your appointment?"

She presses her lips together. "So about six months ago, I was diagnosed with ADHD," she says, watching my face. "I tried a couple of different medications and most of them had too many side effects to be worth it. So, I'm on a pretty mild one right now that helps me through work but it doesn't take away all the..." She motions wildly to her head. "All the distracting things. It works for me, for now, but it was kind of rough for a while, to know that there *is* actually something wrong with me but be unable to fix it. I got a little depressed, and it just wasn't a fun time. So I started coming here, and we've worked on a bunch of mindfulness techniques that have helped with both the depression and the lingering leftovers of the ADHD."

"Steph, I had no idea." I grab her hand where it's resting on the park brake.

She smiles sadly at me. "How would you know if I never told you?" She sighs. "Anyway, when you told me everything that you kept bottled in, I just thought that maybe it would help you talk to someone who's not me about it, you know? As much as I trust you, I'd have trouble articulating exactly what's going on in my mind to you—but my therapist is a pro. And she's really nice, and I think it would be worth it if you took just two or three sessions to talk about everything. And if you hate it, I totally get it. But I think it might be good for you."

"Steph, I appreciate you doing all this, but I don't think I need therapy. I just need—I don't know—a little bit of time to process everything."

She nods and then reaches toward me and snaps my waistband. "If this is your idea of what time will do for you, I don't think you're going in the right direction."

I blink. "Alright, you might have a point there."

"Just try it? If not for yourself, for me? If not for me, for Zeke?"

I breathe out through my nose.

It doesn't feel like a *bad* idea. But it does feel like I'm admitting to being fucked in the head.

"Okay."

"Really?" she claps, which seems like the wrong reaction to someone going to therapy, but I do my best to muster up a smile for her anyway.

"I'll go." I nod, trying desperately to plan out the next hour if I'm actually going to do this. *Where do I even start?*

"Okay, go!" she says, waving me out of the car. "I'll pick you up when you're done. She already knows you're coming so all you have to do is go in and she'll take care of you."

"Okay," I say, suddenly struggling to put together the actions of opening the car door and stepping outside. "I guess I just walk in, then?"

Steph nods. "Seriously, Gabi. Just open the door. She'll take care of you from there, okay? There's a small waiting room, sit right next to the water dispenser—you'll hear her footsteps before you see her from that vantage point so you can have a moment if you need one."

"Okay," I say, pushing open the car door and stepping outside. I throw my bag over my shoulder and take a few hesitant steps toward the building.

I feel like I'm breaking and entering into someone's house.

I push through the front door, and Steph was right—there's a waiting room just ahead, with a little water dispenser and a well-worn chair next to it. I sit gingerly, my bag between my feet, and try to calm my pounding heart.

A few minutes later, I hear her steps and I stand, straightening my hair over my shoulder.

"Gabi?" she asks, her smile wide and welcoming.

I nod. "Hi."

"Dr. Shapiro. But you can call me Gwen." She notches her head toward the hallway behind her. "Follow me this way."

43

ZEKE

I have gotten zero sleep this week.

Okay, so maybe that's an exaggeration. But it's only Tuesday and I feel like I've gotten zero sleep this week because today and yesterday, I've driven ten hours each day to get to Virginia and back to see Gabi for an hour before she falls asleep.

I know it's overkill, but she needs me right now in a way that has me stretched. She needs me in person but she also needs me to go to work, so I'm stuck in a weird limbo where it really feels like the thing I need *least* is sleep.

Except I'm really fucking jonesing for some by the time I get back to my apartment.

I blast through the door with my duffel bag thrown over one shoulder. I throw my jacket in the coat closet and drop my bag on the ground, and I'm halfway through pulling my shirt over my head to *immediately* find Gabi and pull her into bed, when I realize my apartment smells different.

I pause, pulling my shirt back on and turning to the kitchen.

She's sitting at the kitchen counter, the candle in front of her casting her face in a warm glow. She's wearing a dress and her hair is done in those pretty waves she puts in whenever we go somewhere fancy.

"Hey," she says, nudging a glass in front of her that looks to be filled with whiskey. I notice that next to it is a bottle of that melatonin stuff that knocks you right out. "I wasn't sure what you'd want tonight so I got you both."

"Thank you." I smile as I make my way to her, pressing a kiss to her cheek as I sniff the air. "Are you making something?"

She turns on her barstool and pulls me between her legs. God, she's even got *heels* on. *All for me? Wow.* "I'm making you dinner. It's nothing fancy so don't get too excited. Chicken and potatoes. But I kind of wanted to talk to you."

And my heart drops.

And she must see it on my face because she immediately tugs on my shirt, keeping me close. "No no no no no! Not bad talk. Good talk. Nice talk."

I eye her for a second. "If you're done talking like a caveman, can you tell me what all this is about?"

I reach for the whiskey, swallowing it down in one gulp, and she opens the bottle to refill me.

"I want you to stay in Virginia tomorrow."

I search her face. *What about this is a* good *talk?* "Why?"

"Because as much as I love you coming back to make sure I'm okay, you're going to kill yourself in the process. This isn't sustainable, even for a week."

I shake my head. "I don't care. I don't want you spiraling here without me."

She gives me a look. "I already know you're scheduling

Steph and Kelly to check up on me at regular intervals. I'm not *that* delicate." *Oh, but you are. The strongest, most delicate thing I've ever met.* "And neither of them can keep a secret, by the way."

"They don't need to keep it a secret, as long as they keep showing up."

She lets out a short huff. I swallow down another sip of whiskey.

"It's only a week."

"I need you to trust me when I say I'm okay."

I bite my lip. If this isn't a checkmate, I don't know what is. "I do trust you."

"Then stay in Virginia. We can talk on the phone every night. I won't try to go to my apartment alone. I won't give up on yoga or drown myself in wine."

I watch her face as I speak. "You promise?"

She nods. "I promise."

She kisses my chin, and I take the opportunity to wrap an arm around her waist and smother her in kisses like I've been wanting to from the moment I stepped inside.

I'm still worried about her, but I believe her. I don't have that feeling in my gut anymore like leaving is the worst possible thing I can do. I still don't like it, but something about the way she's holding herself and the confidence in her words makes me think she's not just trying to get me to leave.

She's trying to take care of herself, and me in the process.

"Sit," she says, slapping the barstool next to us.

I do as she says, and a second later she's up, pouring herself a glass of wine that she leaves on the counter next to my whiskey. She takes the chicken and potatoes out of the oven and arranges them gracefully on two plates and slides them across the island to our seats.

"I had something else to tell you, too." She takes a seat next to me, carefully cutting a piece of chicken and spearing a potato on top.

"Yeah?" I ask, doing the same, but slower, just in case whatever she's about to tell me has me choking on it.

"I talked to my dad last night," she says.

Gabi was asleep by the time I got home last night, and as much as I wanted to wake her and talk to her, it was enough for me to know that she was okay, snoozing soundly in my bed.

"About what?"

"About what he said about love being nothing more than good timing."

I leave my utensils on my plate and turn to face her.

She swallows and does the same, gathering my hands in her lap and squeezing them. "And he told me this really... sweet story about how when Steph and I were little he was overwhelmed and kind of in awe of the way my mom clicked into motherhood. He thought he was undeserving of her and that she only picked him because he came around at the right time." I watch her face as she speaks. "All that to say, he doesn't believe that anymore. I'm not sure he ever really did. And I'm not sure I did either. I think it was a convenient excuse when I searched for reasons why none of my relationships worked out."

I raise my eyebrows. "I can give a laundry list of reasons, and none of them are you."

She gives me a look. "What I'm trying to say is that what I said in bed the other day stands." I didn't think she was awake enough to know what she was saying. "Finding the right person at the right time is a crock of shit. I want to be your person all the time, and you, mine."

I can't stop myself from kissing her. From wrapping her up in my arms and squeezing her as tight as I can without breaking her. Her tongue tangles with mine, and I find myself sinking into this moment, memorizing her words for the next time that bug sneaks into my head and tells me I'm only good enough for her for *now*.

"I love you, Gabi."

"I love you now and forever."

She rests her head in my neck and lets out a long breath before pulling away and pointing at my plate. "Now eat your chicken."

I turn back to my plate and start spearing another slice of chicken.

"I figure I should also tell you, Steph took me to therapy yesterday."

And I drop it right back on my plate.

"What?" I ask, turning to her.

She shrugs. "Apparently she's been seeing this woman for quite a while, and she gave me her appointment yesterday. To, you know, work through stuff."

"How was it?"

She takes a sip of her wine and then leaves it on the counter. "I'm cautiously optimistic."

"Yeah?"

She nods. "I was kind of opposed to it at first—I mean, people deal with so much worse than I do"—I bite my tongue—"but she seemed nice. And it feels like I might get somewhere. And Steph is leaving for Costa Rica this weekend so that time slot will be open for as long as I need it."

I wrap my arms around her again, and she drops her

fork to her plate. "I'm so proud of you, Gabi. I'm *optimistic* for you," I say, stealing her choice of words.

She presses a kiss to my cheek, taking a breath in like she's going to say something else.

I raise my eyebrows, waiting for her to get it out.

"Something I talked about in therapy was depositing your check and using it as a down payment on a new apartment."

For a moment I'm disappointed that she won't be staying long term. And then I get a little excited that I have someone who I miss enough when she's gone to want around all the time.

But then a little swell of pride warms my chest because she's actually taking the money I've been trying to give her for weeks now. And she's advocating for herself. She's doing what she needs to do to feel comfortable and safe, and she's actually letting me help her.

"I think that's only fair since I broke your lease without consulting you. Even if it was the right thing to do."

She bites her lip. "You're not mad?"

"No way. I'm thrilled. I mean, I'd move you in today if I thought you were ready for that, but I know you're not. So, we'll move you into some other apartment that doesn't have creepy men hanging about, and when you're ready for more, you'll let me know."

"Yeah? You're okay with that?"

"I love it. It sounds like the perfect plan."

She gives me a look.

"What? You'll be happy, comfortable, and safe, and me helping you into the new apartment cancels out me tearing you out of your old one. And if I play my cards right, you'll be foaming at the mouth at the end of this year because you want to move in with me so bad."

She laughs, shaking her head at me, and I throw an arm around her shoulders to pull her close and kiss her cheek. She seems like herself again, and I just want to smother her in hugs.

She rubs my leg, the motion stirring up all sorts of thoughts in my mind. "Thank you for dealing with me."

"You're my favorite thing to deal with."

When she grins at me, it's absolutely everything.

44

GABI

As we sit and eat, the tension slowly disappears from Zeke's shoulders. I hate that I've been stressing him out, but I'm relieved that he'll be able to relax a little for the rest of the week—at least, as much as he can while managing Leanne.

As we clean up dinner, his normal grin returns to his face. He touches me constantly, and I'm reminded of New Year's, when being inches away from me was just too far.

I can feel the relief flowing off of him in waves, and I realize just how necessary this dinner was. I wanted to do something nice for him, to show him that everything he's done for me isn't lost on me and remind him that even though I'm having a tough week, I'm still myself.

And most importantly, I'm not going anywhere.

But I feel like I'm watching that protective outer shell of his break.

I didn't even realize just how tough this week was for him, too.

As I close the dishwasher on the last of our plates, he wraps his arms around me again, his lips trailing little kisses along my neck. A heat instantly builds in my abdomen as I tilt my head to kiss him and feel his tongue slip into my mouth.

He lets out a small groan that I can feel in my lips. "Gabi, I missed you."

"I missed you, too."

He reaches down and lifts me, my legs wrapping easily around him, and sets me on the edge of the island, grabbing my thighs and leaning into me. I can feel just how hard he is through his pants, and it spurs an ache between my legs.

"How do you want me to make you come first?" he asks, his face buried in my neck.

His lips brush over my collarbone, his thumb running along the crevice of my leg. I shiver into his touch, totally incapable of processing his words.

"What?" I mumble as I press myself against him.

His thumb slides beneath my underwear, pressing briefly inside of me before continuing up to the bundle of nerves there.

"Pay attention, Gabi. How do you want me to make you come first?" he repeats, swirling his thumb around me as I cry out. He reaches behind me, tugging down the zipper of my dress, and I push the sleeves down my arms.

"It's kind of hard to pay attention when you're doing that," I say, my eyes lowering to where his hand rubs me.

He takes it away, his wet fingers tailing along my inner thigh, and I wrap my legs tight around him so he can't step away from me. "Wait, wait, wait. Don't stop!"

He leans over me, one arm wrapping around my waist while his other hand cups my breast, pinching my nipple between his fingers. "Gabi," he says, his eyes finding mine. "Tell me how you want to come. Use me."

I'm momentarily stunned, his hand trailing along my

ribs, tugging at my dress to pull me closer. He presses his lips against mine, his tongue swiping inside my mouth and tangling with mine.

"Your mouth," I stutter out.

He groans into my lips. "There's my girl." He tears my underwear down my legs, discarding them somewhere over his shoulder and pushes me down roughly onto the island. He kneels down in front of me, placing my feet on his shoulders.

"Wait, I don't want to hurt you," I say, reaching to unstrap my heels.

He scoffs. "Hurt me, Gabi. I'd love nothing more than a bruise on my shoulder that reminds me just how hard I made you come on my face." He trails a finger down my core, slipping it inside me.

"Jesus, Zeke." My hips grind toward him, but he holds me steady.

He slips another finger inside me, pulsing gently. "So fucking soaked for me."

He leans forward to press a kiss to my thigh. My hips buck toward him, and he drags his teeth along my skin.

"Zeke," I pant.

"Yes, Gabriella?" The smirk he throws me tells me he's enjoying this far too much.

"Please."

His lips leave a trail of kisses along my thigh. "Such good manners."

Every nerve in my body feels like it's on fire as he takes my clit into his mouth.

"Fuck, Zeke," I moan, my hands in his hair. His fingers continue pulsing in and out of me, and with the other hand he bunches up my dress around my waist and tugs, using it to hold me in place.

I cry out as I come around him, my entire body going tense and lifting up off the counter. I'm vaguely aware that my heels are digging into his shoulders, but he doesn't seem to mind. His eyes are on mine, his tongue still moving around me even as I squirm away from him.

When he's certain I'm done, he stands in front of me, one hand trailing along my leg, my stomach. I throw an arm over my head as my breathing slows, and he takes the opportunity to palm my breast.

He pulls his shirt over his head and discards it over his shoulder. The sight of him undressing never fails to make my mouth go dry.

He grabs my hips, pulling me back to the edge of the island, and gently palms my core.

"Zeke," I say, my legs closing around his hand.

"I know you're sensitive," he says, his hand moving so slowly, "but we have to get you ready for me." He undoes his pants with his other hand, pushing his underwear down and freeing himself. "Because I can't wait much longer to fuck you."

His words send another rush of heat through my abdomen, and my legs open on their own.

"That's my good girl," he says, slipping his fingers inside of me again. He pumps himself lazily as his fingers pulse gently into me.

He takes a step toward me, running his dick along my center. He tugs my leg up so it rests on his shoulder, leaving a quick kiss on my shin. He presses into me gently, only giving me a part of him to start.

And then he pushes deeper, filling me, and I let out a long moan.

"Hang on to the counter," he says, and when I look at

him in confusion, he takes my hands, wrapping my fingers along the edge between us. "Don't let go, okay?"

He rolls his hips into me, his hands pulling on my thighs to go deeper. He tips his head back, groaning as his pace ticks faster.

My fingers dig into the granite as he pushes deeper than I've felt him before.

He turns to the side to kiss my leg, dragging his teeth along my skin as he pounds into me harder.

"Fuck, Gabi, I wish you could see the way your tits are bouncing right now."

I take one hand off the counter and his eyes narrow, watching my movement with hesitation. I palm my breast, squeezing it in my hand and pinching my nipple between my fingers.

"Fuck, that's hot," he says, leaning over me slightly to fuck me harder.

I reach down to play with myself, wondering if that will turn him on too, but he slaps my hand away as soon as my fingers make contact with my clit.

"No," he says firmly. "Your pussy is mine."

"What, I can't play with myself?"

"No," he says, his thumb finding my clit and circling it. "I'm making you come tonight." He rocks into me harder. "Now hang on."

I stick my chest out as I reach down, intoxicated by the way his eyes are drawn to me, and wrap my fingers around the edge of the island.

"Good girl."

And he fucks me so hard I start shaking.

My orgasm rips through me so wildly that I can't control the noises jumping from my throat or the way my legs wrap around him and squeeze. I'm warring with him, his body extracting every last bit of pleasure from me that it can, even as I sit up, writhing against his arms holding me in place.

"Gabi," he says, his voice low in my ear. He pulls out of me, giving me a moment to gather myself. "You just came so hard for me." He brushes my hair out of my face, his fingers trailing down my arm and resting on my ribs.

I'm fighting to catch my breath as he kisses me, struggling to understand how he just *did* that.

"Are you okay?" he asks, one hand on my neck.

I nod, unable to come up with words.

I feel dumb.

I think he just fucked all thought out of me.

"I want to do that again."

He grins, his hand finding his dick and pumping it in anticipation. "Well, if you're going to demand a *third* orgasm, you're going to have to do something for me."

"What is that?" I ask, eyeing the way he pumps himself.

"Get on your knees."

I've never been so excited to drop to the floor. I take him eagerly in my mouth, watching as his eyes roll to the back of his head.

"Such a good fucking girl," he says, his fingers weaving into my hair and tugging.

He groans as I take him deeper. I cup his balls, running my fingers along the taut skin. I choke a little as he hits the back of my throat, but it only spurs me on.

"Fuck, Gabi, I'm going to come."

I suck him with determination, swallowing him down as he spills into my throat.

Afterward, he pulls me to my feet. My dress is still wrapped around my waist and he takes the opportunity to push it down over my hips. He plays with my nipples and they pebble in response, my body already ready to go again.

"Give me five minutes, and I'll give you orgasms three and four," he says, wrapping me in his arms and leaving a kiss on my temple. When he pulls away from me, he slaps my ass. "Until then, go get in bed. I'll give you two minutes to show me how you like to play with yourself."

"What about the other three minutes?"

"I get to play."

45

GABI

"Ladies," Corinne says, looking around at each of her students. "I'm pleased to announce that every single one of you passed."

A collective cheer echoes through the room.

"Okay, okay!" she says, reining in the noise. "Your certificates will be mailed out to you in a few weeks. As for today, I just want to thank you all for being such a wonderful first class. It was truly a pleasure to do these two hundred hours with you, and I look forward to doing yoga with each and every one of you at some point in the future. Namaste." She bows quickly to us. "Now go home!"

My heart ticks faster as I gather up my things. We're done early today, and Steph is only a few blocks away at the tattoo convention. I'll be able to see her for a bit tonight, after all.

I pack up my things quickly, but make sure to say a quick goodbye to Corinne before I head out.

"Thanks so much," I say, and she wraps me in a big hug.

"You did great, Gabi. I look forward to good things from you."

I grin. "Still on for Wednesday?"

She nods. "I'll be there."

I managed to convince Corinne into a weekly class at Yogi's Choice. Not that it was hard.

"Are you going to go celebrate?" she asks.

I shrug. "Kind of. My sister is at the tattoo convention, and she's leaving for Costa Rica for an undisclosed amount of time this weekend, so I'm going to go hang out with her while I can."

"Oh, sounds like a fun trip."

"Yeah, it does, but I'm nervous for her. You know, she's this incredibly spirited, fun girl—I just worry about her being all alone in a foreign country." I shake my head. "But she's an adult and she can take care of herself." I laugh. "Big sister problems."

Corinne nods. "She'll be okay."

"Yeah, she'll be okay," I parrot, even though my heart still thumps a little harder when I think of her being there alone.

"Well, go enjoy yourself!" she says. "And congratulations."

"Thank you."

She squeezes my arm as I walk out, and I take a moment on the street to text Steph that I'm on my way over. She sends back a picture of Oliver talking to a tattoo artist, motioning to something on his arm. I'll take that as enthusiasm that I'm able to join them.

When I finally get there and find them in the masses of people, Ollie and Steph are at a booth, crouched over a book of tattoos. He's pointing at something, and she motions to her forearm, drawing a long line from her palm to her elbow.

"Jesus, this place is gigantic," I say, coming up behind them.

"Oh, I'm so happy you came!" Steph wraps me in a hug.

"Stephanie's getting seventeen tattoos," Ollie says.

"I am not! I just can't *decide* between seventeen tattoos!" She elbows him, shaking her head.

He gives her a look. "Whenever you can't decide on what to drink, you end up with five half-drunk drinks."

"You're just mad I took the last of your gin."

He looks at her. "Yeah, because I told you I was really looking forward to it and you proceeded to pour it into a drink that sat out all night."

Steph acts mock-offended. "I made that drink for *you* and you had the audacity to say it was disgusting."

He turns to me. "It was gin with club soda and mashed strawberries, and it was *pink*."

"I mean, it doesn't sound half bad," I say.

"You're no help," he says to me.

"Sorry, only here to support my sister."

"Aw," she says, pulling me into another hug. I squeeze her back, painfully aware that it could be months before I see her again.

"So what are you getting?" I ask, nodding to the book in front of her.

She sighs. "Well, I was thinking of getting something, like, floral and delicate maybe along the inside of my arm. I want to avoid words because I feel like I just—well, you know, I'm not good with words, and putting them on my body just sounds like a disaster. But maybe words are good if they don't make a real sentence but, like, portray a meaning?"

"Like in a sentence?" Ollie asks, and we look at him.

"Just avoid words, Steph. I think you're going in the right direction."

She huffs at him and then turns to me. "I don't know, what do you think?"

I feel like this is a test: have I really overcome my overbearing tendencies enough to let Steph be herself and get something that makes her happy without judging her for it?

"I like the floral idea."

She nods. "Me too."

"Maybe you can get a flower you really identify with. Didn't you really like orchids for a while?"

She shrugs noncommittally. "Yeah, but I had a bunch and I killed them all."

"Well, maybe you can choose a flower that's really pretty but also resilient. Like you."

She smiles for a second. "Are you trying to butter me up so I stay?"

"Absolutely. But I'd say the same thing even if you weren't going on a crazy wild adventure by yourself that makes me really nervous."

"There's my sister," she snaps back. She taps her finger on her chin, thinking. "Roses are pretty resilient."

"Overdone," Ollie says immediately.

"Trumpet vines," I offer, but Steph crinkles her nose at that.

"Wildflowers," Ollie says, and there's a beat of silence between us where Steph raises her eyebrows, considering.

"Wildflowers?"

I nod. "Wildflowers."

She grins, her eyes connecting with Ollie's for a second. "Wildflowers it is." She bites her lip, eyeing him. "Can you draw it?"

He raises his eyebrows. "You want me to draw your tattoo?"

She nods. "I think you know what I'll like. And you're so good at drawing."

Oliver shrugs, his cheeks flooding with the faintest bit of color. "Okay. Sure, I can do that." He grins as he asks to borrow a pen and paper from one of the artists.

I realize with a start that Oliver didn't show up at Stephanie's birthday randomly; she invited him when she realized she wouldn't be having wild birthday sex with Rod.

My heart thrums. Something is happening between them. Something that is being swept under the rug because as far as I know, my sister is still going to Costa Rica for someone else.

I swallow down the excitement that pulses through me. Ollie's a little wild in his own way, but something tells me he would treat my sister well. Maybe he could be the reason she cancels her trip. Maybe he'll be the person she runs to when Rod inevitably disappoints her again.

But if they're playing it cool, I'll play it cool, too. I'm not about to blow up their spot.

But I'm having *so* much trouble keeping my questions to myself.

He draws her a thin bouquet of wildflowers which she takes to the tattoo artist waiting a few feet away. They talk for a minute about placement as the artist scans in the drawing and makes a few quick edits to fill in the stems.

And as she's about to sit in the chair, she turns back to me. "Last chance to get one with me!"

I surprise all of us by pausing. Steph's eyebrows crinkle, and I can feel Ollie's gaze.

"Okay," I say.

Tattoos are not my thing. But my sister is. And this

seems like a moment we can sink our teeth into. A way to memorialize how we've grown apart and back together over the past year—Steph with taking care of her mental health, and me, learning to trust again.

I don't know where we'll go from here, but I know this is a sisterly moment worth clinging to.

Steph turns to the tattoo artist. "Can we hold on like five minutes so we can get ours at the same time?"

He nods. "I think Darya might be able to take you." He calls over to another artist who isn't currently tattooing anyone. She walks over, a genuine smile on her face. I take in all of the tattoos on her body—all of them minimal and tasteful.

And I think I feel good about this.

"Are you able to do something custom?"

She nods. "Sure babe, let's draw something out for you."

She brings me over to a table where she peppers me with questions and draws a few different designs. Meanwhile, Ollie strikes up a conversation with another artist. While poor Darya is still making edits to mine, he's sitting down in a chair only a few feet away from us, his tattoo artist focusing in on his upper arm, just above his elbow.

When we agree on a design, Steph squeals. I glance over at Ollie and see that he's grinning—he gives us a thumbs-up with his other hand.

"Where are you thinking, babe?" Darya asks.

"Maybe right here?" I motion along my ribs, just below my bra.

She nods. "I'm gonna need you to take your shirt off for that, possibly your bra too. Are you okay with that?"

I pause. Good lord, I don't know about that.

"Do it," Steph whispers in my ear.

"We have a sheet to cover you. You don't need to be

exposed, I just don't want your skin to be pulled in a way that could skew the design."

"Okay, don't do it if you're uncomfortable," Steph says, catching my eye. "But I think that'll look really nice."

I turn to Darya. "I'm okay with that as long as my nipples are covered."

She laughs. "Babe, you'll be holding the sheet so that's totally up to you."

I take a deep breath. "Okay. Let's do it."

They set Steph and me up in two chairs right next to each other, pushing them close so we can hear each other. I take off my shirt and Steph holds the sheet over me while I pull my sports bra over my head. She makes sure I'm comfortable and then sits in her own chair.

And then we begin. Alcohol swabs and shaving and design confirmations and pain warnings.

Steph holds my hand with her free one and chatters about all of the things she's planning to do in Costa Rica, the places she's staying and all of the activities she has planned for once Rod gets there. She's booked them zip lining and canoeing and coffee tours and sloth forests.

I'm so concerned about him not showing up that I nearly forget a woman I just met is plowing a needle into my ribs.

Nearly.

Our tattoos don't take very long, but Ollie's is faster. He waits by the foot of our chairs while we finish, a grin on his face as he watches us. Mine takes a little longer than Steph's, but she waits in her chair until I'm done too.

"I *love* the design you got," Steph says, her voice low enough so that only I can hear.

"Thanks, I really like it too."

"Did you get it because of Zeke?"

I shake my head. "No. I mean, he suggested it, but I got it because of me. It *is* me, you know?"

She nods. "It's so perfect for you."

"Thanks, Steph. I'd hug you right now if it weren't for the needle in my ribs."

46

GABI

Today is the first warm day we've had in a week. The snow is melting, the sun is shining, and Stephanie slept in Zeke's bed with me last night to make sure I don't have a mental breakdown before going to yoga.

Because today, I have to teach another class.

I dress in nondescript leggings and a sweatshirt and make coffee and oatmeal while Steph putters sleepily around, one eye on her coffee and the other glued to me. She spends her morning ironing out the last small details of her trip, checking on reservations and showing me the cute little lodge she booked for her first week in Costa Rica.

I don't bother with my routine this morning. Instead, I drink my coffee and look out the window at the street outside, where the snow has been cleared and the piles lining the walkways are already melting down.

By the time noon rolls around, the buzzing is in my head again and I can hardly process what Steph is saying to me as she asks to borrow a change of clothes. I throw her an outfit and she showers quickly before heading to the studio with me.

We get there long before class starts, and Stephanie scrolls mindlessly on her phone while I set up. I prop the doors open, just like Corinne used to when it was nice out.

And fifteen minutes before start time, my anxiety reaches a crescendo. I sit on my mat in front of Steph and force myself to breathe.

"Are you okay?" she asks, throwing her phone on the floor and moving toward me, lying on her stomach.

I nod. "I'm fine. Please don't ask or I'll start not being fine."

Steph rolls her eyes. "It's still early."

"I know."

I force myself to breathe in through my nose, out through my mouth.

And then I hear footsteps in the stairwell. My eyes are glued to the open door as Natalie appears. She waves, smiling as she discards her shoes into cubbies, her jacket onto the rack. She lays out her mats a little bit away from Steph, who doesn't seem to realize yoga isn't really a talking sport.

She introduces herself and moves her mat closer.

"Steph," I warn. She shoots me a look and I shut up, seeing that Natalie doesn't seem to mind Steph's somewhat overbearing welcome.

A minute later, there are more footsteps—Corinne, trailed by two girls from our teacher training classes.

Wow, already a group of five.

Then Annabel, in dark leggings and a polka dot crop top. She sets up on the other side of Steph and they immediately fall into conversation, the noise in this small studio growing exponentially.

Then Kelly, with two girls around her age coming up the steps behind her. She waves politely, and the three of them set up in a second row behind the other girls.

Okay, nine.

And then Mari and Carrie join us, waving excitedly as they roll out their mats.

Okay, eleven. My heart kicks up a notch, apprehension about no one showing up suddenly turning into apprehension that *too many* people have shown up. The teacher training classes are small—I've never taught more than eight people at once.

Stephanie's best friends Kay and Leilani walk in, seemingly unsurprised by the number of people in this room. They crowd in behind Stephanie's mat, the noise level continually growing.

Gemma walks in, waving excitedly when she sees me.

"Gabi, it looks so good!" she says, gesturing to the studio.

"Thank you," I say, trying to swallow down my nerves.

Fourteen people. Fuck.

"I'm so sorry I couldn't make it last week. We managed to get an appointment at this pediatrician who's usually booked solid for months—he had a cancellation because of the storm—and basically I told my husband if he wants another truck after this one, it's gotta earn its keep and get us to that appointment." She pauses for dramatic effect. "Luckily, it did, so he gets to keep the truck, and we're now doing an elimination diet with poor Taylor."

"Oh, well I'm glad you were able to get the appointment. Don't worry about last week."

"I felt so bad," she says. "I really wanted to be here for your big day, but Taylor has to come first. And honestly, I have a good feeling about this. He has a hunch that it's a gluten issue based on what we've already tried—which is wild to me—but if that's what it is, I'll take it. We can become a gluten-free household without issue, if it gets her eating and stops her crying."

"Oh, I'm so glad you have a direction! I know how difficult that was. And really, don't worry about last week. Yoga's an invitation, not an obligation," I say, parroting words Corinne has said to us on numerous occasions.

Gemma smiles at me and gives me a quick hug. "I'm excited for you, Gabi."

"Thank you," I say even though my heart is beating wildly in my chest and I'm not totally sure *I'm* excited for me anymore.

I think I'm just *scared* at this point.

Steph catches my eye and grins at me.

"Did you do this?" I ask, referring to the number of people now in the studio.

She shrugs. "I called Kay and Leilani, but the rest showed up on their own."

I lower my voice so only Stephanie can hear. "I've never taught this many people before."

She grins wider. "What better time to learn than now?"

I swallow as the clock hits the hour.

Here we go.

THE IRONICALLY GOOD part of yoga is that since it was always my safe space, the act of doing begets more doing. It's a self-perpetuating prophecy—as I lead everyone into their peace, I find my own.

I push through the first few minutes on shaky arms, *espe-*

cially since Corinne is here to judge me, but after a few deep breaths, it's almost like I'm able to become a student again. Sure, everyone is watching me, and I have to speak all of my movements out loud, but I have Corinne's notes to guide me if I get lost.

All I really have to do is remember to breathe and bring everyone along with me.

It's not easy by any means, but it's doable, and with every minute that goes by it feels more manageable.

It also helps that most people here are less into yoga than I am, so they probably won't catch if I slip up. And it's not Gemma or Natalie's first class with me, really, so their attention doesn't really bother me. Corinne and the girls from teacher training, however, are making me a little nervous, despite the easygoing smiles on their faces.

But I can tell from their movements that they're not judging me right now, or grading me, or looking for points of feedback they can give me to improve on for the next class.

They're just participating.

As is the rest of class.

I suddenly realize just how little everyone is paying attention to me.

I've become a part of this studio, a part of the lifebreath of the practice that exists outside of a teacher or a movement but within the place itself.

I cue, and people move.

I cue again, and people move again.

I blink as the realization hits me. *I think I've done it. I've become a teacher.*

It feels good.

When class is over, I blow out my candle.

Everyone rolls up their mats and gathers their things, moving slowly en masse toward the door. Chatter grows as footsteps descend, Corinne and the girls from teacher training among the first to leave, then Natalie and Gemma.

Steph eyes me as she talks to Annabel, the two of them making no attempt to clean up their stuff, even as Kay and Leilani mosey out, shouting a quick goodbye over their shoulders.

When I turn back to Steph, she's sitting cross-legged on her mat with a grin on her face.

"So how does it feel, Ms. Yogi?"

I can't help the smile that spreads across my face. "It feels good."

Annabel claps. "Oh yay! Oh good!"

She picks up her phone, calls someone, and presses it to her ear a second later. "You can come in now!"

"Who?" I ask, suddenly suspicious that the four girls left seem to be in no hurry to pack up their things.

And then I hear their voices on the stairs, deep and familiar, and footsteps far too heavy plodding up toward us.

Charlie, first, with two bottles of champagne. Then Oliver, carrying a box of plastic champagne flutes. And then Kick, carrying two more bottles of champagne, and Henry, with a large cardboard box.

Henry heads straight for me, and as he moves, my breath catches. With every second that passes, I think Zeke might just pop out from the stairs, a smile on his face and a bottle of champagne in his hand. He's on his way back from Virginia today, and although he really wanted to be here for this class, we both knew he'd be cutting it close.

But my heart drops with every step Henry takes. There are no more footsteps on the stairs.

Charlie heads for Annabel first, leaving kisses on her cheeks as he assigns her champagne duty. From her mat, she pops open the first bottle and pours, distributing the flutes around to each of us. He comes to me next, wrapping me in a big hug and kissing my cheek.

"You did it, Gabi!" he says. "I'm so proud of you."

I roll my eyes. "Thanks, Charlie."

"We didn't want any of the girls to be creeped out so we waited outside until we got the all-clear, but just know we absolutely would have taken your class too if any one of us had the slightest bit of ability."

"Oh, you guys are always welcome. You don't have to be good at it."

"Okay, maybe I just didn't want to embarrass myself," he says.

"I *wanted* to come," Henry says, plopping the first cardboard box in front of me. "I do yoga all the time, but Oliver said I'd get in trouble."

"I only said you'd get in trouble if you started looking at asses."

"*I'm* actually capable of controlling myself."

Oliver rolls his eyes. "Okay, it happened *one* time, and Steph forgave me in zero-point-two seconds because she was *flattered*."

"Ollie, stop talking. You're digging your own grave," Steph chimes in, taking a sip of her champagne.

The curiosity hits me again—what on *earth* is going on between them?

I push the question aside as Henry pulls the flaps of the box open in front of me and motions for me to look inside.

It's filled with T-shirts. I take one out, and as I unfold it, I notice my logo over the right breast.

"Henry," I say, pulling out shirt after shirt, all with my logo. "Oh my god, I can't believe you did this."

He shrugs. "To be fair, it was Zeke's idea."

"Henry, thank you so much." I wrap him in a hug and afterward, he joins Kick and Ollie on Carrie's mat, where she and Mari are lounging with their champagne. Mari gives him a look like he wasn't welcome in their conversation and quickly crawls over to Annabel, who's chatting with Steph and Charlie.

I pause as I hear another set of stomping footsteps trailing up the stairway.

I glance at Steph, who doesn't bother hiding her grin, and before I know what I'm doing, I'm standing, like there's some invisible magnet pulling me toward him before I even know it's *him*.

He appears at the top of the stairs a moment later, winded and with wild eyes. "Sorry I'm late," he says, a grin on his face. I shake my head as he takes a hesitant step toward me. "How did it go?"

I nod. "It went well."

"Fuck yeah, it did!" Steph shouts, and Annabel shushes her.

A second later, his arms are wrapped around me. He lifts me, pressing kisses to my face and twirling me in a circle before setting me gently back down. "I knew you could do it, Gabs."

I bury my face in his chest as a wave of elation passes through me.

I actually fucking did it. "I couldn't have done it without you."

∽

ZEKE SITS NEXT to me on my mat with a glass of champagne in his hand long after our friends have left. His eyes roam the studio, a small smile on his face.

"I have something to show you," I say, pulling his attention away from the studio and back to me.

"Oh yeah?"

I rest my glass on the floor and slowly pull my shirt over my head.

"Oh, I like where this is going," he says, leaning back on his elbows and watching me shamelessly. I drop my shirt to the floor next to me just as his eyes zero in on the bandage across my ribs. His brow furrows as he sits up again, moving closer to me. "Are you okay?"

I hold up a hand, hoping to pause whatever panic is happening behind those concerned eyes. "I'm fine. It's a fun thing."

He raises his eyebrows, reaching out to touch my waist as I slowly pull the bandage back.

His jaw drops when he sees what's underneath.

"Gabi!" His fingers trail higher, leaving goosebumps along my skin, as he touches the unaffected skin around my new tattoo. "You got a tattoo?"

I nod.

His eyes jump up to mine. "This is the design I suggested."

I nod again, and then pause. "Technically, it's *two* designs you suggested. And I combined them."

He bites his lip, his thumb still trailing along my skin. "Gabi, this is sexy."

"You think?"

He nods, his eyes wide. "Is that a lily?"

"It is."

"And what pose is that?"

"Cobra."

He nods, biting his lips as he stares at it. "I like cobra pose."

A rush of heat runs through me as his fingers trail up, slipping beneath my sports bra.

"I guess it's about time we christen the studio, huh?"

He leaves his champagne on the floor and presses me down on the mat, his fingers trailing along my side but careful to avoid the sensitive skin around my tattoo. He weaves one arm behind me as he kisses me, holding himself above me as he settles between my legs.

As he kisses along my neck, down to my collarbone, he pauses, staring at my tattoo. "You know, I think I might get one."

"Yeah? Of what?" I ask, squeezing my knees around him in the hopes he'll continue kissing me like he was.

"A lily."

He catches my eye, and I can't help but grin at him. "You want to copy me?"

He nods. "I want it right here," he says, hoisting himself up on the arm that's underneath me and using his free hand to point at the spot on the inside of his elbow that presses right up against mine.

I snort. "You want to get matching tattoos in a place they can kiss?"

He grins, nodding at me.

I shake my head. "You're so corny."

"Horny, you mean?" He kisses me before I can answer. A moment later he presses himself into me so I can feel just how hard he is as his hands roam my skin and tug my leggings down. "Because my girl is a fucking badass."

"I didn't realize you were so turned on by tattoos."

He pauses. "I don't think I ever really thought about

them before. But on you, Gabi? Fuck." He shakes his head, his fingers slipping beneath my underwear and slowly pulling them down. He undoes the clasp of his pants as he settles between my legs again, and I can't help my hands dipping beneath his sweater, feeling his strong muscles above me as he frees himself and slowly presses inside me.

He lets out a long breath into my neck as he moves inside me. His eyes dip to my tattoo and he shakes his head, like all of it is just too much.

I wrap my hand around the back of his neck and pull him down to kiss me as my orgasm builds.

"I love you, Gabi," he says, his pace steady as he pushes me over the edge.

"I love you too," I say, as his arms clamp tighter around me and he jerks into me.

Afterward, when we've taken a moment to clean ourselves up and return to our champagne, we sit on the floor and he pulls me up against his chest, leaving a kiss on my shoulder. He lets out a long breath and squeezes me tight.

"What?" I ask, leaning over slightly so I can look at him.

"I'm just so proud of you." He rests his head on my shoulder, one hand trailing along my arm.

I lean my head back against his shoulder. "I kind of can't believe I did it."

"You're actively *doing* it," he corrects.

"I meant it when I said I couldn't have done it without you."

I turn to kiss his cheek, and he deftly moves so I kiss his lips instead.

He grins as I pull away from him. "What's amazing is that this is just the beginning. All of this work, all of the time and heart you put into this place—and it's just the beginning."

I lean my head back against his shoulder and close my eyes. He might be talking about the studio right now, but it feels like he's talking about us.

About everything we are now, and everything we could be. In time.

ZEKE

EPILOGUE

One year later

I do yoga now.

I feel silly and uncoordinated for most of it, but I do it anyway.

And when I'm not actively doing yoga, I'm sitting behind a makeshift desk in the corner of a yoga studio, doing my best to be invisible while other people do yoga.

Over the past few months, Yogi's Choice has gone from a small, neighborhood studio, to one that people travel to from all parts of the city—even a few who come in from the suburbs. Different teachers are in and out at all times of the day, and although Gabi handles most of the coordination, she leaves some midday stuff to me while she's at work.

Which she doesn't need to be anymore. I take care of her taxes and most of the scheduling at this point—she's booked solid a week in advance. Once teacher training was done, she put all of her efforts into marketing, and it paid off. She's not about to retire and move to Florida, but she could live comfortably off the studio if that's what she decides she wants to do.

The current class finishes up, the girls packing up their things and heading slowly out the door. The teacher—one of the girls from Gabi's teacher training—follows shortly after, waving on her way out.

I finish up the report I've been working on for Gabi that pulls data automatically from her website so she knows which classes are consistently booked and which ones aren't. I sliced it a couple different ways—by time of day, by teacher, by weekday. It'll get emailed to her weekly, and I'll spin up a monthly version next.

I check the time—Gabi should be on her way over from work.

I pull out the Swiffer and do a quick clean before she gets here. I wipe down the cubbies on the one side of the room and clean up my own mess around the desk—my bag, headphones, charging cables, the remnants of my lunch.

Gabi had a breakfast meeting with a client this morning who's been exceptionally hard to land and couldn't be here for the morning classes like she prefers, so I've been here for quite a while, slowly working through a website for a new cycling studio a few blocks away whose owner has become good friends with Gabi.

I was planning to head home when she arrived, but when she does she blows past me in a fog of that delicate perfume and corporate attire, her hair long and straight down her back and her heels clicking across the wood floor.

"Sorry I'm late!" she shouts, beelining for the closet in the back that she's claimed as her personal changing room.

"Are you late?"

I follow her in, closing the door most of the way just in case someone wanders in.

She shrugs, pulling her shirt over her head. "I don't know. This whole day went by in a blur. I've felt like I've been late since I got up this morning."

She undoes the clasp on her skirt and pulls it down over her hips.

"Considering you don't teach for another half hour, I think you're right on time."

She straightens, taking a breath. "I knew that. I guess I'm just nervous."

"What about?" I wrap an arm around her and pull her toward me, the lily on my arm pressing up against the one on her ribs.

She takes a deep breath, looking up at me. "I might have made some decisions today."

I raise my eyebrows. "I'm intrigued."

She bites her lip. "We finally closed Marigold."

The client who's been eluding them for the better part of a year.

"You did? Congratulations!"

"Big contract, and they signed. Like, the deal is done."

"That's awesome. I'm so proud of you." I kiss her head.

She nods. "That's not all." She swallows. "I confirmed with Dieter—I'm still going to get commission on it even though afterward, I put in my notice."

My heart skips a beat. "No you didn't."

She nods. "I just can't do both anymore. And you're right, I don't need to. I guess I just needed a little bit of time to get comfortable with the idea, but honestly, Zeke, I'm excited." She's on her tiptoes, the energy thrumming through her as she presses her body into mine.

"I think you desperately needed to quit your job for the sake of your sanity. You know I'll always support you if you need it, but I know your numbers as well as you do, and I don't think you need help at all."

She nods, and the expression on her face tells me that might not be all.

"Something else?"

"I gave notice on my lease today."

It takes me a second to catch up to what she's saying. I've been casually suggesting to Gabi that she start thinking about what she's going to do when her lease is up. She has two months still on the temporary apartment she moved into after the Dustin situation, but knowing her, she needs time and space to comfortably come to her own conclusions. I've learned not to push her.

And she's slowly starting to have more confidence in her own decisions.

But I didn't expect this.

I had already accepted the fact that we'd likely be waiting another year to move in together.

"Oh my god," she says, her body tightening in my arms. "Oh my god, I'm sorry. I thought you were hinting that you wanted me to move in."

"No no no no no," I say quickly, pulling her back when she tries to take a step away from me. "I do want that, but I honestly didn't think you'd be ready yet. I thought for sure it'd be another year. And by then maybe we could find someplace safer than my apartment, you know? A place not in Kensington? But god, if you're ready now, I'm sure as hell not letting you second-guess it. You're moving in with me."

I laugh, her relief palpable as I squeeze her against me.

She grins, standing on her toes to kiss me.

"You have to start carrying your pepper spray again, though. I don't like the idea of you getting home late and walking around there by yourself."

She shrugs, her eyes fixing on mine. "I just thought you might walk me home."

I can't help the smile that spreads across my face.

"Always."

She leaves a kiss on my jaw before pulling on her leggings and a Yogi's Choice T-shirt. I open the door for her as she ties her hair up, and as I grab my things from the desk along one side of the studio, the door at the bottom of the stairs clangs shut, followed by slow footsteps.

Gabi and I glance at each other, wondering who could be here.

And then we hear Gemma's soft voice. "Good job, Tay. Step up to the next one," she says. Then we hear the indiscriminate babbles of a toddler. "Good job. Next one."

Gabi sticks her head in the stairwell. "Hi Gem," she says.

"Hi Gabi! Taylor, say hi to Miss Gabi!"

Taylor babbles at her, and Gabi glances back at me with a look on her face that tells me she's falling head over heels for baby Taylor. If she wasn't already.

When they reach the top of the stairs, Gabi scoops her up in her arms for a hug, and the three of them wander back into the studio.

"Hey Zeke," Gemma says, waving at me.

"Hi Gemma. Hi Taylor," I say, giving the little girl a wave. She throws her face into Gabi's shoulder, suddenly shy, and Gabi makes that face again—the one that shows just how smitten she is.

"Sorry to just drop by unannounced. She's on the move so we've been essentially wandering the neighborhood for the last hour."

"Oh you can always drop by here. Especially if Taylor's with you," Gabi says, taking a moment to tickle the little girl. She erupts into laughter.

"Hey, do you still like high-fives?" I ask, holding my hand over Gabi's shoulder. Taylor immediately punches it. "Nice!"

"Is the new diet still working for her?" Gabi asks, brushing her hand over Taylor's back. They've spent almost a year doing various elimination diets, and Gemma was close to truly losing her shit when they finally started seeing results. It was a tough time for all, but now that they know Taylor has baby IBS and non-celiac gluten intolerance and have been able to build a diet around that, they're in a better place.

Gemma nods. "She's doing much better. Thank god. That was the *worst*."

Gabi nods sympathetically. "Good, I'm so glad."

Gabi sways, Taylor turning to watch the women talk as if she's a part of the conversation.

And something hits me as Gabi rests her cheek so naturally on Taylor's head.

"Fuck, I need to get a ring."

Everyone's attention snaps to me.

Fuck, I said that out loud.

Gemma's jaw drops, and Gabi's eyes go wide. Taylor just smiles.

I clear my throat. "I mean—" I glance around and then shrug. "Sorry."

No sense in denying it. They both heard it.

"Well," Gemma starts and then looks between us as if trying to figure out a way to smooth over this awkwardness. "This was a nice chat." She gestures to Taylor as if asking Gabi if it's okay to take her, and Gabi reluctantly hands her back. "I'll leave you two to—" She shakes her head. "Well, nice seeing you both."

Taylor on one hip, Gemma bustles down the stairs, the door clanging shut behind her.

Gabi turns to me, her hands on her hips. "Zeke, did you just get baby fever?"

"No," I say, even as I tug on her shirt, pulling her in for a kiss.

"You *so* did," she says into my lips. "You got baby fever so hard you made a split-second decision to propose."

I fight the color leaching into my face. "And so what if I did?"

She runs her fingers along my chin. "Well, I guess I'd have to say yes."

GABI
EPILOGUE

Two months later

A year ago, I never would have thought I'd be touring empty studio spaces for a second Yogi's Choice studio.

But here I am. The studio is booked at least a week in advance, constantly, and regulars who have been coming for the past year are starting to get annoyed that their favorite classes aren't always available.

So, I consider it my duty and privilege to give the people what they want: a second, bigger location, with more teachers, more classes, and more parking.

It's walking distance to our new apartment on the safer end of Northern Liberties, and the Realtor texted me the code to the lockbox so I could take a look when I have a spare moment.

They're few and far between these days.

I fish the key out of the box and unlock the door, closing it gently behind me. I'm immediately hit with a strong floral smell that has me warming to this space already.

I must be a little off today because for some reason it smells like lilies.

This studio is similar to the first in that it's a second-floor space with big windows and independently owned by a landlord with a good reputation. That was important to me when we started looking.

I climb the stairs to the second floor, the scent getting stronger with every step, and note the warm light being emitted from the door at the top of the stairs. It doesn't seem like the normal fluorescents I'd expect—it's much dimmer. Almost like candlelight.

When I reach the top of the stairs, I freeze, my heart thumping in my chest.

It *is* candlelight. And the reason I smell lilies is because this studio is absolutely filled with them.

"Hey," he says, a grin spreading across his face as I step into the room. He's standing along the far wall, his hands clasped behind his back, and the candles lining the room give his skin a warm glow.

"Hey," I mock, dropping my bag on the floor by the door. I walk toward him, eyebrows raised. "What's all this?"

"Well, it's a couple things," he says, sliding an arm around my waist. I wrap my arms around his neck as he speaks. "First, I bought you a studio."

My brain struggles to follow his words. I thought I knew where this was going.

And I didn't expect buying me a studio to be a part of it.

"You what?"

"I stole your list of requirements and came to see this place a few weeks ago. It's everything you wanted. So I took a chance and went ahead and bought it."

I struggle to form words. "But I was just going to rent it."

He shrugs. "Now you don't have to."

"Well, now I have to rent from *you*," I say.

"You think?"

I raise my eyebrows.

"I was thinking maybe it could be half yours."

I swallow. "Half mine?"

He takes a step away from me, and my heart catches.

I watch as he lowers down to one knee, withdrawing from his pocket a little velvet box.

"Will you marry me, Gabi?"

I'm nodding before the words are even out of his mouth, kneeling down with him and wrapping my arms tight around him. "Yes, yes, yes, yes, yes!" I kiss him everywhere I can, nearly knocking him over in the process. He puts one hand on the wall to steady himself.

"Gabi, you have to let me put the ring on your finger," he says through his laughter.

I pause my kisses to push my left hand toward him expectantly, and he slides the diamond onto my finger.

And then I don't hold back.

I pull him down to the floor with me, running my thumb along the metal band that now sits on my finger as I tear at his clothing and tug at his hips.

We have hot, sweaty, *engaged* sex on the floor of my new studio, surrounded by candles and lilies and so much love that my heart might actually burst.

Afterward, we lay on the floor entwined, the lily on his arm mashed right up against the one on my ribs. He kisses my hand, his thumb running over my ring.

"This looks right on you," he says, and I nuzzle in closer to his neck. He adjusts the yoga pants he's using as a pillow, and leans over to kiss me on the temple.

"I think so too."

He sighs, leaning his cheek against my forehead. "I was worried it would be too soon for you."

I glance up at him and catch his eye as I shake my head. "Your timing was perfect."